Praise for **Kerriga**

"The romance is 1... ...
satisfying."
—*Publishers Weekly*

"This is a...

"Byrne is...

"Capture...
lush, and s...
—Suzanne Enoch, *New York Times*
bestselling author on *The Highwayman*

"A passionate, lyrical romance that takes your breath away.
From the first page, you'll fall in love."
—Elizabeth Boyle, *New York Times* bestseller

"Byrne makes a stunning debut with a beautifully written,
intensely suspenseful, and deliciously sensual love story."
—Amelia Grey, *New York Times* bestseller

Also by
Kerrigan Byrne

The Scot Beds His Wife
The Duke
The Highlander
The Hunter
The Highwayman

The
Highlander

KERRIGAN BYRNE

St. Martin's Paperbacks

THE HIGHLANDER

Copyright © 2016 by Kerrigan Byrne.

All rights reserved.

For information address St. Martin's Press, 175 Fifth Avenue, New York, NY 10010.

ISBN: 978-1-250-07607-6

Our books may be purchased in bulk for promotional, educational, or business use. Please contact your local bookseller or the Macmillan Corporate and Premium Sales Department at 1-800-221-7945, ext. 5442, or by e-mail at MacmillanSpecialMarkets@macmillan.com.

Printed in the United States of America

St. Martin's Paperbacks edition / August 2016

St. Martin's Paperbacks are published by St. Martin's Press, 175 Fifth Avenue, New York, NY 10010.

10 9 8 7 6 5 4 3

$\mathcal{P}$ROLOGUE

Wester Ross, Scotland

Something has to be done, Liam Mackenzie decided as he stared down at his gruesome discovery.

About the evil man who ruled the Mackenzie of Wester Ross with sadistic whims and cold terror. About the hollow-eyed woman who'd replaced Liam's own wretched mother, haunting the halls of Ravencroft Keep like a thin, tormented specter of regret and fear. About her son, Liam's half brother, who hid in closets and had never learned to smile in his entire young life. About the Mackenzie bastard recently beaten to death in Newgate prison.

Something had to be done about the body that Liam had just fished out of Bryneloch Bog.

Tessa McGrath.

Though she'd been little more than a skeleton covered in sludge, peat, and mud, Liam had known it was her. The moment he'd glimpsed what remained of the wool cloak he'd given her on that terrible night those few years ago, he'd *known*.

That cloak—his final act of kindness—had become her shroud.

Tessa had been a bawdy whore who'd boasted of incomparable skills and dark fetishes. It was why the Laird Hamish Mackenzie had hired her for his sons. Why she'd been chosen to turn boys into men. Nay, not men, but something entirely more terrible.

Tessa had underestimated the abject cruelty of the Marquess of Ravencroft. She'd not known the depth of Hamish Mackenzie's evil.

"She wants it." Liam's father had sneered as he'd strapped a naked, blindfolded Tessa to the bed. "She's begging for it."

The whore *had* been begging for it. For the playful lashes of the buttery-soft whip she'd brought in her satchel of pleasure toys. She made the appropriate noises, writhed in the appropriate ways. She'd said inviting things and given salacious permissions that would send any boy of sixteen into a lustful frenzy.

But not Liam.

It wasn't her fault. She could never have imagined what the laird had in store for her. She liked to play with a little pain, but Hamish Mackenzie didn't stop a game when he'd won, he kept going until his opponents were utterly broken.

Liam had already suspected that Hamish meant to break the girl in front of them. To compel them to watch. He could never have imagined that his father had intended to force his *sons* to break her. To observe with sick, sadistic pleasure as the very lads he'd sired became monsters.

Monsters like himself.

Not until the laird had produced a toy of his own had Liam guessed. An antique, Roman lead-tipped whip with as many leather straps as Medusa had snakes on her head.

Each one of Laird Mackenzie's sons trembled at the sight. Hamish, the laird's namesake bastard. Liam, his heir apparent. And the boy they called "Thorne," the only son of the laird's second wife. They were all intimately acquainted with that whip. They knew the pain of its kiss and missed the flesh it tore away with each lash.

Indeed, they'd stared at it in wide-eyed incredulity as the laird had run it over the purring whore's back. She'd arched and gasped in anticipation . . . at first.

Then she'd screamed and cried, struggled and begged, and that was after only two lashes.

Dark eyes glowing with perverse excitement, Hamish stalked to their side of the bed and held the detested whip's pommel out to his sons, who gaped from a regimental line.

"Two lashes for each of ye," he'd ordered.

"She'll not survive that," Thorne had argued, his pubescent voice cracking against his fear.

The laird answered his son's impudence with his fist, sending Thorne sprawling to the floor. "Two. Lashes. Each," he repeated. "I doona care which of ye gives how many, but she'll not be released until she's been whipped six times."

Laird Hamish Mackenzie, a giant of a man, used to tower over all his sons as he did most men. But on that night, Liam noted that he looked across at his father eye to eye for the first time. Few dared to meet his father's glare, let alone stand against him.

"Ye do it," the laird ordered with an evil smile. "Or I'll do it *myself.*"

It was disconcerting, to say the least, when the person you hated the most wore your own features. To ken that someday, perhaps in two decades past, those same monstrous dark eyes would stare back at Liam from the mirror, a reminder of the rancid cruelty that ran through his tainted Mackenzie blood. Seeing the paternal challenge on the face of his father, Liam realized that one day, he would no longer have to be afraid of this man. He would have to grow just as large, just as cunning, ruthless, and brutal. But one day, he would challenge the monster with a beast of his own.

The glint in his father's eye had told him that he looked forward to that day.

Seizing upon the opportunity to impress his father, Hamish the younger had reached out for the whip, a familiar cruel anticipation building beneath the apprehension on his less compelling features.

Hamish would do what his father said.

And Tessa wouldn't survive it.

"Nay." Liam had stepped forward, wrenching the whip out of his father's hand before Hamish could take it. "*I'll* do it."

The wind screamed over the moors and whipped across Bryneloch Bog with a resonance not dissimilar to the sounds Tessa had made that night as lead-tipped straps flew toward unblemished skin. The confused terror in her sobs had carved what was left of Liam's heart out of his chest until only a raw, cavernous wound was left.

Now, standing over her body, Liam's hand closed around nothing but moist, humid air, his knuckles as white as they had been the night he'd hesitantly gripped the braided handle of the leather whip.

She didn't ken that he was doing her a kindness in the only way he knew how. That by being the one that carried out his father's pitiless orders, he could do his best to mitigate the damage.

How could she have?

Liam wished to God the night had ended there . . . but the laird's cruelty knew no bounds, and it had been a hellish hour full of unspeakable things before Liam had been able to roughly bundle her into that cloak and help her escape.

To her credit, she'd never stopped fighting; indeed, she'd threatened retribution through a bottomless well of frightened tears.

Those threats had been her fatal mistake.

She hadn't been walking right when she'd limped down the stairs, and some of her rosy, pink skin was starting to color with what would become ugly bruises. That had been Hamish's doing.

Even at his young age, Liam had been strong enough to carry her through the night and across the fields to the village, and he'd offered—God, how he'd tried—to reason with her. Apologize to her. Anything to mitigate the shame staining his insides.

She'd hear none of it, not that he could blame her.

"I'm going to turn the clan against ye, and yer wicked family," she spat. "See if I doona. I'll tell everyone, show them what ye barbaric demons have done to me. They'll come for ye. For all of ye!"

But she hadn't had the chance. She'd been silenced.

She'd been *murdered*.

There was no question in Liam's mind who'd committed the deed.

Evil begat evil, did it not?

There was no escaping it. Even Dougan, his father's youngest bastard, who'd been raised away from the red stones of Ravencroft Keep, had killed a priest when he was just a teen.

Dougan. His father had paid to have his youngest son beaten to death in prison. Somehow, the lad had escaped, reinvented himself, and secretly reached out to Liam whilst simultaneously waging a war for supremacy of the London Underworld.

The sons of Hamish Mackenzie had been *bred* to spill blood. The Fates wove violence into their sinew like a gruesome tapestry, and brewed ruthlessness to pour through their veins.

When the king is dead . . . long live the king.

Dougan had written those words in lieu of a signature in the letter that bade Liam to do the one thing he'd always fantasized about.

Liam wrapped what remained of Tessa back into the dissolving cloak, and let the gurgling bog become her grave. As he watched the earth slowly claim her, he felt what was left of his hope, of his humanity, sink with her.

A coal of hatred replaced it, igniting in his empty chest, fanned into an inferno by the rank and sulfurous breath of the devil himself.

Perhaps fantasy hadn't just become a reality, but a necessity.

As he stood and stared across the emerald landscape interrupted by the jagged Kinross Mountains, Liam thought of his mother and how his father had broken her, both in body and spirit. He thought of his clan, the Mackenzie of Wester Ross, who toiled and cowered beneath their laird's merciless iron fist. He thought of his brothers, both bastard and legitimate, none of whom was strong enough to withstand his father's abuse.

So Liam often took it for them.

But who would be here to protect them now that he was off to war?

Liam had grown into a man, not only tall enough to look his father's evil in the eye. His shoulders were finally wide enough to carry the weight of the numerous lashes that shaped the flesh of his back as though carved from brimstone by Satan's own mallet and chisel. His fists were heavy enough to strike in kind.

He'd reported for his commission in Her Majesty's Regimental Army. He'd used the fire in his blood to commit violent acts in service to the crown. Sanctioned by God and country.

It was his only way out.

But first, *something* had to be done about all of this.

The day had come.

Laird Hamish Mackenzie had wanted to craft a monster out of his son and heir. Someone like *him*. But monsters were mythical, the figments of superstitious imaginations and farcical stories of centuries past. Liam decided he'd be no monster. Nay, he'd do one better.

He'd become a demon.

CHAPTER ONE

London, September, 1878
Twenty Years Later

Take off your clothes. It wasn't the first time Lady Philomena St. Vincent, Viscountess Benchley, had heard the
command. She was the wife of a violent libertine, after all.
But as she stared in wide-eyed incomprehension at the
jowly Dr. Percival Rosenblatt, she was at a momentary loss
for words. Surely he couldn't mean that she was to disrobe
in front of *him.* Only female nurses oversaw the ice bath
therapy here at Belle Glen Asylum. To have a male doctor
in attendance was all but unheard of.

"But, Doctor, I—I've been well behaved." She took an
involuntary step back, trepidation flaring in her stomach
when she saw the tub, jagged chunks of ice bobbing on the
surface as horrifically as shards of broken glass. "Surely
I've done nothing to warrant this—this treatment."

Treatment. A peculiar word. One with many meanings
in a place like this.

"You've been at yourself again." Nurse Greta Schopf,
her self-proclaimed nemesis here at Belle Glen, stepped
forward and grasped her wrist, strong fingers sinking into
her flesh, yanking the loose sleeves to her elbow. The large
German woman, clad in a uniform, a high-necked, somber

gown with a white apron and hat, held up the fresh scratches on Mena's forearm for the doctor's inspection. "She's also been at herself in . . . other ways, Doctor. We've had to strap her to the bed at night to stop her from her amoral compulsions."

Mena gaped at the nurse in sheer disbelief.

"That simply isn't true," she gasped, then turned to entreat the doctor. "Please, she's mistaken, Dr. Rosenblatt; it was another patient, Charlotte Pendergast, who scored my arm with her nails. And I swear I've never—" She didn't want to say it, didn't want the heat to flare in his wrinkled, murky eyes at the thought of her touching herself. Though, at this point, she'd do most anything to avoid the ice bath. "I've never once done myself harm . . . and I've likewise refrained from . . . any . . . amoral compulsions."

She'd informed the doctor of this before, of course, in their initial sessions together. She'd confessed that her bruises and scrapes were not, in fact, self-inflicted, but inflicted *upon* her by her sadistic husband, Lord Gordon St. Vincent, the Viscount Benchley. In her first days as an involuntary patient here, she'd done all she could to emphatically deny any madness or lunacy or sexual misconduct, because it was the absolute truth.

In fact, she'd frantically confessed everything about herself upon her arrival here at Belle Glen Asylum, as she'd been frightened and utterly alone.

At first, Dr. Rosenblatt had reminded Mena of her father, doling out the milk of human kindness from behind his stately office desk. Possessed of a pleasant round face complete with chops and an extra chin, jolly red cheeks, and a portly belly, Dr. Rosenblatt seemed to be a mild-mannered, middle-aged professional gentleman.

She should have known never to trust her instincts when it came to others, especially men. Somehow she was always wrong.

Dr. Rosenblatt snapped open her file, reading it as

though he weren't the sole author of the lies contained within its depths. "You're getting agitated, Lady Bench-ley," he said in that soft voice, the one people usually saved for crying children and the insane.

"No!" she cried, louder than she'd meant to, as Nurse Schopf tugged her toward the bath. "No." She schooled her voice into something more pleasant, more ladylike, even though she dug her feet against the tile floor. "Doctor, I'm not at all agitated, but I would very much prefer *not* to take the ice bath. *Please.* I—isn't there something else? The electrodes, perhaps—or just put the mittens on me and send me to bed." She didn't want to consider the alterna-tives she'd just suggested. She dreaded the electrodes, abhorred the chafing little prisons locked about her wrists, rendering her hands useless for anything at all.

But she feared *nothing* so much as the ice baths.

"Please," she entreated again, frightened tears welling behind her eyes.

"You beg so prettily, Lady Benchley." His gaze never touched hers, but drifted lower, to her mouth and then to her breasts that tested the seams of her tight and uncom-fortable black frock. "But, you see, I am your doctor and my first obligation is the treatment of your illness. Now, if you please, remove your clothing without further incident, or they will be removed for you."

Nurse Schopf's grip tightened on Mena's wrist with bruising strength unusual for a woman. She pulled Mena toward the tub, securing her other hand around Mena's up-per arm. "Are you going to fight me today, Countess Fire Quim, or will you behave for once?"

Countess Fire Quim, it was a name one of the patients had given her that first awful day in Belle Glen. They'd been stripped bare in a room full of fifteen or so women, poked, prodded, deloused, and then doused with buckets of cold water. Someone had remarked on the uncommon shade of her red hair, and then on the darker shade of auburn between her legs. Mena had been called many cruel things in her life, most often by her family, the St. Vincents, and generally pertaining to her uncommon height or her wide hips and shoulders, but "Countess Fire Quim" was somehow the most humiliating. Especially when used by the nurses or the staff at Belle Glen.

"I've done nothing wrong." Mena sent one more panicked, entreating stare to Dr. Rosenblatt, who quietly shuffled the papers in her file without even glancing down at them. "Don't put me in there!"

"You're being hysterical," he said softly. "Which only proves to me the extent of your madness."

The nurses, one on either side of her now, dragged her by the arms. Once she was close enough, Mena kicked out at the tub with both feet, hoping to upset it. The sturdy tub didn't move, but as Mena was not a small woman, her struggles were enough to free her from the grasp of the nurses.

"Wot's this 'ere?" The cheerful voice of Mr. Leopold Burns could have brightened any room that he entered. But to the patients of Belle Glen Asylum, his arrival always brought darkness. The ogre-sized orderly was closer to his twenties than his forties, but an unfortunate potato-shaped nose and thinning blond hair belied his youth. "You're no' makin' any trouble, are you, Lady Benchley?" A fist of dread squeezed Mena's lungs as Nurse Schopf's grip was traded for Mr. Burns's. "Now let's take those clothes off."

Mena fought them this time. She'd tried being prim and obedient. All her life, she'd been timid, pliant, and gentle, and it only served to produce the same result. At least this once, she was not a willing participant in her own humiliating tragedy.

She struggled and jerked as the nurse's deft fingers undid the buttons of her coarse frock, yanking it down her waist and over her hips and legs. She cried and pleaded, kicked and stomped when they ripped her chemise away—

no one in an asylum bothered with a corset—exposing her breasts to Mr. Burns's and Dr. Rosenblatt's greedy eyes.

Those eyes drank their fill, and Mena dimly wondered how the nurses, as women, could be a part of this obvious deviancy.

The tears streaming down her cheeks were not only caused by humiliation and fear, but by the acrid, unbearable stench of Mr. Burns's breath. He pulled her back against his body, and secured her in a bearlike grip under the guise of immobilizing her so the nurses could relieve her of her drawers. His hands groped and grasped painfully at her breasts, and he lowered his offensive mouth to press against her ear. "The more ya struggle, Countess Fire Quim, the harder it is to keep me 'ands proper."

"Your hands have *never* been proper," she accused. The frigid air against her flesh told her she was fully naked now. She became less worried about that than the press of Mr. Burns's growing arousal against her back.

He squeezed her with his meaty arms, cutting off her breath. Sharp pain stabbed at her breasts, and a more worrisome twinge lanced her as she felt something like a rib shift in her side, stealing her ability to draw the breath to cry out.

"Wot senseless things these loonies say," Mr. Burns tsked as he lifted her momentarily paralyzed form over the rim of the tub while each of her legs were secured by a nurse.

Mena watched in horror as the ice water came at her slowly. At this juncture, she could do nothing but brace for the impact.

The shards of ice hit her with the puncturing and sudden affliction of a cat's sharp claw, evoking the reflex to snatch back the offended limb. Except her entire body suffered the sensation and when she breached from the original submersion, she was shocked to see that none of her skin had been perforated.

Out of desperation, she flailed for the edge of the tub, her lungs emitting little spasms of shock that escaped her with desperate mewls. Dragging her naked body up, she managed to gain her feet and nearly hop back out of the tub before three sets of strong hands forced her back down.

Her head went under along with the rest of her.

And stayed.

She thrashed and flailed at her captors, but their hands were everywhere, subduing her limbs. After a time, the initial panic subsided and she stilled. Was this to be how it ended, then? Imprisoned along with the empire's forgotten naturals and unfortunates, a Cockney pervert sneaking a squeeze of her breasts, and a sadistic nurse holding her down while a coldhearted doctor looked on?

She wondered if Lady Farah Blackwell, Countess Northwalk, had ever received her letter. Had the countess done anything on her behalf, or merely ignored her pleas for help. Judging by the burning in her lungs, Mena doubted she'd ever find out.

Perhaps it was for the best. She'd leave this world surrounded by cold and merciless shards of suffocating ice. The literal manifestation of what her life had been these past five years.

Could hell really be worse than this? Was there a chance she'd already served some penance for her sins here on this cruel plane? Perhaps the Lord was not such a vengeful God, merely an indifferent one. Be that the case, maybe she could persuade him to let her have a tiny, insignificant corner of heaven. Even the part no one else wanted. An isolated place at the end of a long lane where she could exist in quietude and seclusion. Away from the malevolence of expectation and the judgment of her many failures. Somewhere the clouds hovered low like a canopy and the sun filtered through them on a late summer's day like the pillars thrown down on the southern moors, as majestic and warm as divine forgiveness.

Closing her eyes, Mena found the bravery to draw in a breath of icy water just as the hands holding her under tightened to pull her up. She surfaced and heaved what little of the liquid had made it into her lungs in a series of soul-racking coughs.

Once the spasms had passed, she focused on filling her lungs with air. The moment was gone, that glimpse of peace she'd found beneath the ice. She knew she was too much of a coward to take her own life.

So she sat and shivered, surrendering to her misery, drawing her knees up to her chest in the bath before the cold stole mobility from her limbs.

"See that she's cleaned and then we'll begin," Rosenblatt directed.

The nurses scrubbed her skin with harsh soap and efficient brutality, remarking as they did so that this would account for her weekly bath.

Five minutes had passed once they'd finished, and Mena's skin felt as though a thousand needles pricked it with simultaneous persecution. But she set her jaw, deciding to do what she must to escape the cold now seeping into her bones.

"I'm going to interview you now, Lady Benchley." Dr. Rosenblatt stepped to the foot of the tub. "I want you to tell me how the following information affects you. If I feel you've answered honestly, we'll get you out of the tub. Do you understand?"

Mena nodded.

"Good." He shuffled some of his paperwork, and finding the one he searched for, he placed it on the top of her open file and read. "First we'll dispense with the generals. Do you hear voices in your rooms at night, Lady Benchley? Ones that keep you awake or torment you?"

Mena remained staring straight ahead and answered honestly. "Only the screams of the patients. And the nurses who mock them."

Greta Schopf pinched her shoulder painfully, but Mena didn't so much as wince.

"Quite so." The doctor never looked up from his notes. "Do you ever see things, strange things, apparitions, ghosts, or hallucinations?"

Mena answered this very carefully, as she knew that hallucinations were the mark of true madness. "Never." She shook her head.

"A few questions for statistical purposes, due to your diagnosis," Rosenblatt continued.

The cold had begun to muddle Mena's thoughts. The blood in her veins slowed to a drip and she'd begun to shiver so violently, she had to force her words through teeth clacking together. But she knew which questions were forthcoming. The diagnosis her husband and his mother had paid their family doctor to make was psychosexual hysteria and amoral insanity, and the good Dr. Rosenblatt simply *delighted* in inquiring about it.

"Tell me, again, how often you and Lord Benchley engaged in marital relations."

Mena refused to answer the question in front of an audience. "I've t-told you already."

"Yes, you've told me he used to come to you five times a week at first, and then hardly ever toward the end. That once he realized you could not bear him children, he sought the company of other women." Dr. Rosenblatt leaned forward, capturing her gaze that was beginning to blur due to the cold. "Except when you would ask him to force you. He told me you disgusted him, especially when you would request that he fulfill your violent sexual fantasies, isn't that right, Lady Benchley?"

Mena learned that even in the ice bath she could burn with shame. "He . . . lied. I. Never. W-wanted . . ." The cold leached into her chest, robbing her of her voice.

"I've warned you, only the truth will liberate you from your current state," Rosenblatt reminded her.

The truth. The truth was that her husband was as much a sadist as Dr. Rosenblatt. Gordon St. Vincent enthusiastically tried to figure out what made people cringe. What they truly feared. What they hated about themselves. And he exploited this information to his advantage.

It had started gradually, her hell within the St. Vincent household. And before long, when Gordon had thought her broken, when his jibes and torments no longer seemed to affect her, her husband became violent. Acts that would land a man in prison should he enact them out on the streets were all perfectly legal if he perpetrated them on his wife.

In the span of time and space, a quarter hour is nothing. A grain of sand on an endless beach. But in that tub, it became an eternity, stretching away from the warm rays of the sun. Until there was nothing but cold. Nothing but this white, white room and suffering.

After that, Mena lost the ability to see the arms on the clock. Her joints seized and her muscles contracted with such violent pain, she let out an involuntary wail.

Lord, but she truly did sound mad.

Her hands contorted into strange and painful angles against her chest, and odd convulsions seemed to rack her spine, even as she felt her heart slow to a plodding amble, nearly losing its rhythm.

She was tired. So tired.

It was then they dragged her from the bath, lifting her by the elbows drawn stiff enough to hold her weight. She'd become like the ice, truly frozen. She couldn't even summon the strength to care anymore as Dr. Rosenblatt and Mr. Burns watched while she was toweled dry and a rough cotton shift yanked over her head.

An alarming numbness had begun to spread from Mena's muscles and limbs inward to her organs. She'd never spent more than ten minutes in the ice baths before. She hardly noticed as a comb was jerked through her long hair.

She tried to stumble away, but her knees refused to hold her as the cold had leached all strength from her muscles. Mr. Burns caught her in time to prevent injury, but she'd rather have fallen to the floor.

"She's too heavy for us to carry. You'll have to get her back to her rooms, Mr. Burns," Nurse Schopf ordered.

" 'Appy to, madam," Mr. Burns said cheerfully.

"I'll assist. The bath has seemed to calm her hysteria, and she should be docile for quite some time." Dr. Rosenblatt pushed away from the wall and snapped her file closed. "See that this gets back to my office, Nurse Schopf, and make certain that we aren't disturbed."

Mena's useless feet made terrible noises on the long, uncarpteted floor as the two men "ushered" her down the corridor, scrubbed and painted with that peculiar whiteness that must be reserved for such institutions. Gas lamps spaced precisely between the doors did nothing to warm the glaring emptiness of the place. Even the beams and bolts and the padlocks on the iron doors had been whitewashed. Sterile, like their bedrooms, devoid of warmth, light, or color. Pure, like their nightgowns, high-necked, binding, and modest, but for the fact one could see the shape beneath.

Little shivering whimpers escaped Mena's chest and throat, unbidden and unwanted, but somehow she couldn't stop them. Her jaw ached from the clenching and clacking of her teeth. The asylum night noises grated on her skin. She felt each wail of insanity as though they were nails scoring her flesh. At the sound of heavy boots, some women pressed their faces against the three bars that comprised their tiny windows to the hall. Their stares pricked her like needles. Some were mad, mocking, and terrible. Others, like her, those who did not belong behind these walls, were full of pity and sometimes tears. Mena could acknowledge none of them. At the moment, she couldn't even manage to turn her neck.

"I like that she's clean and meek," Mr. Burns stated. "But I don't relish the idea of sticking my prick into an ice block."

His words speared a sharp clench of panic through Mena. She'd often wondered if rape was their aim. She knew that the doctor and the orderly had used Belle Glen as their own personal playground. She'd listened to the screams of more than one longtime resident as she'd given birth in the middle of the night. She'd cried with them, and thanked her stars for the first time in her life that she was too tall and too round to be considered truly desirable.

"She'll be warm enough on the inside," the doctor replied shortly. "And the muscle convulsions will make things . . . more interesting."

Dread seized hold of her with a grip tighter than either of their cruel, groping hands.

"P-please. Don't," she stuttered, before her jaw clenched shut on another wave of chills. If only she could struggle. It wouldn't help her, she knew that, but at least she wouldn't have this feeling of being bound by her own sinew and skin. Of all the hopeless anger she felt at the moment, most of it was directed at her own useless limbs.

"That's right, milady, we'll be making ya beg for it," Mr. Burns said with apparent relish before addressing the doctor on the other side of her. "I've been wanting to get me 'ands on those tits for months, why'd you make us wait so long?"

"This is no government-run institution, Burns, with poor oversight and crowding. Also, this isn't just any woman. She's a viscountess. I had to make certain her family wouldn't make a fuss about her. That they wouldn't soften or change their minds and take her home. But the Viscount Benchley has just recently assured me that she's well and truly abandoned to our tender mercies."

Mr. Burns made a noise of anticipation that roiled what little food Mena had in her belly. There had been a spider baked into her bread that evening for dinner, so she'd only drunk the rancid broth.

"Never shagged nobili'iy before," he observed.

"Indeed." Dr. Rosenblatt turned to address Mena. "It may please you to know, Lady Benchley, that your husband has parceled off Birch Haven Place and sold it to make a generous contribution to the institution here at Belle Glen. You'll be a guest here . . . indefinitely."

At that terrible news, a sob escaped her, though, sadly, tears never came. It was as though she were incapable of producing any.

Birch Haven Place had been her *home*. Her only refuge. And now she'd well and truly lost everything.

The portly Dr. Rosenblatt was audibly short of breath by the time they reached her room, and her weight was primarily supported by the orderly.

"Not a dainty bird, are ya?" Burns remarked. "Well, that's awright, I s'pose. You're not like to see tits like those 'uns on a delicate lady."

The jangle of the keys the doctor pulled from the pocket of his overcoat finally produced a spurt of panic strong enough to slam her heart against her ribs. A trickle of fire started in her scalp and dripped down her spine until her entire body seemed dipped in acid.

Dr. Rosenblatt's fat fingers seemed clumsy with excitement, his cheeks flushed beneath his gray beard. "I'm going to go first," he said. "I don't know where else you've put that dirty cod."

"And ya don't want to know, neither," Burns joked, and they shared a masculine chuckle.

Hot tears finally managed to gather behind her eyes and they felt more substantial than the rough hands clamped about her numb arms and waist. Mena wished that she had led the kind of life in which their vulgarity still shocked her. That she'd never known what it was to have a man inside her after she'd said no. Or while she'd cried. Or while she'd struggled and fought. Her husband had taken care of that, hadn't he?

By the time the heavy door to her room swung open, Mena was able to twitch her fingers. Her strength and blood flow was returning in terrible increments.

Which meant she might be able to struggle—but could she fend them both off?

She doubted it. They were brutes. Two men who mocked her for her height and size when Mr. Burns's muscle was covered with a layer of softness and Dr. Rosenblatt was simply fat.

They would win, they would overpower her, and then—a gag she was unable to suppress stole her breath.

"Dr. Rosenblatt!" Nurse Schopf's voice echoed down the hallway like a cannon blast. "Doctor, you must come now!"

A cacophony of madness erupted as other patients were roused, the more unstable of them screeching and making their horrid noises.

"We are being invaded!" the nurse screeched.

"Invaded?" Dr. Rosenblatt visibly blanched. "By whom?"

"The police!"

Lip curling in disgust, Rosenblatt made a nasty comment and then tossed the keys to Mr. Burns. "Put this one in her quarters and use the restraints while I deal with this."

"With pleasure!" Burns gathered Mena to him and forced her into the unlocked room that had become the stage for her nightly battles with the abyss.

"Not the restraints," she rasped out, desperation helping her to regain her voice somewhat. "You don't have to do this. Please just leave me be." There was a special kind of fear in not being able to move one's limbs in the night; the fear created its own sort of lunacy as the mind worked while the body could not. Mena imagined all sorts of horrors to combat the chill of being manacled, spread-eagled, on her hard plank bed. An errant fire that she could do nothing about but lie in wait until it consumed her slowly, or London rats chewing on her feet, or spiders crawling on her with no way to brush them off.

And here a new terror was introduced. A man, two men, with unadulterated access to her body and no way for her to struggle, or strain, or even shift to alleviate the pain that came with intercourse.

Some strength began to return to Mena's hips and shoulders, working its way slowly out from the torso. Everywhere he touched it felt like his skin was made of razors and hers of silk. The ripping sensation was almost audible.

Panic flared as mobility began to return, and Mena tugged against Mr. Burns's unyielding grip. She struggled to wrench and yank away from him, but knew her movements were weak. "Don't tie me up, I implore you!" When one of his arms released her to reach for the first buckled leather manacle, Mena's arm flailed out, her elbow catching him in the chin.

He bared his filthy teeth as he whirled her around and smashed the back of his ham-sized knuckles into her face. He released her as his blow connected, sending her crashing to the hard floor in a pile of weak limbs. Pain exploded into Mena's cheek and radiated to her eyes, ears, and down her neck, but she caught herself with trembling hands before her head cracked against the floor. The taste of brine and copper trickled into her mouth from where her teeth had cut into her cheek.

Mr. Burns crouched down, the pleasant, unassuming look fixed back on his unfortunate features. "Let me remind ya of something out of the kindness of me 'eart, Countess Fire Quim." The foul stench of his breath assailed her, causing her already watering eyes to overflow. "Out there, you're a noble lady expecting everyone to lick your boots and kiss your arse. But in 'ere, you're nothing but another loony cunt, locked away because no one can stand ya. I'll tell ya what I tell the others here. If ya make me 'appy, I can make your life easier. If you're difficult, then life will be difficult, and no one will believe that the bruises I leave on ya weren't inflicted by your own self."

All of the large muscles in Mena's body quivered and twitched with returning blood. Her skin burned, yet she was freezing. Despite all that, she was only aware of the raw black emotion swirling in her soul. Something dark and self-destructive, as though one of the many demons she'd fought in her lifetime had finally been set free.

"It's *Viscountess* Fire Quim, you hateful brute," she snapped, surprising herself as much or more than Mr. Burns. "If you all insist on calling me that ridiculous moniker, the very least you can do is affix the correct title." To seal her fate, she spat blood in his repulsive face.

He acted just like she'd expected him to, and his next vicious blow granted her the oblivion she craved.

To Mena, heaven was a difficult notion to comprehend. And, somehow, whenever she pictured it in her mind, she merely conjured an image of home. Her *real* home. Not Benchley Court, the stately, opulent mansion where she'd resided with her husband these five soul-crushing years. Nor Belle Glen Asylum, where she lay now on the stone floor in a puddle of her blood and grief.

But *home*. Birch Haven Place, an idyllic country baronetcy in Hampshire. A place as much a paradise as this asylum had become her purgatory.

Floating in the dark folds of her unconscious, Mena could feel the sunshine of southern England on her face. Could close her eyes and still see the light and shadow playing to her in the shade of her favorite copse of birch trees where she used to picnic and read of a summer's day. She'd gaze over the fields to where the manor house settled, a cozy Georgian structure, too big to be called a cottage and too small for a mansion, with red stone, white windows, and entirely too many chimneys. Her father had once told her he thought the roof rather cluttered. But Mena had loved each seemingly random gable and smokestack right where it was.

When she was growing up, the gardens had been her fairyland, a place to let her imagination roam. The stables, her adolescent refuge, as she was allowed to explore the countryside on horseback until the fields ran into the sea. The grand fireplace in the meager great hall was a warm corner of comfort, where she and her beloved father had huddled their heads together every winter over countless books and shut out the world.

Her father, lovely as he was, had been too low for high society, too gentle for the merchant class, too eccentric to fit in much of anywhere, but too wealthy to ignore. Her mother had died of scarlet fever before Mena could even walk, and Baron Phillip Houghton had protected and pampered his only daughter. Educated her like a man. Treated her like a treasure. And instilled a love of all things intellectual and agricultural.

When the St. Vincents purchased the stately manor of Grandfield bordering Birch Haven, the baron had seen a chance to save his only child from encroaching spinsterhood.

A disease had been eating at his bones, one he'd kept hidden from Philomena until he succumbed to it mere months after her marriage, leaving her alone in this world but for a cruel husband and his hateful family.

Now Birch Haven was gone. Her father, years dead. And there was no sunshine or warmth in this world.

The cold pierced Mena before consciousness fully returned, and she knew for a fact she was not in heaven. Even before she blinked open her eyes and saw the face of the devil calling her name, an eye patch affixed over a grim, scowling, but satirically handsome face.

"Don't move, Lady Benchley," the black-haired, black-eyed devil was saying as he tucked something around her shivering body, something with warmth in its heavy folds. His cloak, perhaps? "Don't look," he softly ordered.

There was a man yelling, not far from her. Mr. Burns? The voice made her skin crawl. Her face throbbed with pain. Screams of madness and cries of joy echoed from women among the chaos of authoritative male voices out in the hall.

A sickening crunch sounded, and despite the devil's orders—despite her own dismay—Mena looked.

Mr. Burns dropped from the grip of a familiar auburn-haired mercenary. The orderly's neck crooked at an impossible angle and his eyes stared sightlessly at the cold, white walls.

Mr. Burns had been terrified in his last moments, and Mena was glad of it.

"He shouldn't have put his hands on you," the killer stated in that toneless, stony way of his.

"Mr. Argent." A fair-haired man in a perfectly pressed suit leaned into her cell from the doorway, his light brows drawn down his forehead with somewhat paternal disapproval. Though he couldn't have been much older than either Dorian Blackwell or Christopher Argent. "Did you just *murder* that man?"

Argent toed at Burns's limp shoulder, his chilling features a smooth, blank mask of innocence. "No, Chief Inspector Morley, I—found him like this."

The chief inspector glanced from Christopher Argent down at Mena, his blue eyes full of compassion, and then to the devil crouched over her. The director of Scotland Yard was no idiot, and Mena could tell that he ascertained the situation within a matter of seconds.

"Blackwell?"

"Bastard must have slipped whilst accosting the lady." Dorian Blackwell, the Blackheart of Ben More, shrugged as he touched gazes with Argent, and then slid his notice back to Morley.

A tense and silent conversation passed between the three men, and after a moment where even Mena forgot to breathe, the chief inspector dropped his shoulders and nodded. "I'll send for a doctor for the viscountess," he muttered through clenched teeth. "A *real* doctor, as I intend to see the one running this institution hanged."

"I'll dispense with this heap of rubbish." Taking Burns by the ankle, Argent dragged the limp and dirty orderly away as though he weighed no more than a gunnysack.

Turning back to Mena, Dorian tilted his head so he was regarding her solely out of his good eye. "Stay still a while longer, Lady Benchley," he said with a gentleness Mena hadn't known such a villain capable of. "My wife, Lady Northwalk, is waiting in the carriage. Once the doctor says it's all right to move you, we're taking you away from here."

Mena fainted again, this time from profound relief.

CHAPTER TWO

Hallucinations. Delusions. Waking dreams. All symptoms of absolute madness.

And yet every time Mena pinched herself, the pain didn't wake her.

This was really happening.

She blinked rapidly against misty-eyed gratitude as she looked at the two women occupying their own chaise longues, enjoying their second day of watching Madame Sandrine and her efficient minions fit Mena with a new wardrobe. If she were to paint them as they were now, she'd name the work *Seraphim and Seductress*.

Farah Leigh Blackwell, Countess Northwalk, perched on Mena's right, a study of feminine, angelic English gentility. Her ivory muslin and lace gown played with the few gold strands in her white-blond coiffure as she sipped tea from a delicate cup. One would never at all suppose that she was the wife of the most notorious Blackheart of Ben More, king of the London Underworld.

On Mena's left, Millicent LeCour draped her scarlet-clad body across her chaise like a luscious libertine, twirling an ebony ringlet about her finger. She narrowed catlike midnight eyes in assessment and bit through a soft truffle, rolling it in her mouth with sensual enjoyment.

"I know you're self-conscious about the breadth of your shoulders, dear, but if you roll them forward like you're doing now, you convey submission and doubt. You've a lovely, statuesque figure and *must* use it to your advantage. Throw your shoulders back and roll them down from your neck, like you have angel wings you need to stow." Unfolding her legs, Millie stood to demonstrate her instruction, her posture the very image of confidence and authority. "And another thing, keep your chin parallel to the floor. Look anywhere you must if you can't meet someone's eye, but whatever you do, don't drop your chin."

Lessons in comportment from the most famous actress on the London stage; Mena could scarce believe it. She did her best to imitate Millie's posture of regal grace and checked her progress in the mirrors surrounding the dais upon which she stood.

Her shoulders were the solid picture of dignity, wide and imposing. Her bosom thrust proudly aloft, although it was crushed into her new corset to make it appear smaller, pressed against the plain, elegant black buttons of her green and gold plaid day dress, the perfect uniform for her new position as governess.

It was her features that killed the effect.

Mena's tongue touched the healing split in her lip and she realized the swelling had gone down dramatically in the three days since she'd been rescued from Belle Glen. Her eye had blackened and swelled until she couldn't see from it. But she'd applied cold compresses provided by Lady Northwalk, and finally her features were beginning to look like her own again. Though the color from both bruises remained angry.

Much like the man who'd put them there.

Millicent LeCour's fiancé, Christopher Argent, had snapped Mr. Burn's neck easy-as-you-please. Mena won-

dered if the actress knew what her intended was capable
of. She must, for one only had to gaze upon Argent to ascertain that he was a lethal man. The arctic chill in his ice-
blue eyes only melted for the actress and her cherubic
son, Jakub. Mena would be ever grateful to the man, as
he'd pulled Mr. Burns off her unconscious body, saving her
from the indignities the monster had intended to inflict.

Mena felt as though she should be horrified at having
witnessed the ending of a life. But she was glad, grateful
even, that Burns was no longer able to torment the helpless. And more thankful, still, that these two women had
taken her under their respective wings, going so far as to
pay for a new trousseau made by the most sought-after
seamstress in all of London, as well as a bevy of undergarments, shoes, and haberdashery.

She suspected that Madame Sandrine was in the employ, as well as a tenant, of Dorian Blackwell, and thereby
likely used to keeping secrets.

"There you have it," Millie encouraged. "I think that
captures the effect precisely. No one would dare to doubt
your confidence and authority."

"I've never had any authority . . . or much in the way
of confidence, for that matter."

"That's why it's called acting," Millicent prompted,
moving to make way for Madame Sandrine as the tiny,
dark-haired Frenchwoman bustled in with a basketful of
frippery. Setting it down, the seamstress bent to check the
hem of the final dress to be added to Mena's new trousseau. "And I've found that, frequently, whatever you convey you can trick yourself into believing."

"Millie's right, dear." Farah abandoned her tea to a side
table and stood to join her friend. "Often we must seem to
have confidence, and in doing so it tends to appear." Her
clear gray eyes inspected Mena's face with just the right
mix of sympathy and encouragement.

"Your wounds will heal," Millie reassured her. "They

already look much better. I think we've concocted a brilliant story with which to explain them."

"A brilliant story all around, I'd wager," Farah agreed. "And this position is not forever. Dorian has already started on your emancipation from the insanity verdict, though the process is infuriatingly slow."

"Let's go over the lines again." Though she had the demeanor of a seductress, Millicent LeCour possessed the single-minded work ethic of an officer drilling a regiment. "What is your new name?"

Mena took a deep breath, trying to be certain everything was stored correctly in her memory to match the entirely new persona Dorian Blackwell had created for her. "My name is Miss Philomena Lockhart."

"And where are you from?"

"From Bournemouth in Dorset originally, but these past four years from London, where I was employed as a governess."

"I still think we should change her name entirely," Farah suggested. "What about something rather common like Jane, Ann, or Mary?"

Millicent shook her head emphatically. "She doesn't *look* like any of those women, and I know that it's easier to keep track of a lie if there is a shred of truth to it. She'll answer to the name Philomena because it is her own. And it's common enough. We selected Bournemouth because it's near Hampshire, where she was raised, and she's familiar with the town and can call it to memory if need be."

Farah considered this, tapping a finger to the divot in her chin before declaring, "You're right, of course."

Miss LeCour's ringlets bounced around her startlingly lovely face when her notice snapped back to Mena. "Whom did you work for in London?"

"T-the Whitehalls, a shipping magnate and his wife."

"Their names?"

"George and Francesca."

"Who were their children?"

"Sebastian, who is off to Eton, and Clara, who is now engaged."

"Engaged to whom?"

Mena stalled, her eyes widening, then she winced as the bruise around her eye twinged with the movement. "I—I don't remember going over that."

"That's because we didn't." The actress selected another truffle with the patient consideration of a chess master. "I was demonstrating that you're sometimes going to have to improvise. Just say the first plausible thing that happens to appear in your head."

"My head seems to be frighteningly empty of late." Mena sighed.

Farah made a sympathetic noise. "You've been under a lot of strain. Millie, perhaps she needs a break."

"No." Mena shook her head, receiving a sharp look from Madame Sandrine. Remembering herself, she stood as still as could be. "No, I'll try harder."

"What is Clara's fiancé's name?" Millie pressed.

"Um—George?" She plucked the first name that arrived in her head.

"That's her papa's name," Madame Sandrine corrected from below her in her thickly accented voice.

A hopeless sound bubbled into her throat; even the seamstress was better at this than she. "I've always been a terrible liar," Mena fretted, pressing a hand to her forehead. "Never mind an actress! I'm never going to be able to pull this off."

"Nonsense!" Millie planted fists on her perfect hips draped with crimson silk. "You are *strong*, Mena. This is going to be nothing at all compared to what you've already survived."

No one had ever called her strong before. In fact, she'd been berated for being such a mouse. Perhaps strength wasn't so much her virtue as survival. And she had survived, hadn't she? Because of the kindness of these exceptional women.

A sudden rush of gratitude filled Mena until her throat swelled with emotion. "I—I don't know how I'll ever be able to thank you both for what you've done. Not just the rescue, but the clothes, the new life, securing me employment. I only hope I don't let you down, that I can remember all we've concocted here and do it justice."

Millie tossed her curls, eyes snapping with sparks. "I wish you didn't have to use it. That we needn't send you far away. But your husband and his parents are on a rampage to find you. Lord, they're *such*—"

Farah put a staying hand on her friend's arm. "You're going to do just fine," she encouraged.

"I still say you can stay with us," Millie offered. "Christopher shot a member of your family to save my life. Our home in Belgravia would be the last place in London anyone would look for you."

Mena's eyes stung again at the unlimited generosity of these women. "You can't know how much your offer means to me, but the police do know that I confessed my family's crimes to save yours. Chief Inspector Morley knows that we are close, I feel that I would be putting your fiancé's new career in danger."

Millie's frown conveyed her frustration, but she didn't argue the point. Christopher Argent had once been the highest-paid assassin in the empire. Now, because of his love for Millie, he was trying a career in law enforcement on for size. Considering what had happened with Mr. Burns, Mena wondered if the big man was suited to the job.

"We all agree that getting you out of London will be safer for you should your husband or agents of the crown come looking for you here," Farah reminded them gently. "And arrangements have been solidified in Scotland. Lord

Ravencroft has already said he would meet your train to-morrow afternoon."

The bottom dropped out of Mena's chest, sending her heart plummeting into her stomach. She still wasn't certain how she'd gone from being a viscountess, to a prisoner at Belle Glen, and then a phony spinster governess in such a short time.

Madame Sandrine stood, the seamstress's eyes wide with disbelief. "You are going to work for the *Demon Highlander*?"

"T-the what?" Mena gasped, unable to keep a telling tremor out of her voice. "The who?"

Farah winced, which did little to allay Mena's growing panic.

Madame Sandrine hurried on, her face luminous with ill-omened dramatics. "They say that the Marquess of Ravencroft went to the crossroads to make a deal with a demon so that he will never die in battle. He is known to charge cannon and rifles head-on, and the bullets and cannonballs curve around him as if he were not there. He has killed so many men that there is a mountain of bones in hell named after him. The most violent man alive, is he. It is said he can murder you with only a touch of—"

"Madame Sandrine," Farah said sharply. "That's quite enough."

"A . . . *mountain* of bones?" Mena stared at the two rather guilty-looking women with pure disbelief. "Just *where* are you sending me?"

Farah stepped forward carefully. "You of all people know how the papers sensationalize these things. Yes, Lord Ravencroft was a soldier some twenty years, and was commended for his uncommon bravery in Asia and the Indies. His children are nearly grown, which means he's a much older man now. He's retired from the army life, and committed to being nothing more than a father and a farmer. I assure you, there's nothing to be frightened of."

But Mena *was* frightened. Her stomach roiled and her legs wanted to give out. What if she'd been tossed from the pot into the flames? What if Farah's perspective was skewed by her own circumstances? She *was* married to the Blackheart of Ben More, after all. He was king of the London Underworld because he'd won the Underworld war by washing the streets of East London with rivers of blood. When one was married to such a lethal man, who would think twice about sending someone to . . . "The—the most violent man alive?" she finished aloud as a shudder of anxiety stole her breath and a tic began to seize in her eyebrow. Mena sank to her knees on the dais, gasping for air. "I don't think I can do this."

Farah sank next to her and rubbed a warm hand across her back. "Mena . . . I know you don't know me very well, but I'm your friend. I wouldn't send you to him if I thought you'd be in danger."

Mena just shook her head, unable to form words around her pounding heart and the heavy lump of fear threatening to choke her.

Farah took something out of her skirt pocket and gave it to Mena. A letter with a broken wax seal. "Read this," Farah prompted. "And then make your final decision. Know that in giving you this letter, I'm entrusting you with information that not many are privy to."

Millie sat on Mena's other side and took her hand. "I've learned something about being in a desperate situation that may help you."

Mena stared at the letter and focused on regaining her breath. The thick paper had Farah's name on it, scrawled in substantial, heavy masculine script. The letters were the precise same height and width. All lined up like little soldiers.

"What is that?" she whispered.

"Sometimes." Millie's usually cheerful voice was low and grave. "When in a predicament like yours, the safest place to be is at the side of a violent man."

Dear Lady Northwalk,

This correspondence is meant to inform you and Dorian that I have retired from military duty to Ravencroft Keep to oversee clan farms, tenements, and to run the distillery.

As you may know, I have been this past decade a widower, and my children little better than orphans, as I have spent the preponderance of their lives abroad in Her Majesty's service.

In my absence, their education has been disastrously neglected.

When a soldier is fortunate enough to reach the age I have, he collects many regrets. Mine are not confined to the atrocities of war, but also to what I have abandoned. Not only in regard to my children, but also to your husband. My own brother.

I have no right to do so, but I wonder if I may call upon your gentle will for a boon.

I am not a man used to prevailing upon the kindness of others. However, as an unrefined soldier, I am ill-equipped to prepare my children for the world in which they will be expected to reside as the heirs of a marquess. Rhianna is due for a season, and Andrew wishes to go away to university when he is of age. They're in need of an exceedingly experienced governess and tutor. I would ask that you find one, not for my benefit, but for theirs. They deserve the very best in civilized education. No matter the cost. Inform her that her relocation expenses will be included, and she can have any salary you deem satisfactory.

> *I will owe you a debt of gratitude for your*
> *assistance.*
> *Please extend your husband my regards.*
> *Yours in gratitude,*
> *Lt. Col. William Grant Ruaridh Mackenzie.*
> Marquess Ravencroft.

Bealach na Bà Pass, Wester Ross, Scotland,
Autumn 1878

Mena considered it a kindness on God's part that the brougham carriage wheel had waited to noisily fracture until they'd crested the treacherous road through the Highland mountains and angled west on the verdant peninsula toward Ravencroft Keep. Had it broken earlier, the carriage would surely have shattered upon the black stones scattered about the moss-covered valley floor.

The kind driver in full livery, Kenneth Mackenzie was his name, had been the only one to meet her at the Strathcarron rail station. Mena never could have guessed the elderly man would climb the switchbacks of the Bealach na Bà Pass with the alacrity of a man chased by Death.

After a cursory inspection of the broken wheel, the driver had muttered something to her in an unintelligible form of English, unhitched one of the four horses from the wagon, and gone for help straightaway, leaving Mena with only three horses and the approaching storm for company. That had been—Mena checked her new pocket watch—more than an hour past now, and the torrential rain had begun to obscure the view by which she'd been captivated in her time alone.

The topography of the Highlands tantalized her until she'd quite forgotten about her tossing stomach caused by the vigorous climb up the switchbacks and the ensuing fear for life and limb.

Mena had seen beautiful countryside before, having been raised in the bucolic paradise of Hampshire. Wester Ross was nothing like the tranquil, organized fields and pastures of South England. Something feral and untamed breathed life into this place. An air of prehistoric mysticism lingered in the very stones. She could sense it as potently as the cling of brine in the air caused by water stirred by the storm, or the last fragrant gasp of the heather and thistle as autumn encroached. Moss and lush vegetation clung to the dark rock and soil, painting the landscape every conceivable spectrum of green.

But now low, rolling clouds climbed the black stone peaks like inevitable conquerors, hiding the tops of the Hebrides from view. Even the rain was different in this place. Unlike the gray storms of London, the moisture didn't fall from the lofty heavens. It crept upon her with the chill of uncovered secrets, surrounding her in a heavy mist tossed about by unruly winds.

She shivered, even in her dress of heavy wool and the blanket the footman had found for her beneath the seat. The cold here reached through her clothing and her flesh, cloying around her bones and causing them to quake.

It wasn't an ice bath. And so she could endure.

Though she wasn't certain for how much longer. What if something had happened to poor old Kenneth Mackenzie in this weather? It was barely possible to see much more than ten paces away, and over terrain like this, one could easily end up in a bog somewhere, or stumble down a ravine.

A sound like the muffled beating of her accelerating heart pounded at the earth, and Mena leaned against the window in time to see several mounted Highlanders melt out of the mists like the specters of Jacobite warriors who had roamed these very moors a hundred years past.

Her breath caught at the sight of them. Heavy cloaks protected brawny shoulders, though their knees remained bared to the elements by matching blue, green, and gold kilts. They reined their horses to a walk and lurked closer to the carriage, letting the mist unveil them to her wide gaze.

Mena was suddenly aware of how *very* alone and vulnerable she was. Chances were, she told herself, this was the help Kenneth Mackenzie had sent for, but she didn't see the driver among the mounted Highlanders.

She counted seven, each one burlier—and *filthier*—than the last. On the other hand, they could be brigands. Highwaymen, rapists, murderers . . .

Oh, dear God.

They circled the carriage, all peering inside the rain-streaked windows with not a little curiosity, speaking the lyrical language of the Highlands. She understood it to be Scots Gaelic, though she comprehended not a word.

Then she saw *him.*

Her mouth became dry as the desert, and a tremor that had nothing to do with the cold rippled through her.

Though he wore a soiled kilt and loose linen shirt beneath his drenched cloak, he sat astride a black Shire steed with the bearing of a king. Dark waves of hair hung long and heavy with moisture down his back, and menace rolled off the mountains of his shoulders in palpable waves.

Whoever he was, he was their undeniable leader. She saw it in the way they looked to him, in the deference they used when speaking. If not by birth, then by physical laws of nature, surely. As the largest, the strongest, and the most fearsome of them all, he towered above the brawny men as he scowled through the window at her.

Even through the mesh of her hat's veil, and the black soot streaked across his features, Mena could see the tension in his strong jaw. The aggression etched into the grooves of his fierce, deep-set eyes. Viewed through the chaotic tracks of rain upon the window, he could have been a savage Pict warrior, bred not only to survive in this beautiful and brutal part of the world, but to conquer it.

Mena gasped at the shocking flash of muscled thigh bared to her as he dismounted, and despaired that even afoot, his astounding height and breadth diminished not at all.

Dear Lord, he was coming closer. He meant to reach for the door.

Lunging forward, she threw the lock and extracted the skeleton key just as his big hand turned the latch.

Their eyes met.

And the rain disappeared. As did everything and everyone else.

Mena knew that there were moments in one's life as significant as an epoch. Existence, as a result, was split into a before, and an after, and whatever was left as a consequence of that moment illuminated who someone really was. It laid one open, exposing the most vulnerable part of one's self for honest and brutal inspection, and the acceptance that inexorable change has been wrought. She'd lived long enough to experience a few of these. Her mother's death when Mena was only nine, her first real taste of tragedy. The first time she galloped on a horse on her father's farm, and experienced true freedom. Her first kiss. The horror of her wedding night. The moment she was told she'd never be a mother.

So she recognized this as one such moment.

The leviathan on the other side of the now seemingly inadequate barrier of the window was not the only one conducting the inspection.

What Mena saw in the striations of amber and ebony in the Highlander's eyes alternately terrified and fascinated her. Here was a man capable of inconceivable violence. And yet . . . a weary sorrow lurked behind the incredulity and subsequent exasperation in his glare. He might even be attractive beneath all that soot and filth, but in the feral and weathered way the Highlands, themselves, were appealing.

Mena blinked, berating herself for noticing such a thing of her probably robber-highwayman-rapist-assassin, and the spell was broken.

"Open the door," he commanded in a deep and booming brogue.

"No," Mena answered, before remembering her manners. "No, thank you."

They called him the Demon Highlander.

Over the course of the previous two decades, Liam Mackenzie had led a number of Her Majesty's infantry, cavalry, and artillery units. He'd stormed countless mobs during the Indian Mutiny and made his fame when the so-called Indian Rebellion had been crushed. He'd facilitated the disbandment of the East India Company with espionage, assassination, and outright warfare, painting the jungles with blood until the crown seized the regime. He led the charge against Chinese cannon in the second Opium War, leaping from his horse over cannonfire and slicing through Asian artillery. He'd secretly conducted rescue missions to Abyssinia and Ashanti, leaving no trace of himself but for a mountain of bodies in his wake. He'd trained killers and killed traitors. He'd toppled dynasties and executed tyrants. He was William Grant Ruaridh Mackenzie, lieutenant colonel of Her Majesty's Royal Secret Highland Watch, Marquess Ravencroft, and ninth laird and thane of clan Mackenzie of Wester Ross. A high agent of the crown and a leader of men was he.

When he gave an order, it was obeyed by patrician and plebian alike. Most often without question.

He had no time for this. A fire had somehow ignited in the east fields this morning and his men were exhausted from frantically fighting it. The rain had been a blessing, one that had saved their winter crops. When Kenneth had ridden up and explained their predicament with the carriage, they'd raced five miles through the sac-shriveling autumn rain to save her pretty hide.

Had she *really* just locked him out of his own carriage and then disobeyed his command with a polite *no, thank you*?

If he'd have been himself, he'd have ripped the door off its hinges and yanked her to attention, taking her to task for her insolence.

He should do it now, lest his men think him weak.

Then again, perhaps not, lest his men think him brutal.

He never knew anymore. These Mackenzie were farmers, not soldiers, and the regulations that had regimented his life didn't apply here at Ravencroft.

More's the pity.

When their eyes had met, he'd felt the earth shift beneath him in a way he'd never experienced before. Not with the unstable feeling of a peat bog or slick silt beneath his boots, but exactly the opposite. As if the land might alter and align to please the cosmos, clicking into place with prophetic finality.

Something about the bruised look glowing from the softness of her vibrant green irises, the only thing about her he could see with any clarity, seemed to have stolen his wits from him.

It was bloody unsettling. Infuriating, even.

He jiggled the handle of the carriage door. "Open up, lass," he hissed through his teeth.

The infernal woman shook her head demurely, her lips quivering behind the heavy veil she wore. Leaning up, she unlatched the small half-window used for ventilation above the larger window and spoke through it in a perfect, cultured British accent.

"I'd rather not, thank you."

Liam's knuckles cracked as he tightened his fist.

"I think we've frightened the wee lassie," Liam's steward, Russell Mackenzie, said in their native Gaelic. "We look a sight after the day we've had."

Liam glanced at his soot-laden steward, then down at his soiled and drenched clothing. "Och, aye," he agreed. Then turned back to the woman. "If ye'll come with us, we'll take ye to Ravencroft Keep and get ye out of the storm. We can send for yer things once ye're safe."

She glanced nervously at the men surrounding the carriage, and Liam thought he caught sight of a wound or a split in her lip when she turned her head. He couldn't be certain. He couldn't see inside as well as he wanted to. And Lord, it irritated him how badly he desired to uncover the rest of her features and perceive if they were as striking as her lovely eyes.

"I do appreciate your kind offer, sir, but I'll wait for someone from the Ravencroft household to collect me. They should be along *any* moment."

That elicited a rumble of amusement from his clansmen.

It occurred to Liam that he couldn't remember the last time he'd been thanked so often in one conversation. Or denied.

"That'd be us, lassie." Thomas Campbell, a bear of a man, gestured to Liam. "And this here be the marquess, himself, isna that right, Laird?"

"Aye." Liam nodded, expecting her to open the door now that that had been cleared up.

Instead of the deference he anticipated, one skeptical brow dropped over her right eye as she took in his appearance. "I think not."

The laughter came louder this time, and Liam set his teeth. "I am Liam Mackenzie, Marquess Ravencroft, laird and thane of the Mackenzie of Wester Ross."

Her tongue snaked out to test what he now knew to be

a split in her lip as she seemed to work a problem out beneath that troubled brow.

Liam shifted restlessly, testing the strength of the latch as her eyes brightened with an idea.

"Do you happen to have any proof of your lordship or nobility?" she suggested, blinking pleased, expectant eyes at him as though she'd offered some sort of foolproof plan. "A signet ring, perhaps, or a seal of—"

"The fact that I havena torn this carriage apart with my bare hands is proof enough of my nobility," he growled through lips drawn tight over his teeth. "Now open the *bloody* door."

"I'm sorry, but no." She shut the window.

His men's chuckles came to an abrupt stop when he whirled to glare at them. Facing her again, he knocked on the window this time, careful not to break it, and she opened it as primly as any English valet.

"Is there something else?" she queried.

"Aye!" Russell Mackenzie hooted before Liam had a chance to finish his intake of breath. "How do ye *know* he's *not* the Mackenzie laird?"

Liam would have growled in kind at Russell, but he had to admit it was a good question.

"Because the marquess is the father of two children nearly grown and lately from a decades-long career in the army. By now he's got to be a retired older man, not this . . . this . . . strapping sort of . . ." The lady flicked those long lashes at him in another nervous gesture before finishing. "Not *him*."

Something Liam had thought long dead rose from the ever-still, ever-dark place within him. Some strange pride belonging to adolescents and young bucks during mating season. At forty, he'd never expected to experience it again. He fended off overt sexual advances regularly, from beautiful women. Younger women. But this veiled lass's insinuation of virility nearly had him flushing like an untried whelp.

Goddammit, was this going to become an issue?

"Coax her out of there, Liam," Russell urged, again in Gaelic, though his voice still conveyed amusement. "It's colder than a witch's tits in a brass corset out here."

Liam took a bracing breath. "What would it take to get ye to Ravencroft Keep?" he asked as though speaking to a simple child.

"Well . . ." She hesitated, glancing at each of his men, then back to him. "Since you asked, I would pay you, of course, if I could prevail upon you . . . gentlemen . . . to perhaps secure the wheel?"

All four mounted Mackenzies and two Campbells exploded into booming spasms of mirth, which drew a frown from the woman. Even Liam had to bite his lip to repress a smile, and he didn't miss how his new governess watched the movement with an arrested expression.

"That's what it takes, does it?" Thomas Campbell chortled whilst wringing the rain from his cap.

"Just slip the wheel back onto the carriage and off ye go!" Russell laughed hard enough to startle his horse into a prance.

"As a matter of fact, *yes*," she huffed.

Highlanders were a jolly lot, but it had been a long time since he'd heard his men laugh quite so heartily. They jibed him in their native tongue.

Ye should send her back. She's not too bright.

Maybe ye could keep her as a mistress, instead, she's entertaining as well as pretty.

Bemused, Liam squinted at her indistinguishable expression through her veil. She did seem rather young judging by her voice and what little of her features he could make out. He wondered why Farah Blackwell had selected her, specifically, to send for the position. Had he not been clear enough in his specifications?

The lass waited with a long-suffering air for the joviality to die before she spoke again. "Do forgive me, sirs, if

I'm mistaken, but I inspected the wheel a little earlier, before it started to rain, and it seemed to me a simple fix if you could use your cumulative strength."

"Well, lassie, *do* educate us on how simple it would be." Russell wiped either a raindrop or a tear of mirth from his ruddy cheek. "We just pop the wheel back on the axle and hold it with what, a prayer?"

Now it was she who smiled. "Well . . . no." She dragged the word in a protracted manner then pointed out of the window with a long, elegant finger. "Upon assessment, you'll find the wheel and axle both in excellent repair. If you gentlemen would look to that two-parted hub there, its principal features are these two linchpins." She rose on her knees to slide her arm out of the window and point downward toward the problem. "They've both been sheared at the top here, you see, which is why the wheel came loose."

Every Highlander, including Liam, stared at her for a full silent minute, all traces of mockery vanished. Partly because of what she said, and partly because her body was now pressed against the larger window of the carriage.

Even through her dyed burgundy wool dress, every man could see she had the figure a lusty Highlander dreamed about at night. She should have looked ridiculous, arm and eyes half out a tiny window. But Liam burned with shame, and quite a few other confusing emotions, when he found himself as slack-jawed as the rest of his men.

Christ, were those breasts real, or were they the creations of some newfangled English contraption?

In that moment, he'd have given his eye to find out. And just as abruptly, he wanted to burn the eyes out of every man who ogled her.

"Well," he snarled at them. "Check the bloody wheel."

It was Russell who dismounted and jogged close to inspect her assessment. "I'll be buggered if she isna right," he muttered to Liam, who stood wondering how in the hell a young gentlewoman, one with breasts like that, would know about carriage mechanics.

"But, lass, we've no linchpin lying around out here on the Bealach na Bà." Russell looked to her as though she might come up with a magical answer for that, too.

"Now that we know the problem," Liam said very evenly, "I would ask ye to again consider riding with me the scant five miles to Ravencroft Keep." His reasons for wanting her on his horse had become much more opaque, but mostly he wanted her away from that fucking window and the wide, lusty gazes of his men.

Her expression actually brightened. "There's really no need." She then addressed Russell, his round, freckled face, ruddy cheeks, and perpetually jolly expression obviously more favorable. "Mightn't you borrow a linchpin from one of the other wheels, as they all have two? That should hold for a scant five miles without incident and then more extensive repairs can be made at the keep." At least she pulled her arm back into the carriage with her, which angled her body away from the window.

Liam wasn't quite sure if he should thank God or curse Him.

Russell considered her words. "We'd need something to secure it with." He rubbed at his russet beard with a thoughtful hand, then winked at her. "Braw as we are, we canna work a linchpin with our bare fingers."

"I've my tool bag." Thomas Campbell's son, Kevin, dismounted and reached into his saddlebags, extracting a leather case.

Liam held up a hand. "It would be easier to deliver ye to Ravencroft and then repair this without the extra weight," he said through clenched teeth.

She gasped, and every married man made a noise of either warning or panic.

"I meant of the bloody trunks lashed to the top of the

carriage!" His famously short temper was fraying rapidly. Liam gestured to his horse, Magnus, and held his hand out to her as though the carriage walls didn't separate them. "Please, lass."

She regarded his outstretched palm for an indecisive moment with such intensity that Liam glanced down at it to see what the bloody issue was. He found nothing but his hand. Callused, square, and unsightly scarred, but nothing extraordinary, except perhaps the size, but there was fuck-all he could do about that.

They weren't like the hands of any marquess she'd have met before. They both knew it.

"I can't . . . I'm afraid."

Liam regarded her for another tense moment as no one moved whilst waiting for his say-so. He'd at first thought her words had been *I can't, I'm afraid*. An expression of polite regret. But upon closer scrutiny, he didn't wonder if the meaning was entirely different. An admission.

I can't. I'm afraid.

Somehow, the ball of frustration in his chest released only slightly. Though something else took its place. Maybe a bit of disappointment? He'd seen that look before in a woman's eyes, the innate suspicion mixed with placating caution. His mother had worn that look around his father.

He glanced back down at his hands. Could she somehow see the blood that stained them? Could she sense the cruelty bred into his black soul? Did she know the vile and unholy urges that, even now, coursed through the very fibers of his muscle?

She was right to fear him.

"All right, lads." Liam inhaled a weary breath and took post by the axle to lift the heaviest part whilst someone affixed the wheel back in place. "Let's get this over with."

He felt her gaze on him as they lifted the carriage and patched it. He couldn't figure out why he was so full of this awareness, but something about her watching him grunt and strain and sweat was damnably erotic.

He didn't allow himself to look at her, though, even when the deed was done. Instead, he swung onto Magnus's back and kicked him into a gallop, leaving one of the others to drive the coach back to Ravencroft.

He needed a bath and a change. If she wanted a proper marquess, she was about to meet one.

CHAPTER THREE

The rain painted the red sandstone of Ravencroft Keep a deep, melancholy shade. Mena loved it immediately, as the roof was, as her father would have said, rather crowded. She counted fourteen turrets and four towers as the carriage trundled over an ancient stone bridge arching above an emerald loch.

Renaissance architecture from the early seventeenth century overlaid defensive ramparts and the original tower that must have dated all the way back to Robert the Bruce. The windows were large and airy for such an imposing stone structure, she supposed, to optimize the view and the occasional sunlight over the sparkling sea beneath the cliffs below. She'd only begun to count the chimneys when they pulled past the fountain around the circular drive and thereby lost sight of the roof.

She'd known the keep would be large, as it was a castle, after all. But this estate had to boast at least a hundred rooms, perhaps more.

Mena took another moment to close her eyes and silently send a whisper of gratitude to the Blackwells for arranging this new life for her. Here might be that isolated place at the end of a lane where she could exist in quietude and seclusion. Just as she'd imagined at Belle Glen.

She hoped the carriage debacle would be her only unpleasant surprise for the rest of the day. If she avoided anyone like the frightening Highlander she'd met on the road, she'd likely succeed.

His men had been nice enough, one of them even going so far as to drive the carriage to Ravencroft. But *his* savage visage had unsettled her, so much so, her heart had yet to slow from its frantic pace.

What was it about a ferocious man that terrified her so? To date, it had been so-called civilized men that had caused her harm.

But the power in the Highlander's body as he'd strained and lifted the carriage with his men had impressed her to a bewildering degree. It had to be his sheer, inconceivable size. And the magnitude wasn't only pertaining to his towering height, but the breadth of his shoulders and the depth of his chest. Some of that had to be the cloak he wore, didn't it?

Mena knew Dorian Blackwell as a well-built man, strong and broad. And likewise Christopher Argent filled a doorway with impossibly wide shoulders, his like not often seen in the boroughs of London. But . . . Mena didn't think she'd ever witnessed a feat of strength to match what she'd seen today. Never cast her eyes upon a man so large and well hewn. His kilt had revealed more than it covered as he'd used his tree-trunk thighs to lift the carriage. His neck had corded and jaw clenched in a most . . . captivating manner. The disturbing notion that something even more intriguing was happening beneath the thick cloak still hadn't abandoned her thoughts.

Lord help her, she hadn't been able to look away.

Once he'd galloped off into the mist, she'd had a strange feeling, much like she'd done after stumbling upon an uncommon creature in the wild, and watching it leap into the shadows. The sense of disenchantment in the knowledge that such a glimpse was rare and extraordinary, and one was likely not to experience it again.

Which was for the best, she decided. Who knew what a man like that was capable of?

Mena sobered a bit when the carriage passed the entrance with the grand stairway and circumvented the keep toward a wide but decidedly less grand portal in the back.

The servants' entrance.

Right. Now was the time to remember not who she had been, but who she was meant to become.

She filled her lungs with a bracing breath, though nothing could have prepared her for the streak of color in the form of what she supposed was a footman, who danced down the few stone steps. He opened the door with a flourish, covering the space with an overlarge umbrella.

"Miss Philomena Lockhart?" He swept her one carpetbag right off her lap before she had the chance to reply, and gave her the most graceful bow she'd ever seen. It was much like being accosted by a sunrise. "I am Rajanikan Dayanand, valet to Laird Liam Mackenzie, Marquess Ravencroft, and I have arrived for the purposes of collecting you and conducting you to the keep."

The word *vibrant* aptly described both the lean young man's manners and his wardrobe. A bright orange and gold silk kurta shimmered from beneath his crimson sherwani, what Mena understood to be the name of the long, lushly embroidered coat favored by the Hindu people. His legs were wrapped in bolts of umber silk, the same color as the long scarf draped around his neck.

Mena took his outstretched hand and ducked under the umbrella with him as they trotted up the stairs and into an alcove off the kitchens that served as a cloakroom.

"Thank you, Mr. Dayanand." She shook a few stray drops of moisture off her wool pelisse as he wrestled the umbrella closed and stowed it in the stand.

"Everyone calls me Jani." His smile was luminous and his black eyes sparkled. Beneath all the opulent drapery he wore, his true age was indecipherable. He could have been fifteen or twenty-five, though his skin was the color of teak, and just as smooth.

"Jani, then." She offered her hand. "I am—"

"Miss Philomena Lockhart, yes, I know. We've all been very curious to meet you." He swept his hand to the cluster of staff gathered in the kitchens on various perches all staring at her in peculiar silence.

A collection of maids were gathered around a large table laid with tea, as a kitchen girl paused in the middle of clearing the evening meal to gawk. A handful of footmen, livery, and ground workers sat on rough-hewn stools at the cooking island, their meaty hands wrapped around tankards of ale as they'd been chatting with a portly cook as he turned a large spit adorned with what appeared to be some sort of lake fowl. They were all filthy and exhausted, peering at her from behind bleary eyes and sooty features.

"How do you do?" Mena pleased herself by saying around the heart beating in her throat as she executed a slight curtsy.

She suddenly felt a pang of guilt for not getting to know her servants better. Though in her husband's household, such familiarity would not have been tolerated. She'd been utterly isolated, even from the kindness of her staff.

The men at the cooking island nodded back to her, their stares oddly concentrated as a few of them mumbled something that she thought was *whit like?*

Hoping it was a local greeting, she replied. "It's a pleasure."

"English." The cook muttered loudly enough for most to hear in his heavy French accent. "Humph."

"That's Jean-Pierre, our ill-tempered chef," Jani informed her by way of introduction.

In this situation, at least, Mena knew what to do. *"Votre*

canard sent la perfection. Je peux seulement espérer goûter quelque chose de si délicieux pendant mon séjour."

All eyes shifted to the chef as his chubby face melted into a smile. "Madame's *French* is perfection. I shall make for you a special dessert tonight. Please tell me you prefer wine to the Scotch swill these Luddites slurp like water." He spat on the floor.

"Truth be told, I am rather partial to the wines of Provence above all else." Mena offered him the most dazzling smile through her veil, painfully aware that the so-called swill sold internationally for more money per volume than gold.

"Then welcome to Ravencroft, mademoiselle!"

"Merci."

"Come, come, Miss Philomena Lockhart." Jani seized her hand and pulled her through the impressive kitchens with startling energy. "Dinner is to be served soon and the marquess has requested your presence there. We must hurry if you are to dress in time."

Mena had barely stepped away from the kitchens before it erupted into chaos. She couldn't understand a thing they said, as they conversed in Gaelic, secure in the knowledge that a proper Englishwoman would not likely have learned their language.

"They like you," Jani informed her as he pulled her down a narrow servants' hall.

"How could you be certain?" Mena wrinkled her brow. But for the good impression she'd left with Jean-Pierre, her welcome had been decidedly cold.

"You must not blame them. There was a fire in the fields earlier today. It was a blessing that the storm came when it did, or this year's winter crop could have been lost. Everyone is recovering from the fear and the excitement of that."

"Oh, dear," Mena exclaimed. "That's terrible, indeed, was anyone injured?"

"No and we are lucky. But the fire is why no one was able to meet you at the train but the driver. I know that the marquess had planned to drive out to collect you, himself, and now, I think, he will be sorry that he did not."

"Why do you say that?" Mena queried.

"Because, Miss Philomena Lockhart, we all expected you to be old and fat, not young and pretty."

"I am not so young." Certainly not pretty. Mena thought of the many times she'd been told she was too fat. A flatterer, this Jani. She liked him immensely. "You may call me Mena."

Jani shook his head. "You are a proper English lady. I am to address you appropriately."

"Miss Mena, then."

Throwing a brilliant smile over his shoulder as he pulled her along, he nodded. "Miss Mena. It is my feeling that the marquess will like you, as well."

Mena worried her lip. She certainly hoped so, because the Marquess Ravencroft, the so-called Demon Highlander, was her only chance for refuge.

Liam couldn't seem to stop himself from glancing into the shadows beyond the door to the dining room. He was famished and furious. It was now three minutes past the hour and everyone at the table waited in silent anticipation for the final dinner guest to arrive.

Miss Philomena Lockhart. His new English governess. What name could be more particularly British than hers?

Philomena.

It belonged to some starched, beak-nosed spinster with a nasal voice and a perpetual wrinkle of disapproval between her stolid brows.

Not the young, buxom creature with emerald eyes that had so charmed and bedeviled his men this afternoon. The shadowy hint of her features he'd spied from beyond the

rain-speckled window and behind the black veil of her hat
had insinuated comeliness. And Liam had spent the entire
time he'd bathed and dressed peering into his memory of
those few maddening moments with her as though they
would reveal her mysterious features to his mind's eye.

He *should* have been thinking of the disastrous fire
today. He should have been contemplating the reasons for
the sheared carriage-wheel linchpins, a cut so clean it
could only have been done on purpose.

Obviously he had enough to occupy his mind without
the addition of Miss Philomena Lockhart and her distracting breasts.

He'd come to the table frustrated, and quickly embarked
on the road to a downright foul mood.

Sharp, rapid clips of a woman's shoes against the stone
floor in the hall echoed the staccato strike of his heart
against his ribs. Liam rose to his feet with such speed, his
chair made an alarming sound on the floor as she rushed
into the dining room, in a breathtaking array of curls and
cleavage.

"Do pardon my tardiness," she puffed as the rest of
the table stood upon her arrival. "For such a square structure, Ravencroft is surprisingly labyrinthine, and I became hopelessly lost . . ." Her words died an abrupt death
as her eyes alighted upon *him* at the head of the table.

Liam had expected a sense of smug satisfaction in this
moment, and he'd taken special care with his appearance tonight in anticipation of the very expression she now
wore. He'd gone so far as to tie his hair back in a queue and
shave a second time to rid himself of a shadow beard.

That he would feel like an imposter at the head of his
own table was not something he'd considered. But didn't
he just? He was yet unaccustomed to this role. He'd been
soldier, he'd been leader. He'd been killer and monster.

But a gentleman? A nobleman?

A noble . . . man?

He'd planned on eviscerating her publically for questioning his word and nobility in front of his men. For costing him precious time in the fields. For making him wait for dinner.

And for dominating his thoughts all bloody afternoon.

But perhaps she'd provoked his ever-ready ire because she gave voice to the doubts that Liam had about his ability to turn a demon into a laird.

He'd waited for that look of wide-eyed, astonished panic all evening. However, it became apparent to him immediately that any intentions he'd had involving thought or speech would have to be reconsidered. As he was bereft of either at the moment.

The blame for that, too, rested squarely on her shoulders. Her lovely *bare* shoulders.

Liam gripped the sturdy table for support. Nothing he'd imagined she hid behind that veil and thick wool pelisse could have prepared him for the unadulterated view of Miss Philomena Lockhart he now enjoyed.

Her dinner dress was a simple, modest green silk affair with little adornment but for some black cording about the bodice and a few black lace ruffles at the hem of the skirts. But on a figure like hers, it was nothing less than a stitched scrap of temptation. The cords, through some magic of tailoring, puffed into translucent sleeves below her shoulders, which met with the edges of her long black dinner gloves. A simple onyx satin ribbon about her lovely throat was her only ornamentation.

There was something about that Liam grudgingly admired. She didn't need any jewels in order to catch the eye.

She was enough all on her own.

Liam knew he'd meet her seamstress in hell for the slew of pure sin racing through his mind and pouring down his body like molten lava. For the wicked fingers that had made this dress knew *exactly* what they were doing to any man who had to submit to the presence of *this* woman in *that* gown. It was crafted to the specifications of propriety, but anyone should know that a woman with breasts like hers should be buttoned to the neck.

The gown had been constructed to make him suffer.

Liam swallowed a rush of profuse hunger flooding his mouth with anticipatory moisture. Philomena Lockhart was, in a word, delectable. Her lips plump and ripe as strawberries. The mounds of her breasts lush and white as Devonshire cream. Her wealth of hair swept back but for a few tantalizing waves spilling down her shoulder like a garnet cabernet.

His eyes snagged on the unrealistically dramatic flare of her hips, at the way her gloves bound to the soft flesh about the upper arm. His hand tightened on the table until the creases of his knuckles turned white. For unlike the oak he gripped to keep his balance, *she'd* be so soft beneath his hands . . . Beneath his—

"Not quite the retired *older* man ye expected, is he, lassie?" A chuckling Russell broke the silence, and Liam glanced to his right, noticing for the first time that his middle-aged steward had also taken more care with his appearance than usual. He'd even trimmed his russet beard, which he rarely did before winter's end.

It was lucky, Liam realized, that everyone's focus remained on her, and no one noticed how affected he was.

Except for, perhaps, the lass.

"I—I confess, I don't know what to say." Her breasts heaved with breath as she obviously prepared for a lengthy apology regarding the afternoon.

The thought pleased Liam a great deal less than he'd anticipated, and so he didn't allow her to finish.

"Permit me to present my children, Miss Lockhart, Rhianna and Andrew Mackenzie." His children, both inherited the Ravencroft ebony hair, had very opposite yet equally inappropriate reactions to the introduction.

"What happened to yer lip?" Rhianna demanded, her chocolate eyes wide as saucers in her angular face. "And are ye wearing cosmetics? Did ye get them from Paris? I heard they're only worn by actresses and prostitutes."

"Haud yer Wheesht, Rhianna," Liam commanded, earning him a glower from his daughter, though she complied. She had no manners and even less respect, Liam was ashamed to admit. In the army, one caned or shot someone for insubordination. With a slip of a daughter, Liam was at a loss for what to do. He dare not raise a hand in anger to his children. There had been enough of that in this house, and Liam refused to be like his father.

"Ye see, Miss Lockhart, how in need we are of your expertise. Rhianna will apologize for her discourtesy."

Everyone held their breath, wondering if Rhianna was about to throw one of her famous tantrums, but she merely slid out her lower lip in a dramatic pout and muttered, "Apologies," without looking up.

Miss Lockhart's glove had gone to her own lip and self-consciously lingered there. After a few surprised blinks, she lowered her hand and gifted his daughter with a kind smile. "I've always had a fondness for an inquisitive mind. I suppose now is the right moment to explain to you all that I was . . . in a carriage accident not a week ago and sustained a few abrasions. The cosmetics were a capitulation to my vanity and maybe a little to my hopes of making a good impression here."

Her voice was the auditory equivalent of warm honey, sweet and languid, and Liam let it coat his senses for a beat longer than he should have.

"A carriage accident?" he repeated, grasping at the vestiges of stoicism. "Ye seem to be rather prone to those of late."

The comment took her more aback than he'd thought it

would. "Yes, well . . ." She blinked at him, at an apparent loss for words.

"We're just glad ye're not hurt," Russell said, gifting the lass with his most charming smile.

"Thank you, Mr. Mackenzie." The appearance of dimples on the edges of her smile was enough to distract Liam from what he was about to say next.

Luckily, Miss Lockhart didn't await a prompting. "It's lovely to make the acquaintance of you both, Rhianna and Andrew. I'm very much looking forward to our time together."

True to form, Andrew muttered a "likewise" and said not another word, but stood when he should stand, and bowed when he should bow, doing just enough to not draw Liam's ire. Which, of course, was beyond irritating.

"Ye dress better than any governess I've ever had," Rhianna remarked artlessly. "Is that the latest in London couture?"

"It is." Miss Lockhart's bosom turned an intriguing pink. "But you'll have a much prettier trousseau once you're of age."

"I *am* of age in most circles," Rhianna huffed. "Father is making me wait another year, and I'm certain to be an old maid by then."

Miss Lockhart only smiled again, but Liam thought he observed a rueful tightening in her eyes. "Don't be in too much of a rush to marry, dear," she said, and then seemed to remember herself. "Give me enough of your time, and you'll be the jewel of next season, I swear it."

Rhianna assessed her new governess with skepticism, but finally nodded.

"Kindly take yer seat, Miss Lockhart, the soup is getting cold." Liam gestured to the seat next to Rhianna, and tried not to notice the sway of the governess's generous hips when she walked. She didn't glide like so many ladies were wont to do. She swayed, each lift of her foot telegraphed by a corresponding movement of her body. A swivel of the hip, a swing of her arm, and a slight, jiggling ripple in the soft skin of her décolletage.

Gritting his teeth, Liam sat. "We're a regimented household, Miss Lockhart, and in the future will start dinner at the stroke of eight."

"Yes, my lord." Soft russet lashes swept down beneath his disapproving look, properly chastised.

Liam winced beneath a ripple of regret that slithered through him.

Jani held her chair out for her, and the governess took it with perfect grace. Liam became absorbed with his soup the moment it was served as it gave him a reason not to look at her.

Dinner was generally a purposeful meal, and they ate in silence save for a few terse items of business discussed with Russell, if any words were spoken at all. So when Miss Lockhart broke the silence, everyone passed uneasiness around the table like a breadbasket.

"Since comportment and conduct are part of my duties, Rhianna, would you permit me to show you the way the ladies eat soup in London?"

Rhianna paused mid-slurp and slid a mutinous look to her new governess. Liam could tell that his daughter absolutely wanted to know, but didn't want to be taught. She was a difficult girl that way. Eschewing authority, but frustrated at not knowing her boundaries and constantly overstepping.

"I suppose," she replied carefully.

They all observed Miss Lockhart as she held her soup spoon delicately, and dipped it into the potato and leek soup. "You scoop it away, rather than toward, and bring it slowly to your mouth, instead of bending over the bowl. The important part is that you sip instead of slurp."

Liam's eyes remained affixed to her lips as she took a delicate sip from her spoon, and returned it to the bowl.

She ate like she did everything else. With elegance and poise. Could it be that she was as unaware of her innate sensuality as she pretended?

"Now you try," she encouraged.

Rhianna echoed her movements perfectly until the grating sound of a slurp filled the expectant silence.

"Tip the spoon to your lips rather than breathing in," Miss Lockhart corrected. "Just thus." She lifted another perfect spoonful, though before it reached her mouth, a tremor in her hand sent half of it spilling onto the bared skin of her chest.

Everyone froze, and that pink color appeared from beneath her gown once more.

An undignified snort of laughter escaped Rhianna and she clapped her hands over her mouth, unable to control the shaking of her shoulders. Even Andrew bit his lips to stop their quivering.

But it was the governess, herself, who broke into a brilliant smile before a merry laugh bubbled up from her throat. Now that her amusement was allowed, Rhianna joined in, as did Andrew, and finally Russell. The tension of the evening dissipated like an unpleasant odor.

It occurred to Liam that laughter was something long missing not just from his table, but from his life. From his keep. But he couldn't possibly join in. Not because he didn't want to, or because he wasn't amused.

It was the perfectly creamy texture of the soup that arrested him. White and slick. It dripped over the curve of her breast, threatening to slide into the valley between as she fished the linen from her lap.

She caught it in time, still enjoying the joviality of the moment.

Salacious, wicked images seized Liam and held him in thrall. He could barely believe he was having such thoughts in the company of his own children, but Liam could only think of that warm, smooth liquid running between her magnificent breasts, and fight the violent lust sizzling through his body.

This had nothing to do with her, personally. It was the Mackenzie appetite to blame for his crass and demeaning fantasies. It was the demon who whispered dark and un-bidden things in his ear.

Mena didn't know if it was the warm meal, the French wine, or the soft glow of the candelabra, but the band of suffocating iron clamped about her chest suddenly re-leased. She filled her lungs for what seemed like the first time in months, and savored the scent of crisp summer apples in the sweet Vouvray Jean-Pierre had sent up to ac-company the dessert soufflé.

Taking another sip of the wine, she regarded the mar-quess over the glass as he discussed the suspicious fire in the barley fields with Russell Mackenzie.

He hadn't so much as acknowledged her presence since the soup course.

Mena still couldn't believe it. The savage Highlander from the road had transformed into a militant marquess. He'd been telling her the truth, after all. Though he'd donned his white-tie finery, bathed, shaved, and slicked his hair back into a neat queue, Mena still expected the bar-barian to somehow rip free of the refined nobleman any moment and threaten to hack her to pieces with a claymore.

Troubled, she set down her wine. Lord, he must think her a fool for how she'd acted this afternoon. But he hadn't mentioned it, and she hoped he wouldn't. Or maybe she needed him to say something, to allow her to explain, to perhaps absolve her, somehow.

Mena watched the muscles of his jaw work ponderously on a bite as he listened to his steward's reports intently. Only a fool would expect absolution from such a man. He was the sort that granted favor sparingly and forgiveness never.

She'd do well to remember that.

He was the Demon Highlander, *elder* brother to the Blackheart of Ben More. These monikers, they were not granted by the happenstance of birth or marriage, like marquess or earl, they were earned by means of ruthless violence and bloodshed. It was easy to forget that fact beneath the grand chandelier of this lofty keep. That was, until the fire in the hearth ignited the amber in his eyes, lending him a ferocity that even his expensive attire couldn't tame.

Suddenly feeling as though she'd taken refuge in a sleeping bear's den, Mena drained the last of her wine much faster than was strictly proper.

When dinner adjourned, she bade the children a fond good night and curtsied to Russell and the marquess.

Rhianna attempted a curtsy, as well, and Mena put that on the list of things to practice with the girl. Andrew merely nodded at her and mumbled an excuse before hurrying away, not once lifting his eyes from the carpet. He was on the tall side of thirteen, and very slim, but his hands and feet were large and ungainly on his frame, hinting that he had the propensity for his father's build.

His aloofness distressed her, and Mena decided, as she made to slip away, that she'd use the next few restless hours in her bed thinking of ways to ingratiate herself to the boy.

"Remain a moment, Miss Lockhart, I would have words with ye."

The vise winched around her lungs once again at Ravencroft's command, squeezing them until her limbs weakened for want of breath. Turning toward him, Mena kept the length of the grand table between them. "Yes, my lord?" she answered, as she watched Russell Mackenzie's retreating back until it disappeared around the entry, abandoning her to the terrifying presence of the so-called Demon Highlander.

"Forgive me, as I'm not the expert, but is it considered

good manners to call a conversation across a room?" His expression revealed nothing. Not an eyebrow lift, a half-smile, or even a scowl. Just an unsettling stoic watchfulness that set every hair of her body on its end with absolute awareness.

He'd not-so-subtly requested for her to approach him, but it sounded like a dare.

Like a temptation.

"No, my lord, it is not." Remembering Millie LeCour's advice, Mena lifted her chin and forced her eyes to remain on his, summoning every iota of British superiority that had been beaten into her since she'd come to London as the Viscountess Benchley.

The flames that reflected in his unblinking eyes licked his gaze with heat and, for a moment, Mena could truly believe that a demon stared out at her from those abysmal depths. He regarded her approach with the same sulfurous glare she imagined the devil used to survey his unholy realm.

To compensate for her apprehension, Mena rolled her shoulders back, as though stowing angel wings, and traversed the length of the table with the deportment of a benevolent royal. Though she kept the corner of the table and one of the high-backed chairs in between them.

She was being brave, not idiotic.

Mena regretted eating quite so much at dinner, as the meal now rolled and tossed inside her stomach, and threatened acid that she had to desperately swallow. Despite that, she didn't allow her gaze to waver, though it cost her more strength than she'd ever credited herself with.

His eyes touched her everywhere, and Mena had to fight the impulse to cover herself, lest he know how exposed she felt in his presence.

"We've not had the opportunity to formally meet," the marquess remarked. "I must say, Miss Lockhart, ye're not what I expected."

Mena attempted a polite smile and fished in her blank

mind for something witty and charming to say. "It seems, my lord, that the circumstance is mutual." Indeed, she hadn't expected him to be so young. So devastatingly virile. So wickedly dark and—dare she think it?—attractive.

She'd meant to be witty, to diffuse some of the intensity between them, but she could tell that her answer hadn't pleased him.

"Aye." He didn't return her smile, and Mena fought the urge to fidget like a child set in the corner.

She'd met precious few people in her lifetime who'd made her feel small. She looked most men straight in the eye, if she didn't tower over them. But Ravencroft dwarfed her so entirely, she had to tilt her head back to meet his stern regard. He stood before her every inch the regimented soldier, posture erect and unyielding with his arms clasped behind him, neither a hair nor stitch out of place. At this close vantage, Mena could identify the familial resemblance between Liam Mackenzie and Dorian Blackwell. The same thick ebony hair, similar dark, haunted eyes, and a raw, almost barbaric bone structure. All hard angles and broad planes and no quarter given to weakness. But where a cruel, sardonic twist adorned Blackwell's lips, Ravencroft's were instead drawn into a perpetual hard line. Unreadable and forbidding. Dorian had the look of a prowling lone beast, hungry and predatory. Ravencroft, however, had never seen a cage that would dare hold him. Nations fell before him. Kings had bowed and tyrants had groveled at his feet.

Mena found herself wondering if those hard lips ever softened. If those heated, merciless, assessing eyes ever became languid and tender.

"I asked Lady Northwalk to send me a capable, experienced, and educated governess and she sent ye, Miss Lockhart, what do ye make of that?" His words pierced her with panic, though his tone remained neutral.

"D-did you not receive my references? My letters of recommendation? I assure you, sir, I am beyond qualified to teach your children comportment. Lady Northwalk informed me that after reading the Whitehalls'—"

"Yer references were impeccable. However, the expectations of my children differ greatly from the Whitehalls', ye ken? They were merchants, *I'm* a marquess, if ye'll believe it now."

"A marquess who dresses like a Jacobite rebel," she reminded him. "Forgive me for not believing you earlier, but you *were* covered in mud and ash from the fields, and I'd never met a marquess who assisted in such—physical labor."

Ravencroft stepped forward, and Mena retreated, her hands covering the flutters in her stomach as though holding back a swarm of butterflies. "I only meant—"

"There are some, Miss Lockhart, who would argue 'tis the responsibility of a noble to oversee every aspect of work on the land he owns. And there are others who would find it mighty strange that a proper London governess kens so much about linchpins and carriage wheels."

Mena recalled Miss LeCour's sage advice, that a lie was best told peppered with truth. "My father was a landed gentleman and avid agriculturist, as well as a scholar. I learned quite a few things at his feet as a child which included—"

"And are ye aware of how far behind schedule my men and I are because we spent all bloody afternoon saving yer stubborn hide? If ye'd allowed me to take ye on my horse, we'd not have lost the daylight."

"I do regret my part in that," Mena said, and meant it. "But as I was a woman traveling *alone* you can't expect—"

"Ye'll need to ken more than farm maintenance and how to distract a man with a pretty dress in order to teach my children what they'll need to know to survive in society," he clipped.

"Well, their first lesson will be on how rude and socially unacceptable it is to consistently interrupt people in the middle of their sentences," Mena snapped.

Oh, sweet Lord. She could hardly believe her own behavior. Here she stood, alone and defenseless before perhaps the deadliest warrior in the history of the British Isles, and she'd just called *him* to answer for his bad manners.

Had she escaped the asylum only to go mad outside its walls?

"Go on then," he commanded, his voice intensifying and a dark, frightening storm gathering in his countenance. "I believe ye were about to apologize for wasting my time."

Mena actually felt her nostrils flare and a galling pit form in her belly. What was this? Temper? She'd quite thought she'd been born without one. Affection and tenderness had made up her idyllic childhood, and acrimony and terror had dominated her adult life. She'd never really had the chance to wrestle with a temper.

And wrestle it she must, or risk losing her means of escape into relative anonymity. Closing her eyes, she summoned her innate gentility along with the submissive humility she'd cultivated over half a decade with a cruel and violent husband. Opening her mouth, she prepared to deliver a finely crafted and masterful apology.

"Why aren't ye married?" the marquess demanded, again effectively cutting her off.

"I—I beg your pardon?"

"Wouldna ye rather have a husband and bairns of yer own than school other people's ill-behaved children?" His glittering eyes roamed her once again, leaving trails of quivering awareness in their wake. "Ye're rather young to wield much authority over my daughter, as ye've not more than a decade on her."

"I have exactly a decade on her."

He ignored her reply, as the corners of his mouth whitened with some sort of strain that Mena couldn't fathom.

"Were ye a Highland lass, ye'd barely seen Rhianna's age before some lad or other had dragged ye to church to claim ye. Whether ye'd consented or not. In fact, they'd likely just take ye to wife in the biblical sense and toss yer father his thirty coin."

Flummoxed, Mena stared at him, her mouth agape. He still seemed irate, in fact his voice continued to rise in volume and intensity. But it sounded as though he'd paid her a compliment.

"So that causes a man to wonder," he continued. "What is a wee bonny English lass like ye doing all the way up here? Why are ye not warming the bed of a wealthy husband and whiling yer hours away on tea and society and the begetting of heirs?"

Had he just called her "wee"? Was she mistaken or didn't that word mean little?

And bonny? *Her?*

A spear of pain pricked her with such force, it stole her ire and her courage along with it. Was he being deliberately cruel? Had she left one household that delighted in her humiliation and sought refuge in another?

"I don't see how that's any of your concern." She hated the weakness in her voice, the fear she'd never quite learned how to hide.

"Everything that happens within the stones of this keep, nay, on Mackenzie lands, are of concern to me. That now includes ye. Especially since ye'll be influencing my children." He took another step forward, and before Mena could retreat, his hand snaked out and cupped her chin.

The small, frightened sound Mena made startled them both.

Ravencroft's gaze sharpened, but he didn't release her.

Her jaw felt as substantive as glass in his hand. Mena knew it would take nothing at all for him to crush her, a simple tightening of his strong, rough fingers. His dark eyes locked on her lips, and they seemed to part of their own volition, exuding the soft rasps of her panicked breath.

He leaned down toward her, crowding her with the proximity of his forceful presence.

She saw him clearly now, as so many must have at the violent ends of their lives. Inhumanely stark features weathered by decades of discipline and brutality frowned down at her now, as though measuring her coffin.

Suddenly the fire and candles cast more shadows in the grand room than light.

Mena knew men like the laird of Ravencroft Keep rarely existed, and when they did, history made gods of them.

Or demons.

The rough pad of his thumb dragged across the split on her lip as light as a whisper. She felt his caress in her bones. And elsewhere. It raised tingling prickles of awareness on her skin and washed all the way to her core, and lower, where something soft and warm bloomed within her.

Was he going to kiss her? Mena's heart sputtered in her chest, then stalled before taking a galloping leap forward.

His own mouth parted, his lids narrowing with something that looked like heat, but also like . . . suspicion. His grip on her chin gentled as he turned her face slowly toward the illumination of the candelabra and lifted an unused linen from the table to gently wipe away the powder she'd applied to hide the bruise beneath her eye.

"Tell me, Miss Lockhart." His voice gentled to a rumble. "Tell me the truth of what happened to ye."

Mena stood stock-still, but for the little trembles seizing her limbs. She was his captive. Though he only held her jaw, she might as well have been bound at every joint.

"I a-already did." She forced herself not to whimper as he revealed more and more of her wounds to him.

"A carriage accident," he repeated evenly.

"Yes." That had sounded like more of a question than an answer, and Mena closed her eyes, fully expecting him to declare his knowledge of her falsehood, to uncover the entire farce.

And what would a man like him do to someone who'd lied as completely as she had?

"My lord?" Mena winced at the breathless panic creeping into her voice.

"Aye?" he rumbled, distracted by his examination of her wounds, particularly that of her lips.

Brittle as she was, in his presence Mena felt enormously fragile and frighteningly transparent. He could do what he would with her and no one would question him. Something about the way he regarded her told her that he knew it as well as she did. She was at his absolute mercy. And she was deceiving him.

"Permit me to . . . that is . . . it isn't seemly for us to . . ." Her hand lifted of its own volition, and rested on his forearm as she attempted to lift her chin from his grip.

He stared at her hand resting on his suit coat for a protracted moment as though it were an insect he feared would sting him.

Then, just as abruptly as he'd seized her, the marquess let her go.

Turning away from her, he curled his hands into tight fists at his sides. "Ye'll find, Miss Lockhart, that I lack many of yer gentle English ways," he said gruffly.

Mena couldn't think of a single reply to that, so she silently regarded the way his dinner coat strained over the uncommon width of his back.

"Ye're here for my children, and I'll thank ye to leave by the wayside any notions of turning me into something I'm not." The firelight gleamed off a few hidden strands of silver in his dark hair as he glanced over his shoulder. "I may be a nobleman by birth, but I'm far from noble. I think it's best we stay out of each other's path. We'll not need to interact but for dinner, or if I have a concern over the children's progress."

Mena knew he was offering her a gift, a chance to live at her discretion, so long as the objective of her employment here was accomplished.

She wanted nothing so much in all the world.

"Yes, my lord."

"Laird," he corrected. "In yer land, I'm the Marquess Ravencroft. In *my* land, I am the laird. *The* Mackenzie."

He'd neglected to mention the Demon Highlander, but that was impossible to forget, especially now that she saw that demon looking out of his eyes.

"Of course." Mena dipped in a curtsy, mostly so she no longer had to look at him. "Laird Mackenzie."

He nodded, the firelight playing with the silhouettes and shadows of his bold features. "Ye may go."

The moment he dismissed her, Mena made her escape, though she didn't break into a run until she'd reached the hallway. Rich brocaded tapestries blurred into a mélange of blues, greens, and golds as she rushed by them. She'd catch sight of a majestic stag, or a frolicking faerie creature, and she'd want to stop and study it, but didn't dare.

She felt the cold kiss of something on the back of her neck. Like she'd left the Highlander behind, but his demon might be following her. In fact, when she glanced behind her, the shadows seemed to merge with the suggestion of movement. She'd catch a glimpse of something—*someone*—before it was gone.

Weaving through the halls of the keep, she didn't slow until she'd found the familiar door of her room. To her surprise, she'd been stationed on the second floor of the west wing, where the family's quarters were located, rather than below stairs with the servants. She supposed, so she'd have more access to the children and they to her.

Bursting into the chamber, she pushed the door closed and turned the key, effectively locking herself inside.

Collapsing against the sturdy oak, she pressed her cheek against the wood, warmed by the crackling fire someone had laid in the hearth.

She willed her galloping heart to slow and her lungs to find their rhythm as she stood against the door frame and trembled. Unbidden, her fingers found her cheek, still tingling from the strong grip of a battle-worn hand. For a man so large, with the capability of such extraordinary strength, he'd handled her gently.

She'd quite forgotten what that was like.

Turning from the door, she ventured on unsteady legs into the bedroom. Before, she'd been in too much of a rush to dress for dinner to truly take account of it. She ran her fingers across the smooth, polished wood of the dressing table and writing desk that seemed to be crafted by the same loving artisan as the mahogany poster bed.

Drifting toward the bed, she pressed on the mattress, relishing the downy softness. Greens and gold and chocolate hues added warmth to the cold stone of the walls. This keep was obviously bereft of a woman's hand, done in masculine tones and clannish draperies. But Mena found that she rather liked the gothic feel of the place. It had housed centuries of Mackenzies of Wester Ross. Its stones had seen the births of heirs, the deaths of rebels, and more than its share of monarchies. Some would claim 'twas an English castle now, with an English titled lord.

And they'd be fools.

Laird Liam Mackenzie was a Highlander to the very marrow of his bones. His people claimed these lands before England, even before the Scots. His blood belonged to Pictish barbarians fortified with that of Viking raiders.

A thoughtful maid had turned down the bed, draped in a quilt made of the Mackenzie plaid, and fluffed the green and gold pillows for her.

Maybe dear Jani was right. Maybe there was hope that they would accept her . . . that she was welcome here.

By those in employ here at the keep, if not its master.

Mena pushed the laird from her mind, thinking instead of how small and simple the room was compared to her suites at Benchley Court. She'd been the lady of the house for five eternal years, and had hated every miserable second. Her husband had insisted she allow his mother, Esther St. Vincent, to decorate the home. Mena's entire suites had been done in wicker and lavender draped in gaudy pink lace.

How she'd hated it.

But even Benchley Court was preferable to the infernal whitewashed walls of Belle Glen Asylum. Pure, cold, and sterile. Full of misery and helplessness. Even through the desperately unhappy years with her husband, she'd never suspected that a pure desolation existed until Belle Glen. She'd never known that inside every soul was a void so dark and lonely that it could take months of falling to find the true end.

And contained in the depths therein was only madness.

She hadn't thought about Belle Glen since she'd left. Hadn't allowed herself a moment to process the fact that she'd truly been rescued from the brink of utter despair. That if Dorian Blackwell had been seconds later, she might have been raped.

No. Mena ripped the ribbon from her neck, as it suddenly felt too confining. She didn't allow herself to consider it. She needn't mourn. Needn't dwell on what was before, or might have been.

She'd stay busy, stay distracted, it was the only way to cope and thereby forget.

Mena remembered that she'd seen a wardrobe tucked in a small round turret just past the fireplace. Perhaps she should unpack. Though it would be better to prepare a plan for the children tomorrow and leave unpacking unnecessary things for later. Thinking of the wardrobe, she swept into the little round turret room.

And froze.

Something inside her shriveled as she spied what sat in the center of the room, awaiting none but her. Her heart kicked over again, and she could feel her features crumpling. Though she didn't want to, she took small, plodding steps forward, forcing herself to approach what might become a nightmare.

What if she'd been dreaming this all along? The dashing and piratical Blackheart of Ben More. Farah and Millie. Her new clothes, her new identity.

Her second chance.

What if awaiting inside that large, gleaming, pristine white bathtub . . . was nothing but ice?

Mena gritted her teeth and ignored the sting of a lone tear as it slipped from eyes blurred with emotion. She pulled the glove from her arm, revealing fingers white and leached of blood. Reaching out trembling fingertips, she forced herself to dip them below the surface of the water.

A sob escaped her. Then another.

Finally her legs could handle her weight no longer, and she crumpled to the floor. But as the strength and courage she'd learned the last few days ripped from her throat in raw, ragged sobs, so did the grief, the rage, and the terror.

The bath, it had been real.

And it had been very, *very* warm.

CHAPTER FOUR

"One, two, three. One, two, three. Ouch!" Mena hopped back on one foot after rescuing her other from beneath the heel of Rhianna's boot.

Again.

"Oh, Miss Lockhart, I'm so sorry!" the girl cried, following her as Mena hobbled away and collapsed onto a plump couch by the window in the solarium. "I'm hopeless at the waltz. I doona think I'll ever become comfortable with dancing backward."

"It's all right." Mena soothed both the girl and her own smarting toes. "The waltz isn't easy to master." She'd picked this room for dancing as its windows and French doors opened onto the balcony overlooking the sea, and a lovely piano hunkered on a plush carpet. The nursery-turned-classroom was a dreary place, and Mena had formulated a plan to relocate to a more cheerful set of rooms.

She'd begun the day with some classic literature and rudimentary French. After she'd found Andrew tucking a penny dreadful behind his Jonathan Swift, and listening to both the children reduce the language of love to the equivalent of a verbal assault, Mena decided that music and a dance lesson would provide a welcome diversion. Often she'd found the mind operated more usefully after dancing. Almost as though the music and rhythmic exercise opened pathways of thought not established on one's own.

Evidently in the case of the Mackenzie children, she'd been mistaken.

Rhianna proved a willing and eager pupil, if not particularly accomplished. Though Andrew treated Mena with a solemnity bordering on contempt. He was, however, a brilliant musician, and played the pianoforte with effortless style and technique.

Mena was able to ascertain that they'd suffered a slew of tutors and governesses intermittently over the years. They'd been taught the basics of reading, writing, arithmetic, and history. But as they grew, their governesses had all deserted them in short order. Their knowledge of economics, refinement, conversation, etiquette, French, music theory, and the social arts was all but nonexistent.

Well, she was a viscountess, by Jove, and a gentleman's daughter before that. She had mastered every British social policy, written and otherwise. There was no one more qualified to guide them than her. She was determined to succeed, not just because she needed this position to guard her secrets, but because the Mackenzie children desperately needed to learn what she could teach them.

And their father knew it.

"Come, Andrew," she prompted. "Why don't you dance with your sister, and let me play the piano? I need a rest."

"I doona dance," he informed her, studying his fingers curled against the piano keys.

"That doesn't matter," she said encouragingly. "I'll teach you, then, while Rhianna practices her piano. We can go slowly."

"Nay, I didna say I doona know how. I said I doona dance." He thrust his jaw forward; his eyes alight with stubborn rebellion.

"But how are you going to impress the young ladies unless you perfect your waltz?" she tempted him.

"I have no desire to impress anyone," he spat.

Mena glanced to the window, longing to bask in the rare autumn sunlight instead of Andrew's dark mood. Clouds loomed in the distance, but right now the sun sparkled off the sea and illuminated the peaks of Skye. After so long in Belle Glen, she yearned to feel the warmth on her face, to wander unimpeded through the forest.

But for now, she must teach.

Gathering as much kindness as she could from behind her frayed nerves, she approached the piano and reached for the boy. "Please, dear," she cajoled. "I confess that I'm not the best at leading, and so it's not fair to your sister. I'm not used to dancing the gentleman's part."

"Ye should be," Andrew muttered, flinching away from her. "Ye've the stature of one."

Mena snatched her hand back as Andrew lunged from the bench and stalked toward the west door of the solarium.

"Andrew, doona be an arse!" Rhianna called after him.

Jani crossed the threshold carrying a tray laden with their afternoon tea. The two nearly collided, ruining Andrew's chance for a dramatic exit and allowing Mena to recover from her astonishment at his hurtful outburst. Andrew made a rude noise at a startled Jani before attempting to circumnavigate him.

"Andrew Mackenzie." Mena enunciated the syllables in his name as she'd heard her father do when she'd been in trouble as a girl. The enunciation, when applied with a low register, always brought her to heel. "If you don't want me to have a lengthy discussion with your father this afternoon, you will apologize to Jani for your haste, relieve him of his tray, and bring it here."

The room was as silent as a mausoleum as they waited for Andrew to move. The youth muttered something that must have been an apology to a wide-eyed Jani, and then took the tea tray from his hands. The threat of his father was an effective one, but not one Mena had wanted to use. This was no way to establish trust, or a genial relationship, but she couldn't allow such behavior. Left unchecked, a boy with such terrible angst could grow into a cruel man.

And the world had enough of those already.

Andrew set the tea tray none too gently on the solarium table and stood before her as rigid as a gallows post.

"When you quit a room with ladies present, you will bow and excuse yourself first." Though confrontation of any kind had always made her feel shaky and ill, Mena narrowed her eyes to meet his discourteous glare with one of authority. "I won't ask for an apology, because I won't accept a disingenuous one, but your father hired me to teach you how to behave in polite society. I intend to do my job, whether you wish me to or not."

Repugnance gathered in his stormy eyes and his thin frame shook with rage, but after a tense moment, wherein Mena didn't allow herself to breathe, he bowed to her. "If ye ladies will excuse me." His voice could have dried the Nile, but Mena gave him a tight nod, and watched him march away with a sadness clenched in her heart. What made the boy so angry?

She read abundant approval in Jani's meaningful look, but it did nothing to lift her spirits. She would rather ingratiate herself to Andrew, or at the very least have a civil interaction. Her unsteady legs gave way, and she plunked onto the piano bench without a modicum of poise or grace.

"Some tea, Miss Rhianna." Jani's voice was smooth as the crimson silk he wore while he poured Rhianna her tea and handed her the dainty china cup. His eyes were pools of liquid bronze as he waited on his mistress.

Intrigued, Mena watched their interaction.

Rhianna barely glanced up at Jani, though she thanked him politely.

He bowed to Mena, and then back to Rhianna, his head dipped in a way that, Mena suspected, hid the worship shining in his eyes. "Do you require anything of me?" he asked, and the hopeful deference in his voice nearly broke Mena's heart.

Oblivious to his reverence, Rhianna shook her head, her dark curls bouncing against her shoulders. "No, thank ye, Jani."

"Summon me, ladies, if there is need." He made no noise as he gracefully strode away.

"Doona listen to a word my brother says, Miss Lockhart," Rhianna pleaded, rushing to her side the moment they were left alone. "I'd *murder* someone to be as tall and elegant as ye. Ye willna let Andrew drive ye away?"

Mena looked into the girl's dark eyes and softened at the desperation she saw there. A girl on the cusp of womanhood, bereft of a mother or any steady governesses to bring her up. To teach her how to be a woman. Mena ran a fond hand over Rhianna's obsidian curls, and then patted her on the hand.

"I'm made of sterner stuff than that, I'm afraid." She smiled. "It'll take more than a few jibes to be rid of me."

Rhianna immediately brightened. "I suppose ye'll have to tell Father," she goaded with an exaggerated sigh.

Mena chewed at her lip while she considered it. "Well, Andrew *did* excuse himself," she said. "I see no reason to bring your father into it."

As she regarded her from behind long black lashes, the lively girl's mouth curved mischievously. "What do ye think of my father, Miss Lockhart? Think ye he is handsome?"

Taken aback, Mena put a hand to her fluttering stomach, willing the sudden upset to quiet. "What a question!" she remarked.

"It's all right to admit it. I willna say a thing." Rhianna wiggled her dark brows. "There are many women in the clan who think my father is quite handsome. I only wanted to know if an Englishwoman would agree."

"Well . . ." Mena floundered, unsure of how to proceed. Ambiguity, she decided, was the most diplomatic route. "I don't believe male aesthetics differ so much between England and Scotland." Though she was beginning to think that female aesthetics did. "It doesn't at all surprise me that your father, being a marquess and a hero of the crown, is an attractive prospect for some women."

"That's not what I asked," Rhianna said cheekily, smoothing the skirt of her lovely yellow frock. "I asked if *ye* find him handsome."

Mena pressed her lips together, an image of the marquess rearing in her mind's eye. His forbidding presence last night at dinner, his abundant black hair caught up in a sleek queue, and his eyes smoldering with dark flames. His massive body contained by the trappings of a gentleman crowding her so close, she could still smell the sweetness of the soufflé on his breath.

Though it was the memory of him as he'd been at their first meeting that often leaped unbidden into her errant thoughts. Rain streaming from his loose hair, his thick legs burnished a tawny hue, as though he often bared them to the sunlight. Eyes that flashed with wrath and temper and masculine potency.

Was he handsome? Not in the traditional sense of the word. Not like Gordon, her husband, was handsome. Lean and elegant with haughty, aristocratic features.

Laird Mackenzie was much too large, his features too fierce and barbaric to be considered elegant. But, she supposed, he held a particular masculine allure. Especially when he spoke. The gravel in his voice lent his brogue an extraordinary depth that delighted her senses like the deep roar of the ocean cresting against stone.

"There's no polite way to tell a sweet girl that her father is brutish, old, and unsightly, is there, Miss Lockhart?" As though he'd been evoked by her improper thoughts of him, the marquess's resonant voice drifted to her from the doorway behind them. "Therefore, Rhianna, it's an impolite question to ask."

Mena leaped to her feet, almost upsetting the piano bench, and whirled to face him.

He stood with his wide shoulder resting against the arched entry. There was a Sisyphean quality to his stature that suggested it was the laird who supported the weight of the castle stones, rather than the other way around.

Lord, but he *was* handsome. There was no denying it, not to herself or anyone. He'd again donned the garb of the clannish rebel warrior. The cotton of his thin shirt molded against the swells of his chest. The rolled cuffs exposed tanned forearms that flexed beneath her stupefied gaze. He'd left his hair loose, and a few strands of silver gleamed in the rays of sun piercing the solarium with warmth. This was a laird she hadn't yet encountered. His expression as casual as the low sling of the Mackenzie kilt on his hips, he sauntered toward them.

Mena fought with a heavy, dry tongue to form a proper greeting as she inched away from Rhianna, trying to put space between her and the approaching marquess. Why, oh why, did he insist on saying things to which there was no proper response?

And why did every nerve in her body seem to stand at attention at his nearness?

"Ye are such a brute, Father," Rhianna teased, rising on her tiptoes to plant a kiss on his stubbled cheek. "But that doesna mean ye arena the most handsomest man in Wester Ross. Or perhaps all of Scotland. Every lass says so."

"*Most* handsome," Mena corrected instinctively over the piano she'd placed in between them.

Ravencroft's eyes sharpened, his features tightened, and Mena met a look so searing, she thought her clothing might catch flame if he did not glance away.

Realizing what her correction had insinuated, she hurried to cover the mistake. "Not *most handsomest*," she elaborated. "But handsomest is also correct."

Rhianna's giggle did little to help the situation.

"That is, *most handsomest* is incorrect . . . in that sentence, not that you're not . . . most . . ." Burning with mortification, Mena puffed out a beleaguered breath.

Though he didn't smile, a dangerous heat lurked beneath the amusement dancing in the laird's eyes.

The longer he stared at her, the tighter her corset became. Mena's hands flew to the lace cravat at her bodice. She thought it had given her an air of professional respectability, but now it just seemed to strangle her over the high neck of her russet gown.

"Andrew refused to dance with Miss Lockhart, Father," Rhianna tattled, ignoring the sharp look from Mena. "He was unaccountably rude."

The merriment in his eyes died. "What? How?" the laird demanded.

Mena took a step forward. "It really wasn't as bad as all that."

"He said that Miss Lockhart was built like a man."

Ravencroft's eyes touched on all the abundant curves that distinctly established Mena as a woman.

"My. Son. Said. *What?*" The careful enunciation of each low word as darkness gathered on the laird's features filled Mena with no small sense of alarm for Andrew.

Gorging on the drama of it all, Rhianna became even more animated, though Mena had previously thought it impossible. "Yes! And Miss Lockhart made him apologize to Jani and excuse himself before he left. Ye should have seen how angry he was."

"Rhianna!" Mena reproached.

"Did she, indeed?" The laird's brows lifted and some of his wrath seemed to flicker and melt away.

"Please." Mena inched around the piano toward the

towering Scot and his daughter. "I was going to let this incident pass quietly. Andrew and I have yet to bond . . . and sometimes, I think, boys at that age have difficulty adjusting to such situations . . ." She paused, her guilt at her lack of true experience with such things making it difficult to meet the sardonic eyes of her employer. "It—it really is quite normal," she lied as she ran a restless hand over the gleaming polished wood of the instrument, following the delicate grain with the sensitive pads of her fingertips in rhythmic strokes.

When she gathered the courage to glance up, she found Ravencroft's eyes also focused on her stroking fingers with an alarming intensity. Curling her fingers, she quickly hid her hand behind her back.

"All right, Miss Lockhart. Ye're the expert." He didn't look entirely convinced. "But I'll not have my son behaving like a barbarian."

"I understand," Mena murmured, thinking that the distinction was strange coming from such a man as him.

Kissing his daughter on the forehead, he finally allowed his hard mouth to curve slightly. "There is only room for one at a time in this keep, eh, *nighean*?"

"Aye, Father," Rhianna replied warmly.

Something tight and fearful unfurled from inside Mena and dissipated as she observed a tender moment bloom between father and daughter. Liam Mackenzie might be the Demon Highlander, but he loved his children. So why, she wondered, had he spent so much time away from them? Surely he could have retired his commission any time over the last several years and returned to Ravencroft Keep to raise his family. Their mother had been gone for nearly a decade, so why pick now to come home?

With one last fond pat of his daughter's arm, he strode to the doorway. "I'll be in the distillery this week," he said, and disappeared around the stone arch.

Mena had barely remembered to breathe again when he

reappeared, a devilish gleam in his eye. "Excuse me, ladies." He executed a perfect bow, his eyes never leaving Mena's, holding her captive with his indefinable intensity.

"There *is* no excuse for ye, Father." Rhianna giggled again, shooing him away.

"But ye ken, even a barbarian can learn the ways of a gentleman if he has the right tutor." With a lingering look that weakened Mena's knees, and a quick wink at his daughter, he quit their company.

To Mena it seemed that every time she chanced to meet the marquess, she was introduced to someone new. The Demon Highlander, the barbaric clan chieftain, the regimented nobleman, and now, the fond and affectionate father. Each incarnation of Ravencroft, however, stared at her in the most disquieting manner. As if she were a mystery he planned to solve, or a secret he intended to uncover.

She'd rather be anything to him than that, for her secrets were too dangerous.

Heaving a deep sigh, Mena turned to Rhianna, who slid a knowing look in her direction.

"What did he call you just then . . . *nighean*?" Mena queried.

"It's a Gaelic endearment for *daughter*."

"Oh." It had been lovely. Mena decided whilst she lived among the Highland people, she'd do well to learn some of their language.

"Well, let's *do* see where your brother has run off to." What she needed was a diversion from the unwelcome intrusion of the laird Mackenzie into almost every waking thought.

"Must we?" Rhianna whined. "He's so dreary all the time."

Mena slid her arm through the girl's and they strolled over the lush carpets of the solarium. "You were very wicked today, tattling on him so," she scolded gently.

"I know." Rhianna shrugged and smirked. "I must get it from my father. He's a *brollachan,* ye know."

"A what?"

"A demon. Hadn't ye heard?"

"You don't really believe that, do you?" Mena scoffed, though a little thrill of anxiety touched the base of her neck. "That your father is a demon?"

"I doona ken whether he is or no, but I do hear what everyone whispers about him. If he's not a demon, then he is a very wicked man, indeed."

"Indeed," Mena murmured. Considering, not for the first time, if she believed in such things as demons.

CHAPTER FIVE

He's a demon. He'll destroy ye.

Mena dropped the edges of the library's drapes and whirled around to face the enormous, *vacant* room.

Who had said that?

A pervasive stillness permeated the gloom as Mena frantically scanned the tapestries and ornate furniture of the library for the source of the unsettling voice.

"H-hello?" Her uncertain whisper echoed off the stones and the windows, though no answer followed. "Is anyone there?"

A chilling silence greeted her, and Mena could think of nothing worse at that moment than the feeling one was not alone in an empty room.

The marquess had taken his children to the village of Fearnloch for the afternoon, and Mena had intended to use her first day off to escape into a good book, and bask in the rare and lovely autumn sunlight in the conservatory. The library had the fewest windows in the castle, though it boasted an impressive fireplace and far too many candelabra. The marquess claimed to be an uneducated man, but he obviously understood that the sun would fade the tomes in his collection, and therefore kept out the light with drawn, heavy velvet drapes.

This part of the keep faced away from the sea and offered a view of Wester Ross and the Kinross Mountains. Mena had wandered to one of the covered windows and pushed aside the drapes. The glimmer of the afternoon rays off the golden waves of barley clinging to the verdant hillsides had diverted her immediately. Perhaps a touch of her distraction had been drawn by the strong backs of the clansmen toiling in said fields, some with nothing but a kilt wrapped around their hips while the light kissed their flesh with amber.

Unsettled, Mena scanned the gloom of the library again. A large, dark shadow caught her eye, but darted away as soon as she thought she'd found it.

"Please," she called. "Show yourself. You're frightening me."

"If I showed myself ye'd be terrified." The masculine voice could only be identified as serpentine. The s*s* drawn out in a bone-chilling hiss that seemed to come at her from everywhere and nowhere at once. "But I mean ye no harm, 'tis the laird ye should fear."

"Why?" Mena asked the shade, inching along the wall toward the door that now seemed miles away rather than across the room. She wanted to call for help, but didn't dare. What would she say once help arrived? That a disembodied voice had accosted her?

She'd be sent back to Belle Glen for certain.

Cold fingers caressed above the high collar of her gown, and Mena let out a strangled scream. Whirling around, she saw nothing but a dark blurred shadow, and the flash of white streaked with veins of startling red surrounding black, abysmal pupils.

Surging back with terror, she somehow forced her legs to move, and bolted from the library.

Mena didn't stop in the hallway, nor did she seek refuge

in the solarium, her room, or the conservatory. Running on pure, heart-pounding fear, she flew down the back stairs and burst from the keep into the embrace of the sun outside.

Racing through the back gardens, she didn't stop until she'd plunged deep into the forest that grew wild on the south and west of Ravencroft lands. She quickly found a deer path that led through the foliage. Picking up her skirts, she allowed her fear to drive her deep into the trees. She'd always taken refuge in the forest back home in Hampshire, and while the sun broke through the dancing leaves, Mena could pretend she was at Birch Haven, and that demons didn't chase her.

When her lungs felt as though they'd burst, Mena reached her arms out and braced them against the trunk of an ancient oak. Clinging to it, she focused on catching her breath, her thoughts racing as if chased by whatever malevolent presence she'd fled.

Had she truly just encountered a ghost? Or a demon?

She couldn't believe it was so, and yet there was no denying the chill bumps that still lifted every fine hair on her body. If she closed her eyes, she could see nothing but those dreadful black pupils rimmed with white and streaked with alarming bolts of red. She'd never in her life encountered eyes like that before.

Because surely no living creature was bestowed of something so horrific.

As she began to catch her breath, another terrible fear pierced her like an icicle as a memory she fought to repress rose to the surface.

Are you hearing voices? Or perhaps seeing things that are not there?

Dr. Rosenblatt's even timbre was as bloodcurdling as a banshee scream, and Mena fought the impulse to clap her hands over her ears.

Could it be? Was she going mad? Hallucinations were the hallmark of true insanity and Mena couldn't decide which was worse. A demon in Ravencroft's library, or one in her mind.

The things he'd said about the laird . . .

A sound permeated the roar of her own blood in her ears. A high-pitched yip and a howl followed by a succession of barks. Lifting her head and peering around the tree, Mena identified the unmistakable roll and crest of the sea.

The canine sounds intensified in strength and pitch until Mena was certain they were distressed. Drifting carefully forward, she climbed over a fallen tree limb and followed the sounds through the thick foliage until the tree line suddenly gave way to a thin, steep grassy knoll. She found that she was at the peak of this hill, though taller, imposing black cliffs rose to to the north, and to the south. A steep path led down some amber-tinged autumn grasses to a hidden cove of golden sand.

Below her, a tall sheepdog and her tiny replica frantically paced at the surf, barking and howling loudly. Occasionally the mother would dive in and attempt to break the pull of the waves to reach an outcropping of rocks, upon which one little black and brown puppy yipped and cried for help.

Demons all but forgotten, Mena checked her surroundings before tucking her skirts into her wide belt and descending the steep and rocky trail to the cove as hastily as she could while still keeping her balance. She guessed the dogs had been playing on a sandbar and frolicking around the rocks when the tide had come in. The mother must have only been able to rescue one pup before the water became too deep and powerful for her to reach the other.

Since the coast of Wester Ross was buffeted by the Hebrides and the Isle of Skye, the surf was not as wild as the open ocean, and Mena felt confident that she could reach the little creature in time.

Abandoning her shoes and stockings the moment she reached the sand, she pulled her skirts even higher as the mother and her puppy raced toward her. They danced at her feet, barking pleas for help, rushing back to the water's edge, and then returning to nudge her legs.

A pang of fear slid between her ribs as she realized how cold and alarming the water would surely be, but it only took one look at the whimpering, stranded puppy for Mena to find her courage.

"I'm here," she told the frantic mother, who wouldn't stand still long enough to be touched. "I'll get your little one."

The icy shock of the autumn ocean drew a gasp from Mena as she plunged into the gentle surf. But as frigid as it was, it had nothing on the asylum's dreaded ice baths. Mena knew exactly how long she could function in water this cold.

Her skirts became heavy as the water engulfed her knees, then her thighs. But she quickly found the sandbar that the dogs must have crossed, and was able to navigate quite a ways to the outcropping of wet rock without the water reaching past her hips.

Once she neared the terrified pup, she reached out just in time as the little creature leaped into her arms. "Come here, my darling," she soothed as the tiny warm body squirmed and whined and burrowed its little face into her neck. "I've got you. You're safe now. Your poor mum is awfully worried." The chill of the water now stung her legs, and the depth began to creep upward toward her waist. Mena cuddled the wet pup to her breast and turned toward the beach.

Then froze.

The mother and pup were no longer alone. A man had joined them, and was even now kicking off his boots and wading into the water toward her.

Suddenly her trembling had little to do with the cold.

He waved a hand as he plunged into the tide, his strong

legs displacing water much more efficiently than hers. "Whit like, lass?" he called in a friendly voice.

Mena knew she had very few options at this juncture. She couldn't very well go farther out to sea, she'd drown or freeze before she swam to the island. And now that her skirts were heavy with water, there was no hope of out-running the man.

Lord, but they did breed a very different kind of male out here in the Highlands, didn't they?

His kilt of Mackenzie plaid tufted out about him in the water, and then sank as his large body shuddered with cold. He was tall and broad, and built like the strong men working in the barley fields. All slopes and swells of mus-cle and not an inch of fat to be found, this becoming more apparent as the moisture seeped into his shirt, causing it to cling to his well-sculpted chest.

"I'm quite all right," she replied as he waded closer.

He ignored her flinch as he swept a brawny arm be-neath her elbow and secured another about her waist as he helped her press toward the beach while simultaneously allowing her the hold on the puppy she clung to.

"I've got ye," he rumbled.

Mena was going to remark on the fact that she hadn't needed to be gotten. Though she had to admit that with the brawny man's help, she didn't have to rely so much on the failing strength of her legs straining against the icy pull of the Atlantic.

Once they began to splash into knee-deep water, they were accosted by the distraught mother, and the creature in her arms yipped and wriggled to be let down.

Mena took a few more steps, grateful the man released her to do so, and waited for a light wave to recede before placing the little thing back into its mother's care. The dogs whined and yelped and tumbled over each other in exu-berant reunion, the mother obsessively licking over both her children who romped toward the tall grasses that eventually led to the forest.

"There's gratitude for ye." The Highlander chuckled from behind her. Mena turned to stare into the most extraordinary green eyes she'd ever seen. Much darker than her own jade irises, his gaze reminded her of the shady canopy of trees that she'd traversed this very afternoon.

Mena's thoughts stalled for a moment at the brilliance of his smile and how it illuminated the rest of his handsome face. A face that seemed familiar, somehow, though she was certain she'd never before been introduced to him. Something about the raw shape of the jaw, or the proud, broad planes of his forehead. He had the look and build of a Mackenzie, she realized, though his coloring was more falcon than raven. Hair the shade of the wet sand beneath them glinted with strands of copper and gold when illuminated by the afternoon sun. He wore it short in the London style, though his garb was that of a Highlander.

"Allow me to thank ye on behalf of my ill-mannered mongrels," he said with a disarming smile. "Trixie is good with the sheep, but has always been a little daft if ye ask me, and shite with swimming."

"Think nothing of it." Mena backed toward the grassy knoll, painfully aware of the peril of her situation. "I really must be going, good afternoon, sir." She wrestled with her water-logged skirts and the give of sand beneath her feet as both impeded a hasty escape.

"Ye're English," he observed affably.

"Quite," she clipped, bending to retrieve her shoes and stockings, grateful that the water had pulled her skirts from where she'd tucked them up before. Mena found herself wondering if the Highlander had spied her when she'd lifted her skirts well above her bare knees earlier.

"I'm Gavin St. James of the clan Mackenzie . . ." He stopped and offered a hand, which Mena pretended not to see as she climbed the knoll toward the forest. She didn't have to look behind her to know he followed her. "And ye are?" he prompted, his voice betraying only amusement rather than ire at her discourtesy.

"I am very tardy," she said over her shoulder. "They were expecting me back at Ravencroft Keep some time ago, and will likely already be looking for me as the hour is late." She crested the hill quickly and, though she was a bit winded, she hurried toward the deer trail, hoping he took the not-so-subtle hint that she didn't welcome company.

No such luck. "Would it make ye feel more at ease if I told ye that I'm foreman at the distillery and I ken who ye are, as I was there that day the linchpin gave on the axle."

Mena paused at the tree line and turned to face him, studying his chiseled features more carefully. "You were?" she queried. "I don't remember you." Though she had been focused on none else but the imposing laird.

"I was mostly behind the carriage," he said sheepishly. "Also, I was wearing a rather dashing hat."

Searching her memory of that day, Mena found him. "The red hat with the dark coat?"

"That would be I," he announced. "And it might further please ye to know that it was yer ward Rhianna who named Trixie when she was a wee lass."

"Oh." Mena tucked a stray tendril back into her knot as the wind caught it. Somehow she found that it did, indeed, make her feel a bit less anxious about finding herself alone with him. "Forgive me if I was rude, I am not accustomed to walking in the forest with strange men."

"Think nothing of it." He repeated her words back to her with the most charming twinkle in his eyes. "Now that we are no longer strangers, would ye allow me to escort ye back to the keep, English? No offense to yer capabilities, but how could I face me own mother knowing I abandoned a half-drowned lass in the woods?"

His eyes were so soulful, his demeanor so earnest, Mena found that she couldn't at all refuse him. And besides, she was in no hurry to return to the keep.

And to the demons she might find there.

"Am I correct in assuming you live around here?" she queried, stooping to pick at a heather bloom at the edge of the forest.

"Aye." he motioned to the north and west as he fell into easy step beside her. "I hie from over to Inverthorne Keep north by Gairloch, though I'm here with the men for the distilling of the summer harvest, and then the sowing of the winter crops."

"Oh? I was unaware another keep resided so close to Ravencroft."

Another of his easy smiles endeared him to her even more. " 'Tis another Mackenzie stronghold, lorded over by the Earl of Thorne."

"I've never met the Earl of Thorne."

"And ye shouldna like to, either." he warned sagely. "Ravencroft's half brother. An incessant hedonist and notorious libertine, that one. Pretty lass like ye would do best to avoid his ilk, lest ye find yerself in trouble."

Mena's eyebrows flew toward her hairline. "I wasn't aware Ravencroft had any *more* brothers."

The Highlander slid a bemused glance her way. "What do ye mean, *more* brothers?"

Oh, blast, why had she allowed this slip of the tongue? Of course no one else knew about Dorian Blackwell. That he'd once been Dougan Mackenzie. She'd never forgive herself if she revealed a secret that was not hers to tell.

Especially when she trusted the Blackwells to keep her own secrets.

"Not very many outsiders know about Hamish," he said

easily, sensing her distress. "I'm surprised ye were told, is all, English."

"I thought Hamish was the name of Ravencroft's father."

"So it was." Gavin nodded, studying her intently. "But it was also the name of Liam's elder brother."

"Good Lord. How many errant Mackenzie brothers are there?"

"Too many." Gavin peered into the woods toward Ravencroft, though they were still too far away to see it through the copse of dense trees.

Mena barely had time to wonder at the shadows that settled over the genial Highlander's features before they were gone.

"The lairdship of Hamish the elder was a dark time for the Mackenzies of Wester Ross," he explained. "Young Hamish was the firstborn of the laird, but he wasna legitimate. Liam followed soon thereafter, and then the marchioness died under what some believe to be suspicious circumstances. There was a rumored bastard or two after that, no one knows who or how many. The laird wasna a kind man, ye ken, he didna always give his mistresses the choice . . ."

Mena nodded, her heart pinching for the poor women left in the late Laird Mackenzie's wake. "I heard as much. So this Earl of Thorne, he's one of these—illegitimate children?"

"Nay, he's the firstborn of the late Laird Mackenzie's second wife, 'tis why he was bequeathed the lesser title and a drafty keep."

"And . . . what happened to young Hamish?" If it was anything as terrible as Dorian Blackwell's fate, she'd almost rather not know.

"He was raised with Liam, mostly. They were close after a fashion, went off to war together, only . . ."

"Only what?"

"Only Liam returned. Hamish died at sea."

"Oh, dear, how very sad." They walked on in silence for a while. Mena gathered a few more late sprigs of heather, some wild lavender, and a small white flower that had fluffy, fernlike leaves. It occurred to her that her bouquet was rather like something someone would place at a grave. "This family has certainly seen its fair share of tragedy. Hamish the elder and younger, the laird's mother, and then his wife, all gone."

"Aye, well . . . Colleen, Liam's wife, was different," Gavin murmured, his eyes still far away.

Mena's eyes drew together at the liberty the Highlander took with the laird's first name. "How so?" she queried.

He took a long time to answer, so long Mena thought he must be lost in a faraway memory. "She just was."

Feeling as though she trod on a clan secret, a sense of unease around the death of two young Mackenzie marchionesses brought another dark fear to mind. "Mr. St. James," Mena began.

"Call me Gavin, please, there's no need to stand on ceremony out here, English." And just like that, his amiable mood and mischievous smirk had returned.

It struck Mena again how handsome he was, so incredibly virile, and she had to fix her gaze firmly on the forest in front of her.

"I wondered if you might tell me, that is, if you've ever heard of . . . or are familiar with . . ." Mena squeezed her eyes shut, feeling utterly foolish. "With the *brollachan*."

Gavin tossed his head back and laughed so heartily, Mena couldn't help but notice how the sinew of his masculine throat and collarbones were exposed to the dancing shade of the late afternoon. "Been listening to clan gossip about the laird, have ye?"

Mena glanced back down with a sheepish smile. "It's not just clan gossip; he's known as the Demon Highlander even in London. I was just . . . wondering if you, if the locals, gave the myth any credence."

The corner of his sensual mouth tilted roguishly. "The *Brollachan* was around before the Christians brought the fear of demons to this land, but the idea is the same, I suppose. It is said he's a wicked cast of Fae that has no shape but for fearsome red eyes. If ye look for him on a deserted road and ye make him a deal, he'll possess ye for a time, gift ye the speed and strength of the Fae. But then he'll drag ye down to perdition when he's finished with ye."

A shadow with red eyes?

"Is he dangerous to . . . to anyone else?" Mena stuttered.

"Only if ye meet him on the road, but not if he's inside a dwelling. A *Brollachan* is said to be good luck if they haunt yer home . . . or yer keep. Grateful spirits, they, and not fond of the chill."

Though Mena felt ridiculous, the information allowed her to peel her tense shoulders away from her ears. "Oh, well, that's good news, I suppose."

"Ye're most likely to see them around this time of year." He studied her again for a moment with that strange, intent expression, before bending down to pluck her another sprig of lavender and add it to her arrangement as they meandered through the forest thick with songbirds and equally boisterous creatures. "Do ye believe in demons, English?"

Mena couldn't stop picturing the horrible red-eyed shadow she'd seen earlier today. She'd like to believe it had been a dream, but would much rather it be real than a hallucination.

"I—I think I'm beginning to," she confessed with a diffident grimace.

"Was it the Mackenzie?" he queried, his tone hardening. "Does he frighten ye, lass?"

"Not at all." He terrified her.

Hiding her features in her bouquet of blooms, she glanced up at her companion. Large and strong as he was, he didn't carry the daunting menace Ravencroft did. His demeanor tended more toward charisma than hostility. In fact, she felt a sense of ease next to him, as though he posed her no threat, whereas the laird was nothing if not intimidating.

"I must admit the Marquess Ravencroft isn't what I anticipated when I accepted the position. He tends to be a bit . . ." Mena stalled, searching her extensive vocabulary for the right word.

Gavin ticked off on his fingers. "Formidable, grim, disagreeable, imperious, overbearing, high-handed, authoritarian . . ."

As the red stones of Ravencroft came into view, Mena found herself laughing, enjoying the answering chuckle of amusement that produced a charming dimple, a surprising and attractive change in the Highlander's chiseled face.

"He's not as bad as *all* that." She surprised herself by defending the laird.

"Aye. He is."

Mena's eyebrows lifted, as the sudden and serious vehemence in his voice caught her unawares. It was as though Gavin St. James were attempting to warn her, somehow, against her enigmatic employer.

Curious, Mena asked, "How well do you know Laird Ravencroft?"

The question produced another lift of his muscular shoulder. "It's been decades since he's settled here for more than a few weeks at a time. I doona think anyone truly knows him, as he's not an easy man to be acquainted with. And it's hard to trust a man who was raised by the hand of Hamish Mackenzie. Who looks so much like him, and shares his apparent gift for . . . brutality."

It was that penchant for violence that caused Mena the most concern in regard to her life here at Ravencroft.

She'd seen enough of it to fill her lifetime. Though, she supposed, thinking of Dorian Blackwell and his cohorts, of Ravencroft himself, and the many men sent off to war . . . She'd been exposed to less than others.

Mena spent a great deal of time not thinking about what kind of brutality might be visited upon her should her deception be exposed.

"Even still . . ." she murmured, more to herself than the man next to her. "He tries very hard to be a good father."

"Aye," Gavin agreed with a noncommittal shrug. "He does love those bairns." With a wave of his hand, the Highlander dispelled the sense of sobriety that threatened their conversation. "It seems to me that people either adore or despise the laird, though all his clan must agree that he's brought fairness and prosperity back to Wester Ross in the short time he's been home."

Adore him or despise him? "Am I to assume you are in the latter camp?"

They broke the tree line and the Highlander expelled a sigh. "I doona despise the laird. Though our interactions have been . . . complicated," he said cryptically.

"Yes, well, he's a complicated man." Mena contemplated the keep and its mysterious laird for a moment until she found her hand captured in a warm grip. The heat of Gavin's skin reminded her of how wet her skirts were, and how chillier every moment became.

"Thank you for the escort." She curtsied to him, her features relaxing into a genuine smile. "I should proceed from here alone."

"Aye," he agreed, his emerald eyes becoming heady and dark. "Ye're shivering, lass, and yer lips are a wee bit blue. May I give ye a kiss to keep ye warm and turn them rosy?"

Flustered, Mena squirmed away, pulling her hand from his. "Certainly not." She'd meant to sound stern, but her smile ruined the effect. "What kind of woman do you take me for?"

He twinkled eyes full of insinuation at her, and Mena did, in fact, feel a little warmth creep from beneath the collar of her dress. "Other than an intelligent lass and a selfless savior of wee beasties, I doona ken what kind of woman ye are, only what kind of woman I was hoping ye'd be."

His smile was devilish and handsome.

"Well." Mena laughed a little breathlessly. "I do hate to dash your hopes, but I am a respectable lady, and do not grant my favors lightly, if at all. Now I must bid you a good afternoon and return to the keep."

He bowed over her hand and pressed a lingering kiss there, the loose collar of his shirt exposing the impressive swells of his chest. "Good evening, then, lass." He gestured to where the sun began to dip below the trees.

Mena turned away and wandered into the gardens, though she smiled when he called after her. "I'll be seeing ye again, English, of that ye can be certain."

Shaking her head at his behavior, she found it impossible to repress a smile. She pressed her nose to her bouquet again and inhaled the loamy scent of the heather, mixed with the pleasant, camphorlike smell of the lavender blossoms.

The probability of another such encounter with Gavin was not just unlikely, it was imprudent. Not only was she still a married woman hiding from the high court of the queen, she was not at all looking to become embroiled with another charming, if devastatingly handsome, man.

She'd learned her lesson the first time.

Though, she had to admit, it had been rather nice to enjoy the attentions of a handsome Highlander. During the years she'd spent as a married woman, her sense of self-worth had been stripped away by means of underhanded jibes and blatant humiliation. Sometimes, the wounds produced thusly were slower to heal than bruised flesh.

It seemed to Mena that the standard of beauty up here in the verdant north was a great deal different than in London. Petite, thin, and delicate ladies had always been the draper's favorite. And though men had tended to pay Mena their more vulgar attentions, they'd always remarked unfavorably on her uncommon height . . . or her weight.

Gordon had been lusty and voracious at first. But that hadn't at all been pleasant. Quite the opposite, in fact. Then, as his mother and sister had done their best to craft her into the woman *they* wanted her to be, he'd turned into a cold and cruel beast.

Other men had approached her. Desired her. Her father-in-law for one, then Dr. Rosenblatt, and the late Mr. Burns. But she'd been nothing but an object to them. A pair of uncommonly large breasts with a few warm orifices attached, to use for their pleasure.

But these Highlanders . . . they roamed their untamed land like giants, and among them she felt like . . . well . . . like more of a *woman* than an object. A feminine creature.

She'd be lying to herself if she couldn't admit that she liked it. The afternoon's flirtation with Gavin St. James somehow felt as rare and warm as the disappearing rays of the sun. Full of impossibility, but lovely nonetheless.

Reaching the edge of the garden, she circumnavigated a thorny everblooming rosebush, and a few fading pink and burgundy blooms caught her eye. The frost was coming and these were, no doubt, the last roses she'd see this season, as Ravencroft had no hothouse.

Reaching in, she carefully plucked the roses and added them to her bundle.

She closed her eyes and enjoyed their sweet, almost ostentatious fragrance as she turned toward the keep. Perhaps once she'd changed for dinner she'd beg Mrs. Grady, the housekeeper, for a vase. Or maybe make a satchel of lavender for her pillow or to soak in the bath—

Large hands clamped around her upper arms like manacles, barely stopping her from plowing into a barrel-chest.

"Forgive me, I wasn't looking where I—"

The hands around her arms twitched with anger, or the

effort it took for him to not snap her bones in two, she couldn't tell. Dark eyes flashed with wrath in the quickly fading afternoon light, and Mena blinked against the savage majesty of the Laird of Ravencroft as he glowered down at her with barely leashed hostility.

"Explain to me, Miss Lockhart, just what *the fuck* ye were doing alone in the woods with *that* man?"

CHAPTER SIX

It was her mouth that did him in, Liam decided, as he glowered down at the startled governess held captured in his hands.

He'd spied her drifting through the gardens like a wayward flower petal, her lush lips tilting up slightly, as though the fragrance of the blooms brought a forbidden secret to mind.

Her mouth not only haunted his dreams, but also his every waking moment. And if that fucking ingrate had charmed her into letting him have a taste, Liam was going to burn Inverthorne Keep to the ground.

With Gavin St. James still inside.

After an enjoyable day out with his children, Liam was surprised to discover how much he looked forward to returning home. Because Miss Lockhart would be there, swishing about the halls of his keep in some lovely gown or other. Charming the staff, tantalizing the men, and smiling that kind but mysterious smile.

He'd anticipated that smile all bloody afternoon.

Once they'd arrived back at the keep, the lass had been disappointingly absent, and Russell had informed him that she'd been seen running into the woods alone, as though chased by the reaper.

Ravencroft was generally a safe place, but peculiar and dangerous things had occurred lately, and he didn't like the idea of a London lass in the Wester Ross woods alone. Concerned, Liam had taken it upon himself to go after her, as the hour began to grow late, and had barely set off when he'd heard the musical cadence of her laughter drift from the tree line.

She'd appeared, and not alone.

The smile in which Liam had meant to bask, she'd bestowed upon someone else. And not just anyone else, the very man who'd already betrayed him once before.

A familiar rage ignited inside him. Liam grasped onto that anger with both hands, calling forth the demon that had been forged in the inferno of his fury. It smothered the pain and suspicion with arrogance and superiority. He couldn't allow himself to notice the soft give of her flesh beneath his rough hands as he held her. Nor could he glance down to see the wet skirts clinging to her legs, outlining every lush curve of her voluptuous body.

"Answer me, woman," he growled. The image of her rolling beneath Gavin St. James in the waves sent a shock of murderous rage through him that lit his blood aflame. "What the bloody hell were ye doing in the forest with *him*?"

"I—I took a walk by the sea." Her eyes searched for anywhere to land but his. "A pup almost drowned and I waded out to save it for poor Trixie, and Mr. St. James was likewise looking for his dog and he offered to escort me home and—um . . ." The words tumbled out of her in desperate chaos bereft of any of her characteristic eloquence.

"It is *dangerous* to lie to me," he roared, giving her a firm shake.

Instead of offering more excuses, as he'd expected, the woman blanched a ghostly shade, and moisture welled to the rim of her lids as angst tightened her soft skin against her lovely features.

Confronted by what seemed to be guilt, Liam felt physically ill. "Is this how you conduct yourself? The second ye're left alone, you run off to whore in the woods with a known scoundrel?"

Her chin snapped up, and her eyes locked onto his, brimming with something other than tears, something he'd never expected to see from such a timid creature.

Fearless defiance.

It turned her irises an intense shade of azure-green and flashed at him with the strength of a sea storm, as though she were Calypso herself readying to unleash her wrath.

"You *will* unhand me, sir." She whispered the order, softly, *slowly,* as she twisted in his grip in such a way that Liam knew it would cause her pain if he didn't let go.

So he released her, though his hands curled at his sides, aching with a sense of loss. With the need to touch her again.

She took a step backward, then another, brandishing her bouquet like a shield as her features became harder and colder with each careful retreat.

Conflicted, provoked, angry, and bemused, Liam advanced, which seemed to fuel her hostility.

"How dare you?" she spat, her voice almost a whisper, and somehow carrying the weight of a Viking's cudgel. "How *dare* you cast such unfounded aspersions at me when I have given you no reason to draw such dreadful conclusions?"

Liam summoned his indignation to smother the shame he felt at handling her roughly. "What other conclusions do ye expect me to draw, Miss Lockhart?"

"Perhaps you should gather information before making wild and ridiculous accusations. Before calling me a *whore*."

Would that she were a whore rather than a governess.

The errant wish shocked Liam so thoroughly that his next words escaped more harshly than intended. "Do ye deny that any of yer pretty London lords and ladies wouldn't suspect the same after witnessing such behavior?"

"Wasn't it *you* who informed me you were different than they are?" she accused.

Liam blinked, momentarily speechless. No one dared to speak to him like this, not in decades. He'd thought this wee lass a timid English mouse. And though her heart-shaped face was leached of color, her eyes burned with a lovely jade fire, fueled by her defensive indignation.

"Mr. St. James treated me with more respectful deference and gentlemanly conduct than you have since the day I arrived at your keep, *my laird,* and *he* kept his hands to himself."

"How do I know that?"

She'd looked so guilty when he'd accused her of being a liar.

"You have my word as a lady."

"I trust no one's word." Besides, she was no lady. Merely a governess.

"That's no fault of mine," she quipped. "What was it Shakespeare said? 'Suspicion always haunts the guilty mind.'"

Liam's head snapped to the side, as though she'd slapped him. He couldn't look at her for a moment, couldn't see the fire in her eyes match the heat burning inside of him.

He'd not be responsible for what he would do next.

Gritting his teeth against his conflicting emotions, he pressed forward, forcing her to step back again, retreating toward the walls of the keep. His demon temper wanted her cornered. Wanted her helpless and trembling before him.

He wanted her to beg. Wanted her to *kneel*. He. Wanted . . . *Her*.

Beneath him. Above him. He didn't care. The thought of her with another man, with *that* man, caused his Mackenzie blood to simmer with dominance.

For such an intelligent lass, she wasn't smart enough to fear him. He needed to change that, for her own good.

He was a monster, after all. A demon. And it was best for all involved that she stay out of his way.

Though . . . hadn't he sought her out?

Pushing that troubling thought to the side, he gave her the look that had sent the most powerful of men to their knees. "If ye wish to retain yer position here, or if ye want Mr. St. James to live with his hands *attached* to his wrists, ye'll make certain they stay away from yer person. I'll not have ye keep company with the likes of him."

"I had no further intention of doing so," she stated, her eyes widening as her back found the stone wall of the keep, impeding further retreat. Yet she stood against him, her chin lifted haughtily, and her shoulders thrown as far back as the wall behind her would allow. "Regardless of my intent, you don't have the right to dictate how I spend my free time, or with whom!"

The leash on his temper snapped and roared to the surface. "Like hell! *I* am laird here!" He threw his arms out wide to illustrate the scope of his domain before gesturing at her. "And whilst in my employ, *ye* will mark me when I order ye to—"

Her reaction turned the flames of his temper into shards of ice. Heated words crowded his throat, suddenly filled with shock and remorse, and turned to ash.

The woman didn't just cringe or wince, like someone who'd been startled, when he'd gestured at her.

She *cowered*.

The bouquet of blossoms scattered to their feet as her hands flew up to protect her face, chin tucked tightly against her chest, and her lovely eyes squeezed shut. Bracing herself. Preparing for him to strike her.

And that wasn't even the worst of it.

From one of her trembling, splayed palms little crimson dots of blood revealed a terrible truth. She hadn't been fearless in her defiance as he'd initially assumed . . .

She'd been brave.

Clutching the flowers with white knuckles, she'd not even winced as the thorns had pierced her delicate flesh.

Because the entire time she'd stood against him, she'd been too terrified to notice.

All suspicion and—he finally admitted to himself— jealousy drained from him as he watched her courage likewise desert her. As the haze of red receded from his vision, he noted the details that supported her story. She smelled like the sea and the forest and late-summer herbs. Beneath that, the unmistakable smell of a wet dog clung to her damp bodice.

Her skirts were soiled and damp, but her blouse remained clean and her hair was undisturbed in its intricate coiffure. If she'd had a proper go with Gavin St. James, she'd be a disheveled mess. An image of her danced into his mind, lips swollen from rough kisses and her luxurious hair wild and spilling down her back. Naked flesh flushed with passion and begging to be touched, tasted, nay, *worshipped*.

"Christ," he whispered.

Never in his long, regret-filled life had he felt like such an unmitigated arse.

Liam tried to stop. Told himself to turn, to march away and leave this conversation for another time. But somehow he was reaching for her again, his fingers circling her wrists with all the infinite gentleness he could muster.

She gave little resistance as he pulled her hands away from her face, revealing her pale, pinched features.

And the haunted eyes of a refugee.

He'd seen the same look on the faces of victims from the Orient to India and Africa. The question in their forlorn gazes lurking behind the exhaustion and despair.

Are you going to be the next one to hurt me?

Hurting people was something he'd always excelled at, something his superiors in the military had noticed right away. They'd honed him from a violent youth into an efficient weapon and had unleashed him upon their enemies. Pain became his arsenal and his ally. In his long life, he'd hurt so very many.

But causing her pain seemed as unfathomable as did erasing the sins of the past.

Liam hated himself almost as much as he loathed whoever had put those shadows in her eyes. He'd relish using his considerable skills to bring the word *pain* a new and horrific perception to that man.

Grappling his temper, he schooled the wrath from his features as he searched his person for a handkerchief.

"Mo àilleachd," he whispered gently.

Her eyes sharpened with a question, but she remained still and watchfully silent as he pressed his handkerchief to the few small wells of blood.

"Tha mi duillch . . . Maith mi."

Forgive me.

Liam had never apologized before, and could only bring himself to do so now in his native tongue. Perhaps because he asked too much? That he was beyond forgiveness.

Had been for years.

Miss Lockhart searched his face with those huge, haunted eyes, her entire body still, yet coiled to spring away, like a rabbit beneath a stroking hand.

Working his jaw as though grinding his pride down

enough so he could swallow it, he flicked her a penitent look. "I vow on my honor as Laird of the Mackenzie clan never to strike ye."

She watched him with care, testing each movement of his muscle, assessing every change in his expression. "I do not question your honor, Laird, but it seems that I, also, may trust no one's word."

She'd heard such a promise before. And it had likely been broken.

So where did that leave them?

A small tendril of her lovely hair escaped its pin, caught the breeze, and snagged over her soft features. Liam released her uninjured wrist to reach up and brush the curl away from the nearly healed bruise on her cheek.

She winced, but did not flinch away.

"I've been the cause of enough such wounds in my life to recognize one made by a fist," he murmured. He wanted to say that he'd never raised his hand to a woman . . . but a terrible night in his youth would have made him a liar, and a familiar shame choked him into silence.

Her throat worked over a swallow, and the tension loosened, if only the slightest measure.

"I'll believe that yer walk through the forest with Gavin St. James was innocent, lass . . . if ye admit ye've been keeping a secret from me."

Her lashes swept down over her pale cheeks, and it warmed Liam that she was a terrible liar. An endearing trait in a woman.

"This was no carriage accident," he prodded. "Some bastard struck ye, did he not?"

The backs of his fingers caressed her cheek, the satin skin cool and unutterably soft beneath his work-roughened hands.

She stared at the space between them for several uncertain moments, and gave a barely perceptible nod.

"Tell me," he urged.

Her features became indescribably bleak. "I—I can't. Please don't ask that of me."

The sun gave one last explosion of light as it finished its dip below the trees, setting fire to her hair. Her jade eyes became luminous with unshed tears.

Never in his life had Liam seen anything so heartrendingly beautiful.

It unsettled him. It was as though when she looked at him, she saw not the man he struggled to be, but the man he truly was.

The demon he tried to keep locked away, but that he'd very nearly unleashed upon her.

A protective instinct welled from deep in his gut and seized his chest. It was wrong, and it was dangerous, but it was as undeniable and inevitable as the coming night. This woman, this stranger Farah Blackwell had sent him, she was intelligent, capable, indescribably lovely . . .

And she was running from something. From someone?

Perhaps that was why her perceptive gaze disturbed him, caused him to wonder what those observant eyes saw when she looked at him. Why did he care? He'd not done so before. Why did he look down at her now and yearn to be the savior she so obviously needed?

Because he'd never been that to anyone before. Indeed, it had always been the opposite. He'd been the one to run from. The Demon Highlander. The man from whom there was no salvation.

Only pain.

God, but he was tired. Tired of the fear he read in the eyes of others. The deference. The expectation.

The English loved him for the atrocities he committed for their empire. His clan hated him for the atrocities committed by his father, but they needed his land, his business, to survive. So they tolerated him, and feared him, and obeyed him. Avoided his temper because his wrath had become legend.

But what if, *just once,* he inspired a different emotion? What if he used what made him hard and dangerous to protect something soft and vulnerable?

Someone rare and brilliant and beautiful.

What if, in return, he found the thing he sought most in this world?

Peace.

Testing the strand of silken hair between his thumb and forefinger, he tucked it behind the shell of her ear.

"Do ye know what this land was called before it was Wester Ross, before it was Scotland even? A name that is still whispered to this day?"

Her brows drew together, creating a little wrinkle of confusion between them. "I confess I do not," she said carefully, her mistrust of this subject change apparent.

"Comraich." He murmured the word with all the reverence it deserved. "It means sanctuary. Protection. People have been climbing the Bealach na Bà Pass to Wester Ross to hide for thousands of years."

She caught her lip in her teeth, and Liam's gaze snagged there. "Is that what ye've done, Miss Lockhart? Have ye come here in search of refuge?"

Her face turned toward his fingers, as though searching for the warmth they would find there. "I don't know what to say." Uncertain eyes met his, looking for direction. For assurance.

"Ye'll find it here." Liam could tell his words had stunned her.

"Why?" she breathed. "You cannot trust me."

Did she mean that he should not trust her? Or that he was incapable? Something about the secrets held in her eyes brought to mind paintings of Renaissance angels hinting at the great, divine mystery.

Why, indeed?

Because he wanted her close. Because the sound of her soft and husky voice did things to him physically that the most exotic whores had failed to provoke. Because she'd only just done what no other seemed brave enough to do. She'd stood against his ire. Put him in his place.

She'd provoked the fire of his temper, of course. But then—somehow—she'd put it out.

"Because, in my blood, before I am the Marquess of Ravencroft, a British title given to my ancestors, I am the Laird of the Mackenzie clan of Wester Ross. Like I said, we lairds have provided sanctuary to anyone who seeks it, even our enemies, and especially against the British. Highland hospitality is our sacred duty." Though he felt as though his smile would crack from disuse, he attempted one, and judging by the complete change in her features, he was pretty certain he'd succeeded.

Her eyes became impossibly wider and one breath of disbelief followed another. "But I *am* British."

"Am I correct in assuming that so is whomever ye're hiding from?"

After a protracted, level look, she nodded. Her first concession, which ignited a spark of hope.

He noted that her hand had relaxed from where she'd gripped his handkerchief, and he began to gently dab her palm. Once the dried blood was gone, it was impossible to tell where the thorns had punctured her.

"I thought you were going to—" She swallowed when he looked at her, and seemed to forget what she was going to say, so he concentrated on her palm. "I thought you were going to dismiss me."

Not a fucking chance in hell would he allow her to leave.

In lieu of that, he said, "Sanctuary aside, I think ye're good for Rhianna and Andrew."

"You do?" He found the surprise in her voice both bemusing and endearing.

"I just spent an entire day with my children, and after only a week, their behavior was better than it's ever been."

Her pleasure at his compliment was palpable, and Liam let it spread over him like a cooling balm.

"I'm so delighted to hear it. I was worried that progress has been rather . . . gradual."

"We Highlanders are a stubborn, hardheaded lot. Gradual is the best ye can expect from us by way of progress."

"You don't say."

Liam glanced up at the dry note of levity in her voice. There it was. *That* smile. The one that made her eyes glimmer with the brilliance of the jade sculptures he'd admired in China. It was all he wanted out of this day . . . and he'd been the cause.

Liam had thought himself too old, too cynical to ever again experience a marvel at his own sense of achievement.

Would wonders never cease?

Apparently not, when it came to his governess.

It was then he noticed her shiver. In fact, her lips had lost some of their rosy color, and some fine veins had become visible beneath her pale, nearly iridescent skin.

She was cold, he realized.

"Come, lass, let's get ye inside."

"Yes, that sounds wonderful." Bending down, she used the hand not clutching his handkerchief to gather the scattered pile of flowers and herbs she'd dropped.

Berating himself, Liam crouched to help.

She flicked a grateful look at him, and Liam noticed that her eyes caught at his shoulders and held, then traveled down the places where his arm strained against his shirtsleeves.

"Blast." She grimaced, and dropped the rose she'd clutched at, as well as his handkerchief.

A thorn remained in the soft pad of her finger, and she reached for it with a wince.

"Och, lass." Liam beat her to it. "These roses are a jealous flower." Cupping her hand with his, he pressed a thumb into her palm to secure it before plucking the thorn out quickly, to cause her the least amount of distress.

A tiny drop of blood welled from her fingertip.

Liam had no other handkerchief to offer her, and didn't want to use the one on the ground, so he did the only other thing he could think of, and slid her finger into his mouth. Closing his lips around the insignificant wound, he watched her reaction with rare pleasure.

She froze, her eyes growing round as two glowing moons.

His body's reaction was just as astonishing, and just as instantaneous.

Her finger was cold inside the heat of his mouth, and he fitted his tongue against it, warming her with a soft sucking motion. He enjoyed her quick intake of breath with a predatory thrill.

She tasted of the sea. A bit of brine mixed with lavender. Liam could see the pulse jump against the thin, delicate skin of her wrist. Could feel the quiver of sensation that washed up her arm when he gave another gentle pull with his mouth.

No more blood welled from the wound; he would have been able to taste it. But he couldn't seem to let her go. Instead, on a dark whim, he ran his tongue up the underside of her finger and reveled in the startled catch of her breath and the dilation of her eyes.

It was then he realized just what a colossal mistake he'd made.

He *never* should have allowed himself to taste her. Never should have glimpsed the way her eyes liquefied and her plump lips parted and softened at the illicit motion of his mouth.

Her gaze ripped from what his lips did to her finger and caught his eyes. His primeval instinct—the same one that made him such an efficient killer—identified the heat he glimpsed beneath the innocent confusion. Her fear, a primal emotion, had become something equally as primitive.

The knowledge that he could fan that soft spark into an inferno set flame to his own blood.

He wanted to be the answer to the questions he saw building inside her. To allay her every curiosity and teach her things she'd never even thought to inquire about. To peel away the wet layers of her clothing and fit her naked body against his, and distinguish the moment when her shivers of cold became shudders of ecstasy.

To allow lust to consume them both.

It was as he'd warned his men when commanding them to avoid the opium dens and pleasure palaces of Asia. It was better to never take that first step.

Because once you tasted the smallest part of something so infinitely sweet, you'd want the rest of it with a fiendish, obsessive hunger. You'd give away every part of yourself to savor it again. Would beg, steal, or kill in order to obtain it.

Miss Philomena Lockhart was exactly that kind of unattainable pleasure.

And he'd just had his first taste.

Velvet shackles wound their way around his bones, locking his soul down with an ominous sound of finality. He'd always been a beast of greater appetites than most men. He understood that he needed too much and too often. He'd been careful, *so fucking careful,* when it came to drink, or gambling, or the myriad other things that men like him lost themselves to.

Even women.

It was because of his consuming need that he held himself in check, even to the point of denial. He was a large man, larger than most. It wasn't just the strength of his temper he feared . . . . it was the idea that he wouldn't be able to temper his strength.

This, he realized, was a great deal of Miss Lockhart's

allure. The wrist beneath the grip of his hand was feminine, but not delicate. Her voluptuous, statuesque build intrigued him. She was strong, hearty, with more dips and hollows, more curves and handfuls, than the women he was accustomed to.

He'd thought that perhaps he could unleash the full force of his voracious lust on a woman such as her . . . and she'd be able to withstand it. She didn't seem so fragile, so easily broken.

But that was wrong, wasn't it? Someone had already tried to break her, and very nearly succeeded.

As though she could sense the direction of his thoughts, she gasped and slid her finger from between his lips, reclaiming her hand and enfolding it to her chest. Blinking rapidly, she rose to her feet.

"Thank you, Laird, for . . ."

Liam watched her grope for the words and wished he could help. Manners dictated that he rise when she did, but he couldn't. Not with his body in the urgent state of arousal it was now.

"Excuse me," she murmured, and rushed around him, flowers forgotten where they lay strewn in colorful chaos.

Liam glared down at the fragrant blossoms. He didn't allow himself to watch her. Couldn't afford to appreciate the sway of her ample arse as she hurried away from him. He didn't dare stand. If he stayed here—stayed low—the predator within wouldn't urge him to chase her as she fled.

Because he *would* catch her . . . and there would be no accounting for what he would do to her once he did. She would be a lamb in the jaws of a lion, and her fate would be the same as any other beautiful, innocent thing he'd dared to care about.

She'd end up dead.

For destruction was the destiny of those he loved. The cost of his glory. The counterweight of the stewardship over this ancient land. He was the result of untold generations of cruelty. And as the world became more civilized, he had less of a place within it.

Nay, he admonished himself, as the cold of the encroaching evening seeped past his flesh and into his soul, but did nothing to erase the shiver of yearning or the flavor of her flesh from his tongue.

He *never* should have allowed himself a taste.

CHAPTER SEVEN

Even though she'd changed into dry clothing, Mena couldn't seem to stop trembling. Perched on a delicate chair next to the hearth, she held her hands out to the fire, though she knew that her quivering no longer had anything to do with the cold.

And everything to do with *heat*.

The fire she'd seen simmering in the eyes of the marquess as he lifted her finger to his lips. The heat of his mouth and the silken rasp of his tongue against her cold skin.

How could she—how *had* she—allowed that to happen? How had the gentle warmth evoked by his offer of protection suddenly flared into a conflagration of the senses that left her feeling—well, scorched?

Her finger still glowed with sensation, so much so that Mena kept checking it to see if he had, indeed, burned it somehow with his sweltering mouth.

Curling her fingers into a fist, Mena leaned back in her chair and pressed her closed hand to her heart. Damn her, but his lips had felt good—too good—and the branding impression of them singed along her blood and carried that heat all the way down to her—

A soft knock ripped her away from her disquieting thoughts. Standing on unsteady legs, Mena smoothed her hair and ran her hands down the front of her green and gold striped dress, making certain the lace on her vest wasn't in disarray.

Jani's brilliantly white smile met her when she answered, the effect almost startling against the brilliance of his attire. "Miss Mena, you have a letter, and I wanted to give it to you myself."

"Thank you, Jani." Mena took the small folded letter and a pang of apprehension shot through her as she instantly recognized Farah Blackwell's small and efficient handwriting. She smiled her gratitude and began to push her door closed.

"Forgive my impertinence, Miss Mena." Jani stood on his tiptoes and stretched his neck to peek around her into her chamber. "But I could not help noticing that you have been here for several days and have yet to fully unpack your trunks."

Glancing behind her, she noted that her trunks, indeed, remained where they'd been placed at the foot of the bed, and she'd not done a great deal to move their contents to the wardrobe. Every time she considered emptying them, something had prevented her from doing so. What if she had the need to flee again? What if she'd failed to impress the marquess and he sacked her? Surely if her things were already in their trunks, it was safer.

"I—I've yet to find the time to truly settle in."

Chocolate eyes lit with the pleasure one found in a grand idea as Jani clapped his hands together. In a liquid movement of violet silk, he somehow slid past her and into her room. "Permit me to assist you, Miss Mena. We will be finished by the time it is for supper."

"That really isn't necessary." Mena tucked the letter into her belt and hovered anxiously by as he hurried to the empty wardrobe in the turret and threw open the ornate doors. Anxious to read her letter, she considered the best way to dismiss him without hurting his feelings.

"I was the valet to the Mackenzie for many years before he brought me here to Ravencroft." Jani announced proudly. "I am exceptional at organization."

"I'm certain you are, but—"

"When he was lieutenant colonel, I kept almost twelve uniforms for him and also his other belongings." Bustling to her trunks, he unlatched one and tossed the lid up and gasped as though he'd found a poisonous serpent.

"What?" Mena asked, her heart rate spiking. "What is it?"

"Oh, no, no, Miss Mena, no, no, no. It is being bad luck to be putting a red garment next to a blue garment," he said gravely.

"It is?" She peered into her own disheveled trunks as though she'd never seen them before.

"Yes. In my village they are two very auspicious colors. One is sensuality and purity, and the other is the color of creation. Very powerful. And they will fight each other, causing you many problems."

She'd certainly seen her share of those. "Fight each other . . ." she echoed. "In—in my closet?" Mena regarded him skeptically, thinking how strange and intriguing it was that sensuality and purity were considered to be close to each other in his culture.

He nodded gravely. "I will fix this, and arrange your garments for optimal placement for colors, seasons, and accessories." Plucking her red wool pelisse from where she'd folded and tucked it, he snapped it out and began to brush the wrinkles and arrange the buttons.

Mena wanted to insist on her privacy, but she had seen that expression of serious determination and kind condescension before. Her father used to wear it often, and when he did, she'd learned that there was no standing in his way. In truth, she'd never had to unpack and organize her own garments before. She'd always had servants to do so, and was both ashamed and grateful for the assistance.

Taking a moment, she turned from him and unfolded the letter, which, it seemed, had been folded and unfolded a few times. Her heart kicked against her ribs as she absorbed Farah's carefully intended words.

Dearest Mena,

It is my fervent hope that you are settling well into your new position. London is frenetic with preparation for the coming holiday season and gossip already abounds. I thought I'd inform you so you don't feel so isolated. The most salacious story on everyone's tongue is that of a viscountess who apparently absconded from Belle Glen Asylum more than a fortnight ago during a recent régime change organized by none other than my husband. She's quite disappeared. No one knows what to make of it.

The viscount and his family appear beside themselves with worry. They've all but torn the city apart looking for her, and have threatened to start searching abroad, going so far as to hire a few detectives. Though I found it curious that her father-in-law has petitioned the high court to begin proceedings toward proclaiming her deceased. I find myself hoping that she is careful, that she is never found by these horrible people. Though my dear husband has improved upon the situation at Belle Glen, I should not like to see her back there.

Write and tell me how Scotland agrees with you. I do so miss Ben More Castle. Perhaps in the summer when we return, I will come to visit you.

Please take care, dear Mena.

Your ardent friend,

Lady Farah Blackwell, Countess Northwalk.

"You have gone very, very pale, Miss Mena," Jani observed. "I fear you are fainting."

He reached to help her and Mena put out her arm. "No. *No,* I'm just fine, Jani. Just a bit of bad news, is all."

"Did someone die?" he queried, dark eyes liquid with concern.

Myself, perhaps, she thought acerbically, tucking the letter back into her wide belt.

"No, Jani, it's nothing of consequence," she lied. Extracting the bodice of the green dress she'd worn to dinner the first evening, she arranged it to be hung neatly, mirroring Jani's efficient movements and hoping to distract him from the letter. "I don't often think of the marquess as a lieutenant colonel," Mena remarked, picking up a scrap of conversation he'd dropped earlier. "Were we in England, he'd be referred to as such, but I rarely hear of it here at Ravencroft."

"Perhaps, Miss Mena, that is because most of the Mackenzie people do not think so well of the British or their armies and corresponding titles," Jani said sagely, hanging her pelisse and returning to the trunk.

"Just so," Mena murmured. It had been a hundred years since the Jacobite rebellion, and yet in places like this, where tradition ran through the bones of every baby born, prejudices remained strong. She'd never been particularly political, but she remembered her father's strident opinions against what he considered the English empire's overreach.

Curious about Jani and his relationship to the marquess, Mena asked, "How long have you been in the laird's employ?"

"Ten years," he answered cheerfully.

"How much of that time have you spent here at the keep?"

"Very little, though I am quite happy to be staying. I have seen many countries and many wars, and somehow they were all in places that are very hot. I am not meaning to be complaining, but I admit that I am excited to see the snow." He beamed at her before lifting one of her thin, white undergarments from her trunk and examining it curiously.

Mena snatched it from him and hid it behind her.

Dark eyes sparkling with naughtiness, Jani allowed himself to be directed toward the trunk containing her shoe boxes.

Sorting through her own underthings, she shoved them in a few dresser drawers before turning back to him. "May I inquire . . . that is . . . do you remember much about the late Marchioness of Ravencroft?" she ventured.

He nodded, stacking boxes dangerously high on one arm. "Lady Colleen. She was quite mad."

"Mad?" Mena's heart started. "As in, she belonged in an asylum."

"Yes."

Oh, no. Mena turned, so he could not see the fear tightening her features. Though she doubted he could over the mountain of boxes he hauled toward the turret.

My, but Millie LeCour did get carried away at the cobblers.

Biting her lip, Mena remembered back to her encounter in the library earlier that morning. An encounter with a demon? Or with her own madness?

She struggled to keep her voice casual as she asked, "Would it be terrible of me to inquire about how she . . . how she died? I've heard the children discuss it, but I'm not certain of the particulars, and I thought it cruel to ask."

"They are ignorant of the particulars, as well," he called from around the dividing wall. "For they are too brutal."

"Oh?" Her heart bumped against her chest. She burned to know, but didn't dare ask him to elaborate, so she remained quiet, hoping he'd fill the silence.

Luckily, he did just that. "She had terrible fits. So bad

that the marquess had to keep her from the children. One night, she climbed up to the widow's walk, and threw herself from it."

Oh, dear Lord.

"Why?" Mena whispered, horrified. "Were the children in residence?" Had the marquess been?

Jani appeared around the wall shaking his head. "The children were with their maternal grandmother in London, and the laird and I were not even in the country. The marquess was called back from Rajanpour for the funeral. That was maybe more than nine years ago. Though the children think that an illness took her, and the marquess would be very angry if he found out they knew different."

"They won't hear it from me," she promised.

So what had been the meaning of the ghostly encounter in the darkness of the library this morning? She'd been so tired, hadn't she? So utterly exhausted, perhaps she'd imagined it. Perhaps she was remembering it wrong and this was all the fault of an overwrought imagination.

Needing a change of subject, she asked, "What about you, Jani? How old were you ten years ago?"

"I was a very small boy, maybe seven."

Working alongside him to pull out all her skirts, she pressed, "That's awfully young. Your parents allowed you to work for the marquess at that age?"

"My parents were part of a rebel force that fought the British *and* the East India Company. They were killed when the laird's regiment . . . moved on our village. *Everyone* was killed, but me." His voice remained genial, pleasant even, but his features darkened with something bleak and indefinable.

"Dear God, Jani!" she gasped. The petticoat Mena had been folding slid from her fingers and fell in a heap at her feet.

He shook his head, the deft movements of his fingers

never ceasing. "It was so long ago. Time has a way of softening all tragedies, and after a while, it is easier to forget the pain of it."

Horrified, Mena tried to focus on their task, but she simply couldn't bear it. "But Jani, how can you bring yourself to work for him? To live under his roof and serve him?"

His dark, gentle eyes lit on her as he smiled sadly. "Because he offered me revenge."

"What?" Mena could hardly believe what she was hearing.

"The marquess was a captain then. He and his lieutenant found me picking through the rubble searching for food. I was so angry that when I saw them I threw things, even glass. I screamed at them and spat at them. His superior took out his pistol and was about to put me down when Ravencroft stopped him. I remember being very frightened when he approached me. I never had seen a person so big before. So tall and wide. He subdued me and picked me up. Then he took me to his tent and fed me. I was so angry, but also starving." Even in the dim light of the fading evening, the youth's hair gleamed a brilliant black, and it matched the darkness in his eyes. "Do you know what he said to me while I ate?"

Mena shook her head, astounded. "I can't even *imagine*."

"He said that if I wished, he'd feed me, train me, and protect me. He promised that if my anger grew to hatred as I grew into a man, he would be always close, and I could have my revenge whenever I wanted to take it. He said he would not fight me."

Plunking onto the bed behind her, Mena just shook her head in disbelief. "You had to have been tempted."

Jani's eyes lost some of their luster as they gazed into the past. "I would sit on my cot eating the supper he brought me. He always provided a sharp knife, even when there was no meat to cut, and we'd eat in silence. For years

I went to bed, fully intending to slit his throat while he slept."

"What stopped you?" Mena breathed.

"I think it was the way he looked at me every night before he blew out the lantern . . ." Jani paused, glancing up at Mena as though remembering that they were not so well acquainted.

"How was that?" she inquired, unable to stop herself from asking.

"Like he wanted me to do it." Jani gathered an armful of her new skirts and carried them to the wardrobe, leaving her to stare after him in dumbfounded amazement until he glided back for more.

"But he has children."

"Yes, he does." Jani's expression turned contemplative. "But he's never really allowed them to know him."

With movements that felt stilted and stiff, Mena rose to help, but her mind wouldn't stop racing. "Even after all these years, you can't have just . . . forgiven him."

"The marquess, he has kept his promise. He took me with him all over the wide world, and even provided for me in his will should he die. I do not know, Miss Mena, if he's responsible for the deaths of my parents, but I do know that we were both part of an empirical war machine that was built long before that day." Jani paused in his work to look out her window and over the forest that rolled down to the sea. "The first time he brought me to this place, I understood that Ravencroft was bred to be a warrior, it was his destiny." He turned back to her with that white smile, though this time it was not so bright. "Can you imagine him as anything else?"

"No," Mena admitted, her heart bleeding for the pure tragedy of it all. "No, I don't suppose I can."

"I did not mean to distress you, Miss Mena," the young man said earnestly. "I am content with my life here, and there are . . . other reasons for me to stay."

It was strange, Mena thought, that for the first time in their entire conversation, Jani truly seemed sad.

She had a good idea as to why. "Rhianna?" she prompted softly.

He looked at her, and his heart was revealed.

"Does she return your feelings?"

"She does not know." Fear crept over his features and Mena hurried to comfort him.

"It's all right," she murmured to him, placing a hand on his silk sleeve. "I've mentioned it to no one. I have secrets of my own to keep, and would never betray a confidence of a friend."

He searched her gaze, then nodded. "It is not to be, Miss Mena. The daughter of a marquess doesn't marry a valet, especially a foreigner. I mean, is that not why you are here, to teach her how to be the wife of a gentleman and a nobleman?"

Mena lifted her hand to his smooth cheek and rested it there, a lump of emotion in her throat. "I think, sweet Jani, that there may be no man alive more gentle and noble than you."

A curious sheen glimmered in his dark eyes before he quickly turned away. "Then you will allow me to arrange your writing desk to further maximize your efficiency," he said with forced brightness. "When you reply to your letter, you will be thanking me."

"If you must." She offered him a tremulous smile, allowing him to alter the course of the conversation. She stepped back to her trunks to finish sorting and unpacking them. She and Jani worked in relative but comfortable silence, though, she suspected, their thoughts were anything but.

The dinner bell interrupted them not long after, and Mena decided she and the sweet valet had made sufficient progress.

"Miss Mena," Jani exclaimed upon opening the door.

She looked up from her dressing table, where she hastened to tidy her coiffure.

"This was left in the hallway outside your room."

What lay in his hands instantly softened the sharp edges of her heavy thoughts, and brought back the memory of her encounter with the marquess.

And the heat.

Standing, Mena reached for the tidy, if indelicately arranged, bouquet of the very same flowers she'd abandoned that afternoon. There was no note, no card, and nothing but a small knot made from the Mackenzie plaid to hold them together.

But there was no question as to just who had left them at her door. And as she wrapped careful fingers around the fat stems of the few roses, Mena noticed something that melted the very cockles of her careful heart.

Ravencroft had stripped them of every thorn.

CHAPTER EIGHT

Liam ran his hands through the soft green of the fresh peat moss and tried not to compare it to the vibrant shade of Miss Lockhart's eyes. Was this the newest torment to his endless search for peace? Was there no escaping the lass? He couldn't even examine something as innocuous as fucking moss without conjuring some part of her to his mind. She'd been at Ravencroft two weeks, and he could barely get through dinner every night without hiding arousal beneath the table.

Crushing the soft little buds in his hand, he growled at Russell. "Just *how* many barrels of peat did Grindall order?"

"Enough to roast the entire harvest," his steward said carefully. "He said he discussed it with ye."

"I've no memory of that."

Russell swiped his hat off, revealing tufts of wild orange hair, and scratched his scalp nervously. "Well, if ye doona mind me saying so, my laird, ye've been a bit . . . distracted lately."

Distracted by a ripe mouth and a round arse.

"I *do* mind ye saying so." Because it was true. He'd always been a focused, driven, and determined man, and no tempting wee English lass was going to change that.

The Ravencroft distillery had almost collapsed under the drunken tyranny of his father, and Liam would be goddamned if he added the failure of the livelihood of so many to his already tainted legacy.

Employing a breathing technique he'd learned from an Indian guru, he took a breath in through his nose, and counted slowly as he controlled the exhale with his throat.

Russell likewise employed another tactic. "This shipment was expensive, and we could barely afford it due to the new copper mash tuns for the barley we acquired last year without dipping into the tenant rents. Grindall said that the peat would hasten the kiln fire of the barley and add smoke to the taste. So many of the Highland distilleries are implementing the practice."

Goddammit. He'd wanted the distillery to be self-sustaining. He'd do anything to avoid dipping into his other sources of income.

Liam looked to his right, counting a few bricks of the warehouse which held rows upon rows of aging Scotch in their blond oak casks, then back to the kiln fires over which he was aiding Thomas Campbell, the cooper, in assembling and charring the insides of the imported casks for this year's offering of spirits. The work was backbreaking for most men, but Liam found that he appreciated the mental monotony of it. Once Andrew fit the wet slats of oak into the bottom ring, he passed them to Thomas Campbell to char the inside over the flame.

Liam would then take one of the already charred barrels and bend the slats of wood to fit into the iron rings, and employ the blacksmith's hammer to pound them into place. He enjoyed the need to sweat and strain, found a sort of physical release in the force it required of him.

A physical release that he was sorely in need of.

This peat business was an unwelcome interruption.

Taking another breath, he tossed the peat back into the crate. "There are three—and *no more* than *three*—ingredients in Ravencroft Single Malt Scotch. What are they, Andrew?"

He turned to his son, who stood behind him. The boy's mood was as black as the soot smudged across his fine shirt and stubborn, miserable features. He'd brought Andrew down to experience the jolly frenzy of work that came after the barley harvest. The milling and mashing of the barley into grist, the import and assembly of the casks, the careful fermentation in the mash tuns, the distillation processes, and finally the stacking of the finished barrels where they would sit for no less than three years and one day, and sometimes more than two decades.

"I doona ken what they are," Andrew mumbled.

"Aye, ye do, lad. They've been the same for centuries." Liam tried to keep his rising temper from his voice.

Glowering at the crates of moss, his son lifted a shoulder. "I canna remember."

Setting his teeth against his frustration with his son, his steward, and his fucking buyer, he ticked the answer off on his own fingers. "Malted barley, water from the river Glan, and yeast. That's it," he informed them both. "I'm not adding the taste of the slag ye collect from the bogs to my whisky."

"This peat is special grown for Scotch," Russell said. "It's hardly from the bogs."

Unused to repeating himself, Liam enunciated his words very slowly. *"Barley. Water. Yeast."*

Russell took one look at Liam and hopped to cover the crates. "What do ye like we should do with all this?"

"Burn it. Throw it in the sea. Wipe yer arse with it! I care not," Liam snarled. "But I'll flay the skin from any man's hide that puts it near my whisky."

"You know, Mr. Mackenzie." A soft, husky feminine voice from behind him vibrated through every hair on

Liam's body until lust dripped like warm oil straight to his loins. "I've heard that peat makes an excellent addition to compost. Perhaps you can add it to the fertilizer you're mixing in with the top layer of soil before the frost."

"Miss Lockhart, Lady Rhianna." Russell beamed at her, wiping a self-conscious hand over his hair and replacing the cap. "What an unexpected pleasure."

There was no amount of controlled breath that could have prepared Liam for the sight of Miss Lockhart swathed in a simple dark gold day dress the exact color of the barley roasting in the kiln. A woolen shawl of the blue, green, and gold Mackenzie plaid rested casually over her head and shoulders. Only a little of her hair peeked from beneath it, but Liam thought that she might have worn some of it down.

How long is it? he wondered. And was it truly as silky as it appeared?

Beneath the slate-gray autumn sky, she was as vibrant as a sunset. Judging by the instantaneous change in productivity around the crop of buildings that comprised the distillery, he wasn't the only man to notice.

The lass had addressed Russell, but her gaze traveled the length of Liam from the top of his loosely bound hair, to his open shirt, soiled kilt, and filthy boots. When she'd finished her inspection, her eyes returned to meet his, and he couldn't exactly name what he saw there before she flicked her lashes down, but his body responded to it.

Violently.

Miss Lockhart elbowed Rhianna who stood next to her, dark curls tumbling over a lavender dress. His daughter stepped forward and performed a perfect curtsy. "Mr. Russell, Mr. Campbell, Father," she addressed them all kindly. "Good afternoon."

Liam reached for his daughter, then noted the soot on his hands and staining the cuffs of his shirt and kilt, and thought better of it. "Ye look like a fine grown lass today, *nighean*."

Philomena Lockhart had begun to turn his wild wee daughter into a lady. She never ceased to impress him.

Goddammit.

Russell sidled closer to the governess, a solicitous smile affixed beneath his beard. "So, Miss Lockhart, what were ye saying about the peat making compost?"

"Well, Mr. Mackenzie—"

"We're most of us 'Mr. Mackenzie' around here. Call me Russell." He offered her his arm and the charismatic smile that had gotten him many prettier lasses than he deserved.

"Then you must call me Mena." She took Russell's offered arm and drifted with him toward the crates of moss in the yard.

Mena.

Liam had to clench his teeth to stop himself from testing the name out loud. The word was soft and round, lovely and feminine. Just like everything else about her.

The sight of her clean, soft hands resting on the sleeve of Russell's grubby work clothes set a shimmer of antipathy through him.

Abandoning his post at the open fire to Campbell, Liam followed them over to the crates. "A governess, a carriage mechanic, and now an agriculturalist? Is there aught ye doona do, Miss Lockhart?" he challenged.

She met his antagonism with a modest smile that deepened the distracting dimple next to her lush lips. "I'm no agriculturalist, but my father did have me practice my reading from an American publication entitled *The Farmer's Almanac*. While I don't remember everything I read, I do recall that often American barley farmers would import Scottish peat moss to fertilize their fields and help stave off the blight."

"She's ever so clever, isna she, Father?" Rhianna exclaimed solicitously.

"Ever so." Liam nodded, though his features tightened. "But she forgets our Scottish soil is already full of peat, and thereby adding too much can create a buildup of ammonia."

"There is that," Russell ceded, sliding Mena an apologetic look and patting her hand with his. "But it was a good idea, especially for a lass."

Liam noted, with no small amount of pleasure, that Mena gently but resolutely extricated herself from Russell's arm. Apparently, she'd had enough of his masculine supremacy.

"I have it on good authority that the extra ammonia is easily balanced with an agent like sodium bicarbonate," she observed. "Which is not at all expensive, and you can order such a substance from most any alchemical farming supply these days and it's shipped by train. It might put you a few days behind, but the money you would save on wasting the moss would be worth it to the operation. Not to mention the benefits you'd reap next year with abundant crops."

A stunned silence followed her declaration in which she seemed to take great pleasure. However, instead of saying something smug, which he'd fully expected her to do, she turned to Andrew, and dismissed them altogether.

"This all looks so exciting." She addressed Andrew with a cheeky smile. "I'll bet you're enjoying working with your father rather than conjugating your French verbs."

Andrew shrugged, turning to address his sister. "What are *ye* doing down here?"

"I wanted to see what this is all about," Rhianna insisted. "It isna fair that only *ye* get to work at the distillery."

Russell chuffed Rhianna under the chin. "The lad is going to inherit Ravencroft someday. He needs to learn the business. Ye'll move into yer husband's house, so there's no need to worry yer pretty head about the dirty work done here."

Russell's words chafed Liam, even before he saw the governess surreptitiously reach for his daughter before Rhianna gave words to her mutinous look.

Liam could see that Mena's conciliatory smile was of the practiced variety, and didn't reach her eyes. "That might be so, sir, but I am of the opinion that it does all individuals credit to understand the operation that is responsible for their livelihood, be they lads or *lasses*."

Liam's eyes crinkled with amusement at his people's colloquialisms spoken in her unmistakably crisp British tongue. He also had to admit that this particular *lass* had a point.

All eyes looked to him for his blessing or refusal, but Liam could only feel one gaze, in particular, and all the hope contained within its verdant luminosity.

"Russell," he said, finally coming to a decision. "Gavin is in with the stills. Take Rhianna to him. She can start there."

Rhianna's pleased and victorious smile warmed him. "Oh, thank you, Father!" She moved to embrace him, then seemed to remember how dirty he was. "Come, Miss Lockhart."

"Miss Lockhart will remain here." Liam enjoyed the drain of color from her face. "I need a word."

"Yes, Father." Rhianna bounced away, scrambling after Russell.

"Can *I* go now?" Andrew asked.

Liam glanced at him sharply. "Nay, ye canna go, there is work yet to be done, and ye doona quit until it's finished."

"*Ye're* quitting." Andrew threw his arm out toward Campbell. "And this is the cooper's work, *not* ours."

Liam set his jaw against his son's impertinence, his hands curling at his sides as the rage that had been his one constant companion simmered through him. "I'll have no son of mine be a useless laze-about. If ye're to run this business, ye'll have to learn every detail, and have done *every* job."

"But—"

"It's past time, Andrew, that ye learn to be responsible for something other than yer own selfish desires," Liam snarled. "Mark me, lad, ye'll not leave here until these barrels are assembled, do ye ken?"

The visible ripples of heat in the air between them could have been caused by their clashing wills as much as the open barrel flames.

"Aye," his son said through bared teeth, then turned his back.

Liam nodded to Thomas Campbell, who smirked with both knowledge and approval, being the father of his own three sons.

"Follow me, Miss Lockhart," he barked, and stalked through the square toward the warehouse.

Her shoes made quicker sounds than his on the earth beneath them, but she kept pace with his punishing march until he stalked under the wide arched entry to the brick warehouse. Liam let the perpetual chill generated by the brick cool his work- and fire-heated body, as well as his ire. Halting mid-march, he whirled about and nearly knocked over his startled governess, who caught herself just in time.

"*That lad* is going to be the death of me," he raged, running his hands through his hair. "He stomps around the castle like a dark cloud, glowering at everyone in his path. Stubborn, angry, obstinate, willful . . ." He trailed off as that dimple appeared in her cheek once again. "Ye find this amusing, do ye?" He scowled down at her, crossing his arms over his chest.

She wrapped the shawl tighter around her shoulders, and lifted a meaningful brow. "I'm sorry, my laird, I'm just confused as to *which* of the Ravencroft men you are referring." A soft smile teased at the corner of her full mouth, and lessened the effect the veracity of her words had on him.

And just like that, his anger dispelled into a vapor, much like the angel's cut of Scotch would once any one of these barrels were open. How did she manage to do that? It was like some queer sort of feminine magic, a spell she worked with a flash of that dimple and a merry twinkle in her eye. Suddenly the flames of his wrath were doused, and he could breathe again.

A caustic sound escaped his throat, half amusement, half bewilderment. "Am I truly such an ogre?"

"Not an ogre, per se." Her smile deepened. "But I recall a story I read as a child about a rather distempered troll—who lived under a bridge and frightened all who crossed it—to whom I could possibly perceive a resemblance."

A laugh warmed his throat but didn't quite escape, as a hopeless sound of frustration smothered it. He rubbed at a blooming tightness in his forehead, then noted the soot still on his hand. Covered in the filth of the day, he must, indeed, appear like a troll.

A simple white linen handkerchief appeared in his hand, and Liam lifted it to wipe the grime from his face without thinking.

It came away black and ruined, and he found he couldn't tear his gaze away from what he'd done to her clean, dainty cloth. "I always did make a better soldier than a father," he admitted grimly.

"I'm certain you're excellent at both." She placed an encouraging hand on his arm, and Liam stared at it, wondering if anyone had ever done that before. "Perhaps being a father and being a lieutenant colonel are not so different, just require separate tactics."

Liam's entire existence became the weight of her lily-white hand covering his flesh. He watched her long, elegant fingers as they rested over the muscle they found there, and pictured them curling over something else.

Gripping him. Stroking him. And suddenly, the inferno that threatened to consume him, the fire he fought every godforsaken day, was redirected.

To his cock.

As though she sensed the shift in him, she snatched her hand away, smoothing the movement over by turning to the ceiling-high rows of whisky barrels and running her fingers over the Ravencroft crest branded into the lid where the tap would go.

"Miss Lockhart," he started, reaching for her shawl with the intention of revealing her hair. "*Mena,* I—"

"You said there was something you wanted to discuss with me?" she said with false brilliance, retreating a step.

Liam let his hand drop and whatever he was about to say became like Scotch vapor. Intangible until ignited by a single spark. "Jani mentioned today that ye received some bad news from London a few days past. I've figured it was the reason ye've kept to yerself, and I wanted to inquire after ye."

"It was nothing, I assure you. Just . . . the gossip of mutual acquaintances. Trifles, really."

She was lying again. Liam had taken part in, and been the victim of, enough interrogations to easily identify deception.

Jani had also mentioned the letter had been from Liam's own sister-in-law, Farah Blackwell. Normally, he would have assumed the contents had something to do with trifles. Farah had procured his governess the position so correspondence wasn't, in itself, troubling.

But something restless and suspicious stirred inside Liam. Some instinct of danger and unrest that he had relied upon in his military days, which had saved his life on more than one occasion, pulsed red with warning.

Danger lurked nearby; he could feel it in his bones. A malevolent menace stalked his keep, but identifying it was like searching for shadows in the darkness.

It was more than a purposely sheared linchpin on a carriage he was supposed to take to meet her the day she arrived. More than the fire that could have destroyed his entire east crop of barley. And more than the violence against his governess and the frightened pain he glimpsed in her eyes.

On top of everything, there was the way Jani looked at his daughter, or Andrew looked at Liam, or Gavin and Russell looked at Mena.

The banked fire in everyone's eyes simmered with the risk of eventual combustion.

Except for her eyes . . . They held nothing but shadows.

"Everyone, it seems, is hiding something from me," he said darkly, stepping toward her. Of all the secrets he felt haunting Ravencroft like erstwhile ghosts, he found he wanted to discover hers the very most.

At first he'd thought her features contorted in terror because he'd advanced toward her, but then the sounds of splintering wood preceded the deafening, unmistakable crash of a whisky barrel.

Liam lunged forward, grasping Mena around the waist and lifting her from the ground. He drove them both into the alcove between the shelves and the door, plastering her body against his as the four-hundred-and-fifty-pound barrel rolled past them with the cacophony of a herd of wild horses.

They stood like that for a moment, his arms on either side of her head. Their chests heaving together with frantic breath. God, but she was as soft as she'd been in his fantasies. Her lush breasts were yielding pillows against the hardness of his own chest. Every hair on his body rose, not just from the danger they'd survived, but the unexplainable electric sensation of her body against him. Beneath him, for all intents and purposes.

"Did ye see what happened?" he panted.

She stared at him with wide, moist eyes for a beat longer than she should have before they darted away and she shook her head. "It was all so fast."

A panicked ruckus from the square told him that the barrel had rolled right out of the open doors and into the yard. It would pick up momentum down the yard, heading straight for . . .

Andrew.

Liam leaped away from Mena and bolted after it, dashing into the square and chasing it toward the open barrel fires. *Nay,* if it reached the flames with as much alcohol as was inside the barrel, the consequences would be as explosive as a barrel full of gunpowder.

Bellowing his son's name, Liam lunged for the runaway barrel, ready to throw himself beneath it if need be to ensure his son's survival. Others reached it at the same time, and between them they were able to grapple it into stillness inches away from the open-framed building where the fires burned.

Frantically searching the distillery yard, Liam called for Andrew, the need to cast eyes on his son first and foremost in his mind.

"Where is he?" he demanded of Thomas Campbell.

"I doona ken where he went, Laird." Thomas stumbled out of the forge on unsteady legs, obviously shaken by how close he'd come to death. "He disappeared right after ye did."

A sick fear lodged in his gut as Liam turned and rushed back toward the warehouse. Mena flattened herself against the door to get out of his way as he stalked past her to check the shadows and corners below the place where the barrel had landed.

No Andrew. He was safe. But as Liam inspected the shelf from where the whisky had fallen, one thing became staggeringly clear. The barrel had been pushed by someone. And if Liam hadn't stepped toward Mena when he did . . .

It would have crushed him.

CHAPTER Nine

"Andrew?" Mena pushed open the door to Andrew's bedroom only to find him bent over in the corner scrubbing the stones with a bucket and brush. "Whatever are you doing?"

"Miss Lockhart." He scrambled to his feet and scowled at her. "What are *ye* doing in my room? Is my father with ye?"

Mena read something beneath the aversion in his voice. Anxiety, maybe, or guilt, as though she'd caught him doing something wrong. The farther she ventured into his chamber, the more concerned she became. It was done entirely in red and black, but for the goose down fluffs that now covered the floor and almost every other surface of the otherwise tidy room. They rolled across the stones and carpets in the slightest breeze caused by her skirts. The disemboweled corpses of his pillows lay strewn at the foot of his bed, and one or two hung limply by the wardrobe.

"There was an . . . *incident* at the distillery. Your father is dealing with it now," she explained. She didn't feel comfortable calling it an accident. Because she'd become certain that it wasn't. She'd seen more than she'd let on. A figure in the darkness.

The *Brollachan*?

"Andrew. Tell me what happened here. Did you . . . did you do this?" Motioning to the chaos, she bent to pick up a shoe that appeared to have been torn apart. Just what was going on in this ancient keep?

"Aye. It was me." He hadn't moved from whatever he protected on the floor in the corner, though he regarded her with the frozen, unsure expression of a culpable party in a crime.

Heart squeezing with concern, Mena stopped at his writing desk, where charcoal renderings of dark shadows and red eyes stared up at her with spine-chilling familiarity. That shadow. She'd seen it before the ledge supporting the Scotch barrel had given way and nearly crushed Ravencroft. How terrible it was, to not trust your own eyes. Had Andrew seen the demon as well? Did he have something to do with this?

"Andrew, do you mind explaining to me—"

A commotion interrupted her. It came from the wardrobe, the heavy wood doors trembling as something pressed against them, struggling to be released. Was all this some kind of elaborate prank? Or something entirely more sinister?

"Miss Lockhart, doona open—"

Ready to be done with this mystery once and for all, Mena hurried for the wardrobe and flung the doors open. She gave a startled cry as a familiar form lunged for her.

And began to enthusiastically lick her face.

Utterly relieved, she stroked and cuddled the wriggling puppy in her arms as everything suddenly began to make sense. "So lovely to see you again, darling!" She laughed, enjoying the silky black and brown fur against her cheek, much as she had the day she'd pulled the poor thing off the rocks. "You wicked thing," she scolded. "Look at that face, not one bit of guilt over the absolute chaos you've wrought." Tucking the cheerful puppy into her bosom, she turned. "You never told me that—"

The tears streaming down Andrew's crumpled face astonished her into stillness.

"Everything's a disaster," he sobbed, the scrub brush clattering to the floor. "It's all ruined. He'll take Rune from me. The only thing I love. The only one that loves me back. And then he'll leave again, and ye'll go, too, because I've been beastly to ye. Rhianna will be off getting a husband. I'll be alone!"

Recovering from her initial speechless incredulity, Mena rushed to Andrew and wrapped her arm around his shoulder, handing him little Rune, who instantly went to work on lapping up his tears.

"I don't see why your father should take her," she cajoled. "What's a few ruined pillows? We can clean up the mess in no time. Don't worry if she wee'd on the stones, at least it wasn't the carpets. I can't even smell it."

"You doona understand!" he wailed, his newly deepening voice cracking with emotion. "He will take her from me. He told me nay when I asked if I could have her. But I told Uncle Thorne that Father said I could."

"I see." Troubled, Mena led Andrew to the bed, clearing away some unruly down feathers so they could sit, though she kept her arm around his slim shoulders. He collapsed against her side, his cheek buried into her shoulder, as he cried and clutched the squirming pup.

Fighting against a quiver in her own chin, Mena stroked his thick dark hair, so much like his father's. "Darling, first of all, let me promise you that I'm going nowhere, and neither is your father. He retired his commission to stay here with you because he loves you. Very much. You should have seen him today when a barrel fell and he thought you were in danger. He couldn't find you and he was so worried. Frantic."

"Worried my work wouldna get done." The bitterness in his tone was at once too adult for one so young, and yet completely adolescent.

"That's not fair," Mena said gently. "The things he is trying to impart to you are so important. In fact, your father and I might be teaching you very different things, but it's all for an identical reason. Do you know what that is?"

Andrew shook his head, though he didn't lift his eyes from where he stroked Rune, who kept trying to gnaw on his hand.

"Because the more information you have, the better, *easier,* your life will be. I don't know if you know this, but things are changing out there in the world, Andrew. Engines and steam power and factories are making the world a much smaller place. Land isn't the most precious commodity anymore, and the life of the idle lord, living off his tenants and properties, is going to be obsolete before too long. Your father is trying to secure you a legacy, *a living,* and teach you to do the same for the generations that come after you. That means learning how to work hard to keep it. He wouldn't do that if he didn't love you a great deal." Mena imagined it surprised her more than poor Andrew that she defended the marquess.

Fresh tears leaked from Andrew's eyes, and he sat up from her shoulder. "Doona tell him about Rune," he begged.

"I really don't feel comfortable lying to your father." It was hard enough keeping her own secrets from the laird. "He's going to find out eventually," she pointed out.

"She's been here for two weeks already and he hasna found her," he argued desperately. "I take her out back at night, and while he's in the fields. But I couldna while I was down at the distillery. She only went on the floor the once. Well, there was today, but it was just wet. And it was on the stones, so it isna hard to clean. He said that I need to learn to take care of something other than myself. And so I am." The earnest love in his eyes for the little creature in his arms broke Mena's heart. She was glad he had the pet, that he could show it love and veneration. She'd begun to worry that his darkness was more than just sullen. That it was, indeed, the beginnings of a cruel man. That he could have such tender feelings for the small animal gave her hope.

"It's not as though you can hide poor Rune in this room for the entirety of her life," she said, taking a different approach. "She'll go mad. She needs to romp about outdoors."

Andrew's shoulders sagged, but she could see the moment he accepted the truth of her words. "I'll tell him," he consented. "But give me a few days. Until he isna angry about today anymore. He told me not to leave, but I had to check on her."

Mena considered it. What if the laird discovered their secret before then? What if she was dismissed?

Andrew took her hand. "Please, Miss Lockhart. I'll do anything. I'll rework my figures, read any book you want, even the ridiculously boring ones."

"What is it about classic literature that you find so boring?" she queried defensively.

"Everything." He sniffed, his despair replaced by disgust. "I read penny dreadfuls because they have intrigue and monsters and murder. All of the things that thrill and inspire. We read about love and melancholy and it's so dull."

"Indeed?" Mena asked, an idea beginning to stir. "What if I told you that I would keep your secret for three days, if you read three separate works that I specifically pick out for you?"

"I'll do it." Andrew sighed and looked down at Rune,

who'd just wiped a streak of drool on his trousers. "Which ones?" he asked skeptically.

"What if I said that in one of them, a woman is violently raped by two men, and they cut off her hands and her tongue to keep their secret? Then her father kills them and bakes them into a pie which he feeds to his enemy? Would you find that interesting?"

"Aye." Andrew nodded vehemently, his eyes round with shock.

"Well, that's Shakespeare for you."

"Nay!" he said in disbelief.

"Titus Andronicus." Mena nodded, feeling a thrill at having enraptured the attention of one previously so morose. "Or what about a novel that accounts a man who was betrayed by an evil villain and is wrongly imprisoned for being a Bonapartist. This man escapes from prison and exacts terrible and sometimes violent revenge on all those who wronged him."

"I'll read that one." Andrew nodded.

"Yes, you will." Mena smiled victoriously. "But you can only read *The Count of Monte Cristo* in French."

His face fell into a droll sort of acceptance. "All right, Miss Lockhart, ye win, I'll learn my French."

"Excellent!" Mena stood and beamed at him. "Thank you for being a darling, and I promise that you can trust me with your secret . . . for *three* days, Andrew. That is all I dare give you."

Andrew nodded solemnly. "Three days."

Looking around the messy room, she brushed an errant puff of goose down from her skirts. "Well, let's tidy up in here, shall we? Before one of the staff discovers our intrigue."

"Aye." Andrew set the puppy on the floor, and Rune chased a ball of fluff under the bed. "Ye know, Miss Lockhart," he mumbled as he turned back to his bucket and retrieved the scrub brush. "I'm glad ye're here."

"Thank you, Andrew," she said, turning to hide eyes grown misty. "I am, too. Very glad, indeed."

Liam had never been the kind of man to kneel, even in a church. The old oak pew groaned beneath his weight as he sat, and he glanced around Ravencroft's chapel to ensure his solitude. Centuries had tarnished the ornate candelabra on the decorated altar, and the late afternoon light filtered through the stained glass that surrounded it on three sides. The window depicting a compassionate and loving Redeemer, resplendent in red robes, glowed in the middle of adjacent renderings of Saint George, the patron saint of warriors, and Saint Andrew, the patron saint of Scotland.

He would not be welcomed into their exalted presence, Liam knew that. His very existence was an affront to the man they called the Prince of Peace. But something in his restless soul had drawn him to this silent, hallowed place. Guilt, maybe. A sense of contrition tinged with emptiness. When one was haunted by the ghosts of the past, or faced with a horrible possibility, where did one turn to find clarity?

He could think of nowhere else.

It was no ghost who'd tried to kill him today. But a man. Someone strong enough to push that barrel from its nest.

It had been his personal consideration of all the people who might want him dead that had driven him to this place, beneath which several generations of Mackenzie lairds were entombed.

His brother Thorne, who still saw their father when he looked at Liam. Who blamed him for so much, including Colleen's death.

The ever-present Jani, who'd truly glimpsed the Demon Highlander more than any other person on this earth. The gentle boy had scrubbed the blood of his own countrymen off Liam's uniform more times than he could count. Had he been biding his time, waiting until Liam felt not only safe, but affectionate toward the boy, to take the revenge he rightfully deserved?

Then . . . there was his own child. His heir. Though Andrew was of smaller stature than him, he teetered on the cusp of manhood. He was sturdy . . . but was he strong enough? Maybe his hatred had lent him the might he'd needed to push that barrel. Maybe he wouldn't wait until he could look Liam in the eye to challenge him, but would use his cunning and intellect, instead of brute strength and physical prowess.

The thought lodged in the cavity of his chest, driven like a wedge with a mallet, until the pressure was more than Liam could possibly bear. His chest refused to expand. Guilt and regret were heavy mantles, smothering him until he fought for breath.

Lost in his struggle, Liam barely noted the whisper of soft slippers against the long violet carpet leading up the aisle until the ruffle of a golden skirt teased at his peripheral vision.

He didn't want to look at *her*. She was a temptation that didn't belong in this sacred place. To gaze upon her was to commit a dozen sins at least. How was it that God could grant someone so angelic a body crafted for little else but wickedness?

"Forgive me if I'm disturbing you." His governess's voice permeated the stillness and warmed the cold stones of the walls with a sacrosanct melody. Like the song of a seraphim in spoken form. "I confess I didn't expect to find you here."

Why would the Demon Highlander be in a church? There was nothing for him here . . . No forgiveness, nor redemption.

He'd been beyond that for longer than he could remember.

"I doona often find *myself* in this place." Liam neither

moved nor dared to glance at her. He wanted her to go, but not as badly as he wanted her to remain.

"I can leave—"

"Nay." He spoke with more haste than he'd meant to. "Nay . . . say yer prayers, lass. I'll go." When Liam would have stood, she sat. The soft, gilded fabric of her skirt pressed against the rough material of his kilt. Liam stared at the tiny loose fibers of his wool plaid as they rose to touch her silken skirts, drawn by some unseen current toward her.

Just as he was.

"Are you here to give confession?" she queried uncertainly.

Liam's scoff grated roughly against the smooth stones. "I keep no priest at Ravencroft." He had no desire to confess his sins to a man who would take it upon himself to deem him worthy or damned. In his life, men had only been judged by battle where there was no good or evil, only strong or weak. He had no use for priests. He knew what he was, and where he was headed once this life was through with him.

"Then . . . do you come here to be closer to God?"

"Nay, lass, only farther from my demons."

"Oh." They sat in silence a moment while she smoothed an imaginary wrinkle from her skirts before primly returning her hands to fold in her lap.

It occurred to Liam that *she* may have been seeking a priest. "Have ye sins to confess, Miss Lockhart?" He doubted she was Catholic, but he knew curious little about the mysterious woman next to him.

"I come here sometimes to pray for forgiveness."

"Forgiveness?" he echoed. "What possible atrocities could ye have committed that need forgiving?"

"Perhaps I don't ask to be forgiven, but to be granted the ability to forgive."

She was looking at him with level eyes when Liam finally

lifted his head. In the dim room, cast only in the illumination of the sun filtered through stained glass, she was a kaleidoscopic study in blasphemy. No artist could have given her face a more cherubic shape, but the rendering of her plump lips brought to mind only the most profane acts a man could devise.

The moment his gaze lowered to those lips, she turned away and bowed her head.

"That isn't to say I'm not without sin," she continued. "We all have things we've done in the past that haunt us. Of which we feel ashamed."

Some more than most, he thought darkly. "Do ye believe, Miss Lockhart, that we may be forgiven our sins? That the past can ever be left behind us?"

She shook her head. "We may try to leave the past, but I don't think the past ever truly leaves us. It is a part of us; it shapes us into who we are. I don't think any of us escape that fate, my laird."

Then I am damned. He finally looked up to the window, and met a stained-glass gaze that no longer seemed compassionate.

"Why do you believe you are damned?"

It startled Liam that he'd spoken his thoughts aloud. If she only knew. She'd run from this place. From him. "Ye've heard what they call me, have ye not?"

"Yes. The Demon Highlander." Spoken with her honeyed inflection, it didn't sound so derogatory.

"Even here, in my own land, they think I've been possessed by the *Brollachan.* Do ye believe that of me?"

He expected a practical woman like her to deny it. So when she lifted a hand to her forehead and let it trail to her cheek in an anxious motion, he was actually taken aback.

"Truly, my laird, I don't know what I believe these days. I hardly trust my own eyes . . ." She blinked as if she might say something, and then obviously changed her mind. "Did you do what they say? Did you go to the crossroads and make a deal with a demon?"

He made a bitter sound. "Nay, lass, 'tis only a myth about me. Though that doesna mean I'm not possessed of a demon. I think it's been with me since birth. That it's in my tainted blood and turns everything I do into a transgression. There has never been salvation for me."

"You don't really think that, do you?" She gasped.

"Aye, I do."

"But why?"

A bleak and arctic chill pressed in on him as a few of his darkest deeds rose unbidden to his mind's eye. "Because, lass, there are such sins heaped onto my shoulders, it would kill me to turn and face them."

"It is a good thing, then, my laird, that you have the strength in your shoulders to carry them."

The lack of gravity in her voice astounded him into looking down at her again. She was staring at him again, half of that tempting mouth quirked into a careful smile. Liam basked in it like a winter bloom would soak up the first rays of spring. Blue light from the windows fell across her hair and turned it the most fantastical shade of violet. Greens and golds softened her features and illuminated her pale eyes until they seemed to smolder.

She'd never looked lovelier than she did at this moment.

"How can there be salvation, *redemption,* unless there is first sin?" she asked, her face soft with concern for him. "The devil is in all of us, I think. That's what makes us human rather than divine. I believe there is a tenuous balance between redemption and damnation. You cannot have one without testing the limits of the other. No light, without first conquering darkness. No courage, without battling your fear. No mercy, unless you experience suffering." She turned to gaze at the golden cross gleaming on the altar, her mouth pressing into a line. "No forgiveness without someone having wronged you."

"Who wronged ye?" Liam asked, briefly forgetting his own troubles. "Who do ye come here to pray for?" And why did he want to send that person to meet his final judgment?

"You wouldn't believe me if I told you," she murmured, staring down into her lap.

"Try me," he prompted, surprised by how much he wanted her to trust him, to confide in him.

To confess to him.

"All I can say, my laird, is that I have demons of my own." She met his eyes again, hers shining with suspicious moisture. "And because of your protection, your . . . *comraich,* I like to think that they cannot find me here at Ravencroft."

Something within him melted. Perhaps it was his native language so adorably mispronounced by her British tongue. Or the self-effacing smile that produced that dimple he wanted to explore with his lips. Or her words. Words that provoked a tiny well of light in a subject he'd thought had become hopeless. A part of Liam hated the effect she had on him, that she made his heart soft and his body hard. Though it was life affirming, in a way, this sense of anticipation between them. Of . . . inevitability.

She turned back to the altar and leaned closer to the side of the pew. Away from him, killing the effect. "I just left Andrew," she said brightly. "He is doing much better."

His frown became so grave, so hard, he feared his own features would crack with strain. "With him, I feel there is no forgiveness for me." He scored his scalp with heavy fingers as he ran a frustrated hand through his unbound hair. "All I've ever been is a man without mercy. An agent of cruelty and darkness and fear. My entire life, I've wrought nothing but destruction. I suppose that's why I came back to Ravencroft. The idea of growing things, of building a life, and leaving a thriving legacy for my children, the two beings I helped to create, suddenly held great appeal. As if in doing so I might find some deliverance, if not redemption. Perhaps chase away the terrible memories haunting the halls of this place. But I fear it's too late."

"It's *never* too late to make things right."

She had no idea of what she spoke.

"Miss Lockhart—Mena—I must ask ye. Did ye see what happened today? Could it have been Andrew that pushed that barrel?"

As though realizing what must have been troubling him, his greatest fear, Mena's eyes widened and she shook her head vehemently. "I'm still not certain what I saw, but I'm positive it wasn't him, my laird. I know your son has been a dark and angry cloud. But I found Andrew in his bedroom directly after the incident. He'd already made it back to the keep." She perked, rushing to cover his skepticism. "In fact, we had a rather splendid moment, and made unprecedented progress. I think that you will be pleased with him in the days to come. He'll approach you, I know it, and you'll find a reason to mend things between you."

Liam slumped back against the pew, more relieved than even he'd expected.

"You can't be inclined to believe that your own son would take actions to cause you harm," she said in disbelief.

He wouldn't be the first Mackenzie son to do so.

Liam dipped his head. "I'm inclined to believe that ye're an angel sent to look after them, Mena. The ballast to the devil that sired them."

He couldn't be certain, but he thought a blush tinged her cheeks.

"Hardly an angel," she whispered, and seemed to lean toward him in a way that told him she wasn't aware of her action. "Your children, they have been so lonely for you. Would it be unforgivable of me to ask you what kept you from them all these years?"

His heart thumped so hard, he wondered if she couldn't hear it. He'd never had someone dare to ask him such a question. His gaze darted about the chapel, until it landed on the long unused dark wood box with its royal-blue curtains. Perhaps, Liam thought, now *was* the time for confession. Maybe he could, just this once, unburden his soul.

His voice felt like gravel in his throat as he gave words to his darkest thoughts. "As I said before, there *is* a demon, of a more figurative kind, that has tainted the blood of the men in this family for generations. It burns through us until there's nothing left but ash and char. I've fought innumerable battles in my life, but none as difficult as the one I wage with myself. Ye canna know what it is to live with this much fire. With so much anger and hatred that it chews through ye until ye're nothing but a black void. I would save my children from knowing that kind of cruelty. I would protect them from the abject violence of it. For decades I thought that dark abyss would swallow me whole, and until I stepped away from its edge, I couldna risk taking them into it with me. And so I did whatever I had to do to keep it away from them, even if it meant . . . keeping myself away."

"I don't think you ever would have hurt them," she reassured him after a thoughtful moment.

He shook his head. "But I couldna return until I was certain."

"What changed?" she asked softly. "When were you convinced?"

Liam knew the exact moment; it was branded onto his soul. It haunted his nightmares. "When I lost my brother."

"Hamish?"

A bitter sound escaped him. Of course she'd have heard about Hamish. He'd been a part of this clan. A part of their lives. Their father's not-so-secret shame, and the man that their father would have preferred over Liam to be his heir.

"Our company was sent on a mission to put down a secret sect of Irish insurgents that had been hiding in Canada since the Fenian Rebellion. They'd taken a ship full of people and packed it with explosives. Their plan was to drive it into an English port and detonate it, killing masses of innocent people. We couldna stop the ship, but we boarded it, executed the mutineers, and Hamish was able to steer it back out to sea whilst the rest of us evacuated the civilians. It took longer than we thought to get them a safe distance from the blast radius. I was returning for Hamish, when I realized we'd run out of time. There was a fire on board, the fuse had been lit, and in that moment I knew if I boarded that ship, I'd not make it off again. That my luck as the Demon Highlander had run out."

"Poor Hamish," Mena murmured.

"Aye."

"Was he a good man?"

"Nay, not really. But neither am I. We were forged by the same brutal father, though, and so I suppose ye could say we were bound in that way." Liam let his shoulders lift and fall with a weighty breath. "I wanted to go back for him. I considered it, even though it would have been the end of me. But the only thing I could think of as the explosion ripped the ship apart was that I had to see my children. That I had so much to make up for." His hand curled into a fist at the memory of his brother, begging for rescue. Pleading to be saved. "Something shifted the day Hamish . . . I just knew I needed to come home."

When Mena laid her pale, elegant hand over his rough knuckles, it felt like a miracle.

"I'm truly sorry for all you suffered, and for all you lost. But regardless of the struggles you have with your children, they're better for you having returned. It was the greatest choice you ever made. You must know that."

The fervency in her voice tightened his throat, and for the second time that night he had to look away from her. "I made certain they never knew my father. I shielded them from their mother's madness. All they've known of family is me, and Thorne, I suppose. But I *never* want them to meet my demon. My greatest fear is of them bearing witness to the evil of which I am capable. Of which I've *proven* myself capable."

She squeezed his hand. "When you are subjected to such misfortune, it is difficult for those who are closest to you to comprehend it because you appear to be ordinary. Outwardly, you seem what you have always been, who you strive to show them that you are. But inside you are inconceivably altered, and perhaps you don't even recognize yourself." Her other hand joined the first, and she wrapped them around his palm, her voice growing with ardor. "I think, once you discover who you've decided to become, your children, your people, will get to know that man. And I have no doubt they will grow to love him. You are a good man, Laird Mackenzie, despite what you believe. I think your clan, and your children, know that more than you do."

There it was, that reassuring smile again. The slight tilt of her sensual lips that coaxed a dimple into her cheek. Lord, but to look at her was pleasant. And to be touched by her, divine.

Bless her for what she believed of him, but Liam knew better. The maelstrom of emotion whirling through him at the depth of his confession suddenly flared into a physical inferno. His demon burst into flames of lust. Liam knew she could read it in his eyes, as she released his hands with a shocked gasp and made to rise. To retreat.

Well, if he was already damned, he might as well follow his wicked impulses all the way to hell.

At least he'd get to taste her again.

Liam sprang toward her, grasping her wrists and pulling her back down to him. He sank his fingers into her luxurious hair, loosening the intricate coiffure there, and pinned her head between his two strong palms as he took her wicked mouth with his own.

It was in the joining of their lips that Liam found what he'd come to the chapel seeking. He kissed Mena with a reverence he'd never felt in the entirety of his life. Driven by a hunger that welled from the darkest, most heretical depths of his soul, he knew he'd finally found something worthy of his worship.

Though he didn't want to do so with soft prayers and humble words. He wanted to pay her homage in the most primitive way his Pict ancestors would have. With drums that beat with the rampant frenzy of his heart. With fire that licked at the black sky, ablaze with the strength of the heat spilling into his loins. Passion, years denied, clawed to the surface of his iron will as he feasted on her. Laid siege to her defenses as vigorously and mercilessly as he had so many walls and armies. He used the ruthlessness that had vanquished legions until he was the one man standing in the midst of the fallen.

Her hands closed around his wrists. She didn't pull away, though he knew she wanted to.

They both knew she *should*.

Instead, a soft sound of surrender escaped her as she arched her neck, and opened her mouth to accept him.

Victorious heat surged through him, as he claimed her with his tongue, a delicious thrill spearing that dark place he'd always imagined had housed the Mackenzie demon. Her sweetness overwhelmed and stupefied him, and Liam realized that if anything, anyone, could bring him to his knees, it would be this singular woman. She could accept him deep into her body, and perhaps her soul. She could temper his fire, while illuminating the darkness.

God, but he had burned his entire forsaken existence . . . but had never felt true warmth until this moment.

And never felt true loss until she ripped her lips from

his and pulled his hands down away from where they cupped her face.

The air between them vibrated with needful frenzy, and the frightened tears in her eyes only dampened the fire of a lust that would never truly be extinguished. *"Mena."* Her name became a prayer.

A plea.

"Forgive me," she whispered, surging to her feet and turning away from him. "You *can't* know how wrong this is."

She took the warmth with her as she gathered her skirts and fled.

CHAPTER TEN

Every day at sunrise, Laird Liam Mackenzie courted death.

He'd strap on his low-heeled deerhide boots and run the few miles across the moors until he had to scale Ben Crossan, the mountain which the river Crossan had to divert around to reach the sea. Though the way was rocky and treacherous at times, the true danger didn't begin until he reached the abrupt pinnacle called Craeg Cunnartach, the Dangerous Cliff.

Many a tragic, lovelorn Highland lass had tossed herself to her death from this very place. It was said among the Mackenzie that these women became *Fuathan,* water wraiths, and should a man venture into their waters, the vengeful lasses would drag him to the depths of the sea, and devour him as he drowned, trying to fill the eternal void of their broken hearts. Even fishermen, divers, and merchants avoided the mouth of the Crossan River and the water beneath Craeg Cunnartach.

Liam, of course, didn't believe in the superstition, but knew that a strong current lurked beneath the deep waters, as did sharks, rocks, and numerous other hazards.

The way he figured it, he owed the devil a chance to take him. He also understood that he was not an easy man to kill, and therefore sought the one place he could think of where he was not the alpha predator, the dominant warrior, or the Laird of the Land.

And so it was to the sea that he commended his life.

Almost.

Winded as he was once he climbed to the cliff's edge, he never hesitated to leap, using his momentum to clear whatever juts and crags of the rock face that reached for him on his way down. For in his extensive experience with death, it was in the hesitation that a man often made his most fatal mistakes.

To say that he gave the Prince of Darkness a chance to take him didn't suggest he meant to make it easy on the devil to collect his due. Warrior that he was, Liam fought the current with all his hard-won strength. Once he surfaced, he waited with patience for his breath to return to him—as the cold always stole it—before swimming with lithe, powerful strokes toward the Ravencroft Cove.

He'd never clocked the distance, precisely, but it took him a little over a half hour of hard swimming on most days. He'd performed this ritual since he was a lad.

Since the morning after he'd taken a whip to innocent flesh. His first true sin against another.

The first of many.

When abroad with his regiment, he'd plunged into any waters he could, when possible. He'd forged crocodile-infested jungle rivers, icy Prussian lakes, and just about every ocean on the map.

But this stretch of Highland coast was his favorite. Submerged in the sea that surrounded his home, the water which Druids had blessed and his Viking and Pict ancestors had profaned with the blood of the ancients, he turned his existential struggle into a physical one, as he battled against all that would claim him. That would pull him into the black depths and suffocate him. The guilt. The pain. The hatred. Burdens he carried every day.

He felt as though he invited the gods to strike him, or the devil to take him, and when they didn't, he emerged from the briny water with a semblance of peace or, dare he say, permission. Not so much like a baptism, wherein his soul would be cleansed, but more like a figurative bath. He would live and toil another day, and the refuse, soil, and filth would paint his soul black again, and so he would repeat the ritual the next morning.

This particular morning, he made the journey in perhaps the shortest time since he could remember. A peculiar disquiet chased him up the mountain, and he fled from it with such speed, his legs burned as they propelled him to go ever faster.

You can't know how wrong this is . . .

The autumn wind screamed her words through the canyon until they whipped against his scarred flesh, and stung lashes already healed. He ran and swam shirtless, even though the cold turned his skin white and pink as it drove the blood inward to protect his heart and vital organs.

There was a lesson to be learned here. He would do well to protect his heart. And hers.

She was safe here from everyone that would do her harm. Everyone but him.

She'd been mistaken, his governess, he *did* ken how wrong it was to have kissed her, to have awakened these desires, almost violent in their ardency. This obsessive, wicked curiosity he had about her bordered on the profane. She made him want things. Dark things. Had him considering sins that would not just condemn his soul, but hers as well.

Mena Lockhart.

A name? A state of being? A woman with a locked heart.

Was it her innocence or mystery that drew him? Her

keen intellect? Her troubling secrets? The depth of the understanding in her eyes, or the depth of her warm, lush body?

He wanted all of it. All of her. He wanted to uncover her, body and soul. To lay her bare and wide and make a conquest of her.

He wanted to own her. To claim her. To brand her skin with his mark and to see the same, violent desire mirrored in her eyes.

Aye, he knew how wrong it was. He knew that he must master these wicked thoughts and temper these sinful urges before they burned out of control and consumed him.

She made him hard, so fucking hard that he couldn't think.

But she made him soft, too. In those spaces he'd built walls and fortresses, around those places where memories, sins, and pain lay scattered about like shards of glass in a dark room, waiting for an unsuspecting victim to venture forth. And therein lay the danger.

Every time her hand found his skin, or his lips found her mouth, something forged into cold steel by the heat of his temper . . . melted.

The problem was, he hadn't erected those walls to keep those he loved out, but to keep something from escaping.

The devil is in all of us, I think, she'd said.

Nay, mo ailleachd. No, my beauty, he thought as he leaped from the Craeg and let the icy Atlantic steal the breath from his lungs and the fire from his arousal. *Not all of us . . .*

Only me.

Though she hadn't slept in two days, a pervasive agitation drove Mena to haunt the halls of Ravencroft Keep like a restless ghost. She knew the cause, of course.

The inescapable Laird Mackenzie. An undefeated warrior with profound wounds and hidden depths.

It was as though he'd branded her. Seared his delectable, masculine taste to her lips and marked her skin with only the gentle hold of his large hands.

Mena had been marked and bruised by her husband, Gordon, many times over, and those wounds could last a week or more. The pain, of course, lingered even longer.

But the undeniable impact of Liam Mackenzie's kiss was infinite. She'd live a thousand years and still feel the possession of his lips.

What distressed her the most was how he hadn't allowed her a moment's escape. When he wasn't busy at the distillery, he seemed to be everywhere she was. Just yesterday, he interrupted her waltzing lessons with the children, sweeping his daughter up for a few dances. He proved to be a more than adequate dancer, but would occasionally trip Rhianna and catch her, cursing his clumsy feet whilst the girl berated him for obviously doing it on purpose.

Laughter had filled the keep with the most beautiful cacophony, and it made Mena's heart ache for some reason she couldn't define.

Ravencroft had also taken to having tea with them while they lounged in their favorite solarium, and read from *The Count of Monte Cristo* in French. He would listen with rapt attention, never asking questions or clarifying words as the children did. He merely sat and stared at her with those unnerving dark eyes, jaw perched on his templed fingers.

He prowled about her like a great, rapacious cat, his huge body filling every room so completely, she felt crowded and overwrought. In his presence, her own body was in a constant state of awareness. His gaze, as tangible as a caress, lifted the fine hairs on her flesh until they tingled and pricked with warning when he entered the room.

Here is a dangerous creature, her primitive instincts told her. A beast. A predator. She'd do well to run.

To hide.

Mena would often look up to find him fixated on her

lips, or her breasts. The words would seize in her throat and she'd have to pause to catch her breath. A dark, sexual promise lurked in his eyes, and robbed her of her every thought. Yet he said nothing and hid nothing. When she caught his stare, he did not avert his eyes, nor did he try to hide his frank appreciation of her. He merely looked at her with enough heat to melt the stones of the keep, while remaining still and silent as a statue chiseled by the loving hands of an artisan. Hard. Smooth.

Flawless.

Damn him for kissing her!

Damn *her* for wanting him to do it again.

Despite all that, his constant presence likewise caused more difficulties when attempting to collude with Andrew about his care of the pup. They'd had to devise all sorts of inventive ways to excuse themselves from his company.

And then there was the incident this very morning, from which Mena hadn't seemed able to recover.

"You *have* to tell him, Andrew," Mena had reminded the boy as they'd taken Rune out for her morning romp and piddle. "Tomorrow is the third day."

"I will," he'd vowed. "I'll go to his study with her in the morning." Calling Rune back as she'd begun to follow her nose too far away, Andrew had said, "It's going well with him, doona ye think? My father. These last two days have been . . . well, they've been good, havena they?"

"Yes, Andrew, they have." She'd smiled fondly, drifting back toward him. "And you've done likewise, very admirable. How do you like *The Count of Monte Cristo*? Is it as promised?"

"Aye." Andrew nodded. "It's much more interesting and naughty than anything our other governesses would have allowed us to read."

A worry had struck her then. "Oh, dear. Do you think your father minds that we're reading it?" she wondered aloud as she watched the sunrise lick the amber autumn grasses with gold. "I would imagine that he'd say something if he had an issue with the content."

"Miss Lockhart." Andrew had the oddest look on his face, a curious mix between mischief and epiphany. "My father doesna know what the book is about."

Her eyes had widened. "What do you mean?"

"He doesna ken a lick of French."

He was there to see the *children* every day. That was the only possible explanation for why he joined them as they read from a book he didn't understand. He'd taken the words she'd spoken in the chapel to heart. That was all.

Wasn't it?

Had the alternative not already stolen her breath, Mena would have been rendered witless by Andrew's next words. "Miss Lockhart, my father is coming this way."

"What?" she squeaked.

Panicked, she'd scooped up little Rune and shoved her into Andrew's arms, all but tossing them through the door before turning to ascertain if they'd been caught out.

He was only a specter against the tree line, but his form was unmistakable. Ravencroft ran with surprising speed and an astonishing amount of skin bared to the autumn elements. From her far vantage, Mena couldn't tell where his burnished torso ended and his fawn trousers began.

He'd been an advancing leviathan of warm male flesh and hot Scottish blood. The closer he'd come, the more inevitable a conversation seemed to become. Considering how the last one had ended, with his mouth upon hers, Mena had known she should retreat. There was no shame in doing so, she told herself. Not when countless armies had done just that very thing upon the Demon Highlander's approach.

He was not to be trusted. And, judging by the extra beats of her heart and the tremor suffusing her at the sight of him, even so very far away, neither was she.

She couldn't help but watch for an unguarded moment

as he jogged from the direction of the cove. His head wasn't down, exactly, but tilted in a way that suggested he was intent on a place straight ahead of him, the next span of ground he was about to conquer.

He hadn't seen her yet, but she could certainly see plenty of him.

The closer he came, the more detail Mena discovered. The visible ribbons of sinew and strength clinging to his heavy bones flexed and rippled with movement. The wide discs of muscle on his chest rebounded with each heavy footfall. Long legs ate up the distance between them with a flawless sense of rhythm. His hair was loose and clung to his shoulders with moisture, as though he'd been in the sea. She'd known that she should turn away, lest she be discovered gawking, but her shoes had seemed to be glued to the ground, and her eyes similarly glued to *him*. He'd saved her from a rather awkward altercation when he veered to the left at the hedges, and made his way down the west hill toward the distillery.

It was then that Mena had made a shocking discovery. The Marquess Ravencroft had, at some time in his life, been tortured. Long, horrific scars marred the otherwise smooth flesh of his back. They'd have to be rather large for her to see them from this distance. Her hand flew to her chest to contain an ache that had bloomed there.

Breathless, Mena had taken refuge in Ravencroft Keep, making certain Andrew had Rune spirited safely away, before starting her morning with the children. She'd attempted a regular day of instruction with them, but had proved utterly useless. Who had so egregiously wounded Ravencroft? Perhaps he'd been a prisoner of war at some point. Maybe he'd been tortured for information. Or whipped for insubordination. But surely, the army wasn't in the practice of whipping peers of the realm, especially those as high-ranking as a marquess.

Mena couldn't help it, a well of tenderness bloomed beneath the apprehension and suspicion she felt toward the Laird of the Mackenzie. Was the laird going to appear today, she'd wondered, full of lithe carnality and meaningful glances?

When he didn't, she couldn't tell if it was relief or disappointment that flooded her breast. But after a while, her nerves had threaded so taut that one more mispronounced French verb promised to make her snap. So she'd concocted a few vague excuses to the children, put a book in their hands, and wandered the halls of Ravencroft, grateful for a moment alone to collect the thoughts, fears, and fantasies threatening to gallop away with her.

Mena found herself at the top of the grand staircase that led to the front entry, as she closely perused the luxurious tapestries that warmed the cold stone of the castle walls. The sky outside had become an endless sheet of drab steel curtaining the sun as a storm pelted the earth with rhythmic hostility. She'd dressed in a heavy wool gray frock with tiny pearl buttons down the front. Piling her hair on top of her head in a loose chignon, she thought she'd made a perfectly macabre reflection. Half to match the weather, and half to match her mood.

Her gaze snagged on an imposing oil canvas located above the middle of the grand stairway. It was as tall as her and maybe ten times as wide. This one depicted a great battle, with a large and ferocious Mackenzie war chieftain leading a cadre of kilt-clad Highlanders into battle against the English. Their claymores brandished high, and their hair flying wildly about them, they looked awe-inspiring and inescapable. The battle of Culloden, perhaps? However had such fierce men been defeated?

She pictured the marquess rushing into ancient battles, a dark figure of retribution and prowess, incomparably fearsome because of his unrivaled strength and magnificent form. His fathomless black eyes would flash with rage in the heat of battle, and his thick ebony hair would gather riotously about his face as he vanquished his enemies in bloody and mortal combat.

Spellbound by the beauty of the illustration in this particular painting, she reached out trembling fingers and brushed them against the vicious rendering of the ancient chieftain.

He'd been painted with a heavy hand, all square angles and dark, rough strokes. Almost the exact image of the current Laird Mackenzie. The same fire. The same ferocity.

The same untamed beauty.

Mena realized, as she allowed her fingertips to absorb the insignificant striations in the paint, that a wicked part of her regretted not allowing the marquess a deeper kiss.

No other man had beckoned to her fingertips like the physical marvel that was Liam Mackenzie. She wondered, if she'd wrapped her arms around him, would she have felt the scars on his back through his shirt? Would he have shared with her another intimacy of his past, adding a thread to the cord of complex emotion he'd begun to weave?

Lord, he held all of the fascinating curiosity and thrilling peril of a lightning storm. Of course he'd garnered a mythical sort of reputation because myths were how the common man struggled to explicate someone so extraordinary.

She'd been a willing captive of his hands, of his lips. He'd cupped her face with utter tenderness, but it was her own desire, her own curious temptation, that had kept her a prisoner of the moment.

Because his hard mouth had been softer against hers than she'd imagined. And, Lord help her, but she'd imagined it happening again. More than once. Nothing her fanciful mind could have invented came close to the illicit and primitive heat that she hadn't been able to rid herself of for two blasted days.

The disquieting warmth kept her awake more than anything else. A slow burn that would begin just below her belly and spread lower and out until her limbs smoldered and squirmed with needs she couldn't begin to contemplate.

That she shouldn't even *consider.* She had too many secrets. Secrets that would salt the ground, preventing anything from growing between them. Because even though she'd never return to her husband, she *was* a married woman, and would do well to remember it.

What had happened between them could never happen again. The consequences of such an entanglement were simply too disastrous.

But, oh, did she want to—

"English!"

Mena snatched her hand away from the painting with a guilty start at the pleased exclamation that echoed right next to her. She would have lost her balance and toppled down the stairs if a pair of strong hands hadn't reached out to steady her.

Moss-green eyes smiled down from the alarmingly handsome features of Gavin St. James. He stood two steps above her, and Mena couldn't imagine how he'd gotten so close without her noting his presence.

She couldn't have been *that* entranced with the painting, could she? No, her distraction had nothing at all to do with the canvas, said a hateful inner voice, and everything to do with the laird who owned it.

"I told ye I'd be seeing ye again, English," the Highlander purred in his silky brogue. "And let me tell ye, it's a thorough pleasure to have saved yer life."

"You did no such thing," Mena argued, though she couldn't hide the answering smile he elicited.

"Ye'd have toppled hide over head down the stairs had I not caught ye," he bragged.

"Yes, but 'twas you who crept up on me in the first place

and startled me half to death. That was very wicked of you," she scolded.

"I wasna creeping. It was ye who was lost in yer thoughts." He chuckled, his eyes glimmering with impish delight as he glanced at the painting. "That isna to say I'm not a wicked man."

"Of that, I have no doubt." She laughed. "Not that it isn't a genuine pleasure to meet you again, Mr. St. James, but might I inquire as to what you are doing here dressed to the nines?"

His expression turned sheepish as he brushed at the cravat of his fine suit. "A wee bit of distillery business is all. I just returned from London with some good news for the marquess." He leaned in conspiratorially. "Though it'd take a bleeding miracle to coax a compliment from the old goat, if ye ask me."

"Oh, do go on with you." Mena suppressed a nervous laugh, scandalized by his audacity.

"I gather no introductions are necessary." Ravencroft's cavernous voice could have turned the lush Highlands into a brittle desert.

Blood deserted Mena's extremities as she noted that Gavin St. James still held her arm above the elbow from when he'd reached to steady her. She pulled away from him, reaching for the solidity of the stone banister to hold her up as her suddenly trembling legs no longer seemed to feel the need to fulfill their occupation.

The marquess stood at the top of the staircase, legs splayed and arms folded over his wide chest as he glared down at them both in contemptuous condemnation. Though he was dressed in an impeccable suit, his ebony hair combed back into a tight queue, he appeared as stark and sinister as ever. Mena found herself concerned over the integrity of his suit, as his tense muscles strained the seams.

Now she knew what beauty lay beneath, and had to look away.

"Ye're actually mistaken, Liam, as yer lovely governess and I have shared a previous . . . encounter, but have yet to be formally introduced." He winked at Mena, who considered hurling herself down the stairs rather than glancing up to see the withering glare Ravencroft surely focused on them both.

Who was this man to address a marquess in so informal a manner? And why did he insist on making playful insinuations about their previous "encounter" in the woods? She'd nearly been sacked over the whole ordeal.

Gavin didn't give her a chance to recover from her astonishment before he took her hand again and bowed theatrically low over it. "Allow me to introduce myself, English, as Lord Gavin St. James, Earl of Thorne and half brother to the *most illustrious* Marquess of Ravencroft, Laird Liam Mackenzie of Wester Ross."

He pressed his lips to her hand, but Mena hardly felt it as she could have sworn she actually heard a growl rumble from the top of the stairs.

Snatching her hand back, she winced at the perceptive glance the earl gave her from behind amber lashes.

"Brother?" She wagged an incensed finger at the smirking Lord Thorne. "You cad! You led me to believe you were nothing more than the foreman at the distillery."

"I beg yer pardon, English, but I didna lie to ye." He flashed her a devastatingly handsome smile, and Mena found herself forgiving him instantly, not that she'd been that angry in the first place. "I spoke the truth when I said I was the distillery foreman. Had ye inquired about me, ye would have learned that I'm part owner and the rest." Thorne shrugged, his eyes glinting with mirth. "I admit to being a wee bit wounded that ye didna."

"It was, nevertheless, a falsehood by omission, Thorne." Ravencroft censured him as he descended the stairs, his glare jumping back and forth between the two of them, narrowed with suspicion.

Mena actually retreated down a step, inwardly cringing at his undeniable position on the particular subject of omission.

Brothers, she marveled. Though she supposed she could see the resemblance now that they stood close to one another. As far as she could discern, their height was similar, though Ravencroft was undoubtedly the larger of the two. Like Dorian Blackwell, Liam was swarthy, where Gavin's hair shone even more lambent than before, now that it wasn't darkened by sea water.

Something electric crackled in the air between the men, charging it with such masculine tension, she could scarcely breathe.

Blessedly, the half-hour-to-dinner bell reverberated through the waves of aggression rolling off the brothers, and Mena blessed the chef and his compulsive timeliness.

Perceptibly pulling an air of geniality about him like a cloak, Lord Thorne turned once again to Mena. "Will I be seeing ye at dinner, English?"

"I—I suppose," Mena answered, glancing uncertainly to her employer.

"In my house, you will address her as Miss Lockhart, as is appropriate," the marquess ordered. "And I *never* invite ye to dinner."

"And yet I always stay to dine." Gavin flashed his brother another of his roguish smiles. "Come now, Liam, ye wouldna deprive my niece and nephew of my charming company, would ye? Now if ye'll excuse me, I'm going to see what culinary delights that French genius of yers has in store for me tonight." Turning on his heel, he jogged down the stairs, and strode in the direction of the kitchens. Not a retreat, per se, but a strategic withdrawal, in Mena's opinion.

Judging by the wrath glittering in Ravencroft's obsidian eyes, she applauded Lord Thorne's decision.

Knuckles white on the banister and a vein pulsing above his flexed jaw, the marquess captured her attention with his furious glare. He said nothing, but scrutinized her features as if searching for the answer to a question he dare not ask.

Mena watched in fascination as a narrow spectrum of emotion played across his savage expression. Irritation, suspicion, fury, and . . . bleak misery?

The last one caused her no small amount of confusion and distress.

"My laird, I—"

"Doona I pay ye to spend yer days with my children, Miss Lockhart?" The insinuation that she shirked her duties stung.

Dumbfounded, she could do little but nod.

"Well, then," he clipped, and dismissed her by descending the rest of the stairs two at a time, as though one didn't pose enough of a challenge for his long stride.

Mena couldn't bring herself to move until she started at the slam of a door.

For the first time in as long as she could remember, Mena couldn't bring herself to eat. Stomach churning with nerves, she kept glancing toward the obsequious Earl of Thorne who insisted on saying something flirtatious every couple of minutes. Then she'd peek at the ominously silent marquess, whose glare gathered more dark fire with every refill of his whisky glass.

The aroma of parsnip and leek soup with white fish in a cream sauce tempted her appetite, but Mena could hardly look at it without feeling ill. Not only was she nervous about this strange dynamic between her and the two Mackenzie brothers, but Andrew was perched on her right squirming with apprehension about whether Lord Thorne would bring up the puppy.

Everyone, it seemed, was wound tight as a bowstring. The sound of the rain lashing against the windows and the clink of fine silver were the only sounds that permeated the uneasy silence that settled around the room like a thick blanket.

Only Rhianna ate with vigor, oblivious to the tension around her as she sat across from Russell, who watched everyone very carefully, obviously trying to ascertain just what he was missing.

"Uncle Gavin," Rhianna asked once her initial hunger had been sated and she slowed to allow conversation. "Did ye meet any refined, available ladies whilst in London?"

The earl smiled indulgently at his niece. "None I'd consider making a countess." He wiped at his mouth with a napkin and revealed an impish smile that intensified the sparkle in his eye. "And none so refined as your Miss Lockhart, here."

"Miss Lockhart is *most* sophisticated," Rhianna readily agreed. "She's the first governess who ever *made* Andrew read." She elbowed her brother sharply.

"She's not *making* me read, Rhianna," Andrew argued, though he looked up at Mena with heart-melting admiration. "She just made me want to. We have an agreement."

"A distinguished governess, to be sure," Lord Thorne murmured. "Though she wasna so refined the first time I met her."

"You didna mention meeting Uncle Gavin before," Rhianna exclaimed, unaware of the supreme interest the conversation had garnered from all other occupants of the table. "When were ye two introduced?"

Had Mena been eating, she would have choked. She implored the unrepentant earl with her eyes, not even daring to glance toward the head of the table.

Her discomfiture only seemed to encourage the scoundrel. "I happened upon the lass exploring the Kinross Cove. She swam halfway out to sea like she'd done it a million times before, her skirts hiked to her knees, to save yer wee—"

"I didn't mention it because I didn't know he was your uncle at the time, and I thought it of *little* consequence." Mena interrupted what might have been a reveal about the puppy. This was what came of deceit. A stomach full of guilt and a heart full of lead. She never should have allowed herself to be talked into it. If she could survive tonight, it would all be over in the morning.

Mena glared a warning at him, hoping it would work better than a plea. What in the devil did he think he was doing? Did he not understand that her position depended on the appearance of virtue and respectability?

"It wasna of little consequence to me." He slanted her his own look full of meaning. "I very much enjoyed escorting her home. Yer governess is as witty and entertaining as she is lovely."

"Ye should hear her read," Andrew agreed. "She entertains us all the time."

The child was an absolute angel.

"Aye, and she's taught me to waltz," Rhianna added, not to be outdone.

"Everyone here at Ravencroft agrees that Miss Lockhart is an excellent and bonny addition to the staff." Russell joined the conversation, his beard splitting into a ruddy smile. "It's good for us Highland heathens to see what real manners are like, eh, Laird?"

Mena gathered the fortitude to look at her employer and instantly wished she hadn't. Ravencroft sat stock-still, a knife in one hand and his fork in another, a bite frozen halfway to his mouth. He glared at his brother, black eyes glittering with malevolence.

"You are all too kind," Mena said in a breathless rush.

"Ye must tell me when ye are planning to take another swim in the sea, Miss Lockhart," the earl said with no small amount of insinuation.

Ravencroft's utensils clattered to his plate.

"Yes, and ye must take us with ye!" Rhianna insisted with palpable eagerness. "Ye can teach me how to swim."

Mena also had to set down her fork lest everyone see how her hands trembled. She couldn't remember the last time she'd been so distressed by a simple dinner since her days at Benchley Court. "The weather will be much too cold for swimming for some time." Calling upon her so-called refinement, she turned to a universally accepted topic for salvation. "Russell, is the climate in this part of Scotland always so unpredictable in the autumn?"

"I'm afraid so," Russell answered slowly, seeming as relieved for the change of topic as she was. He studied the mottled red beginning to journey up from beneath Ravencroft's collar with russet brows drawn low before turning to address her. "It'll frost before long, but I hope the rain shadow of the Isle of Skye clears things up around Samhain as it's like to do."

"Samhain?" Mena asked.

"My favorite festival of the entire year." Rhianna said, sighing.

"Aye," Andrew agreed, his features the most animated Mena had ever seen them. "When the spirits of the dead rise to cause mischief and we call the Druid spells to keep the demons away."

"Likely known to ye as All Hallows' Eve," Lord Thorne supplied helpfully.

"There's a festival, you say?" Mena queried.

"It marks the end of the harvest, distillery work, and sowing of the winter crop," Russell explained. "We open an old cask of whisky or two for all the Mackenzie of Wester Ross and a few visiting clans and their lairds, and have a feast and ritual."

"There's dancing and games!" Rhianna almost knocked over her glass in exaltation.

"And we sacrifice animals over bonfires," Andrew chimed in.

"More of a roast and feast, than an actual sacrifice," Russell corrected with a smirk.

Mena smiled for what seemed like the first time that evening. "Sounds delightful. I am so looking forward to my first Samhain in the Highlands."

"Ye'll have to save a dance for me, English," Thorne said around a bite, offering her that cheeky smile of his. "Perhaps I'll teach ye a thing or two."

Ravencroft planted his fists on the table with enough force to rattle the china, causing everyone to jump. His chair made a sharp, grating sound as he stood and advanced around the table toward Thorne.

"A word," he gritted out as he grabbed his younger brother by the shoulder and all but hauled him out of his seat.

Thorne's smile barely faltered as he partly walked and was partly dragged toward the door by a furious Ravencroft. "Excuse us for a moment," he called jovially as they disappeared into the shadows of the hall.

Mena blinked profusely in sheer astonishment before Russell rushed to comfort her. "Doona worry, lass. The earl is always trying to get under the laird's skin. Been that way since they were lads."

"Oh?" Mena smoothed her hands over her waist and sat straighter in her chair. She found the entire exchange quite vexing. In fact, she didn't know if she'd ever feel steady again. Not until she put this to rest with both the Laird Mackenzie and Lord Thorne.

"Miss Lockhart." Andrew put his hand over hers. "I'd like to be excused. I doona feel well." He gestured with his eyes to his room.

Rune would need to be let out before bed, and now was a perfect time. "All right, Andrew. I'll accompany you."

She said good night to Rhianna with a kiss on the cheek, and then excused herself from Russell's company.

"You *must* tell him," she fervently reminded Andrew once again as they found themselves alone in the hall. "Or I'm going to have to."

"I will, I promise, but I think it's best to wait until the morning." Andrew gallantly offered his arm at the base of the back stairs and escorted her up. "Miss Lockhart, do ye know why my father would be so angry with Uncle Gavin over what he said?"

She truly didn't understand what it was Ravencroft wanted from her. What he saw in her. Why he would be . . . be what? Jealous? Surely he could see that she didn't return the Earl of Thorne's flirtations.

"I can't imagine," she murmured.

Andrew flicked her a perceptive look from beneath his lashes and his slash of a mouth quirked up just a little. "I can."

CHAPTER ELEVEN

Liam stopped short of shoving his brother into his study, and he slammed the door behind him. His hands shook with dark needs and murderous impulses. Fury sizzled through his blood, riding the waves of the whisky he'd downed at dinner to keep from hurling his knife across the table at Thorne.

Pacing the room, he wrestled with the seething beast clawing its way through him. The study was too small. Why had he chosen to do this here? *Oh aye,* because this was the only room that didn't carry the essence of *that* woman. She'd never been in here. Never left her sweet floral scent to invoke the enticing memory of her skin.

God, he felt as though he'd truly been possessed. A great number of the deadly sins surged within him and fought for supremacy when it came to Mena. Pride, envy, greed, lust. And at the moment . . . *wrath.*

He couldn't even bring himself to look at his vainglorious brother for fear of what he would do. Gavin St. James was handsome in that disarming way the lasses melted for. He'd always been thus. Every time Liam looked at his brother, he imagined Mena Lockhart pressed against him.

Was that why she'd run from Liam after he'd kissed her? Why she had avoided him after that day in the chapel? Why she seemed so guilty and secretive tonight, as if she were frightened of discovery?

Was there something between his brother and his governess? Was he being lied to?

Again?

"Did ye fuck her in the woods, Thorne?" He posited the question in such a low register, he wasn't even certain he'd heard *himself* correctly.

"What?"

"My governess, ye daft bastard, did ye put yer sullied hands on her?" he thundered. Had he tasted of her sweetness? Did her lips part for his plunder as they had for Liam's? He *had* to know, even if the knowledge might just push him past the edge of his own sanity.

"Technically I'm legitimate, so not a bastard in the truest sense of the word." The laconic flippancy in Thorne's tone lit fire to the alcohol already in Liam's veins.

"Stop saying nonsense to sound clever," he barked.

"I doona know, brother, ye should try it sometime."

Liam spun around. Thorne still hadn't wiped that sly smirk away from his mouth. Though when Liam took a step forward, the smile quickly died.

"Mark me, Gavin, I will rip yer spine out through yer throat and not feel a thing—"

"All right." The earl put his hands up in a gesture of surrender, knowing that when Liam used his real name, he'd hit his mark. "Nay, I left the woman as untouched as I found her, I promise ye."

Liam leaned in; his generally uncanny ability to identify a lie with abject clarity had somehow become maddeningly obscure. "Then why talk to her like ye made her yer mistress in *my* house, at *my* table?" he demanded through clenched teeth.

Thorne's shrug was meant to be conciliatory. "I was

flirting is all, Liam. I'm a wee sweet on the lass. She's a bonny lady with a pair of tits I'm not like to get a chance to—"

Liam seized two handfuls of his brother's suit and nigh yanked the man off his feet. "Open yer filthy gob about her again and I'll see yer guts spilled on the flagstones."

Thorne's verdant eyes widened, not just with fear, but with disbelief. "Ye want her," he marveled.

"Haud yer wheesht." Releasing him roughly enough to make his brother stumble, Liam turned to his desk, trying his best to slow the frantic hammering of his heart.

"My *God,* Liam. After all this time of self-imposed isolation, ye're hard for the *governess*?"

"I said. *Haud. Yer. Wheesht!*" Unable to stand it, Liam lashed at the closest thing he could get his hands on. A sheaf of papers, their brass paperweight, and a box of writing implements flew into the bookcase behind the desk and clattered to the ground in chaotic disarray. Struggling to fill his lungs beneath the pressure tightening about his ribs like a vise, Liam stalked to the sideboard and grappled with the stopper in the decanter while looking for a glass big enough for his desperate thirst.

"Are ye starting to have a problem with the drink, brother?" Thorne asked coolly.

"My only problem is that I doona have any."

Fuck the glass. Liam tipped his head back, taking a large gulp of the Scotch that bore his own title. He allowed the liquid fire to slide down his chest and ease the way for the subsequent inhales. At this point, his breath was likely flammable, but he didn't care. It was drinking or fratricide, and he didn't want Jani to have to clean blood off the study floor.

"A man like ye canna have a woman like her, Liam." Not many people denied him and lived to tell about it. It surprised Liam his brother had the stones. "Any man can see that someone's handled her roughly. In hands like yers, she'd be broken, just like every woman who dared love a Laird of Ravencroft."

His brother's words landed on his turned back like daggers. The truth shredded through his flesh, his bones, and into the heart they protected. A masterfully wielded blade, was his brother's tongue. As it had ever been.

"Do ye not think I know that?" Liam asked darkly as he now took the time to find a whisky glass. "Do ye think she'd fare any better in yer hands? A gambler. A libertine. A fickle reprobate who collects women like trinkets. Who has no compunction about taking his own brother's wife?"

The tightening in Thorne's features told Liam his own blade had struck true. "Doona bring Colleen into this." He pushed off the arm of the chair he'd been pretending to lounge against. "If ye remember, brother, ye took her from *me* first."

"Ye know full well I didna ken she was yers. Father hid it from me, ye never said a thing, and that—" Liam had thought many terrible things about his late wife over the course of the years. But he never dared utter them, lest he escalate the dangerous hostility that had formed between them. Now, it would just be speaking ill of the dead. "That *woman* married me over ye because I was a marquess and ye merely an earl. She only wanted the brother who would inherit. How could ye still love her after that?"

Gavin looked away, a soul-deep pain cutting through his permanently sardonic expression. "There is no stopping yer soul once it finds its mate. We *both* know she wasna right. That she wasna . . . well. But there were days she was lucid. When she was . . . luminous." Thorne's eyes softened as they gazed into the past. "Those days were worth the pain I bore on her behalf." He looked up at Liam. His hair gleaming the color of the malted barley they shoveled from the kilns, his eyes darkened with rare sobriety. "I like to think that if she'd been. . . . of sound mind, she'd have married me."

"Think what ye want." Liam turned and regarded his brother over another numbing sip. They'd already had this out a decade ago. Colleen had been mad, and that madness had turned her into something hateful. Spiteful. Someone . . . not altogether human. Or perhaps the constant duality of humanity had been too much for her. Maybe she'd just not learned to lock away the wretchedness of it like most tend to do. "Ye'd have been welcome to her," he snarled. "Hell, ye *helped* yerself to her anyway."

Thorne's eyes flashed like a blanket of lightning over the emerald moors. "*One night,* Liam. Ye'd been gone so long. She was lonely and I was in love. It was only ever that night."

"So ye say."

"So. It. *Is.* We've been over this before, brother. I told her that we'd made a mistake. That I had to confess the sin we'd committed against ye." Thorne's teeth were clenched now, his handsome features contorting into something cruel and malicious.

"I bled for ye," Liam said, so low it was almost a whisper. There it was. The bleak truth left to fester between them. Liam's back bore the scars that should have been his brother's. He had taken on so much cruelty, so much pain for the boy he tried to protect from their evil father. "I bled for ye and ye still betrayed me."

"We all bled plenty." Thorne's register also dropped dangerously low.

"Ye doona ken the half of what I've done . . ." He couldn't bring himself to say the words. "Ye were too young to remember—"

"Oh, I remember many of yer deeds, brother. I remember ye whipping that whore. I remember that no one has seen her since."

"Are ye accusing me of—"

"I remember what happened to Colleen when I told her we had to confess. She was so afraid of ye, of the *Demon*

Highlander, that she threw herself off the roof. What does that tell ye about what kind of husband you were to her? What does that say about what kind of man ye *are*?"

To Liam's surprise, a bitter sense of amusement permeated the rage fueled by pain and alcohol. "I ken *exactly* what kind of man I am. I am a monster. A monster who has *earned* the title of *demon.* I've killed more men with my bare hands than most soldiers have the opportunity to shoot at. I have done every evil deed required of me without question. Without hesitation. I've wiped out *bloodlines,* Gavin, and ridden through entire cities like the angel of death. I've spilled enough blood to turn the sea red. I've heard enough screams to fill eternity with their echoes." His grip tightened on his glass. "I am *tired* of being reminded of just who and what I am, not because I doona want to remember, but because I've never forgotten. And doona intend to."

Liam took perverse enjoyment out of the darkness gathering across Thorne's usually light features. "But I ken what ye are as well, and I will see ye hanged before I'd see ye with Miss Lockhart. So mark me when I order ye to leave her alone."

"You mean leave her to ye?" Thorne spat, his own fire igniting behind the mask of geniality. "I'm not one of yer sycophantic soldiers, Liam. Ye canna sanction me. Ye canna fire me from the distillery. And ye sure as fuck canna order me away from whomever I wish to keep company with."

He could kill the lad. This wasn't the first time he'd considered it. "She is in my employ. Not only that, she's under my protection."

"How noble of ye," Thorne mocked. "But I doubt ye've learned the difference between protection and command. If she seeks my company, ye canna very well physically stop her from doing so."

"Ye'll not take her," Liam growled. "Not this time."

Thorne's smile showed entirely too many teeth. "What is that charming expression? Oh, yes. All's fair in love and war."

Liam advanced, prowling forward until he was toe to toe and nose to nose with his brother, whose usual smile had been replaced by a sardonic twist. But Liam was able to look past that. To see what his brother hid behind all his bravado and pride.

There was fear. And perhaps regret, if he looked deeply enough. But love?

"It would be the last mistake ye ever made, *little brother,* to go to war with me."

The arrogant smirk returned. "The war would have ended before it even began, Liam. Though she's a kind and good woman, Philomena Lockhart has secrets. A lass like her could never put her heart in hands like yers. And a man like ye couldna love a woman he didna trust. Ye would dominate her, smother her, and finally ye would break her, fail her, and ultimately *ruin* her." Thorne drew himself up to his full height, the eyes he used to charm and disarm so many glittering with unmistakable meaning. "Just like ye ruined Colleen. Like ye failed Hamish. Just like *our father* broke both our mothers. Have another drink, my laird, ye grow more like *him* every day."

Liam's beast reared like a wild stallion. "Get out," he seethed.

"With pleasure." Thorne's look of disgust preceded his lengthy stride to the door. He wrenched it open, pausing with his hand on the knob. Though he didn't turn around, he touched his chin to his shoulder, obviously not comprehending how close to death he stood.

"There is treachery in this keep, Liam. Something nefarious is going on right beneath yer nose and ye're too blind or too proud to see it. *Someone's* trying to sabotage ye, to turn those closest to ye against ye. I'd look to my own. I'd be questioning whom I could trust."

"Believe me, I already am." Liam's muscles tensed to the point of breaking. It was as though he turned to stone beneath his skin. His rage was a volcano, the lava dousing him and hardening, building upon itself until it had become a living thing.

"Ye sit on top of a lonely mountain, Laird," Thorne continued. "Ye've fortified it well so ye keep out all yer enemies, and barricade yourself against the screams and blood in your past. But no one else is in there with ye, Liam, and ye'll die alone. Just like our father did."

"I said get. The fuck. *Out*," he roared. The door closed behind his brother just in time for Liam's whisky glass to shatter against it rather than the back of Thorne's skull.

And then he *was* alone. Alone and seething. Like coals shoveled onto a boiler fire, a myriad of memories, needs, and failings heaped into the flames of his rage, fanning it into something familiar and lethal.

But there was no one here to kill.

Head swimming with the heady rush of intoxicated fury, Liam stared at the flames in his fireplace, the only sound the whoosh of the fire as it devoured the air surrounding it. Would that he could control his own inferno . . . contain it within a casing of mortar and stone. Feeding it just enough to keep those he protected, those he loved, warm and safe.

Would that it didn't consume him, this unquenchable rage. That his very flesh wouldn't burn with it, becoming mottled and red from the force of its heat.

His blood, it boiled. His wounds, they burned. The lashes on his back itched and stung as though flayed open once again.

His head pounded in time to the beating of his heart.

Unable to stare at the flames any longer, or allow his own demons to scream at him through the silence, Liam stalked to the sideboard and reached for more Scotch.

Finding the decanter empty, he surmised that the closest bottle would be in the library.

As he prowled his own keep, it seemed that the castle bent and swayed with malevolent shadows. The shades of his demons waiting impatiently to drag him down to his final judgment. They were behind every tapestry. Slithering beneath the carpets and the cold stones. They were in the rain, hurled at the castle turrets by an unforgiving wind. Lightning sliced through the storm, slashing into the hall and casting a nightmare in terrible white.

The specter of a black-cloaked figure with demon-red eyes lurked not two spans in front of him. The lightning passed, plunging the hall again into darkness.

Liam had a knife in his hand before the thunder shook the stones of the keep. "Are ye the devil come to take me?" he demanded. Or was it the *Brollachan* seeking shelter from the storm? The hair on Liam's body lifted with awareness, with warning. The fetid stench of death cloyed about his senses as though the reaper breathed in his direction.

Those eyes. That form. They'd been familiar and yet so utterly foreign.

"I wondered if it would be ye who came to drag me to hell," Liam slurred, feeling both relieved and unsteady, as the Scotch seemed to release into his blood all at once and cause his world to tilt on its axis.

A high, soft feminine voice permeated the darkness from the direction of the library, along with a gentle but unintelligible masculine reply.

The lightning flashed again, and Liam found himself alone in the hall, his blood pounding through his veins with the force and fury of a blacksmith's hammer.

Had his sullied conscience begun to conjure apparitions?

"Father?" Rhianna called from the library. "Is that ye out there?"

Liam made the few steps to the library door and reached for the frame to steady himself.

Rhianna and Jani sat across a chessboard from each other. A cup of fragrant tea filled with Indian spices steamed at his daughter's elbow, and a fire crackled in the hearth.

Jani leaped to his feet and away from the table with all the alacrity of a guilty scoundrel. Rhianna, completely relaxed, turned in her chair and smiled brilliantly.

Liam loved her so much it ached. "What are ye about?" He attempted to keep his voice gentle, though he'd yet to cull the fury swimming through him.

"Ye know I canna sleep in a storm," she said with a saucy toss of her curls. "So Jani made me tea and I'm teaching him to play chess, which he's hilariously deplorable at."

"Is he?" Liam met Jani's wide, dark eyes over the expanse of the library. The fire threw flecks of light into his black hair and gleamed off the cream and gold kurta he wore.

Liam had spent many a night playing chess with his valet, and Jani had long since learned to best him at it. His eyes narrowed at the boy he knew better than his own son. Another one of his sins he carried with him. A reminder of his own damnation, but one that he esteemed.

He'd thought the hatred had faded from the boy's eyes over the years. But Jani was becoming a man. Had he just learned to hide it? It seemed unlikely, as Jani never was adept at keeping the emotion from his expressive features. Especially now, when his eyes shone brilliantly with guilt and not a small amount of anxiety.

"Is there anything you require, Laird?" Jani asked.

Suddenly Liam very much didn't like the idea of his valet and his daughter being alone in the night together. "Where is Miss Lockhart?" He squinted around the room, wishing the shadows would cease their shifting dance. It made his Scotch-soaked head swim.

He'd thought if he found anyone here, it would be his prim governess. She came to this room often. Liam had spied her more than once, poring over titles and mumbling to the books as though they were old friends.

"Well, you sound intriguing," she'd observe as she scanned the pages. "But perhaps I'm not in the mood for something so loquacious. What about you?" She'd select another title. "A mystery might be in order." Liam watched her, unobserved, as she fastidiously returned every book to its proper place, lining the spines just so. She never read in the library, favoring the conservatory that looked out over the hill leading down to the sea.

A creature of the sunlight was Miss Lockhart. The very memory of her voice calmed and inflamed him at the same time.

"Miss Lockhart took Andrew up to bed right after you left," Jani informed him.

"Aye," Rhianna confirmed. "He said he wasna feeling well, which solves a mystery because they disappeared twice today and I couldna find them. They were likely down in the kitchens going through the apothecary cabinet."

Liam nodded, speared with a pang of guilt that he'd been too preoccupied to notice that his son may have been ill. "I'll go look in on him," he muttered, his notice snagging on the intimate coziness of the room. The crackling fire, the soft light, the fragrant spices.

The glow in Jani's eyes when he looked at Rhianna.

"I trust that ye'll not be up late," he said carefully. "I'll send Miss Lockhart down to keep ye company."

To make certain they weren't alone together for too long.

"We can stop now, if you would rather," Jani said alertly.

"No!" Rhianna protested. "Ye only want to stop because

ye're losing. Miss Lockhart says ye'll never learn unless ye see it to the end. Now sit back down and take yer medicine like a man."

Jani remained standing, his eyes locked on Liam's as he awaited his orders. As always deferential. Faithful. Suspicion melted into a gruff sort of affection and Liam cleared his throat, cursing the fact that drink always brought the emotion that constantly roiled within him bubbling to the surface and threatening to overflow.

"Take it easy on him, *nighean*." Liam summoned a smile for his daughter.

"Ha! Never!" She pointed to Jani's vacated seat. "I'm going to wallop ye, see if I don't."

Liam turned away, thinking morosely that no one had ever regarded him with the patient tenderness the evening fire illuminated on Jani's sharp, young features when he looked at Rhianna.

Concern for Andrew propelled him up the grand staircase and to the west wing of the castle where his family slept. Where his governess resided. His stride faltered when he passed her closed door. Candlelight slanted over the dark hall from beneath it, and Liam found himself wondering, not for the first time, what she did in the privacy of her own chamber. He would picture her there, letting her hair down and brushing it with long, thoughtful strokes. Or perhaps she'd be in the bath, soaping her creamy skin, her shoulders, her breasts, her white thighs.

And higher. Running her fingers through soft auburn curls, shades darker than her hair and slipping into the folds of—

Liam growled as a twinge of lust seized the muscles beneath his belt and drove blood south until he clenched his teeth against the swelling beneath his kilt.

Now was not the time for that. In fact, it would never be time for that. Not when it came to her.

Andrew's suite was three doors past the governess's,

and Liam knocked first, in case the boy was still awake.
When no response was issued from inside, he swung the
door open.

"Andrew?" His voice echoed in the quiet darkness.
Venturing forward, he made a quick perusal of the disheveled sheets of his son's vacant bed.

A deep intake of breath followed the paroxysm of an
illogical suspicion. Liam tried to push it away, but it em-
bedded in his skull like the sharp end of a pick, driven with
such force he winced.

Since that day in the distillery yard, when the Scotch
barrel . . . escaped, Andrew and his lovely governess had
been thick as thieves. They thought Liam didn't notice
their surreptitious glances. The warmth and pleasure that
touched Mena's pretty mouth when she smiled and winked
at his son had, on more than one occasion, licked him with
troubling and unreasonable notions.

He'd thought the covetousness had been aroused by the
obvious fondness blooming amid the two. Because of the
distance between Liam and his son, and the intensity between him and Miss Lockhart, the ease and affection with
which Andrew and she treated each other these past few
days had been enviable.

But what if he'd been blind to something altogether
more illicit? What if, in his own desire for the luscious
woman, he'd missed a blooming dynamic that was not only
troubling, but predatory?

Liam's own initial sexual experience had been with an
older woman. Like Andrew, he'd been a tall boy. Pretty,
angular, and rapacious. He'd drawn the attentions of girls
and women alike, and had learned quickly what they'd
wanted from him.

And what he could take from them.

Something dark and brutal twisted in his gut. A stab of
murderous rage that caused a red jealousy to bleed into the
wound. Would a woman like Mena Lockhart dare trifle

with the son of the Demon Highlander? He wasn't certain. Hadn't Rhianna said Andrew and Mena had disappeared together today? Liam, himself, had noticed that they'd seemed to avoid him more than once.

Head swimming with the Scotch he'd had with dinner— had it been three or four snifters?—and whatever had been in the decanter thereafter, Liam stalked out of his son's empty room and pointed his boots at the light beneath Mena Lockhart's door. He let the dread that weighed down his organs bloom into the familiar anger that he usually fought, but now embraced.

Ravencroft Keep was full of secrets, and one by one, he was determined to ferret them out.

And deliver swift and retributive justice.

Chapter Twelve

Mena had been dressing for bed, and therefore was completely nude when her door exploded open with such force that it rattled the stones of the keep.

She was too startled to even scream.

Incomprehension stole the ability of movement from her limbs as she recognized the swarthy figure filling her door frame. He was the size of a small mountain. Dark as the night that surrounded them, and every bit as tempestuous.

Their gazes clashed and held as he stood equally as solid at her threshold. Hers wide and horrified, his narrowed and furious.

He was so savagely masculine. Relentless. Unstoppable. For a moment, as Mena stood lit by the lone lantern on the writing desk, she couldn't bring herself to move. It was the *naked* hunger etched into his chiseled features that arrested her for a breath longer than it should have. She'd never in her life had someone look at her like that. Like his yearning caused him physical pain. His skin drew tighter against the sharp bones, lending the intensity of his stare a stark, ruthless cast.

His hard mouth went slack at the sight of her, and his

chest rattled as though he struggled to fill it with breath. He looked every inch the barbaric Highlander from the painting on the stairs. Hair wild down to his shoulders, eyes flashing with the ferocity of an apex predator, and muscles cording with incomparable strength. Nothing moved but the flare of his nostrils as he stared at her.

His eyes touched every part of her. Even parts that may never have been touched before. They flashed with lightning, singing along her nerves with electric currents of heat. A sultry, answering thunder whipped through her, calling forth a storm so unexpected, she almost felt betrayed by her own body.

Her nipples, already tight from the chill, budded painfully. The sensation drew a shocked gasp from her as it tingled and flushed from her breasts all the way down her belly to settle in a wet rush between her thighs.

Jesus, *God,* what was she doing? What must he think?

Scrambling for the bed, she stood behind it, yanking her counterpane up to her neck and struggling to wrap it around her exposed body.

Perhaps she misinterpreted his stare. It was anger, not hunger, surely. Now that he'd seen her without her corset, he'd have marked the softness of her belly, the round flares of her thighs, and the grotesque way everything jiggled as she ran for the cover.

"What—what the devil are you doing here?" she gasped around a lump of mortification in her throat. His boot made a foreboding heavy sound as, instead of apologizing or explaining, he breached the threshold of her room.

Her mind instantly went from blank with shock to racing with terror. Had he found out who she was, somehow? Was he here to demand answers? To force her back to London and once again into bondage? Dear God, *what*?

"Where is he?" the marquess boomed in a voice loud enough to shake the windows in their frames. She could make out the question, though the edges of the words ran together, as though he had a hard time enunciating them.

"Who on earth do you mean?" she asked, as his eyes tore away from her and searched her room with frenetic observation.

"Ye ken full well who I mean." He stalked toward her turret, searched in the tub, and opened the doors to her wardrobe.

"I have—I have no idea who you're talking about," she breathed around the disbelief trying to paralyze her tongue.

"Doona play coy with me," he threatened, batting his way through the silk, crinoline, and cotton he found, parting the folds of her clothing as he would dense foliage. "The two of ye have been thick as thieves. I doona know why I failed to see it before now."

Distraught, Mena tried to make sense of his slurred accusations whilst also yanking the blanket from where it was tucked beneath the mattress so she could wrap herself in it more completely. Had Gavin—Lord Thorne—told him lies about what had or, more appropriately, *hadn't* occurred between them? Closing her eyes against a wave of panic, she prayed such was not the case.

"You won't find him here," she said, hating the desperation in her voice. "I'm quite alone."

He slammed the door to her wardrobe, and it bespoke the craftsmanship that the furniture remained intact. "I know ye're hiding something from me," he thundered, his long stride eating up the distance between them until he towered over her.

Mena shrank back from him, tears of terror pricking behind her eyes.

He sank to his knees and flipped the bed skirt up to check beneath it.

"I promise, there's no one in this room but you and me. Please," she pleaded. "Please leave."

"I know what ye've done." In a swift and graceful move, he rose and seized her, his hand clamping around her upper arm. Not hard enough to hurt, but Mena knew she had no chance to escape. "Confess, and I will be lenient, but lie to me . . ." He let the threat trail away, though his eyes vowed retribution.

Mena's limbs went numb with fear and all the moisture deserted her mouth. She'd been threatened before. Struck. Shoved. Even choked once. She remembered the sickening sounds of fists connecting with her flesh. The strange way it took the pain a delayed moment to register. The sight of her own blood. The taste of it in her mouth. How the pain used to confuse and astound her. She'd been treated so gently as a child, and she'd always wanted to do well. To please those she loved and lived with.

But she learned soon enough. To expect the pain, to anticipate it. To see it coming and mitigate the damage.

Such skills would be useless against the brutal-featured giant gripping her arm. He could kill her with a single blow; snap her bones with a flick of his wrist.

"T-tell me what you think is going on here," she cried. "I swear to you, my laird, I've never had anyone in here with me."

Even in his inebriated state, he seemed to register the terror in her voice, because he instantly released her. "Then where is my son?" he demanded. "Where is Andrew?"

She blinked. Opened her mouth, closed it. Then blinked again.

"Andrew?" she echoed, quite mystified. Had he misspoken? Didn't he refer to his brother, Gavin St. James?

Whirling away from her, Liam skirted her bed and stalked back to the door. "He's not in his room, or the ground floor. I was told he was ill. I need to find my son."

A new fear dawned on Mena as the unsteady Scot disappeared into the hall. Andrew was likely still outside with Rune, and if Liam was on alert—

"Just what the bloody hell is this?" the marquess roared.

Oh, no. Dropping the counterpane, Mena dashed across the room to the stand where her robe hung, and she snatched, donned, and belted it in one frenzied move.

"Doona be angry, Father," Andrew was saying, as Mena nearly stumbled over her feet in her haste to reach the door. She turned the corner to see Andrew facing her, clutching a squirming puppy in the crook of his chest and crossing his other arm over his body as though to shield Rune from his father's infamous wrath.

"Angry doesna begin to describe it," Ravencroft bit out. "How long have ye been keeping the beast from me?"

Both father and son's blue-black hair gleamed beneath the gas lamps in the hall, and Mena saw a temper that could mature to rival that of his father's flashing in Andrew's paler eyes. "She's been in the keep for two weeks now," the boy stated. "And ye havena even noticed. What harm is there in keeping her?"

"Two. *Weeks?*" The words were growled from deep below the marquess's ribs. A preternatural stillness settled upon Ravencroft's enormous shoulders like the shroud of death as Mena hurried to place herself between the boy and his fuming father.

Once Mena faced off with the Demon Highlander, she came to understand that the more still he became, the wider his lids peeled away from his deep-set eyes, the more true danger they faced.

Lord, but he was the most fearsome man. Had Andrew not been behind her, she would have stepped back. But she drew what strength she must to protect the boy from his anger.

This was the worst thing that could possibly have happened. The absolute worst way he could have discovered them. Now, all she could think to do was to delay this terrible discussion until the light of day.

"Perhaps, my laird, we should leave this conversation for the morning," she suggested evenly.

Ravencroft assessed her with eyes almost shrewd enough to be sober. "Ye knew." It was a statement, not a question, though he posed it to her breasts rather than her eyes.

Mena glanced down, and noted that her nipples still pebbled through the thin silk of her peach robe. She crossed her arms over them and scowled at the man. How he could notice such a thing at a time like this was inconceivable.

"I found out recently," she admitted. "I wanted Andrew to tell you, instead of tattling on him. And he was planning to talk to you about it, tomorrow, in fact."

"Tomorrow. How convenient." Ravencroft's scowl deepened. "This is inexcusable, Andrew. The rule has been, and forever will be, no beasts in the house. No pets. Especially dogs. Now get rid of it."

Mena's own brows drew together as she felt the desperation of the boy behind her, could sense the gathering storm. "Let's not be hasty," she cajoled. "Andrew's taken good care of the little thing, and shown great responsibility."

"Responsibility? He lied!"

"And—and that should be addressed," she conceded around the heart beating in her throat. "But you said yourself he should learn to care for something other than his own desires, and he's worked very hard to—"

"Uncle Thorne said I could keep her." Andrew found his courage, hurling the argument from behind her shoulder.

Mena squeezed her eyes shut. It was the worst excuse he could have made. She knew what she would find when she again opened them and faced the rage that had ignited behind the laird's eyes, watching his fists curl into white knuckles with trepidation.

"I doona give a bloody shite what *Gavin* told ye," he

roared, gesturing wildly. "*I'm* yer father, and *I* already told ye, *nay*." He thumped his chest for emphasis.

"Some father," Andrew muttered.

Every muscle in Mena's body tensed.

"What did ye say?" Liam took a dangerous step forward, all his fire turning to ice as he regarded his son as though he were a stranger. An intruder.

"With a father like ye, I'd rather be an orphan," Andrew spat, and must have clenched his grip in his anger, because the puppy let out a whimper.

"*Andrew*," she gasped, though her eyes flew to the laird's face to gauge his reaction. The rage hadn't deserted him, but something tormented and bleak had dampened the fire there.

"That's right." Andrew's voice gathered strength and volume, yet shook with anger and probably more than a little fear. "I wish all the time that ye'd never come home. Or that ye'd died at war so that all the years we spent missing ye, *hating* ye for leaving us, would have meant something."

That was it. She'd had about enough of hotheaded Highlanders. It was time for cooler British sensibility to make order of this mess.

Mena whirled on Andrew, drawing herself up to her full height, which at this point was still barely taller than him. "Don't you *ever* talk to your father in such a manner. How *dare* you?"

His mouth fell open in the exact gesticulation of shock his father had demonstrated only moments ago.

Mena wagged her finger, much as her beloved father had done the rare times he'd had to scold her. "He lives to protect your legacy. To protect you and keep you safe and happy and you simply refuse. He is a soldier—no—is a *hero*, and though you've made sacrifices as his son, he deserves your respect if not your ardent admiration." Grief over the loss of her own father seized her so acutely, she wanted to collapse beneath the weight of it. She was able to fight the tears that threatened by seizing hold of her righteous indignation. "One day, you'll have outlived him and, God willing, you'll have children of your own. You'll see what is out there in that dark, cruel world. You'll know the horrors that people can inflict upon each other, and what dastardly things he protected you from. There will be so many words you'll want to say. So much gratitude to express and so many questions to ask, and an understanding that you'll want to share with him and . . . he won't be there anymore. So you will take Rune and march yourself to bed, and when you wake up in the morning, you will draft the most heartfelt apology you've ever given in your life, do you understand me, Andrew Mackenzie?"

Silence jangled about in the hall until she planted her fists on her hips.

"Well?"

After a moment, the boy nodded mutely.

"And *you.*" She directed her wrath back at the Mackenzie laird, who regarded her as though she'd become an oddity he'd never before seen. Astonishment smothered his anger, before his eyes dipped to her breasts once again.

Crossing her arms, she scowled at him. "Don't you understand that there is nothing better for a lonely child than a loving pet? Perhaps if you'd had the company and unconditional regard of such a sweet dog you wouldn't be such an incurable ogre all the time." His lashes flicked down, shadowing his glare with the same boyish petulance his son had conveyed.

"Now." She stood between the two males staring at identical points on the carpet. *"You* are drunk." She gestured to Ravencroft. "And *you* are tired." She pointed to Andrew. "And we all need to deal with this after a good night's sleep. So off to bed with both of you, or so help me . . ." She let her own threat trail off, mostly because she hadn't the first idea what recourse she would take should one of them disagree with her.

Liam lifted his dark eyes to pin her with the most peculiar stare for a breathless moment before he about-faced with the precision of a brigadier general, and marched away.

Mena turned back to Andrew, who now regarded her with eyes as round as tea saucers.

Wordlessly, she pointed to his room, and followed him inside when he dragged the toes of his shoes with the air of a man being led to the gallows.

"I didna mean it," he said after a long while as Mena bustled in and smoothed his rumpled bedclothes before yanking them aside, needing an active vocation as an outlet.

"I know you didn't," she said crisply, though her ire was beginning to cool. A part of her was astonished at her own actions. What a mouse she'd been her entire life. And here she'd stood up to not one, but two people. Men, even.

One of them who famously was wont to kill people who angered him, so she was going to count that as double.

"Do ye think he knows?" Andrew set the subdued puppy on the floor and she plunked her little bottom on the rug with a whine. "That I truly doona wish him dead."

"I think so," she finally soothed, fluffing the pillow on his bed. "Your words were cruel, and I think they wounded your father. But he of all people understands that we all say things we don't mean when we're angry."

"Ye were brave." The veneration in his voice brought a caustic sound to her throat.

"I was reckless." She sighed, turning to him. "I'm sorry I spoke so harshly."

He shrugged his forgiveness. "He was really angry."

"Yes, he was." There was no use denying it.

"What do ye think he'll do?"

Mena stared at the adorable little creature biting at some itch on her rump and falling over in her exuberance. Her heart squeezed with dread and not a little bit of hope. "He might feel differently about Rune in the light of day. He's quick-tempered, to be sure, but he's a reasonable man. There is hope . . ."

"Nay." Andrew hurried forward. "I mean, do ye think he'll send ye away?"

"Oh." Mena wondered that herself. Perhaps she'd gone too far. Perhaps she'd wake to Jani at her door offering to pack her things and go.

She should have been more careful. Just what had gotten into her? Why had she found her voice, her courage, and the strength to stand up for herself at perhaps the worst moment ever?

Touched by the worry glimmering in Andrew's eyes, Mena reached for him, squeezing his shoulder. "I really don't know, darling. I hope not."

The boy's features hardened. "I'll *never* forgive him if he does." He visibly fought angry tears so hard he shook with them. "I swear it. I'll hate him until the day he dies, no matter what ye said, if he sends ye away."

Aching, Mena pulled him to her, resting his head on her shoulder, her own eyes brimming with tears. "That would be a tragedy, Andrew," she said, wondering why she still had an instinct to defend his father. "Trust was broken by me. He'd be well within his rights to send me packing. This is why lying is so dreadful. Do you understand now?" Wonderful, now she was not only a liar, but a hypocrite. Lord, what a mess she'd made.

"Aye." Andrew nodded against her shoulder.

"Crawl into bed," she soothed, drawing back. She scooped Rune up from the floor and set the little creature into his arms where the pup promptly went to work licking his neck. "Everything will look better in the morning. We'll sort it out. Don't worry."

Tears still leaked into Andrew's hair as he put his head on the pillow and allowed her to tuck him in. She stroked his silky hair. "No matter what, know that I'm on your side, all right, darling? And that, in the end, your father is, too. We both want what's best for you."

Andrew's jaw was still set in a stubborn line, but he nodded.

She turned down the lantern before sweeping to the threshold.

"Good night, Miss Lockhart."

"Good night, Andrew." She stopped herself from saying she loved him, though she felt as though she really did. What a dear boy Ravencroft had made.

Closing the door softly behind her, Mena released a bone-weary sigh as she peered through the flickering light down the hallway. Finding it empty of both demons and marquesses, she padded toward her room.

Andrew wasn't the only one anxious regarding her fate on the morrow. The evening's wait would be torture. She already knew sleep would elude her like a wary thief. Perhaps she should steal to the library and find some book or other to distract her.

Mena decided against that course immediately, as she knew that no book would keep her attention. Besides, the room still unsettled her, after her . . . encounter? Hallucination? Waking dream?

She didn't have to turn her knob, as the door to her room stood slightly ajar, the latch splintered from the wood.

She pushed it closed behind her, and did what she could to secure it, trying to forget the suspicious accusations Ravencroft had hurled at her earlier. She'd been such a fool to allow Andrew to talk her into this folly. Blinded by the kinship blossoming between her and the boy, she'd *lied* to her employer. Again. It seemed that once she'd agreed to live this ruse of a life, it was easier to compound it with more secrets, more fraud. She was most frightened of losing her integrity altogether.

In truth, she couldn't blame the marquess one bit for his displeasure. For being suspicious of her and the Earl of Thorne. Unlike her, *he* was no fool, and he knew that she'd been keeping something from him.

Lord save her if Ravencroft ever truly found out the depths of her deception.

The candle had gone out, somehow. Only silvery moonlight streamed into her bedroom from the large window, painting a crooked cross from the windowpane on the carpets.

Mena drifted over to gaze up at the glowing orb that hung low in the sky, mesmerized by the iridescent gray clouds as they allowed the autumn wind to toss them in front of the waxing moon. The wisps fragmented its glow to illuminate the lush landscape of Wester Ross and the sea beyond.

Wrapping her arms around herself, Mena pondered her situation with a melancholy desperation.

What a mire she'd become trapped in. She'd thought, initially, that her lies were victimless, that they served no purpose but to keep her safe. That she would hide here in this gothic Highland stronghold until the danger had somehow passed. When she'd been lost in the fear and pain of the aftermath of Belle Glen, the future had been this miasma of gloom and uncertainty. She'd run as fast as she could, headlong toward whatever sanctuary had been offered her.

Never would she have expected to become so attached to this wild, wonderful place. And—she could only admit this to herself here in the dark—to its wild, willful laird. To his children, his staff, and even the cold stones of this castle. Now, perhaps, she'd be forced to leave because of her idiocy.

Maybe she'd won a personal victory tonight, standing

up to the marquess's unreasonable temper; but the cost of such a victory might well be regrettably high.

"Ye were wrong." The pain and shame in the deep voice ripped through the stillness of the night with enough force to leave a wound.

Both hands flew to her mouth to contain a scream as Mena whirled around.

Moonlight rimmed the dark silhouette of the marquess in silver. His visage remained masked by the night, though his body dwarfed the chair in which he reclined, obscured by the shadows that seemed to embrace him as one of their own.

The Demon Highlander was not one to wait until the light of day when cooler heads prevailed. He'd never leave a challenge unanswered.

Mena swallowed around a throat closing with fear. No, he'd deal her fate to her here in the dark.

CHAPTER THIRTEEN

"Ye were wrong," Liam repeated, though he hadn't wanted to say anything at all. Nay, he'd wished to be a ghost, an invisible specter who could play voyeur to her mysterious feminine nighttime rituals. But she'd have turned and found him eventually, and every moment that passed without a word between them became more dangerous to them both.

To *her* body. To *his* soul.

She was a goddess shrouded in silver beams. Naked beneath her wrapper, her lush form was perfectly outlined by the moonlight piercing the thin fabric.

Liam had known she was a voluptuous woman, had often speculated in his quiet moments about the body she might be hiding beneath her corset and many skirts. But nothing in his life could have prepared him for what he'd witnessed mere minutes ago before the debacle in the hallway. Her nude form would forever be the image branded on the inside of his eyelids. Her creamy shoulders glowing in the candlelight as her luxurious hair fell in loose waves down her back, vibrant as a sunset reflecting off a waterfall. He'd known her breasts were generous, but his palms itched at the memory of their ripe, rosy-tipped perfection, quivering with the force of her astonishment.

They'd even fill hands as large as his, maybe to overflowing. The thought caused his mouth to water and his eyes to close against the unadulterated lust that rocked him to his core.

It wasn't fair. To see her thus was to be a damned soul given a glimpse of heaven. Forever denied. The cruelty of it was enough to break him.

"I know." Her humble admission confused him for a moment, and he opened his eyes to see her lower her hands from her mouth to wrap them around her middle.

"I was wrong, *unutterably* wrong to keep Andrew's secret from you. There is no excusing my decision, and—"

"Nay." He lifted a hand to stop her and didn't miss the way she flinched, even though the length of an entire room lay between them. The reflexive action set his teeth on edge. "I meant, ye were mistaken about . . . I *did* have a dog when I was a lad."

Backlit by the moon as she was, Liam couldn't make out her expression, though her bewilderment seemed as tangible as the floor beneath him.

"You did?" she asked.

"Aye."

"And . . . you returned to my room to inform me of that?"

Liam hated the careful evenness in her voice. The uncertainty and apprehension his actions had stirred within her. He wanted that to cease, but it seemed everything he did exacerbated her fear of him.

"Aye," he answered again.

"That I was wrong?"

"Aye. *Nay.* That is . . . not *only* that . . . I . . ." He sifted through thoughts as dark and muddled as the evening air.

It seemed all the alcohol had gone to his head and all the blood had settled in his groin and nothing was working as it should.

"Then why else did you come, my laird?" she queried softly. "What are you doing here in the dark?"

"I . . ." He knew he owed both of them the answer to that question. After she'd stunned him by dressing him down in the middle of his own keep, he'd planted his boots firmly in the direction of his rooms at the opposite end of the long west wing. But, the farther his feet had carried him away from her, the colder he'd become. The heavier his burdens had weighed upon him, until his shoulders and neck felt as though they'd snap from the strain. So he'd turned around, not at all understanding his own actions, and stumbled back into her room.

The scent of lavender and roses had lingered in the air, and his knees had given out when he'd spied the drying bouquet of the flowers he'd sent her tied to a metal accent of her vanity. Dried but fragrant, displayed like a treasure.

He'd sat where he'd landed in the chair, knowing the husky register of her voice would soothe the restless beast inside of him. That her feminine presence would remind him that he was human. That he was capable of not just temper and fire and fury, but of amusement and tenderness and . . . whatever it was that expanded in his chest when she was nearby.

She seemed to be the soft place his thoughts landed whenever they would wander. Hers was the sweet voice he clung to when the demons of his past screamed in his head. When he thought of beauty, he saw her face. When he felt hard and cold as iron, it was the fantasy of her supple pliability that warmed his blood. She seemed to be the only being that could temper the flames of his rage.

What *was* he doing here in the dark? He knew not, only that he'd followed some kind of instinct to find her, like a wounded animal searching for a safe haven.

"His name was Brutus, and my father killed him." The confession ripped from Liam's lips before he could call it back, and hung in between them with a weighty vibration.

Her arms dropped to her sides, and Liam wondered if she realized that she'd taken a tentative step toward him.

"Your . . . dog?"

He nodded, abruptly feeling too raw and exposed to realize that she might not see the movement in the dark. He wanted to retreat from what he'd just told her, to draw back inside of himself. But the memories lived in there, and he didn't want their company tonight.

Only hers.

"Why would your father do something so awful?" The curiosity in her voice was devoid of pity or censure, and so he was able to answer.

"Because Brutus was something I loved, and my father reveled in destroying anything I treasured, in denying me anything I wanted, and punishing me if I showed any weakness or attachment."

She made a sympathetic noise in the back of her throat, and it washed over Liam like a balm over a smarting burn.

"My father wanted to break me down so that he could craft and fabricate me into his likeness. He wanted a cohort to his evil. A maniacal copy of his cruelty. I never stopped fighting him, but in some ways, I fear, he succeeded in making me like him. A very large, very strong, very *violent* man. Of all the lashes he dealt me, and all the bones he broke, it was the loss of Brutus that caused me the most pain." *Christ,* why was he saying this? He was a man not only grown but aged, and he buried such things in the darkness of decades past and swept them beneath greater atrocities. Maybe it was the drink that loosened his tongue, the night, or the moon, or some sort of feminine magic that pulled the narrative from his throat. A panicked part of him wanted to stop, and something else pressed him forward, the part that sensed the burden begin to lift from his shoulders with a spoken revelation.

Mena ventured even closer, gliding over the carpets with a tentative sensuality that Liam wasn't certain he knew how to process. He almost wanted her to stay where she was, safe out of arm's reach. But to be approached by her was as miraculous as the proverbial lamb with the lion.

"The scars on your back . . . they were inflicted *before* the military. By your own father?"

"Most of them," he answered honestly, simultaneously dreading and resigning himself to her pity.

She showed him neither, though she paused and gave an audible swallow. "Would you permit me to ask you something?" she inquired.

She could say whatever she wanted if she'd only keep using that voice, the one that reached for him through the shades and memories to caress the tension from his muscle, sinew, and bone.

When he didn't answer she proceeded anyway. "If your father's treachery caused you such a wound, would you then hurt Andrew in the same fashion?"

He stiffened. "Nay, lass, doona ye ken I'm trying to protect him from such a loss? I had Brutus less than year before he was . . . slaughtered in front of my eyes. What if my son had such an attachment for ten or fifteen years, and then the wee beastie died or ran away? Is it not kinder of me to circumvent the pain of that altogether?"

"Wasn't it Lord Tennyson who first said that 'it is better to have loved and lost, than never to have loved at all'?" Slowly, his governess lowered her frame onto the dainty bench of her vanity. She was within an arm's reach now, and Liam kept his hands fisted in his lap.

"I doona know, lass. I've never read much poetry."

"Well, that must be remedied." She sighed softly and leaned toward him in the darkness. "The point you make is frankly absolute nonsense, and yet I feel as though I am finally beginning to understand you, Laird Ravencroft." The whisper of a smile warmed her voice and Liam thought that if he sat very still he could feel that warmth radiating from her skin, though she didn't touch him.

Liam's brows drew together as he tried to figure whether her words pleased or offended him.

"You know that I'm acquainted with Farah Blackwell, the Countess Northwalk," she continued.

"Aye."

"Well, I will confess that she has taken me into her confidence, and I know that she is not only an association, but your sister-in-law. You see, I understood your father to be a vicious man before I came here, because Farah told me that he paid to have your brother, his own son, beaten to death by the guards at Newgate Prison where he was wrongly incarcerated."

She'd uncovered another guilt he carried locked beneath his ribs. Something he should have been able to stop, somehow, had he acted sooner. Had he become the Demon Highlander back when Dougan Mackenzie, the boy who had become Dorian Blackwell, had needed him, might he have saved his brother from becoming the Blackheart of Ben More?

"I felt so much sorrow for your brother all those years ago." Mena's voice caught for a moment before she cleared the emotion from it. "I mourn for all of the ill-treated and illegitimate children of Hamish Mackenzie and men like him. But what I realize now is if that was the awful fate of the *unwanted* boy, what must it have been like for the child who had to *reside* with such a man?"

No one, not even Liam, himself, had thought of it in those terms before. He'd always mourned for the countless victims of his father. Never had he thought to count himself among their ranks. He'd been the heir apparent. The legitimate issue who at least had inherited a castle, fertile land, a title, and a business, one he'd built from failing to thriving. He'd always thought that of all Hamish Mackenzie's offspring, he'd received the most reparation, and therefore had little entitlement to his pain.

Liam raked his hands through his hair before returning them to his lap, finding it impossible to lift his gaze. For the first time since he'd been a child he felt brittle. Breakable. As though he were stretched out on the rack and the last turn of the screws would tear his limbs apart.

"I hated my father," Liam admitted. "I promised to never become like him and yet, though I've never laid a hand on my son in anger, he still wishes me dead."

The whisper of her touch caressed him before her hand rested tentatively in his open palm. Again he had to close his eyes because, even in the dimness, the moon illuminated too much.

"Your father was unspeakably cruel to you, and I am so very sorry for it." Her fingers curled around his hand and exerted a soft, comforting pressure. Her voice warmed the chilly evening. "If I know one thing, Andrew is *your* son. Hot-blooded and hardheaded, but tender for all that. I think he speaks from a place of injury rather than conviction."

"How do I tell him that Gavin was right? That I stayed away because, even though my father is dead, through me he somehow seems able to destroy everything or everyone in my path . . ." An aching void opened up in Liam's chest that stole his breath. One by one, he allowed his fingers to curl around hers.

"I became the Demon Highlander for *them,* ye ken? Not for the glory of the empire. Or the Mackenzie clan. Not to make a name or fortune for myself. Ye see, as a young man, I always thought if I died at war, if I left this world a hero, my children would remember me fondly. Not only that, their futures in society would be secure.

'Tis why I always led the charge, why I jumped into the most dangerous circumstances without a thought. Every mission, *every battle,* I expected to be my last. I think Andrew and I both anticipated that I would be nothing but a distant memory for him, not an ill-tempered man he'd have to live with. Someone he'd wished had never come home . . ."

"He didn't mean what he said," she crooned to him.

"He's within his right to," Liam murmured, troubled and yet transfixed by the soft, small hand tucked into his.

"No he isn't." She tightened her hold again, and oddly enough he felt a little bit of the pressure in his chest ease so he could take a deep breath. "He loves you. It's why he's so angry. He wants you to love him. He wants you to teach him. I think he needs to know that he can be difficult and you will not abandon him."

Liam clung to her, his only salvation in the crashing and eddying tides of emotion he never allowed himself to examine. "What if it's too late?" His fear amalgamated into something solid. Tangible. And once he'd given it voice, it grew with enough force to crush him.

"I'm not of the opinion that anything with Andrew was broken tonight that cannot be repaired as swiftly and thoroughly as my door can." She'd pushed a bit of cheek into her voice; to lighten the moment, he assumed.

Despite that, shame weighted down the edges of Liam's mouth as he thought of the physical force he'd used against her door. The only illusion she had of safety. "I shouldna have acted so barbaric. I doona want ye to fear me, lass. I'll have the door fixed in the morning."

She was silent for a breathless moment. "Think no more of it," she said. "We'll hopefully both wipe it from our memory and move forward."

Liam hoped like hell she'd be able to, though he knew he'd be tormented by the memory of her sumptuous flesh for countless days to come. His eyes had adjusted to the

lack of light, and whatever the shadows concealed, his rec-
ollection of her perfection filled in the spaces.

"I know this is a sore subject between us," she ventured.
"It's only that I don't know what Lord Thorne said to
make you think I'd allow him into my room, but I want to
assure you that I have no intentions toward your brother,
and wouldn't dream of conducting myself in a manner
that—"

"I knew Gavin wasna in yer room," Liam assured her.
"He wouldna dare. I forbade him from bothering ye further, and he left."

"Forbade?" Liam could tell she didn't like the word by
the perplexed lethargy with which she said it. "If the earl
went home, then who did you think . . . ?" It took her
mind two very quick seconds to put it all together and
snatch her hand out of his. "You came to my *bedroom*
looking for . . . *Andrew*? You kicked the door in because
you thought your *son* was in here with *me* in the middle
of the night?" She'd moved past perplexed to mystified,
and Liam had to sort through his Scotch-muddled thoughts
for something to say.

"Oh, my God." She stood and turned away from him,
retreating a few paces and wrapping her arms back around
her middle in that protective gesture.

The loss of her comforting touch drove Liam to his feet.
"Rhianna said ye'd both gone upstairs to bed at the same
time. The two of ye had been avoiding me for days. When
ye werena sneaking away together ye were whispering secrets. I didna ken at the time that it was regarding a wee
beastie."

She slowly twisted to face him, and Liam was glad he
couldn't see whatever awful emotion her gaze contained.
"So you thought I . . . Lord, I can't even say it." Her hand
flew to her forehead and dragged across it as though to
wipe away the offending thought.

Liam groped for something, anything that might make

her understand. "Andrew's sullen moods have driven away every governess he's ever had, and suddenly he started treating ye like ye'd hung the moon."

"It's called fondness," she hissed. "Affection. We can feel that, you know, without it being some kind of perversion."

"I ken that." He took a step toward her, and again she retreated. "But he's a handsome lad on the cusp of manhood who thinks of little else but women, and ye're young and damned desirable. Ye canna blame me for suspecting—"

"You had to feel a little more than *suspicion* to kick my bloody door in!"

Liam said nothing. At first because no one ever dared to interrupt him, and then because he couldn't ever remember hearing her curse. The lass was right, of course, he'd been quite a bit more than suspicious.

He'd been jealous.

"I should leave," she whispered, her hand still resting on her forehead as though she were now afraid her mind would escape her if she let it.

Liam pinched the bridge of his own nose. He was turning a misunderstanding into a catastrophe. "Nay, I'll go, we'll discuss this in the morning." They'd sort out the mess when he was thinking more clearly. Every emotion he had simmered right below the surface of his skin, some that he battled constantly such as lust, anger, need, and regret. Others he'd buried with his father, and he should wait until the light of day to sort through them.

And then there were these new foreign ones which needed to be inspected. Softer, tender, almost . . .

"No," she lamented, bringing his attention snapping back to her. "There's no discussing this. I *have* to depart first thing. I cannot stay here any longer. Not now."

Alarm seized him. "Ye mean, leave Ravencroft?"

"Yes, I mean leave Ravencroft." She hurried to her

wardrobe with stilting, uncertain steps, blindly reached in, and yanked down an armful of clothing. It was too dark for either of them to truly ascertain what color they were, but she didn't seem to care as she flung open the trunk at the foot of her bed and began to shove them in.

When she looked as though she'd return for more, Liam placed his body in her path. "Ye're staying," he ordered.

She stepped around him. "If your opinion of me is so low that you think I could take advantage of a *child,* this will *never* work. I'll find a different situation."

"I was . . ." He didn't want to say *wrong,* though he knew it to be the appropriate word. He trailed her to the wardrobe wondering how he'd managed to halt armies in their tracks, but this one wee governess refused to cooperate. "Ye're not leaving." He tried a command, which in his book was a bit higher than an order. That ought to work.

"But I must." She hurried away from him, thrusting her second armful into the trunk.

He shut the wardrobe and advanced on her. "I willna allow it," he threatened. "Ye'll *remain* here in my employ, and that is my final word on the matter."

She whirled around and stomped in his direction until they met in the center of the room beneath the silver gaze of the moonlight streaming through her window. She could have been the goddess Danu, her red hair billowing around her, her robe flowing with the force of her truncated movements.

"Don't you think for *one minute* that you can order me about like one of your subordinates." She spoke slowly, enunciating her indignant words with abject clarity. "You may be a Highland laird, and you *may* be a marquess, but that doesn't give you one ounce of dominion over me, Liam Mackenzie." Her breasts heaved with her increasingly forceful breaths. Her voice shook with anger and her pale jade eyes flashed silver with wrath and moonlight.

Something about her temper gave Liam the most excruciating erection he'd ever had. He stepped forward, wanting to reach for her, but for every move he made to close in, she took a step back.

"I might be afraid of you," she confessed, her voice losing some of its fervency as he stalked her in the dark. "But mark me, I'll *never* cower to another man. I am my own self. I am a woman with free and independent will. I deserve to live for no one's whims and pleasures but my own, and I don't have to follow your commands." Her back found the wall, and suddenly there was nowhere to go. Liam knew it. And so did the lass.

"Do what you will, you high-handed, imperious, overbearing brute, but if I want to leave, you'll not sto—"

Liam cut off her words with his mouth.

It was a movement born of panic and instinct. He hadn't been thinking. He just . . . couldn't *bear* to hear her say that she was leaving one more fucking time.

He'd kissed her before, and still he hadn't been prepared for the complexity of sweetness that he found on her lips. It inflamed him. It humbled him. It held him in a thrall he knew full well he'd never escape. So here he stood, a willing slave to his own desire. A helpless victim of the debilitating lust that flared in his loins and boiled through his blood. He was hard as a diamond, the cords and sinew at his hips rolling forward to press against the softness of her belly.

Liam would never have enough of her, not if he fused their mouths for an eternity. Each drugging sweep of their lips only intensified his hunger. Nibbling at her lower lip, he sampled the flavor of her skin, then licked at the seam of her full mouth, silently requesting admittance into the honeyed heat he was certain to find inside.

He swallowed her shocked gasp and plundered her with his tongue as though she were a lifelong conquest. Digging his fingers into her ribs to keep from taking what she did not offer him, he deepened the kiss, using his tongue to convey what he could not find the words to say.

She wasn't the only one who was afraid. Liam was *terrified*.

Of losing her.

Of loving her.

And at this moment, he was in mortal danger of both.

CHAPTER FOURTEEN

The flavor of Ravencroft's lips pushed Mena past shocked to absolutely witless. She wasn't pliant so much as thunderstruck. She didn't kiss him back, but neither did she push him away.

The sweet burn of whisky on his tongue caused her jaw to sting with overwhelming thirst as her mouth flooded with moisture. She closed her lips to swallow convulsively, and instantly his hands were there, his thumbs dragging the corners of her mouth open so he could thrust his slick tongue back inside.

A growl caught in his throat, quickly turning into a groan. The calluses of his palms abraded her skin as he cupped the side of her face, lifting her to give him better access.

He might be a little drunk, but Mena knew *she* was on the edge of pure, carnal intoxication.

It was impossible to tell what was harder, the wall behind her, the man trapping her against it, or the length of his sex pulsing as hot as a branding iron against her belly. His arousal was as incomprehensively large as the rest of him, enough to send her thoughts scattering to the most indecent places. Its purpose unmistakable, his desire inescapable, Mena found herself rocked by sensation so thoroughly that she feared she would lose consciousness. Dizzying chills racked her frame until she trembled as though she'd been left out in the bone-chilling cold. But it was liquid heat spreading through her, settling in her core and causing a rush of alarming moisture to pool there.

She'd been angry, hadn't she? Mortified, hurt, and . . . leaving? She'd been afraid. Should *be* afraid. This was wrong, though she couldn't at all remember why. Somehow Liam Mackenzie was able to dissolve her ever-churning thoughts into a puddle of nothing. With one kiss, he'd morphed her into a creature as instinctual and primal as he, with just as much difficulty controlling her most secret and basic of needs.

The sharp scent of his soap and the musk of something darker, earthier, invaded her senses and Mena breathed it in, making it a part of her. His kiss gentled from bruising to merely relentless. His movements against her lips were urgent and greedy, but strangely unhurried as he penetrated her deeply, searching the recesses of her mouth with a tender sort of aggression.

Mena waited to feel the inevitable revulsion that came with intimacy, the forbearance, the distaste and apprehension. As hands trailed down the fragile skin of her neck, evoking shiver after shiver, she couldn't believe those terrible emotions never found her. It was only anticipation that coursed through her as his powerful fingers curved down her shoulders.

"Kiss me, Mena," he moaned against her mouth, his hot, sweet breath fanning over the moisture on her lips. "Touch me. Teach me to keep the demon at bay."

She could only see the whites of his eyes in the dim light, circling the obsidian of his pupil and iris in such a way that truly seemed demonic.

With trembling fingers, she reached up to softly test the

shape of his masculine jaw. Bristle scraped against her fingertips as they explored the raw, hard features that she'd always wanted to study, but didn't even allow herself to look at for too long, lest she be lost.

How fierce he was all the time. How strong and capable and remote he had to be. Never showing weakness, never allowing vulnerability.

Except in this moment. With her.

He turned into the press of her fingers, seeking more of her touch as a primitive sound escaped him on a shaken breath.

She *was* lost. Never in her life had she been able to turn away a wounded animal.

Liam Mackenzie was no different. The scars he carried upon his soul were horrid and deep as those on his back. Some of the wounds remained open and bleeding, poisoning his chances at happiness or peace.

What a tragedy they both were. Bruised and beaten by those who were supposed to have loved and protected them. Tossed upon a sea of cruelty, and seeking refuge in this unforgiving world. Seeking sanctuary, but hoping for redemption.

Shivering and impassioned, Mena lifted to her toes, pressing her lips against the hardness of his mouth. This time, her tongue met his with welcoming heat as she dragged her hands down the swells of his chest and around his broad torso to wrap what she could of his big frame in her embrace. Her hands searched for a place to settle, light as moth wings at first, and then stronger as she clutched him to her.

A shudder coursed down his spine as she smoothed her fingers over the powerful stretch of his back. The wide muscles flinched and flexed beneath her touch and he groaned his approval into her mouth. She noted the scars, but only the man beneath them registered to her tantalized senses.

His hunger became a tangible thing, escalating his breath until it heaved against her. Hands were everywhere, cupping her breasts, shaping them as the tips instantly hardened and ached against his palms. Testing them with gentle, insistent pressure, molding until she could no longer think past the sensation gathering there.

A whimper of surprise escaped her as her hips tightened and jerked against a stab of need she'd not even thought herself capable of. Wet and swollen, her body called to him.

And his answered.

Chilly air kissed her ankles as his hands gathered her filmy robe until it parted. His knee gently pressed between her legs as he ravaged her with deep, drugging kisses. His solid weight pinned her in place as her robe gave way and he replaced it with his body.

The marquess swallowed her gasp as she realized his kilt had also ridden up between them, and with one smooth and sinuous movement, he'd split her legs and pressed the flesh of his naked thigh against her exposed sex.

He uttered a curse in a language she didn't know as he moved against her, replacing her flare of panic with one of pleasure. Suddenly the hard muscle of his leg was also drenched and slick as he undulated again, creating a strange and delicious friction. His shaft pressed against her hip as he rocked against her. She knew he wanted it inside her, that if she opened to him, he'd sink every hot inch as deep as he could.

"Wait," she said. Or perhaps didn't say, as he never let up the pressure of his mouth, even as her lips moved. She wanted him to stop. She *never* wanted him to stop.

Then his hand was there, clever fingers slipping into the wet cleft and touching a place no one had ever before paid attention to. He somehow ignited frenzy into her blood with infuriatingly slow strokes. A curious heat unfolded in her core and quickly caught into a blaze of sensation.

Mena writhed helplessly against him, riding his strong thigh as more heat created more friction, which in turn built the flames even higher. What sort of pagan magic was this? How could hands so rough and raw create such smooth, silken sensations against her most tender skin?

Something was . . . happening. Her muscles contracted and expanded, her body seemed to open, to prepare, to warn her to brace herself against his strength because she wouldn't be able to stand against what he was about to do. Her hands groped at his back, then his shoulders, clutching at him, then pushing him away. He ignored her feeble struggles, silently pressing her higher with his leg until she was forced to lean on his limitless strength as her toes seemed to no longer touch the ground. He held her there, suspended on the exquisite edge of a dark and unknown abyss. She could feel it reaching for her, a pulsing oblivion that knew no limit, that gave no quarter and had no end.

All she needed to do was let it take her away.

"Come for me, lass." He breathed the order against her throat as he trailed his hot lips down the sensitive column of her neck.

And she would have, had his fingers not tangled in her hair. A thrill of fear pierced her with its icy arrow, and leached the heat from her liquid bones.

Gordon used to pull her hair.

He'd used it as a tool of submission, to lock her head where he wanted, to compel her to be still as he forced himself into her mouth. Sometimes her hair would rip from her scalp, and the sound of it would echo through her ears from the inside.

Whatever desolate, frightened sound she made when she wrenched her mouth away from his and turned her head to the side was enough to pull him out of his aroused stupor.

"Please," she begged in an uneasy whimper. "I can't."

She found herself released as abruptly as he'd seized

her, and Mena would have fallen if the wall hadn't caught her.

Ravencroft flung himself to the opposite side of the room, where he braced his hands against the far wall. His head hung below his shoulders as his wide back expanded with panting breaths.

Dazed by a maelstrom of fear, lust, and shame, Mena gripped the sagging folds of her robe and wrapped them back over her inflamed body, belting it closed.

"Forgive me," he finally said. "I've had too much to drink. I wasna thinking." His voice was thicker than usual, the accent more pronounced. The few seconds of silence between them stretched on for an eternity as Mena desperately groped for the thoughts that had scattered about the darkness of her room like a child's errant marbles.

"Ye canna go, Mena," he ordered.

She couldn't think of a thing to say. Leaving would be safer in some ways, and utterly dangerous in others. Her husband was still out there, searching for her.

But if she stayed . . .

"Andrew can keep his beast," he rumbled, pushing from the wall and moving to the broken door.

Mena remained silent, still trying to catch her own breath. Trying to ignore the pulses of need still throbbing between her legs, and the pulses of fear threatening to stop her heart.

"And . . ." Ravencroft continued, still refusing to turn around. "I'll not dictate how ye spend yer free time . . . or with whom." He said this as though the words cost him a great deal.

Dumbfounded, Mena could still think of no reply until a polite "Thank you," escaped her out of sheer habit.

"Doona leave." It had to have been the gentlest command he'd ever issued, as close to a request as she'd ever get from the Demon Highlander. "Doona abandon them as I have, as everyone has."

He'd used the most devious and effective weapon in his arsenal to get what he wanted. His children. They did need her help and, in truth, she needed them. Needed Ravencroft. Not just the man but the stones of the fortress around them. She remained a fugitive from the crown, and returning to England was simply out of the question.

"Ye'll stay," he prompted again. "And I'll . . . leave ye alone."

That should have made her feel safer, but it didn't.

"I'll stay," she whispered, and didn't allow herself to slide to the floor until he'd left the room, shutting the splintered door firmly behind him.

Mena dreamed of the *Brollachan* that night.

She tossed and writhed about in her sleep as though afflicted with a fever. Rough, callused hands soothed her until she settled from thrashing to merely fitful.

"Liam?" she whispered through the miasma of dream mist and moonlight.

"Nay, lass," a dark voice rasped back at her. "Ye should go. Leave this place. If ye stay with the Demon Highlander, it'll mean the end of ye."

In her dream she was on her bed, but it was not as before. A cold mist billowed inside her room. It fragmented the moonlight and obscured her vision. Her lungs filled with ice and it coursed through her blood blooming with fear.

"Is he going to hurt me?" Mena whispered to the dark, her eyes searching the mist for the frightening demon-red eyes.

"Aye." The word came from behind her, but she dare not turn around from where she lay curled on her side. "He takes what he desires, and then he crushes it. He canna help it, lass, it is in his *blood*." The voice seemed closer now, stronger. "Ye are the object of his desire now, which means ye are in danger. Run before he claims ye, too."

Mena shook her head in emphatic denial. "He does not

mean to claim me. He was drunk and I was weak, but nothing will come of it, I'm only the governess."

"We both know ye're more than that."

Panicked tears pricked her eyes and she yearned to run, but in her dream, her muscles didn't seem to be working.

"Who are you?" she whispered, frightened tears springing to her eyes. "How—how do you know what I am?"

Mena thought she felt the whisper of a breath against the tendrils of hair at the nape of her neck. She released a terrified gasp that escaped as a whimper.

"I am the horrible embodiment of the Mackenzie's many sins. The specter of his demon. He'll not escape the promise he made me."

"What did he promise you?" she couldn't stop herself from asking.

"Everything, lass. *Everything*. And I'll collect what I'm owed."

CHAPTER FIFTEEN

Liam had gone to Andrew's room in the morning and had done what he could to make things right before he left on business that very afternoon. He and his son had traded apologies, something that may have never been done in the Ravencroft household for generations.

He'd left feeling both heavier and more hopeful than he had in a lifetime, and the conflicting emotions set him more on edge than ever.

It took the entire train journey from Strathcarron to Dingwall for Liam to decide upon the woman he'd use to fuck the memory of Philomena Lockhart away. How would he ever make it through the tedium of the Agriculture Council of Highland Lairds as randy and distracted as a pubescent schoolboy? There was no concentrating on late-summer harvest reports, the sowing of winter crops, settling on export prices, or meeting with the Fraser's French cousins to purchase next year's oak sherry casks if he couldn't get his runaway libido under control.

'Twas the reason he left Ravencroft two days early; it would take that long in bed, at least, to erase the memory of her incomparable body, of her slick desire on his skin.

Mary Munroe flung her door open before he had the chance to knock. Her lovely face alight with a welcoming smile, she fanned herself coquettishly and gave him a saucy wink.

"Well, if it isna the Demon Highlander, himself, come to take my virtue." Twirling a dark ringlet around her finger, Mary laughed at her own joke. It had been many years since Mary Monroe had been a virgin, or virtuous for that matter.

She was the most expensive courtesan in the Highlands. It was rumored she stayed in Dingwall because the lord of Tulloch Castle kept her in these lavish apartments.

But as long as she was at his leisure, she could keep her own appointments, as well.

Mary Munroe only held in reserve the most exclusive clientele, and Liam was lucky enough to be counted among their few numbers. He not only enjoyed her dexterity, he enjoyed her company. He could say that about very few people.

She gave a delighted squeal as he crowded her into her apartments, slammed the door, shoved her against the garishly papered wall, and kissed her.

This was what he wanted, was it not? A bout of hot, sweaty, desperate fucking. She'd let him take his fill. She'd done it before. But even as she bloomed for him, swirling her tongue inside his mouth with expert skill, he suddenly knew hers were not the lips he craved. Her breasts beneath his searching hands felt small and unexciting.

Liam's body was hard and ready, had been since the night before. So why did he have to close his eyes and picture Mena in order to make the idea of bedding one of the most beautiful women in Scotland seem more than passing attractive?

She broke the kiss with no small amount of reluctance and studied him with eyes the color of his rich whisky. "All right, Laird Mackenzie, who is she?"

He stepped back as she pushed at his jacket.

"Who?" He kept the question deceptively mild, as he ran a frustrated hand over the hair he'd tied back for his journey.

"The woman ye've come to me to forget." She raised a knowing eyebrow at him and sashayed down the hall, her voluminous bustled skirts trailing after her.

Mena's back also arched just thus, and Liam knew she didn't have to employ a bustle to achieve the shape that Miss Munroe and so many women paid good money for. Mena's arse was a thing of beauty. If he could just mold his hands around it, he'd die a happy man.

He scowled, exasperated by the unbidden direction of his thoughts. He followed the courtesan into her receiving room, and grabbed her from behind, turning her to face him. "Doona talk nonsense, woman."

A painted lip tilted up. "I'm skilled in many things, my laird, but nonsense is not one of them. If ye want a stupid whore, ye'll have to look elsewhere."

"It's not yer sense I'm paying ye for, lass, now take this off." His fingers went to the laces of her dress.

She covered his big hands with her dainty ones, and Liam had a hard time meeting the understanding that lurked in her eyes. "I've known ye a long time, Liam Mackenzie. And I've wanted ye since before ye came to me, back when ye were still faithful to yer mad wife."

"Careful, lass," he warned, pulling his hands from hers.

"Ye wanted me, too, wanted me something fierce if I remember correctly." She turned and moved deeper into her sumptuous parlor, draping herself across a soft green chaise that matched the extravagant gold drapes. Even the room was decorated to make her look more fetching. The colors illuminating her own dusky shades and contrasting with the dark bronze of her dress.

Flicking her fan a few times, she made her loose ringlets flutter with a practiced grace. "I knew that when ye

finally gave in to come and take me, it would be the kind
of encounter that would require recovery. As usual, I was
right. I didna walk the same for a week." Her face glowed
with the fond memory.

So why were they wasting time? "Get naked and I'll no
let yer feet touch the ground for days."

She shook her head, her eyes glimmering with regret
and a fond sort of pity. "Nay. If ye're not already in love
with whoever she is, ye're nigh to falling. I'd have ye off
one time and then ye'd be so full of shame and regret that
ye'd leave. I doona want us to part like that."

"Tell me," he asked acerbically, "does fortune-telling
pay as much as prostitution?"

"Don't be cruel because I'm right," she said sharply.

He glared at her, and she gave as well as she got.

"Sit down, my laird, and have a drink," she invited. "Ye
can tell me about her."

"No, thank ye." He was wary of drink at the moment.

"Tea then." She motioned toward the set at her elbow
and Liam acquiesced, settling himself in the lone high-
backed leather chair next to the fire, the only furnishing
obviously placed for a male visitor.

She poured silently and he watched her, his insides
churning with need, disappointment, and, if he was honest, a great deal of relief.

He took the delicate ivory china cup from her when she
handed it across the small table, and tried his best not to
drink the brew in one sip. He'd never been much for tea,
or comfortable with breakable things in his hands.

She was regarding him with shrewd affection when he
looked up. "I like that I can never quite figure ye out," she
said. "Ye are Lieutenant Colonel Mackenzie, the Demon
Highlander. Ye dash toward the fray, ye charge into the
most dangerous situations with not even a blink. But car-
ing for a *woman* . . . *that* will frighten ye enough to run?"

Liam said nothing, setting his tea down. It wasn't merely

Mena he'd run from. It was himself. The mortification caused by the admissions he'd given her in the dark. He'd shared some of his own secrets with her. Imparted his pain. Unleashed the force of his need . . .

And it had frightened her.

So he'd promised to leave her be, but even as he'd said it he knew he'd been lying. There was no leaving her alone. Miss Lockhart had somehow become a part of him.

"Is it love?" Mary asked gently.

"It's . . . complicated."

"Love is *always* complicated, darling." She laughed. "That's why I do what I do instead of falling for someone who deserves it. Complications are tedious, unless they're happening to someone else, of course."

Liam thought it was her casual attitude toward the situation that allowed him to admit to her what he not only feared, but suspected.

"She doesna want the Demon Highlander."

"You have a great many other titles," she reminded him wryly.

"She doesna seem to be interested in those, either." A fact he found he admired about Mena, though he'd gladly use them to get what he wanted from her if he thought it would help.

The woman shrugged. "Then be Liam Mackenzie," she said simply. "The man."

"I . . . doona ken who that is."

"If she's a good woman, she'll help you find out."

He could only shake his head as his heart became heavier and heavier in his chest. "She's been mistreated and she knows I'm a violent man. She's terrified of me . . ."

"And yet?" Mary prompted.

"She *yelled* at me," he said incredulously. "It's been decades since anyone dared . . . she told me I couldna issue her orders, and that she was a woman with free and independent will. She called me an overbearing brute."

"Oh, Lord." She hid a laughing smile behind her fan. "What did ye say to that?"

"I kissed her. And she kissed me back."

"Marry her, Liam," she ordered, snapping the lace fan closed. "As soon as you can. Tomorrow if possible."

"She'd not have me," he said, rather dazedly.

"Doona be ridiculous, any woman would have you." Mary regarded him curiously over a sip of her tea.

"Not her. She has secrets, painful ones. She avoids me, I think. But sometimes . . . she looks at me like . . ." Like she desired him. Like she understood him.

"Every woman has her secrets." With an impatient sigh, Mary set her teacup next to his none too gently and rapped him on the knuckles with her closed fan to get his attention. "It *still* shocks me that this comes as a surprise to most men, adorable idiots that ye are, but doona ye ken a woman who is not after you for yer title and yer fortune needs to be wooed?"

"Wooed?" The word tasted as foreign in his mouth as the idea was to his thoughts. "Ye mean, gifts and jewelry—"

"Nay, dammit." She pressed a beleaguered and dramatic hand to her forehead. "The most precious thing you can give a woman, a *worthy* woman, is intimacy, time, truth, safety, and friendship."

"Friendship?" He lifted his own hand to his temple, pressing at the place where his head was starting to pound.

"Talk to her. *Know* her and let her know ye, as well. Intimacy is not only in the bedroom, ye know. To love each other, ye must first *like* each other. Do ye like her?"

Liam considered that. He liked the way she treated and talked with his children. He liked the way that, for such a practical woman, she was rather idealistic. He liked the way she ate, with as much relish as manners. He liked how she did her hair and the way she wrinkled her nose, the books she read, even the ones he didn't understand. He liked that he could spill his secrets to her in the dark, and she never shamed him. That she treated him with sympathy that never smacked of pity.

He liked what his heart did when he heard the clip of her shoes against the floors of his keep. In fact, he couldn't think of one thing that he *didn't* like about her.

Her secrets, he supposed. Whatever put the shadows behind her eyes and caused her to fear him.

"Aye," he admitted. "I like her."

"Then ye must go to her, claim her, right away." She stood, as though ready to shoo him from her house.

"Ye make it sound so easy." He stood as well, feeling large and encumbered in her dainty room.

"Nothing worthwhile is easy," she quipped. "Ye helped to dismantle the East India Company. Ye've stormed castles and replaced entire regimes. Should she resist ye, lay siege to her defenses and scale her walls, *Lieutenant Colonel,* it's not as if ye doona ken how to do that."

That drew a dry sound of amusement from him. "I canna go *now,* I have a weeklong summit to reside over here in Dingwall. It's an obligation to my kin and clan I canna ignore."

"Then ye have a week to figure out how ye're going to win her heart, Laird Mackenzie, I suggest ye use it wisely."

Russell had been right about the rain, Mena thought as she stood on the roof of Ravencroft Keep's northwest parapet and surveyed the festivities below her. The chilly October breeze whispered of moisture, but not a drop had fallen.

The Mackenzie laird had returned from Dingwall two days ago and, it seemed, had brought most of the Highlands home with him for the Samhain celebration. Mena hadn't the opportunity to see or speak to Ravencroft alone as he was always surrounded by guests or on some errand or another. Today he'd taken the children and the visiting lairds Monroe and Fraser with their families to the village of Fearnloch, leaving Mena to her own devices.

She'd spent the day helping poor harried Jani and the housekeeper, Mrs. Grady, with menial tasks to ease the burden of the household staff. Soon, though, she found herself more in the way than accommodating, and she sought a moment of solitude before the commencement of the evening's revelry.

Ravencroft had come alive with Highlanders, rustic and noble alike. Many of them slept indoors in any one of the lavish guest rooms, but more still pitched grand and colorful tents on the grounds, heating them with pungent peat fires and enough Scotch and ale to drown an entire ship of pirates.

Mena had Jani familiarize her with the plaids and flags proudly displayed on the tents and tartans of the people. Guests from the neighboring MacDonnell and MacBean clans feasted with the MacKinnon of Skye and the Mac-Neil of the Outer Hebrides. Campbells threaded among them, as did a few Ross and Frasier clansmen, as well.

Mena didn't own a Halloween costume, but she did don her black cloak with the fox-fur collar for the occasion, and settled it over her finest green silk dress.

With its looming red stone grandeur, extensive grounds, and spires that pierced the gothic gray skies, Ravencroft Keep was the perfect setting for the macabre holiday. Though, from what Mena could see from her vantage, the costumed carousers were much too cheerful to be considered ghoulish in the least.

Mena had been afraid of heights, once upon a time, but locked away in her tiny white room in Belle Glen, she'd gained more than a passing appreciation for the open sky. She'd yearned for it in the cruel hours of darkness. During times she'd been confined alone for the entirety of the day, she'd watched the sun move a tiny circle across the floor from a little porthole window that was too high to see out of. Those days she'd yearned for the beauty of a sunset, or a glimpse of a moonlit night.

Now Mena breathed in the fragrant evening air as she watched the sun dip below the trees and the isles beyond, wishing she could be the raven she'd spied soaring over the fires that dotted the autumn terrain of Wester Ross. Starting in the east, the sky had become black, the closest stars appearing as pinpricks on the eternal canvas of the Highland firmament. As she followed the arc of the dusky sky to the west, Mena observed the ribbon of azure still illuminating the horizon above the shadow of the Hebrides. The stars had only become a suggestion of light and Mena planned on remaining until the night sky shimmered with constellations as she'd only seen it do here in the Highlands.

The trees and stones of the keep sheltered those below from the biting wind, but where she stood on the balustrade, it teased wisps of her hair and the hem of her dress. Feeling silly and fanciful, Mena held open the seams of her cloak and let the breezes billow it out from her spread arms, imagining that she truly had wings.

The bitter chill sent a delicious thrill through her, and Mena let out a delighted gasp as she looked below her, the dizzying height intensifying her reckless sensation of freedom. If her body couldn't fly, at least her soul might, and she released it into the wind with a contented sigh.

Once the cold turned from invigorating to uncomfortable, she lowered herself to perch on the waist-high stone wall and play voyeur to the night.

The crash of the heavy tower door against the stone wall nearly shocked her out of her skin, and she almost flung herself backward onto the parapet's walkway.

Mena's heart threatened to leap out of her chest as Ravencroft stood framed by the stone arch, his shoulders heaving as though he'd run a great distance. He looked like some pagan deity, long ebony hair loose around his wide shoulders, but for two braids swinging from right above his temple. A linen shirt, dark vest, and kilt peeked from where his own cloak parted.

Onyx eyes gleamed at her, lit from below by the growing number of fires. His heavy boots made gravelly sounds as he stalked closer.

She should stand and curtsy, or turn and flee, but the abject relief in his eyes held her quite transfixed.

"I saw yer shadow on the roof," he said as though out of breath. "Holding yer cloak out like ye meant to fly away, and I thought—"

Mena gasped and berated herself for her utter stupidity. She hadn't expected anyone to see her up here as the eastern sky behind her was dark. Apparently she'd still cast some sort of shadow, and anyone looking up at just the right moment might be worried that she'd fall from the roof.

Or jump, as the previous Lady Ravencroft had done.

Liam was out of breath now because he'd raced from the grounds below up to the towers to save her life.

"My Laird Ravencroft, I'm so very sorry," she began earnestly. "I didn't at all mean to cause you distress, you must believe me . . . I would never . . . that is . . . I wasn't thinking . . ."

He stopped an arm's length from where she sat, twisting to face him. Shadows played off his flexing jaw as his gaze touched her from the top of her hair all the way down to the hem of her skirts as they rippled beneath her swinging feet from where she perched.

"Please forgive me," she begged, searching his savage features for a sense of how angry she'd made him.

To her utter astonishment, his expression relaxed and his shoulders sagged, though the intensity never left his dark eyes.

"Lass, I'd forgive ye just about anything in that dress."

Flushing, Mena pulled the edges of her cloak around her, sinking her neck into the fur collar and covering the deep cleft of her décolletage.

The laird frowned, but said nothing.

Unable to look at him and still maintain her breath, Mena turned back to the tableau beneath them, a pang of happiness tugging at her heart when she spied Andrew romping about the grounds with little Rune yapping at his heels.

"May I join ye?" Ravencroft murmured from beside her, his breath a warm puff of white against the growing chill of the evening.

"It's your castle," she replied. She wished he wouldn't, and yet she didn't want him to leave. The last time she'd been alone with him she'd allowed him the most illicit liberties. Liam Mackenzie turned her into someone who was not herself. Every moment in his presence was fraught with intensity and heart-stopping emotion.

Mena didn't watch as he kicked his leg over the wall, and then the other, settling in next to her close enough that her shoulder pressed against his arm. She'd have to scoot away from him in order to maintain a respectable distance, and though the rules of conduct dictated that she should, it would still be unaccountably rude.

Either way she couldn't win, and Mena had the distinct impression that he'd put her in that position on purpose.

Glancing at him sharply from under her lashes, she found she could not look away. What must it be like, she wondered, to sit atop such a grand castle and lord over all that was below him? Every soul in the village, every grain in the field, every beast in the pasture all relied upon his land, his will, his honor, and his word. No wonder Ravencroft surveyed the scene with a look of fierce possession, as stolid and stony as a gargoyle, and every bit as formidable.

"This must be how the world looked in the beginning," he observed in a voice as smooth as silk and hard as iron.

She knew exactly what he meant. What had life been

like when the pleasures of night and the seduction of fire could culminate in orgiastic revelry that wasn't impeded by the structures of society?

"Perhaps this is what it will look like at the end," she hypothesized, feeling strangely reckless as though the spirit of the holiday was somehow contagious.

"What *are* ye doing up here, Miss Lockhart?" he asked, without looking down at her. "Why are ye not with the others at the feast?"

Just as quickly as heat had abandoned her face, it crept back from beneath her cloak. "You'll think me ridiculous."

"Never." The sound escaped on an exhale of his, too soft to be a word, too deep to be a sigh.

"I find myself here often," she confessed. "One of my favorite things in the world is to watch day turn into night. First the brilliance of the sunset, then the quiet blues of twilight, and then this final moment." She tilted her head back to look above her, feeling the muscles in her throat slightly stretch in a pleasant way. "It's as though the sky disappears and some sort of heavenly curtain is pulled back, unveiling the stars. Some people find the night sky melancholy, but I've always thought of the stars as familiar as old friends, always right where they're supposed to be. It gives me a sense of the same, I think." Mena lowered her chin, and glanced to the side where Ravencroft stared at her neck with the oddest of expressions before he lifted his unreadable eyes to hers.

"I told you." She lowered her lashes, feeling self-conscious and very small next to him. "It's silly. Tedious, even."

"Nay, I ken just what ye mean, lass." Ravencroft leaned forward, his own neck arched to turn his face to the sky. "I feel as though I've been everywhere in this world. There were days at war, or on a ship, where I would think that maybe home was nothing more than a memory, or a dream. I would wake at night afraid that I'd forgotten where I hied from or who I truly was. I thought I'd lose Liam Mackenzie to the Demon Highlander. It was then I began to study the constellations."

"Did it help?" Mena wondered aloud.

He glanced down at her as though her question had pleased him. "Aye, it did. In a world where men paint the ground with blood, the stars gave me a reason to look up. They're a map when ye're lost, and points of light when all is dark. I ken why you think it makes them seem friendly."

"Yes," she agreed. "I suppose that they remind me that the world always turns. That things are constantly changing. This moment, every moment, whether good or terrible, will pass into oblivion and so I must live it. I must see it through. And, eventually, a new day will come again. Another chance for something better."

Mena thought his face, turned down as it was, half to the light, and the other half to shadow, should remind her that she conversed with the Demon Highlander, the dangerous man she'd promised to avoid as much as possible.

But something about the arrangement of his features belied any of her reservations. His lips seemed fuller, drawn out of their hard line into something resembling a lazy half-smile. The tilt of his deep-set eyes and angle of the brow above wasn't stern or scowling, as usual, but relaxed and at ease and, if her gaze didn't deceive her, perhaps a bit unsure or—dare she think it?—shy.

He seemed younger like this, with his hair loose and his shoulders free of their customary tension. Mena thought that when he smiled, he must be the most handsome man God had ever molded of this earth.

She swallowed, doing her best to ignore the warmth beginning to glow deep in her belly, and lower.

"I think I'd be more comfortable in perpetual darkness," he murmured.

"Why?"

His shoulders heaved with a weighty breath, pressing

deeper against hers. "Do ye believe that the things we've done in the dark will be answered for in the light of day?"

"I certainly hope so." She nodded.

He searched her face then, lifting a hand to draw away a tendril of hair the breeze had blown across her cheek. "Perhaps because ye have a clear conscience."

"I don't, I assure you." She turned away from his fingers, unable to bear the sweet memory of his skin against hers. Unwilling to give words to the message in his eyes.

He dropped his hand to his lap. "Perhaps, then, because ye hope that someone answer for their crimes against ye."

Tears burned behind her eyes, and Mena dipped her chin against her chest. It was the darkest desire in her heart. That her husband answer for all the times he'd caused her terror and pain.

How had he guessed?

"Because," he answered gently, alarming her with the discovery she'd spoken the question out loud. "I ken what it's like to fear the darkness, Mena, and to hate the man who beat that fear into me."

Mena felt the rough pads of his fingers drift over her down-turned cheek. When he reached her chin, he gripped it softly between his thumb and forefinger, lifting her face toward his.

"I find myself in the middle of a dance I doona ken the steps to," he admitted, his eyes gilded by an unholy light as they searched hers for something she could not give him. "When ye're near me, I doona know what to say or how to act. I canna figure what platitudes to give ye. I never learned the soft words that would reach through the walls that ye've built around yer heart."

Though she didn't allow herself to blink, Mena could still feel tears gathering in her lashes. She needed him to stop. She should pull away. But God help her, she couldn't tear her gaze from the abject beauty of his face.

"I doona know which urge to act upon and which to

suppress, but I want ye with a strength that even the gods canna understand . . . even though I canna always tell if it's fear or desire I see reflected in yer eyes."

Because it was both, Mena knew. Fear of him. Fear of the desire she felt for him. Of the things she wanted to do again in the dark.

"It was written in those stars that we meet." His voice gathered a tender fervency that unstitched something from inside Mena's soul. "We are bound in some inescapable way, thee and me. I've known it since I first laid eyes on ye in *that* dress."

Mena wanted to deny it. To shake her head and make him stop whatever it was he was about to say. But she knew she could not. Though her heart threatened to gallop away, her body was frozen in place. A captive of his warm, gentle hand.

"Don't." She whispered a tortured plea as she wrapped her fingers around his wrist, meaning to push his hand away. "It's impossible." She was married. She was a fugitive.

She was unworthy of a man such as this.

"It's impossible to deny it, lass." He smiled down at her, and Mena suddenly knew that one could feel the warm rays of the sun even in the dark of night. "Try as ye will to resist me, I'm after ye, Mena, and I willna claim ye until ye yield. But I'll not stop until every last one of yer defenses are in ashes at my feet."

Down below, a large horn blared loud and long enough to break the spell he'd cast over her.

"They're calling for me, lass." Before she could move, he brushed his lips against hers, then turned over the wall and leaped to his feet. "Ye will be, too, before I'm done with ye."

CHAPTER SIXTEEN

Twin bonfires roared and crackled amidst the festival grounds, blazing as high as a two-story London row house and half as wide. Mena sipped on the spiced cider she'd mixed with Scotch and hoped no one had noticed. Highlanders seemed very adamantly against blending their Scotch with nectars and such, but she hadn't the constitution yet to sip it alone, though she was trying to build to it.

A crowd of several hundred guests circled the twin infernos as gamekeepers and farmers drove their most prized livestock between the fires to purify and bless herds through winter. Bones of the cows, pigs, and various fowl used to feed so many were dried, kissed, blessed, and tossed into the flames, lending the air a succulent aroma. If Mena hadn't already been full to sick from her copious meal, her mouth would have watered.

"You are in luck, Miss Mena, they are about to start the ritual." Jani appeared at her elbow, dressed this evening as a glittering gold maharaja. His turban shimmered with gems, the largest in the center of the headdress, from which a tall peacock feather sprouted.

"Jani, don't you look regal?" Mena exclaimed.

His dusky skin glowed with pleasure. "You are kind, Miss Mena, but I am muted next to your beautiful self."

"Go on, you." She elbowed him good-naturedly and went back to watching the increasingly foreign ceremony. "What ritual is this, exactly? I've never seen the like."

Jani's black eyes reflected the light of the bonfire, turning a tiger gold. "Even in this modern age, Highlanders are superstitious people. The harsh Scottish winters are especially dangerous for livestock, and this ritual the Mackenzie is about to perform will petition the gods to protect the cattle and sheep."

"I see," she breathed, before the ability to speak was stolen from her.

A lone pipe blared, silencing the crowd with its piercing, mystical song. Then the Mackenzie Laird appeared between the fires, and a reverent murmur weaved through the night.

Here stood her ancient barbarian. The one from the canvas in the hall. Clad in nothing but his kilt and boots, Liam Mackenzie radiated primitive, elemental power. His arms and torso were packed with even more muscle than Mena had remembered, and gleamed like tawny velvet in the firelight.

Something dark and unbidden unfurled in Mena's body, tightening her features with a primal hunger and softening her feminine muscles to welcome him. She'd fought the very idea when he'd warned her of his impossible intentions on the roof. But looking at him as he was now, the incarnation of an ancient Druid warrior, she couldn't remember any impediment to his absolute possession of her.

The fire illuminated black and blue runes adorning his chest and arms starting just beneath his rib cage and knotting over and around his nipples, his shoulders, his throat, and finely crawling up his sculpted jaw.

Cuffs of solid gold circled above the swells of his biceps, his wrists, and his neck. His hair ruffled in the breezes, but as close to the flames as he stood, there was no conceivable way he marked the chill of the evening. The ebony of his unbound hair fell to the middle of his back and matched the shadow stubbling his jaw. The two braids over his shoulder teased at his beruned collarbone.

Surveying his people with unabashed pride and satisfaction, Liam found her where she stood at the crowd's periphery. The look he sent her was so full of sensual promise, Mena's body released a wet flood of thigh-clenching arousal.

How could he provoke her with just a look? How on earth was she to ever resist such temptation?

Because you must, she admonished herself.

Whatever he read on her features inspired a glance of such victorious self-satisfaction on his face, she suddenly wanted to throw something at him.

Something like herself, perhaps.

Jani waved to him, oblivious to their unspoken interaction. "The laird has only missed one Samhain since his father died," he informed her, "and on that year, there was blight on the cattle. So the people demand that every year he is here for the ritual."

Mena tore her gaze away from the overwhelming sight that was the Laird of the Mackenzie clan. "You don't really believe that driving a few cattle through two bonfires and saying a spell has anything to do with the survival of the livestock herds, do you?" she asked skeptically.

Jani shrugged. "Who is to say, Miss Mena? The story is that Liam Mackenzie, his father, and all Lairds of the Mackenzie of Wester Ross are descended from an ancient royal Pictish line that mingled with invaders from the north. It is said they carry the blood of the Lachlan berserker in their veins."

"Berserker?" Mena queried.

"Yes, a mythic Nordic warrior who gains the strength of ten men and incomparable ferocity at the sight of blood." He sent her a meaningful glance. "Sound familiar?"

"I thought it was said he was possessed of a *Brollachan*."

Jani gave another of his very quick shrugs. "Highlanders say lots of things. Telling stories is one of their favorite pastimes."

She glanced back at the laird, who lifted his face to the stars, as did his congregation, and sang in a surprisingly lovely baritone to the sky in that lyrical language Mena didn't understand. His delicious brogue lent such a potent sensuality to the prayer that he could very well be seducing a lover rather than symbolically blessing herds of livestock.

Mena was struck not just by his masculine beauty, but also by the beauty of his people gathered around, their faces warm with whisky, ale, and rapture as they repeated parts of the lovely verses, cheering as each herder finished driving his choice few symbolic animals between the fires to finish the blessing.

The rite wasn't long, formal, or ponderous as the mild Protestant services she'd attended growing up had been, and before she knew it, the spell was over. A bagpipe blared, and then another, until four pipers placed at the north, south, east, and western points of the circle lifted their wailing tunes in perfect synchronization.

A young child toddled too close to one of the bonfires, and Ravencroft swept her up and flung her high before settling her giggling body on his massive shoulders. He patiently ignored her playful tugs on his braids as, one by one, middle-aged or wizened women stepped forward to light torches in the fire before leading entire families in their wake.

"What are they doing now?" Mena asked Jani.

Jani gestured to the older women. "The reigning matriarch of each family must take the ritual fire home to her hearth. If their house is close, then she'll take it to the village tonight. If not, she'll take it to the tent and tend the coals until they travel safely home and ignite in their own dark fireplace. The Druid-blessed Samhain fire keeps them safe over the coming winter."

"How lovely," Mena murmured, as she marveled at how quickly the crowd began to disperse, each family following their matriarch back to where she would take the blessed flame.

She noted that the young father of the errant child affixed to Liam's shoulders had wound his way to his laird. Liam tossed the little one up, eliciting one last squeal of delight, before he settled her back in the young man's grateful arms. The men exchanged what Mena imagined to be paternal smiles and words of exasperation over mischievous young daughters before they locked forearms in a traditional show of kinship.

An emotion gathered in Mena's throat in the form of a lump that refused to be swallowed. Did Ravencroft want more babies? Would he like another chance to raise children from the beginning? Were he ever to marry again, he was most definitely virile enough to father many sweet, dark-haired little ones.

Little ones she could never have.

Frustrated tears welled in her eyes. *It didn't matter,* she reminded herself firmly. None of it mattered, as a relationship between them was as unattainable as the stars. She knew it, and eventually, he would as well.

Miserably, she watched him move through the throngs of his clan. Women doted on him, using any excuse to touch his exposed skin the color of his own famous whisky. She could see from her vantage that though some people feared him, the women desired him, and the men respected him. Be he the *Brollachan* or the berserker, his people flourished beneath his leadership, and they *loved* him for it. How could he not know that?

A man like him would be easy to love.

Once the word amalgamated out of the universal impossibilities of the future and the terrifying rifts of the past, Mena realized that she was utterly lost.

She hadn't *fallen* in love with Liam Mackenzie. No, she'd drifted into it in subtle shifts. The moment they'd met had been like the whisper of a storm kissing a hot, humid day with a blessed chill. The promise of something dark and exciting gathered on the horizon, and Mena had watched that storm rumble closer with every instant they'd spent together. Every time she'd banked the fires that blazed in his eyes. Every time he'd ignited heat into her cold heart. He'd chipped a bit of her resistance away and replaced it with the force of his raw, unbridled passion. He shared with her what men rarely did, and he unveiled the darkest parts of himself for her to see. Illuminating them not only to her eyes, but to his own and his children's in an attempt to try and be better. He wanted her to understand him more so that she feared him less.

And Mena loved him for it.

She *loved* him.

Dear God, what did she do now?

"Miss Lockhart! Jani!" An animated cry broke Mena away from her astonished revelation as she felt Jani tense beside her.

Rhianna raced up the subtle hill toward them, draped in the costume of a Grecian goddess. The effect was slightly ruined by her thick lamb's-wool wrap, but in frigid weather such as this, it couldn't be helped. Flanked by two equally red-faced and exuberant girls, she nearly bowled over Jani, but he stopped her just in time with two steadying hands on either arm.

The moment she was stable, he dropped his hands to curl them into fists at his sides.

"Whit like, Jani?" The younger girls giggled, casting not-so-subtle coquettish looks at the young Hindu. Mena had to admit, Jani was an exotically handsome young man, and it broke her heart that he only had eyes for her oblivious charge. Especially when she noted that *he* caught the notice of many a lass.

"Are ye all right, Miss Lockhart? Ye look like ye're about to cry," Rhianna observed with her usual lack of tact, though her dark eyes were filled with concern.

"Just a bit of ash from the fires drifted over," Mena lied as she greeted Rhianna's friends, remembering their names as Liza and Kayleigh, though she couldn't recall which was which. "What's this, then?" She gestured to the charred remains of what she'd surmised to be an apple peel in the girl's hands.

"It's a *C,* Miss Lockhart, and *C* is for Campbell." The sad-looking apple peel was shoved beneath her nose for inspection, and it did, indeed, seem to have been singed into the shape of a *C*. Though there was a suspicious hook at the bottom of the peel that could have been a *J* if reversed.

Rhianna had explained earlier that a long-standing Samhain tradition of divination claimed that if a woman were to peel an apple, then stand with her back to the ceremonial bonfires and throw the peel over her shoulder into the flames, said peel would spell out the first letter of her future husband's name.

"Campbell, indeed?" Mena smiled into Rhianna's glowing features and glanced at Jani, who scowled at the peel as though it were his enemy.

"As in *Kevin* Campbell," the brunette taunted in a sing-song voice.

"Nay, Rhianna, it wouldna be Kevin Campbell," the redhead—Mena thought *she* was Kayleigh—argued. "The letter only pertains to the first name of your husband, surnames doona count."

Rhianna pouted at her friend. "But there's no way an apple peel can spell out the letter *K*!" she protested loudly.

"Exceptions have to be made, isna that right, Miss Lockhart?"

Three sets of expectant young eyes turned on her and Mena couldn't help but laugh out loud, abruptly grateful for the distraction. "I would imagine that in such a case, an exception could be made. Else it would make many an unfortunate man with a name starting with the letter *K* very lonely, indeed."

"Right!" With her raven hair glittering in the firelight, Rhianna triumphantly held the charred peel up as if it were a trophy of war, and whooped like a savage.

"What about ye, Miss Lockhart?" the brunette, who must then be Liza, asked shyly. "What did yer apple peel say? Mine was an *N . . .* or an *S,* I suppose."

Mena forced a laugh. "I'm much too old for such games, and I'm not of a mind to be married."

Because she already was, and it had been a nightmare.

"It doesna matter!" Rhianna insisted, her dark eyes glittering with mischief. "It's not like you *have* to marry. The apple peel just tells who ye *would* marry if ye were *of a mind.*" She repeated her words with a mocking giggle.

"Really, I—"

"Oh, come on, Miss Lockhart!" they all begged, pulling at her sleeves and half dragging her toward the fires.

"Just try it once!"

"It'll be fun!"

"Please?"

Feeling rather harassed, yet enjoying the barrage of attention from energetic young women, Mena shrugged. What harm could it do?

She glanced at Jani who still studied the apple peel with a fierce expression. Though when he turned back to her, he summoned a smile that didn't quite reach his eyes.

Mena reached out and gave his hand one soft squeeze.

"Andrew!" Rhianna bellowed in a rather unladylike fashion across the fires to her brother, who lingered with

Rune by the handsome tables laden with food. "Bob an apple for Miss Lockhart!"

Dark hair already gleaming with moisture, Andrew flashed a rare smile, tossed whatever he'd been snacking on to Rune, and lustily dove into the dark liquid of the nearby barrel face-first. His skinny legs kicked comically in his struggle, and even the solemn Jani laughed at his antics.

After emerging victorious, he slicked his hair back once more, and pilfered a knife from the tables. Simultaneously peeling and walking, Andrew presented her with a brilliant smile and the smooth red flesh of an autumn apple. "Ye have to throw it over yer shoulder and doona look until it starts to burn, or it willna work," he whispered.

"Got it." Mena winked and turned her back to the fire and was ready to throw the peel behind her.

"Wait!" Rhianna stopped her. "We have to say the spell over it first."

All the youngsters nodded in solemn agreement.

"The spell?" Mena echoed.

To the Maiden Goddess of the land
The Crone please bless with divine hand
From the Mother's fruit I hold
My future soul mate's name is told.

Each of the girls' voices blended to the verse beautifully and Mena figured that it should count for her peel. She backed closer to the fire until its searing warmth glowed through the back of her dress. Closing her eyes, she flicked the peel over her shoulder and was rewarded with a hiss.

When her eyes opened, all those who had previously been in front of her had vanished. Turning, she found them bent as close as they dared to read her theoretical fortune.

"Look! It's a *C* like mine!" Rhianna pulled her close.

As it singed and cooked, the peel did seem to be curling in upon itself.

"That's not a *C,* look at that corner there!" Kayleigh pointed to where a flaw in the corner of the peel caused it to jut out, making a specific point. "It seems more like an *L* to me."

"Let me look," Andrew demanded, leaning closer and inspecting it with a scrupulous eye.

Mena's heart pounded audibly when he turned to her with a look of solemn authentication. "Most definitely an *L,*" he confirmed.

The girls giggled and began to make lists of *L* names.

"Lucas or Lionel," Kayleigh suggested.

"Aye," Rhianna agreed vehemently, ticking off names on her fingers. "Or Lawrence, Logan, Lucius—"

"Liam," Andrew offered quietly.

Mena froze as the party almost simultaneously made the connection, and their eyes searched each other's, trying wordlessly to surmise what their reaction should be. The laird and the governess? Dare someone even suggest it?

After a breathless moment, Andrew's face melted into the warmest smile she'd ever seen and Mena's heart broke into gossamer pieces. She swallowed the shards and forced a smile.

"Liam is short for William, dear," she reminded brightly. "I don't imagine that counts."

"Besides, she needs the name of a Brit," the all-knowing Kayleigh interjected.

They all bent back over the apple peel, though something in Andrew's eyes told Mena that he wasn't convinced.

As people filtered out of the grounds, the sounds of horses and carts and the chatter of excitable children and exhausted parents began to dwindle. Liam turned to look for his family. After only a moment of searching firelit faces, he chuckled a little at the sight of six bent arses huddled in a neat little row around the base of the north bonfire. One particular bottom caught his attention, sheathed in a full green skirt and deliciously plumper than the others displayed. Mena's shapely legs were longer than the children's and Jani's. This pushed her round derriere higher, made it more tantalizingly accessible.

Liam silently ambled up to them until he found himself directly behind the object of his desire. If he bent his knees just a little, and pressed his pelvis forward, his erection would be nestled in the sweet cleft. Shaking his head, he stepped back, reminding himself it wouldn't do to turn into a raging tornado of primal lust in front of his clan, his children, and the visiting Highland nobles.

Animated giggles erupted from the girls and they were talking softly among themselves, observing some undetermined spot on the fire.

"What's this, then?" he asked, keeping his voice deceptively light.

Six bodies simultaneously sprang around in surprise, but the line didn't break. Mena wouldn't meet his eyes, but kept her horrified gaze locked on his bare chest.

"Father! We were just—" Rhianna was cut off by her brother.

"We were just playing a silly *girl's* game." Andrew shot his sister a quelling look and Liam watched as confusion and then epiphany played across his daughter's features. Her gaze flew to him and then bounced to Miss Lockhart, who had still yet to move.

"Whit like, Laird Mackenzie?" Rhianna's friends chorused with matching curtsies.

"Good evening, lassies." He gently smiled down at them. "The hour is late, I'm sure that yer families are looking for ye now."

The pleasantly blank looks on their faces told him that

they were not privy to the private thoughts of his children and therefore would be of no use to him.

They left with pleasant *fare-ye-well*s after a quick exchange of hugs and promises with Rhianna.

"Father, we were just tossing apple peels," Rhianna said brightly, taking his arm and maneuvering around the still-frozen Miss Lockhart. "My husband's initial is a *C.* Look!" She pointed to the fire and he saw a smoldering apple peel perilously close to turning to ash.

He squinted into the fire and pretended to study the apple peel with a frown. "Now I know the initial of the man that I'm going to murder."

Rhianna planted her hands on her hips. "Father!"

"But if I'm no' mistaken, this peel more closely resembles an *L* than a *C.*" He gestured to the point at the corner.

His children exchanged excited glances and then huddled close to him, making a big display out of studying the peel for themselves.

"Hmmmm," was all Rhianna replied with an exaggerated nod. "So it does."

"What do ye think, Miss Lockhart?" He turned to include her in their study, but her retreating form was out of earshot as she swiftly walked toward the growing city of tents on the far end of the grounds.

"She thought that it looked like an *L,* too." Andrew murmured seriously, squinting after his governess.

"There ye have it, then." Liam offered his arm to Rhianna and put a hand on his son's shoulder, wondering at their strange and guilty behavior. "What do ye say that we put ye two miscreants to bed? 'Tis almost time for the in-between masquerade."

"Canna I stay up for it this time?" Rhianna begged. "*Please,* Father, I'm seventeen, isna that old enough?"

Liam shook his head. "Next year, *nighean,*" he promised. "Now come with me."

He nodded to Jani and led his children toward the keep,

noting that his brother Gavin ambled in the direction of the tables where Mena had escaped to seek the respectable company of Mrs. Grady.

All's fair in love and war, his brother's voice taunted.

A dark knowledge drifted to him from where his demon stirred. Tonight he would begin the most important battle he'd ever waged.

The one for Mena's heart.

CHAPTER SEVENTEEN

After the matriarchs carried the flames to their hearths, Mena had thought the evening's festivities over.

Oh, how wrong she'd been.

She was wrong about a lot of things, wasn't she? Ravencroft was supposed to have been a place of quiet escape, not of sensual awakening. The laird was supposed to have been a retired old officer, not this commanding, virile mountain of walking sin and temptation.

And whatever was in her new glass was supposed to have been cider, though she had a sneaking suspicion it was anything but.

Torches wended their way through the night, and once they were left in their respective places, the grown men and women of Wester Ross emerged from their tents, tenements, manors, and mires and congregated in the city of fine canvas shelters that had sprung up on the western hill of the Ravencroft estate.

"The children are abed, safe from the in-between. Now the *real* festival begins!" Gavin St. James, Earl of Thorne, loped to catch up with her, falling into easy step with his long stride as Mena wandered to investigate the gathering. "What do ye make of that, English?"

He swept his arm to encompass the ribbons, banners, and all forms of bohemian decoration that ornamented the rather Gypsy-like dwellings which were arranged in a circle stacked about five or so deep. In the center of the large circle was another bonfire. Though not as big as the ones that smoldered next to Ravencroft Keep, the fires were accompanied by strategically placed torches to lend a darker, more intimate glow to the night's festivities.

"What are they doing?" Mena queried. "What is the in-between?" A brightly played fiddle-and-flute melody reached across the night to her and the accompanying drums called out to her spirit until her feet ached to dance.

Gavin swiped a mask from the table lorded over by Mrs. Grady, and tied it over his handsome features, smiling as he did so. His voice took on a bardish eeriness as he explained. "Before the Christians came, we Scots had two halves to the year, the light half and the dark half. The light half belongs to the living. The dark half belongs to the dead and the denizens of the Other World."

"Oh?" Mena glanced around her, watching people in black cloaks and painted skin affix dark masks to their faces. Gowns fit for a London ball and simple homespun dresses alike were rendered exotic by hip scarves and outlandish jewelry. "Let me guess, Samhain marks the dark half of the year."

Strains of strange pipes and drums began a dark rhythmic reel with no distinguishable beginning or end. More ale, Scotch, and other spirits flowed and lent the festival a reckless sort of apocalyptic frenzy. Some ladies had relieved themselves of their bodices altogether and danced around the fire with their chemises hanging from their shoulders, barely covering their unbound breasts.

No one seemed necessarily scandalized, so Mena decided not to be, either. The matching black masks that everyone wore lent a certain amount of anonymity to the occasion, and thereby some sort of wicked consent to such outlandish behavior.

"Clever lass," Gavin crooned, magically appropriating two more glasses of cider, one of which he traded with the nearly empty one in her hand. "Samhain literally means 'summer's end.' Tomorrow, November first, is our traditional New Year. We're both leery and respectful of borders and transitions here in the Highlands. Bridges, clan boundaries, crossroads, thresholds, these are our holy places. Places where those of the Other World tend to linger. Likewise twilight, dawn, Samhain, and Beltaine, the hinges of the year, are our most mystical and often most precarious times."

Mena accepted the mask he handed her, toying with the ribbons. "You celebrate these times because you fear them?" she assessed.

"Exactly that." He grinned, the effect turned a bit ghoulish by the black mask above his sensual lips. "Come midnight, we turn ourselves into that which we fear and we drink and dance and philander like there is no tomorrow. We do so to welcome the ghosts, the demons, the faerie, and the witches to cavort with us, in hopes they doona turn their magic against us when they are most powerful. *This* is the time of the *in-between*."

A shiver of delicious anticipation slid through Mena as crofters, farmers, ranchers, milkmaids, land owners, and lairds all became black-masked apparitions of the mysterious Scottish "Other World." That place where all blessing and all misfortune had its genesis, and therefore the devil could take the consequences of this night.

Warm from the dubious contents of her cider, Mena gave in to the giddy, reckless spirit that seemed to ripple through the crowd, and allowed Gavin to help her affix her mask to her eyes.

"Do ye know any reels, lass?" Gavin queried as they

reached the edge of the circle of revelers who'd begun to dance around the bonfire.

Mena grinned. "Do I know any reels?" she scoffed, tapping her toes along with the quick and merry music. "*Please,* I'm from Hampshire. We invented the reel."

"I thought ye said ye were from Dorset," a masked merrymaker interceded; the red beard and jowly smile identified him unmistakably as the steward, Russell.

Mena almost dropped her tankard of cider, blanching at her mistake. "That's right, I did," she breathed, groping for a way to recover.

A busty young woman twirled from the arms of her overenthusiastic partner, stumbling into Gavin and causing his drink to splash onto his shirt. Giggling a slew of blurry apologies, she ran her hands down the vest covering his muscled torso, and trailed a brazen finger along the belt of his sporran, slung low on his kilted waist.

"All's forgiven, lass, believe ye me," Gavin murmured with a silken intonation full of unmistakable innuendo.

"Come find me if ye change yer mind." She nearly sang the invitation. "I'll make reparations to ye." She kissed him full on the mouth just as she accepted the hand of her unsteady partner and let him swing her away, leaving Russell and Gavin chuckling and Mena dumbstruck.

"I do believe she just propositioned you," Mena marveled.

"I do believe ye're right." Russell laughed merrily.

"And kissed you, in front of her husband and everything!" she exclaimed. "I'm astonished that he didn't call you out."

Gavin's laughter mingled with Russell's, creating a warm, masculine sound. "Och, lass, that's not her husband, he's over there." He gestured with his drink to the edge of the woods, where a short but wide fair-haired man had a tall woman against a tree, feasting upon her neck like a creature out of one of Andrew's penny dreadfuls.

"Goodness," was all Mena could think to say.

"Doona worry, lass." Gavin leaned down to murmur in her ear, eliciting a pleasant chill that raced along her skin. "No one remembers they're married on Samhain, and Beltaine is even worse."

"Gods bless that decadent fertility holiday." Russell crowed lustily and lifted his glass, and Gavin met it with a merry cheer of *slàinte mhath*.

For lack of else to do, Mena touched her glass to theirs and drank deeply, though the unhappy thought that the laird was not among the crowd dampened her spirits.

Masked and cloaked or not, he'd have been unmistakable, and his tall, broad form was conspicuously absent. Had he drifted into the woods with someone to take advantage of the bacchanalian holiday?

In-between some willing tart's thighs?

The unbidden thought drew her brows together with a surprising rush of displeasure.

"Would ye care to teach me a reel, English?" Gavin asked, his green eyes sparkling with mischief from behind his mask. "Be it Hampshire or Dorset or wherever ye hie from?"

Mena placed her hand in Gavin's outstretched one, thinking that his grip didn't elicit the thrills of awareness in the places that Liam's did, and so a dance with him was safer. Permissible. If everyone else was drinking, dancing, flirting, and . . . carrying on, why shouldn't she join in? The witching hour was almost upon them, and it seemed that the later the hour, the more steeped in debauchery the evening became.

And if no one remembered they were married on Samhain here in the Highlands, then neither would she.

Finding Mena in the teeming crowd of people wasn't at all difficult for Liam as he stalked the periphery of the dancing ghoulish Highlanders. She was unmistakable. Her glinting auburn hair had been swept up into a prim do, but was now in shambles. The front of the coiffure was still intact, but the rest tumbled down her back, nearly reaching her waist in a riot of loose glossy curls. Firelight glittered off the emerald satin ribbons threaded about the bit of black lace that passed for a bodice. Her alabaster breasts were splashed with golden light as she danced about the fire in a circle of forty, a man on each side vying for her attention as they taught her the steps.

His children had been right, she was a beautiful dancer.

She laughed gaily when she stumbled; her throaty, lilting sound of amusement evoking the lusty smiles of the men around her. Their hands went wherever they could as they helped her regain her footing.

Torturous black daggers twisted into his gut as he watched her enjoy the masculine attentions. Who'd have thought that his sweet, proper governess could move her body with all the sumptuous grace of a succubus?

The operative word here being *his*.

Hadn't he made it clear enough to her, to his clan, that he meant to claim her?

Eyes glued to her voluptuous shape, he prowled around the edges of the firelight, stalking her prancing, laughing form and watching the glow from the fire set her hair ablaze with color.

Gavin came up behind her and cut into the circle, grasping her hand and smiling at her as if he were perfectly enchanted. Mena's smile was just as brilliant as she turned her head to acknowledge him. The circle broke, and everyone grabbed a partner as the liveliest part of the reel had couples swirling about, their bodies only just managing to keep up with their flying feet.

His blood pounded through his ears and he had to crush the idea of murdering his brother and dragging her home by her luxurious hair.

This was the age of enlightenment, and the modern woman required a more deft seduction.

She needed to be wooed.

Lurking on the outskirts of the encampment, Liam snatched a mask from the table and fastened it to his eyes, letting it rest on the bridge of his nose as he made his way toward the musicians. A piper, a drummer, and two fiddlers played in the near darkness, careful not to get their instruments too close to the heat of the fire. Bending his head toward them, he gave a request for the next dance, and then bided his time until the reel wound down.

He still wore no cloak or shirt, proudly displaying the runes painted in the ancient wode on his skin. He felt like a Druid. Like the mythical Stag King about to claim his mate.

The crowd parted for him as the slow, writhing waltz emerged from the instruments, replacing the dizzy reel. His clan whispered their exclamations as he reached from behind Mena, and placed a hand on her shoulder.

She turned to him and her brilliant smile dimmed, then faltered.

"May I have this dance, *my* lady?" He bowed to her with all the deference of a disciple to his master.

Or mistress, in this case.

The infinitesimal widening of her eyes told him she didn't miss his not-so-subtle emphasis on the possessive word.

The increasingly drunk and cheerful crowd delighted in this turn of events, heckled and crowed, nudging her forward until she was nigh shoved into his arms.

"I don't see how I can refuse," she muttered.

Liam tensed as their bodies connected at many electrifying points, as did she. Every place his heated skin pressed against that infernal dress pulsed with awareness. The tips of her incredible breasts rubbed just beneath his chest. Her thighs pressed to his, the folds of his kilt meshing between her skirts.

Gripping her hand, he slid his other around her waist to span the small of her back and pressed her closer. They would have been hip to hip had he not been so tall, but still she fitted into his arms as if she'd been made for them. Her every generous curve and dramatic dip gave to the jutting angles and hard swells of his own body.

They began the rhythmic steps, their bodies moving seamlessly even though he could tell he'd put her more than a little off kilter. Her hand fluttered over the bare skin of his arm like the wings of a butterfly unwilling to land.

She swallowed a few nervous times before asking, "Shouldn't you don a shirt, my laird? This cannot be seemly."

A dark chuckle spilled from his throat. Always the proper lass, his charming Miss Philomena Lockhart. "Look around ye, woman," he challenged. "Dancing with a half-naked marquess is the least unseemly thing happening at this very moment."

As he led her in the slow, undulating dance, she glanced at the other couples, and then to the periphery of the tent city and even the woods beyond, where more hedonistic goings-on filled the shadows with writhing forms and suspect sounds.

Distracted, she stumbled, and Liam used the opportunity to stabilize her against his body, pulling her in tighter.

"What do you think you are doing?" she asked rather breathlessly, as she tried with little success to regain a respectful distance between them.

"Just being careful of your toes, lass," Liam replied with mock innocence, enjoying her discomfiture more than he should. "I'm a clumsy ogre sometimes and might cause ye harm."

"I know you would never hurt me," she said, covering her gaze with her long lashes.

"Ye think me a better dancer than I am," he jested.

"No." The word sounded like a lament, and she had yet to relax into his arms, despite his efforts to lighten the mood. "You think of *me* better than I am . . ." Her voice hitched, and she made as if to turn away. "Please excuse me, my laird, but I think it's time I retired for the evening."

Liam tightened his hold on her, refusing to let her escape. "Doona run away from me, Mena." The intimacy of her name on his tongue tasted sweeter than the finest Scotch. "Doona run from this. From us."

"There *is* no us," she hissed. "Now please, let me go without a scene, I beg you."

"Ye'll listen to me first, woman," he ordered. And for once, she complied, though her brows snapped together in a mutinous scowl that she directed right at his collarbone.

He gentled his words as he spoke from the heart. "I meant what I said, that I want Ravencroft to be yer sanctuary." He kept his voice and his hands gentle, though his grasp on her was unbreakable. "These stones. They will always be here. They are the clan. They have strength and integrity and have withstood the weapons of countless enemies. This is a place to build a life, Mena. And this is a night of new beginnings."

"There *are* no new beginnings for me," she said in such a soft voice, he had to strain to hear her. "It would be better for you, for us both, if you stopped this now, before you or anyone else gets hurt."

"I'll not stop until ye order me to, lass, and likely not even then," he admitted, pressing her harder against his aroused body. Letting her feel the pulse of his desire against her. "Tell me you doona want *this*. Tell me that ye didna feel this storm brewing between us since the very first day we met. That a part of ye didna know that this was an inevitability. I knew from the first time I saw ye that it was my destiny to claim ye here in the mists. And ye must take me, Mena . . . all of me. Make demands of yer own. Lay claim to the pleasure I'm willing to offer ye."

Her body quivered at his words. Her muscles clenched and seemed to swell inside of her dress. Her hand went from tentatively resting on his arm to gripping it desperately, as though to keep herself upright.

When her face lifted to his, her jade eyes shimmered with unshed tears. The bleak despair surprised and confounded him. Of any effect he'd anticipated his words to have, this was most definitely not it.

"I—I must confess to you something that might change your feelings." Threatening tears lent her voice an even lower register, and Liam spun her away from the dancers and the musicians to occupy the shadows next to a deserted table piled with two empty casks and countless empty tankards.

"There is nothing you can say—"

"There was a man," she said fervently. "Back in London, he—"

Liam pressed a single rough finger against the ripe ridges of her lips. "I know this," he soothed.

She turned her neck and twisted her face away from his touch. "No, you *don't*. You can't possibly know. He laid claim *already*, don't you understand? He hurt me, Liam, but he didn't force me. I let him. *I had to.* He did things to my body, to my soul, that changed me utterly."

Liam's demon rose within him, and he did his best to fight it back. "Give me his name, and I'll see his bloody, broken corpse delivered at yer feet."

She shook her head, taking a step back against the rage that must have gathered on his features. "No. *No,* don't you see? My only means of escape is to be other than I was. You *know* I have a secret. A terrible secret. You can't imagine the depth of it. The scope of it. You don't know who I am . . . what I've become. To tell you would be the end of me." Her last words escaped on a broken voice.

He reached for her, pulling her close. He wanted to erase every bad memory from her tortured thoughts. To ease every fear she had and smite all her dragons. He wanted to destroy this man who'd caused her such pain, such shame. If only she'd give him the means with which to do so.

Unable to go to war, as was his first instinct, he tried to give her some modicum of peace, instead. "I have secrets of my own, lass. Terrible ones. The kind that will damn me in the end. Let us leave our secrets to the past where they belong, and let us have this moment. Tomorrow is tomorrow, yesterday is yesterday. But tonight. Tonight is for us."

She searched his eyes as though his was a face she didn't recognize. "Don't you remember what we talked about that day in the chapel? The past isn't just the past. It stays with us, it makes us who we are. The sins we commit tonight we will have to answer for in the light of day."

He reached out, brushing his knuckles against the downy softness of her cheek, right below where her ugly bruise used to be. "They say the past is etched in stone," he murmured. "But ye've made me believe that it isn't. It's merely mist and mirrors, lass. Time passes and it becomes cloudy and unclear, and we can learn to leave our pain behind."

"But certain things linger, don't they?" she asked bitterly. "Like the acrid smell of peat smoke. The choices you make . . . there are so many that are impossible to escape."

"Ye told me once that evil can make itself seem light. Good can do the same." He leaned down to her, crowding her with his body against the table, pressing his cheek against hers as he gathered her close. "Ye make me yearn to be a good man. Let me show you how redemption can be found, even in the darkness, lass. Doona let tomorrow dawn, with all its dangerous unknowns without having let me love ye. For it canna be a sin beneath such friendly stars."

A tear dropped onto his bare skin, scalding him as it ran into the grooves of his chest. "Don't you understand what I'm trying to tell you? I'm not a *virgin*."

"Hush, lass," he soothed, pressing a kiss to her brow. "For I will share a confession of my own." He tilted his head down toward hers, his hot breath hitting her ear. "Neither am I."

Something about the obvious absurdity of his answer caused her a small hiccup of laughter. The thought of another man above Mena, inside of her, tightened every possessive instinct with such a force he thought he would snap beneath the weight. And yet . . .

"It changes nothing about the fact that I want ye," he told her. "I am not a man who holds his women to an impossible standard of chastity. That's not been our way out here in the Highlands. This is a place of handfasts and fishwives, we like to be certain of our desire before we bind our lives." He pulled away, using a few fingers to lift her unsteady chin up toward him.

"Look into my eyes and say that yer body does not call to mine. Tell me ye doona want me."

Her eyes shone brilliantly from her porcelain skin. "I—I can't."

"Then go to the north woods in five minutes. I'll wait for a few minutes, so we are not marked as leaving together, and then I'll find ye." He'd not only find her, he'd assault her with such pleasure, he'd wipe the memory of any other man from her mind.

Permanently.

CHAPTER EIGHTEEN

The Highland woods were a mystical place on any given night, but to Mena, Samhain had taken on a distinct dreamlike quality. An iridescent mist crept in from the sea and settled on the soft floor of the forest. The dense fog, turned an eerie shade of blue by the moonlight and some unexplainable force of nature, carried the scent of loamy brine and evergreens.

Mena's skirts displaced the vapor as she picked her way through the thickest parts of undergrowth, wondering just where she should pause.

And wait for him to come for her.

Dear Lord, what was she doing? It had been easy enough to look deep into Liam's dark eyes and to drown in the desire she saw burning there. To let the scent of him arouse and intoxicate her. Soap, whisky, autumn spices, and that masculine essence that was so unique to him. The one that told her she was safe.

Or that she wasn't.

Whatever it was, she knew that scent—her soul knew it—and she'd inhaled him deep, as though she could hold a memory in the most minuscule fibers of her body, like she could a breath.

How a man like him could seduce her so easily, so absolutely, still astounded her. He was an enigma. A man with a great deal of sense and the temper of a demon. A good man with a frightening past. A violent man with a wish for peace.

It was the paradox that drew her. He was a puzzle, a complication, someone whom she didn't understand and who was not at all like her but who, in his own way, arrived at the very same conclusions she did. About many things.

It worried her how incompatible they were.

It amazed her how perfect they were for each other.

Liam was a hero who'd come to hate himself for the sins of his past, and she was a refugee with a secret shame. How fitting that they should find redemption in each other's arms.

And passion, one couldn't forget that.

She'd never known a man with such passion. Riddled with so much fathomless need. She'd never been the object of such ardent, fervent attentions. Mena shivered more from the memory of his touch than the chill in the air. Some womanly instinct whispered that the passion he'd shown her thus far was merely the surface of a roiling volcano. The pressure was building, boiling, and churning the air between them until it'd reached the point of eruption. There was simply no containing it anymore.

No denying it. He was relentless, the Demon Highlander. He would not be resisted. He would not be deterred. And Mena was tired. In the absolute way that even her bones felt tired of supporting not just her body, but the weight she carried within her soul. Tired of pretending not to want him, tired of fearing what may occur in the morning. And above all, tired of being alone and afraid.

There was going to be a moment when she regretted the

decision to surrender to Liam Mackenzie. But tonight was not that night, and this moment was not that moment.

Mena stumbled upon a small clearing. As she drifted into it, soft mosses cushioned her boots, muffling the sound of her footfalls. A rock the length of a tall man leaned against two shorter, hulking stones in such a way, it reminded Mena of an altar that she'd seen in one of the Great Hall tapestries.

This was the place.

The moonlight slanted down on the tiny glen, lending its azure magic to the enchanted atmosphere of the site. Mena felt every bit the sacrificial virgin being led to meet her fate at the hands of some demanding god. The altar would be the perfect spot to make herself into an offering.

Virgin or not.

For if ever a pagan deity roamed the earth, he surely would take the form of Liam Mackenzie.

A ripple of anticipation seized her, followed by a chill of apprehension, and the mist seemed to respond, swirling as though scattered by a form much bigger and stronger than she. His name escaped her lips on a husky whisper, and she turned to greet Liam, her would-be lover.

Red eyes stared back at her from a face so hideously disfigured, that revulsion rose just as suddenly as terror. Both reactions closed her throat against a scream.

The Brollachan.

He wore no hood this time, no cloak to cover the horror that was his face. The creature had no nose to protect the two dark slits beneath the bridge between his eyes. A gleaming web of flesh dripped down the right side of his head. The left was oddly flat, as though he'd lain on one side for an eternity, and the skin had decided to melt in that direction after a time.

"How sad, lass, that ye didna heed my warning," the demon hissed from behind lips that couldn't really close, and thereby didn't deserve the distinction. "For now, I fear, it is too late.

The demon seized her, and the scream of fright turned into a cry of pain as he wrenched her around and yanked her neck to the side. He pressed her back against his chest, as he twisted one arm painfully behind her in a brutal hold.

"Scream all ye like, lass," he hissed, drawing another desperate sound from her throat as he pulled on her arm hard enough for pain to rip through her shoulder. "Yer screams are just what he wanted to hear tonight. And we should oblige the Demon Highlander, should we not?" An unmistakable metallic grind was as loud as any scream to her ear. Mena knew what that sound meant before she felt the kiss of his unsheathed dagger beneath her neck.

Frozen against the very hard, very real body of the specter who'd stalked the shadows of Ravencroft Keep since she'd arrived, an absurd question permeated the cold terror coursing through her.

What would a demon need with a blade?

Now that Mena knew he wanted her to scream, to summon Liam, she pressed her lips together. The hold he had on her arm wasn't immobilizing, but the dagger point he held beneath her throat certainly was.

She found it a mercy that she didn't have to look at him, that his horrific features wouldn't be the last thing she saw in this world.

"He's not coming for me," she lied, hating how small and frightened her voice made her sound. "You're mistaken. He remained at the festival."

It was the dark chuckle that confirmed to Mena who he was. Rough, caustic, full of rasping masculinity and devoid of any humor. Only three other men on this earth had ever made a sound like that.

Liam Mackenzie, Gavin St. James, and Dorian Blackwell.

Brothers.

"*Hamish,*" Mena whispered. "You're alive?"

"And ye're a clever sort." His serpentine head lowered so that she could hear the slight whistle of air through the pitiable slits in the center of his face. "Though not so clever as ye think if you consider *this* a life."

The blade against her throat radiated the chill of the evening, paradoxically burning against the soft, tender skin of her throat. Mena was terrified, but felt oddly detached. A frigid chill that put the ice baths to shame washed over her, but instead of seizing her mind with those fingers of ice, it somehow liberated her.

She'd survived violence before. She'd been struck, threatened, choked, and terrorized. Somehow, through it all, she'd learned to keep her head in a dangerous situation. To cycle through the fear and pain threatening to cloud her thoughts, and pluck from the nebula of knowledge, instead.

Her newfound strength would be priceless in this situation.

Mena knew she wasn't his true quarry, that she was a means to an end. Which could prove to be her salvation, unless *she* proved to be useless to him. First she must ascertain what his motives were, and then she could formulate a plan.

"That night I thought I dreamed of you." A chill speared her at the memory, and she had to straighten her spine to keep it at bay. "You were in my bedroom?"

"I tried to warn ye then, woman," he confirmed. "I told ye to run. I had revenge to reap and ye were in my way. I regret it had to come to this."

"It still doesn't have to," Mena ventured. "You said that night that Liam promised you something. That you felt he owed you."

"He *does* owe me," Hamish insisted, his pressure tightening on her neck, the blade biting into the soft skin right beneath her chin.

"What?" The question sounded shrill and desperate, even to her. "What did he promise you? I'm certain he'll give it, he's a man of his word."

A crack sounded in the woods beyond the feeble reach of the moon. The snap of a tree limb, perhaps?

Mena's heart caught. Could it be Liam? She both desired and dreaded the sight of his sinister features.

Hamish had heard it, as well.

"I know ye're out there, brother." That terrible, almost beautiful laugh vibrated the air around them, and seemed to even disturb the mists now rising past their knees and inching up their thighs as though meaning to swallow them.

"How quick yer woman is to defend ye," he taunted. "I wonder, Miss Lockhart, if ye would still think so highly of him if ye'd ever seen him as I have. Bathed in the blood of his quarry, drunk on his own rage, the indiscriminate killer. The Demon Highlander."

A shadow moved in the trees, and Hamish brandished her at the night like a shield.

"Come forward and I spill her blood!" he called, tucking the knife tighter against her, this time nicking the skin. "Stay out there and I'll spill yer secrets. Ye decide, Liam."

His hand released her arm from behind her, sliding up her spine with sickening lethargy. Mena didn't dare move; the blade at her throat rendered her an absolute prisoner.

His hand wrenched her neck to the side so she could no longer scan the tree line in front of them, only the inky darkness that led down to the western sea.

"Ye decide!" He laughed again, this time maniacally. "Either way she dies."

At the sound of Mena's scream, Liam had dropped low into the mist and pulled his dirk from his boot. The blood that simmered with the heat of anticipatory arousal instantly boiled with the lust for vengeance.

His predatory instincts flared, and he prowled forward with all the sleek stealth of a wolf, hungry to rip out the throat of an enemy.

But the blood he would spill was blood he shared.

Hamish.

Skirting the moonlit clearing, Liam ducked errant tree branches and navigated his way through the mist. He processed a multitude of terrors as fast as his disbelieving eyes allowed.

His brother, alive. A scarred mass of rage and retribution. He had Mena. Held a dagger to her throat.

Fury threatened to smother all sense of reason or thought. Primal instinct screamed at him to attack, to lunge forward and slash at his brother until nothing was left of the monster but bones and carnage.

But Mena would never make it, Liam knew. Hamish was a terror with a blade.

Almost as good as Liam, himself.

Moving as close as he dared, Liam conducted a quick assessment of Mena. Moonlight turned her hair into waves of dark crimson, the color of spilled blood. Her porcelain features glowed with an ethereal purity. Through the mist and the darkness, he couldn't tell if she was injured. Something had made her scream, and there had been pain in the sound. That fact tortured him with a violence he'd never thought possible.

Her voice wavered as she spoke, but there was a calm to it, an evenness that he hung all his hope for salvation on.

Somewhere to the east, the sound of a twig snapping rang through the forest like a cannon blast.

"I know ye're out there, brother!" Hamish had screamed, as Liam maneuvered to the west, away from the sound, never allowing his head to rise above the line of the gathering mist.

His dirk felt solid in his hand, every bit as sharp and lethal as Hamish's, but it was useless until he found exactly the right time. He could try to get Hamish from behind, but then he'd lose sight of Mena, and thereby wouldn't know when to strike.

Then he heard the words that instantly turned his blood from molten iron to shards of ice in his veins.

"Either way, she dies."

Hamish had no intention of setting her free.

For the first time in his adult life, abject terror threatened to paralyze him. Why Mena? Why now? Hamish had been a morally corrupt man over the course of his life, but then, he'd had to be. Liam had always known that. He was a bastard, the eldest son who would inherit nothing from their father but a taste for blood and fear.

Liam had to calculate the strategy of his next move perfectly, because he would die before Mena became another casualty of his many sins.

Using a trick he'd learned from a Turkish puppeteer, Liam flattened his back against the trunk of an old elm and threw his voice across the meadow, making it seem to vault off the tree line in the east.

"Let her go, Hamish," he said. "She has nothing to do with this business between us."

His ruse was successful. Hamish's neck whipped in the direction Liam had hoped it would.

"We do have business, Liam." Hamish said his name as though it were a rotten thing on his tongue that he needed to spit out. "Ye didna keep yer end of the bargain. Ye were supposed to die on the battlefield. To leave Ravencroft to *me*."

"I tried." Liam volleyed his voice farther this time, hoping to get Hamish to turn toward it.

He might be trying to distract his brother long enough for him to take the knife from Mena's throat, but he also spoke the truth. He'd set everything up perfectly to make reparations upon the event of his inevitable demise.

Hamish would overtake Ravencroft Keep and the distillery, and the Wester Ross lands would be kept in trust for Andrew when Hamish died. Rhianna and Andrew would go to London to live with their maternal grandmother, Lady Eloise Gleason, a kindly old woman who was very fond of her tragically ill only daughter's children. Andrew would become marquess, and would maintain all London holdings.

But Hamish had been killed in that ship explosion, or so everyone had assumed, and Liam had proven damnably hard to exterminate. His recklessness only brought him glory.

"They were supposed to hate ye," Hamish hissed. "The clan was supposed to think ye cursed by the *Brollachan,* to turn against ye. But despite my best efforts, it seems ye truly have made some deal with the devil."

"The fire in the fields and the toppled barrel at the distillery," Liam realized aloud. "That was ye?"

"Thwarted by a rainstorm and a bit of luck," Hamish spat. "And it was a pure miracle that carriage didna tumble down the Bealach na Bá with a shorn linchpin."

"Ye put innocent people in harm's way just to get yer revenge," Liam growled. For that he would pay.

"Doona let this so-called Demon Highlander play the hero for yer benefit." His bastard older brother almost sounded gleeful as he addressed Mena. "Innocent lives have never meant much to either of us. We are similar creatures with different predilections."

"I was never like ye." Liam's hard voice echoed around the glen now, before it dissipated through the canopy of trees.

"Nonsense, whatever monstrous things Father neglected to teach me, ye filled in the spaces," Hamish said conversationally. "Doona ye remember the things ye said? That open battle is effective for casualties, but that the battles we wage with terror gain us even greater results. That the personal kill is the most satisfying. Ye taught me that if ye snap a bone just right, it makes a clean, crisp sound that ye can feel ricochet in yer own skeleton. Ye taught me that ye attain glory on the battlefield, but to gain true infamy, ye attack at dinner, or a party. Or maybe when yer enemy is putting their children to bed . . . Or . . . *making love.*" Hamish bared his teeth from behind those hideously disfigured lips, and made as though he were going to bite into Mena's bare shoulder.

"Ye're wrong." Liam battled the desperation threatening to creep into his tone, convinced his brother's injuries, and his hatred, had tainted his memory. "Ye're confused," he corrected as evenly as he could. "That was his grace, Lord Trenwyth. *I* was the demon on the battlefield, *he* was the phantom in the darkness. It was always thus."

"Collin Talmage, the sodding Duke of Trenwyth." Hamish spat into the mist. "I'll settle that score once I'm through here."

Liam didn't take the time to wonder what his brother meant. His every thought, every molecule in his body, was focused on Mena. "Let her go," Liam had meant to cajole, but it escaped as a command. "I'll trade ye across, my life for hers. I'll take ye to Trenwyth if ye want."

Hamish made a snide sound of victory. "Why this sudden weakness for women?" he sneered. "Could kill yer own father in cold blood, and whip a whore to death. But watching the English bitch die will break ye?"

Liam closed his eyes for a brief moment, unable to bring himself to face the look of horror and terror Mena must be wearing. That *alone* would break him. He wouldn't survive her loss. Not the part of him that was human, anyhow. Liam somehow knew that seeing her blood would turn him into the monster he'd spent forty years trying not to become.

He didn't miss her sharp gasp, though, and neither did Hamish. Now she knew his darkest secrets, the two main reasons his soul was eternally damned.

It started with Tessa McGrath, and patricide had sealed his eternal fate.

He'd killed his own father, left his brother for dead, and helplessly allowed his mad wife to take her own life.

He truly did destroy those closest to him.

But he'd die before letting the woman he loved fall prey to his demon curse.

"Father *deserved* to die for what he did." Liam had forgotten to misdirect his voice that time, and Hamish's head swiveled in his direction. "For what he forced *us* to do."

Mena's calm had deserted her. She'd become a shivering pile of liquid bones and frozen blood. Only the blade at her throat and the monster behind her kept her from dissolving into a puddle of panic and soaking into the marshy ground.

Liam seemed to be everywhere at once. First to the east, and then in the shadows where her imprisoned gaze was trained to the west.

He'd offered himself for her. Mena's heart swelled at the fervency in his voice. A part of her wished Hamish would take the offer. That he'd toss her away. But in her heart, she knew that she'd never be able to live with herself if she'd had any hand in Liam's demise. His children needed him. His clan and kin relied on his leadership.

She, however, could disappear into the mist and none would be the wiser. She had no family but the one who had locked her away. A handful of people would mourn her tragedy, hold their loved ones closer, and then move on.

Hamish's words pulled her from her encroaching despondency.

Liam had whipped a woman . . . and killed his own evil father. *Dear God.* She'd assumed it was any number of heinous war crimes that haunted him. Or the circumstances of Hamish's death. But no, Liam hadn't only killed people in the name of queen and country, he'd committed *murder.*

Her breath caught as she considered his answer. What had the elder Hamish Mackenzie done to incur Liam's wrath?

"It was one tavern slut, Liam, and she was paid handsomely for her services." Hamish almost moved the hand with the blade at her throat, as though he wanted to make a frustrated gesture. Remembering himself, he tightened his hold on her, repositioning the dagger in a more dangerous place than before.

Mena would have whimpered, but she refrained, fearing that even the slightest swallow would impale her upon its point.

"No amount of money could prove recompense for what he made us do to her." Even through the confines of her own terror, Mena wept for the hollow shame in Liam's voice. Wept for the poor girl and the humiliations that were too awful even for the Demon Highlander to lend them words. The hot tears scalded her chilly skin and ran down the cold blade.

"He was turning us into men," Hamish spat.

"He was turning us into monsters."

"I still doona see why ye felt ye had to do away with him," Hamish expounded. "Ye canna really rape a whore, can ye? Besides, ye were weak even then. Ye couldna go through with it."

Hearing that caused a tear of relief to join the steady trickle of moisture from Mena's eyes.

"I found her body in Bryneloch Bog." Liam's temper

was overcoming his caution; she could tell by the heat in his voice. "Ye know he murdered her to keep her silent, so she wouldna stir the clan against him."

"That's what's always been wrong with ye, Liam. Ye think that her insignificant life was worth the death of a great man."

"He was an evil man," Liam snarled. "He *killed* innocent people. His own clan."

Hamish scoffed at that. "All great men do evil things."

"Ye're wrong."

"How would ye know? Ye're neither a great man nor a righteous one. But ye're not famous for yer good deeds, are ye?"

The darkness was silent for several heartbeats. Hamish's taunt had hit its mark.

"What about Dougan?" Liam's soft, tortured question barely traversed the distance between them. "Father ordered the death of his own son."

"Dougan was just as much a monster as any of us. Worse, I'd wager. He murdered a bloody priest before he saw the age of fifteen."

Mena's heart bled. She wanted to tell Liam that she still thought he was a good man. A great man. That she was glad his father had answered for all the vicious, unspeakable things he did. She hesitated because it seemed that Hamish had all but forgotten her. His hold didn't waver, but he no longer seemed to be focused on her death.

"One would think, dear brother, that ye ought to have more sympathy for our father's bastards." Gavin St. James startled both Mena and Hamish as he strode into the clearing from the east, looking relaxed as you please. "Seeing as ye are one."

"Sod off, Thorne," Hamish snarled. Every muscle in his mangled body tensed, and Mena cried out as his grip on the back of her neck tightened. He blessedly took the knife he held beneath Mena's chin and brandished it at Gavin. "I should have smothered ye the second yer wretched mother whelped ye into this—"

Mena heard the slight whoosh of air as the dagger left the shadows, twirling end over end until it whirled by her ear.

Hamish screamed as it found its mark, and Mena was released just in time to duck as the Demon Highlander rose from the mist, leaped to the altar rock, and vaulted for his brother.

CHAPTER NINETEEN

The impact was like two leviathans colliding, and it shook the earth. They went down, swallowed by the vapor, and Mena scrambled away. The cold rasp of stone abraded her fingertips as she pulled herself up by the altar rock and clung to it. The terrible sounds of flesh connecting with flesh in violence echoed through the clearing, and a little part of her died every second she couldn't see Liam. She wanted to do anything but stand and watch the events unfold before her, but knew the smartest thing to do was to stay out of Liam's way. She would help no one by putting herself in danger. There were two daggers down there in the mist, and Lord only knew what damage was being done.

Thorne rushed forward, and it was then she realized that he was not alone. Russell barreled in behind him, followed by a stern-looking Thomas Campbell.

"We heard ye scream, lass," Russell called. "Are ye hurt?"

"No, but the laird—"

Before the clansmen had a chance to reach her, Liam surged out of the mist, his own dirk poised where Hamish's neck met his mangled shoulder. The laird's powerful arm bulged with the strain of keeping his wounded brother in check.

"I should kill ye for laying yer hands on her," he snarled.

"Doona do it, brother." Thorne approached the two furious Highlanders cautiously. "He has many crimes to answer for."

"And his justice should be swift," Liam insisted through clenched teeth. His dark eyes were wide and wild with furious frenzy as the muscles in his arm clenched with the restraint it took not to slide the blade home.

"Hamish. It canna be," Russell marveled, wearing an identically stricken look to Campbell's as he took in Hamish's distorted form. They were seeing a ghost. A hideous, disfigured specter of a man they all once knew. If he wasn't so evil, he'd have been pitiable.

"Finish what he started if ye have the stones," Hamish hissed, though he was out of breath. "Ye could just work through slaughtering yer entire family. First yer father, then me." He turned to Gavin, his lips pulled away from a few sharp teeth. "Ye'll be next," he predicted ominously. His face was bleeding from a cut on his head, but in all the chaos of his scars, Mena couldn't find the source of the wound.

Thorne's expression faltered, at the revelation of what Liam had done.

He hadn't known, Mena realized. He hadn't known that his brother had killed their father.

The earl took his belt off, and gestured for Russell to do the same, his movements methodical. "Let us take him to the dungeon, Liam. We'll deliver him to the regiment tomorrow by train. I'm certain Trenwyth will have more than a few charges to bring."

"They'll only hang him," Liam gritted out.

"Liam." Mena stepped forward, reaching for him.

"Stay *back,*" he ordered. "Doona get close."

Mena hesitated, letting her hand drop to her side. She wondered who he truly warned her away from. Hamish? Or himself.

"Do ye think I'm finished with ye?" Hamish taunted. "That I'm the only one who would see ye dead?"

"I know you're angry now." Mena tried to ballast the poison spewed by Hamish. "But you don't want your own brother to be just another sin that haunts you."

She couldn't tell if she was getting through to him, didn't know if her words penetrated the haze of pure, white-hot fury radiating from the Demon Highlander's massive frame.

"I'm sure yer tormentors are legion," Hamish drawled. "I've killed many, but none so much as ye. I admit that I see them at night, the faces of my victims. I find them in my dreams, and sometimes when I'm awake. Do ye see their faces, Liam? Do ye find them in the darkness?"

Ignoring his order, Mena stepped behind Liam and pressed a hand to his back, the soft skin of her palm settling over the interruptions of long-ago wounds that never truly healed. She said nothing as the muscles twitched and shuddered beneath her chilled fingers.

"Nay, brother," Liam finally said, maneuvering himself so Gavin could bind Hamish's hands behind him. "I doona find them. . . . They find me."

Liam watched his brothers disappear into the forest, aided by Thomas and Russell. He tried to feel the things he understood that he should be feeling. But he'd grieved for Hamish already. He'd alternately hated and loved his elder brother with the same complicated feelings he'd possessed for his father. They battled the same monstrous rage, only Liam put up more of a fight against it, instead of letting it dissolve his soul completely.

The moment Hamish had touched Mena in violence, his

life had become forfeit, just like that fucking bastard who'd harmed her in London, whoever he was.

He could feel Mena's gaze from behind him as tangible as her kind hand had been on his back. She'd done it again. Bedeviled him with her gentle magic and smothered the flames of his fury with one simple caress.

Anger and aggression still pounded through his veins and thrummed through his muscle, but it was joined by relief and fear.

What must she think of him now? Now that she knew his darkest sins. Now that she completely understood just exactly how damned his soul was. What would he find in her eyes? Revulsion? Terror?

Condemnation?

Awareness prickled along his spine and stung beneath his scars. He knew he was mostly bare, but never had he felt so naked. So exposed. Only one scar in a hundred had remained on his skin, but every single one had lashed at his soul.

Nothing Liam had ever done—no danger he'd ever faced—had taken as much courage as did turning around to meet her unflinching gaze.

Mena used the altar rock to support herself. The indigo mists climbed and caressed her body as though trying to seduce her with embracing wisps of moisture.

She was the most beautiful creature ever crafted of the mystifying and enchanted elements that made up a woman. If he was stone and steel, she was serenity and softness. The long tendrils of her luxurious hair tumbled down her arms and grazed the dramatic flare of her round hips. The flimsy material of her bodice—God love whatever it was called—enhanced more than concealed her breasts as they heaved with her own panting, unsteady breaths.

Christ, he could have lost her tonight. Liam's knees weakened as he truly realized how close that blade had been held to her delicate throat.

He saw his severe relief mirrored in her lovely, pale eyes.

An ache throbbed deep in his body, as a shudder coursed down the length of his spine, starting at the shoulders and landing at the base, sending heat and desire into his loins. A raw, unbidden sound rose from deep in his chest, and escaped on a breath of undiluted need.

She tilted unsteadily forward, like a siren beckoning him to his destruction. He had about as much power against her.

In that moment, they both knew it.

Nothing else need be said between them. No words or platitudes uttered. No fears or sins confessed. He saw absolution in her eyes. Understanding. Acceptance.

And still he gave her a moment. A warning. A chance to escape.

Because once he got his hands on her, there would be no stopping him.

His body screamed for her, driven with a need to touch and taste that teetered on the brink of madness. Every lurid, wet, aching, shocking, demanding thing he could do to her body raced through his mind and incapacitated him with lust. The drive to fuck overcame every other rational thought or biological need. There wasn't enough time left in his life to try everything he wanted to do to her, but damned if he wasn't about to attempt it.

Her lashes swept down for a breathless moment, and then she raised her gaze back to meet his, eyes hooded and lips parted.

Desire.

There was no mistaking it. Not this time.

He surged forward, planted his hands against the rock on either side of her head, and took her offered lips with the desperate hunger of a man denied sustenance for too long.

She surged against him, pressing every curve of her

voluptuous body to his. Her full breasts were a delicious crush against his rib cage, and his entire being focused on the weight of them against his bare skin. Her warm mouth opened to him in silken welcome, accepting the possession of his tongue with a soft sigh of capitulation.

This time she was no passive recipient of his kiss. She met his tongue with her own, pressing her mouth against his with the same fervent sense of frenzy.

She clung to him as if he were her only stability in an uncertain world. As though she somehow knew that if she let go of him, everything would fall apart. The gesture was his undoing. The sheer, heartrending honesty in the action. She was unguarded in her passions, uninhibited by the usual wall that surrounded her. It drew him to her, made him want to uncover all her secrets, to lay her bare for him to soothe and soften the rough edges of her life. To offer himself as a guardian, as a vigilant sentinel against all that would cause her pain.

Their mouths fused with reckless passion, he lost himself to his reverent worship of her. He found salvation in her surrender, and he knew that in offering it to him, she'd gained an ardent devotee.

His hands explored her lush body with all the eagerness of an untried boy and all the patient skill of an adept. Only a fragile layer of silk and lace separated his hands and her skin. Pausing at the swell of her cleavage, he stroked the cleft, and drew his finger along the lacy line of her bodice. He knew the nipples beneath her corset pebbled, and the need to take them in his mouth drove him mad with anticipation.

She moaned her pleasure, dissolving into liquid shivers beneath his fingertips.

Needing no further provocation, he slipped the tiny capped sleeves of her emerald dress off her shoulders and peeled her bodice down to her waist. A black corset hoisted her generous breasts into half orbs of alabaster flesh, and Liam reluctantly broke the kiss to enjoy the vision.

He stared at her, momentarily paralyzed by a hushed and splendid wonder. The world seemed to recede, to cease spinning on its axis, as if her beauty could command the cosmos to hold its breath in deference to her magnificence.

"Save me, lass." His groan rumbled from somewhere deeper than he could physically imagine as he finally found the voice to plead for what his soul could not. "I'm drowning in my need and I— Say the words that willna make me a monster in the morning."

One refusal from her lips would shatter him into a thousand pieces.

She rested her head back against the stone with an ardent sigh, and splayed her fingers right above the warm skin over his heart.

"I want you, Liam," she said in a clear voice turned husky by desire. "Take me."

His dark soul exalted and every last bit of restraint caught fire and became ash. He was going to claim her so thoroughly she'd never be the same. He wanted no other name on her lips. No other lips on her skin. He wanted no other man to touch her the way he was about to touch her.

And come the morning, they'd all leave for London, where he would rid himself of the last of his ghosts, and claim her not just as his lover, but as his wife.

Mena felt every bit of his low, strangled growl in her loins as he surged against her once more and took her lips with a primitive possession. Something about the way he looked at her, as if she were a morsel about to be devoured, was alternately exalting and petrifying.

But his kiss set her body aflame with electrifying, life-affirming need.

She was acutely aware of the power in his arms as they roamed her body, and only made a small sound of shock when he broke her corset, freeing her breasts to the kiss of the autumn night. His mouth branded a trail down her jaw to lave at the hollow between her shoulder and her throat before moving lower.

His hand lifted her breast to his mouth, and Mena's surprise turned into pure, sensual astonishment as he closed his hot lips over the cool skin of her taut nipple. His mouth was both hungry and unhurried as he sucked and nipped. Teasing and tantalizing until she no longer felt the chill of the night, he paid each of her breasts equal attention. She felt dazed and feverish, threading her fingers in his glossy black hair as she watched him feast on her abundant flesh.

A steady, insistent throbbing clenched her feminine muscles around pervasive emptiness. An acute ache speared her until she arched her back against the novel and unbearable intensity of it, and struggled to draw breath.

He straightened, his skin glowing with a sheen of mist and his hair tousled by her kneading fingers, and his dark, questioning gaze searched hers.

The cuffs at his arms and neck gleamed metallic in the moonlight. The runes he'd painted on his skin little more than darker knots on the muscled planes of his body.

She couldn't believe a man this magnificent could wear a look of such worship when making love to *her*. She, who'd always been taunted for her height, her weight, her lack of feminine fragility, felt as substantial as a scrap of lace, unstitched by the unparalleled force of his masculinity.

The mystic night lent her a boldness she'd never before possessed as she reached out to again splay her hand over steely muscle that covered his racing heart, caress up to his iron-sculpted shoulders, and down the swells of his liberally veined arms.

Never again would she have the opportunity to appreciate such a rare and primal specimen of lethal virility, and she wanted to take a moment to savor the feel of all that smooth skin stretched taut over unyielding strength.

Suddenly her hands were pinned above her head, and he was filling her mouth with his tongue. She tasted the salt of her skin on his lips and the pervasive ache between her legs became a flooding, insistent sort of pain. He kissed her with such scorching thoroughness, he quite erased the last vestiges of rational thought.

"Now," she sobbed against his mouth, too distressed to feel shame at the pleading note in her voice.

His dark noise was full of masculine victory as he continued his seductive assault on her lips, caressing down the soft curve of her hip, then slid lower, gathering the folds of her skirts in his hand, tugging them up her leg.

Mena's fingers blindly gripped the stone behind her as frantically as she grasped for her sanity.

Then he dropped to his knees.

"What are you doing?" she gasped, reaching for him, meaning to pull him back against her.

"Doona touch me, lass," he commanded, sliding his hands up beneath her dress, his calluses rasping against the silk of her stockings with a delightfully wicked sensation. "I'll not be able to stop myself from taking ye."

Her brows drew together in bemused consternation. "But I told you that you could take me." She was almost panting now, as though she'd run a great length.

"Aye." He chuckled, his clever fingers stopping to toy with a garter, effectively rendering her witless. "I give before I take, lass. It'll always be thus."

"But I don't unders—" The rest of her breath left her on a rush as his hand found its way inside of her drawers and sifted through her damp curls. Pleasure spiraled through her as his hand found the flesh that had been causing her such aching distress. Her breath became nothing but broken gasps as he rent her intimate garments and delved within the swollen folds, his fingers becoming instantly slippery with the abundant wetness he found there. Any thoughts of embarrassment disintegrated into the stunning pleasure he expertly coaxed from her with the slightest of movements.

His head dipped below the mists and disappeared. Her skirts lifted. His hair grazed the tender skin of her thighs for a shocking moment before he made a fluid, magical movement that buckled her knees and eased her thighs apart.

Then he was there between them, settling her thighs against his shoulders.

In all her life as a married woman, she'd never experienced the brutish, straining satisfaction she'd glimpsed on her husband's face as he attained his climax on her. And though she'd been forced to submit to any indignity he could devise, he'd never even considered *her* pleasure.

Touched, scandalized, apprehensive, and unbearably aroused, Mena opened her mouth to protest when his wicked, sinuous lips nudged against her closed body, and then licked it open, delving into her sex.

His moan vibrated against her, driving little tendrils of bliss through her core before letting them escape to her limbs. His tongue was at once lewd and unutterably sweet as it glided against the swollen nub that throbbed with torturous need.

Incredible agony slammed into her as he parted her folds with his fingers and suckled the aperture. He breathed only in moans as he tasted her, and the hedonistic pleasure conveyed in the sounds brought her to the edge of madness.

"I can't," she cried, feeling her knees melt.

His lips left her with a wet, wicked sound. "Ye will," he breathed against her most intimate flesh.

"I'm going to fall," she warned weakly, her hips undulating toward his mouth with mortifying wantonness.

"Fall apart in my arms, lass," he soothed, his hands caressing around to fill his palms with the flesh of her backside, making a cradle of her hips. "I'll not let ye go."

Then he burrowed his mouth inside her slick folds once again.

Mena shivered with carnal bliss, then tensed with the building, aching pulses as each glide of his swirling tongue elicited sensations she'd not known herself capable of. A cataclysm of pleasure seized her with such force, she truly did feel as though it unmade her.

Distantly, she heard the low, lurid sounds that ripped their way out of her as she shuddered and pulsed with unparalleled, unfathomable bliss. Tension rushed from her, released with slick pulses of rolling, cresting delight. She whimpered and arched, strained and bucked, and still he pressed against her with that gentle, hot tongue, ever the conqueror, until she pleaded with him for mercy.

He finally relented, his wicked mouth reluctantly leaving her. But as he again rose from the mist, his sinister features were anything but merciful. Dark eyes glittered at her from a face etched with animalistic hunger.

Mena was too boneless to be afraid. Too drugged with pleasure to either anticipate or hesitate until the moonlight briefly reflected off the storm that had gathered in his onyx eyes.

This was the Demon Highlander, and he was about to take not only her body, but her soul. The force of his passion seemed to reach her a moment before his lips did. He backed her fully against the stone, devouring her with lips that tasted of sweet musk and intimacy.

Her gown was suddenly above her waist, and he pushed his kilt aside before seizing her thighs and splitting them around his lean hips, supporting her with his shocking strength. The smooth head of his cock caressed the still-pulsating flesh of her sex, becoming instantly wet with the evidence of her release.

He was large. So devastatingly thick that a flash of fear speared her just as he slid into her with a swift, desperate stroke. There was pressure, there was even pain, but as soon as she would have cringed away, he withdrew. As though understanding her dilemma, he feathered kisses over her clenched eyelids, crooning low words to her in that indescribably beautiful language of his before plunging forward again. Even though he moved even deeper, she felt her body open to accept him, enclosing him in warm, slippery flesh.

Pressure morphed into pleasure, radiating from where their bodies joined in such a way that she felt awash in a pool of wet desire, held together only by the warm, hard masculine flesh around her.

And inside her.

"Can ye take more of me?" he panted.

Mena's eyes flew open. How could there possibly be more? He withdrew yet again, gazing down at her with dilated eyes as he surged forward. He touched a place inside her she'd not known existed, and Mena tossed her head from one side to the other, letting out a high cry of ecstasy.

"Yes," he whispered fervently. "I knew ye would take all of me, Mena." He drove forward again. And again. Thrusting with controlled urgency, the storm gathering into gale, and then a hurricane. Lifting her incredibly higher, he angled his cock so that it slid along that place deep inside her, the one that made her scream and clamp around him, bearing down on his hard length as it penetrated her again and again.

Using the rock to press back against him, Mena found herself straining to meet his thrusts, setting a rhythm. She anticipated each slippery invasion with eager delight and mourned his every withdrawal. It was as though a bond weaved between them within the Samhain mist, pledging themselves to this night, to this act, to the pleasure they found in each other's bodies and the ease they gave to the other's wounded soul.

When another climax blinded her with pure bliss, she locked her legs around his pistoning hips, pulling him impossibly deeper. Shivering pleasure assaulted her in wave after unrelenting wave.

He roared her name to the sky as her pulsing body gripped and stroked at the swelling length of him. Hot spurts of his release spilled inside her. His great body locked with spasms as he crushed her to him and joined her in that place where right and wrong no longer mattered. Where consequences didn't exist. Where tomorrow was an opportunity instead of a liability.

They stayed in that place for a long time after the storm of pleasure had passed. She locked in the strength of his arms, and he cradled within the softness of her body.

"I find, lass, that I doona want to let ye go," he confessed.

Mena's fingers tenderly searched the stark angles and planes of his beloved features. What a man this was. A rare, brilliant, incredible man, and, as of this moment, he belonged to her.

The wondrousness of it was unfathomable.

At her touch, he rolled his hips forward once again, and Mena's eyes peeled wide as she realized that he was still hard, still reaching that quivering swath of pure, burning sensation deep within her.

He'd . . . finished. She'd been certain of it.

His teeth flashed a brilliant white in his swarthy face as he shrugged. "It's a Mackenzie trait," he said blithely by way of explanation, before he began to move in slow, but insistent thrusts. "Once I'm done here, we'll probably only make it back to the keep before I'm ready to take ye again."

"Oh, my," was all she could say as teasing heat and pleasure stole all her capacity for speech as he began his tireless climb toward bliss once again.

CHAPTER TWENTY

The last time Mena had peered through the black mesh of this veil, she had been traversing the Bealach na Bà Pass toward Ravencroft. It had felt much like it did now, more a funereal veil than anything glamorous or stylish. Something behind which to hide her shame, her face, and her very self. Though she'd taken off the hat, a veil of secrecy had remained for her entire tenure at Ravencroft Keep. For the slightest, happiest time, even Mena had forgotten who she truly was.

The Lady Philomena St. Vincent, Viscountess Benchley.

Purported madwoman, and a ward of Belle Glen Asylum. Fugitive from the crown, her noble husband, and certain insanity. A woman she'd come to despise over the course of her enchanted autumn in Wester Ross. A weak-willed, soft-spoken ninny. A victim of violence. A perpetrator of silence. Ephemeral, unwanted, and thoroughly unhappy.

Mena Lockhart, on the other hand, had become more natural to her in the first five days than the viscountess had been in five years. As the spinster governess, she'd faced down multiple fears. She'd laughed, danced, scolded, healed, and imparted of her hard-won wisdom.

She'd even stood her ground in a quarrel with the Demon Highlander, and not only emerged the victor of their skirmish, but won his wounded heart.

Though, in doing so, she'd lost her own.

Her reflection in the train window showed no traces of the softness and contentment she'd cautiously begun to allow herself to feel whilst hiding in the Highlands. Her full lips drew into a line of prim restraint, her eyes became pinched and dull, her skin wan and pale rather than porcelain tinged with pink.

She'd retreated to a tiny, unoccupied box in a sparsely populated railcar to gather her thoughts. To brood, was more like it.

How in God's name had she ever allowed herself to board a train back to London? Was she truly mad? Why had she not portended some rank and incurable illness, forcing everyone to leave her behind?

Partly, she admitted to herself, because she'd been pleasured into witless oblivion more times than a human being could possibly be expected to endure and still hold a thought in her head. The hour had struck half past two in the morning before Liam and she had stumbled into her room, and even then they hadn't slept for some time. He'd thrown the drapes open wide and peeled her dress from her body with curious and infinite languor. He'd taken special care with her stockings, fingering the ribbons and garters and caressing them down her long, sturdy legs.

His rough fingers were infinitely gentle as he discovered every inch of her skin with patient and arousing caresses in the moonlight. They'd talked of amusing things while he undressed her. And insignificant things while she washed the runes and mist from his bare skin.

Then they said nothing at all when he pulled her above

him and split her legs over his lean, sinuous hips. They'd communicated only in gasps and sighs as she'd ridden him with sensual rolls of her body. He'd palmed her breasts in his warm hands and said wicked things in his people's native tongue while she pleasured herself upon his sleek and magnificent body. Then, when he could stand it no more, he'd dug his strong fingers into the flesh of her hips and driven upward until he'd bowed with such shocking pleasure, Mena had thought his back would break.

In the darkness, he'd held her close against his slowing heartbeat, and spoke of serious things, of his brothers and the fear her capture had caused him. Of his intentions to bring Hamish to London and have him face the military tribunal that was doubtless waiting for him. He'd told her stories of Collin Talmage, the Duke of Trenwyth. As Liam had been gaining glory on the battlefield, Trenwyth had been a secret agent, spilling blood in the dark. After Hamish's presumed death, it turned out Trenwyth had made Liam aware of several war crimes he'd previously been ignorant of. His status as the Demon Highlander had shielded his brother from facing justice.

But justice awaited Hamish now, and it promised to be swift and merciless.

"How strange," Mena had commented, while stroking her hands through the soft and sparse hair on Liam's chest, enjoying the feel of his masculine skin. "That a duke like Trenwyth would be in such service to the crown. If I remember correctly, he's something like seventeenth in line, practically a royal."

"Trenwyth is no royal dandy. He's one of the most dangerous men I've ever met, with a self-destructive streak twice as long as my own."

"Oh, my." Mena yawned.

"He was born a second or third son, though, and didn't take on the mantle of duke until he'd already been in Her Majesty's service for quite some time. I imagine Trenwyth spends little time in the field now, though, as he lost his hand on a cover mission to Afghanistan."

"Poor soul," Mena murmured. "Did Hamish have anything to do with it?"

"I imagine Thorne and I are about to find out."

Though Liam was the Marquess of Ravencroft, Laird of the clan Mackenzie, and a retired lieutenant colonel, Gavin St. James, the Earl of Thorne, acted as local magistrate, and so they were both to transport Hamish as their prisoner in the morning.

Exhausted beyond physical comprehension, Mena must have fallen asleep before the part where Liam had mentioned he intended for his children, and thereby, Mena, to accompany him on the journey.

It wasn't until an ecstatic Rhianna had accosted her in her bed, where she'd awoken alone with pillars of late-morning sun slanting in through her open windows, that she'd found out the panic-inducing news.

The dear girl exuberantly informed her that her father had accepted their grandmother's request for them to join her in London for a few small soirees before she would whisk them off to spend Christmas in Paris and celebrate the New Year in Florence.

Mena's reaction had been the antithesis of Rhianna's exaltation. Nausea had risen above a haze of denial choking off her throat. The suffocating steel band of dread, of which she'd thought herself rid, had clamped back around her rib cage.

She'd barely had time to don her robe before Jani arrived with a bevy of maids to pack her things and help her dress.

Mena had penned a frantic plea for help to Farah Blackwell, Lady Northwalk, and thrust it into Jani's hands, begging him to have it delivered to the telegraph office in Strathcarron. She'd paid him a full week's wages, and he'd scampered off to comply.

She'd gone in search of Liam, but he and Gavin had

taken Hamish to the station early to secure a locked car and spare the children the traumatic verity of his tragic return and, even worse, his eventual fate.

They'd lost him already, it wouldn't do to see the creature he'd become.

Before she'd quite gathered her wits, Mena had quickly cleaned and dressed, the children were gathered, and they bundled into a carriage that raced down the Bealach na Bà at a dizzying and at times stomach-dropping pace.

Liam had met them at the train station, and Mena's fraying composure faltered at the knee-weakening sight of him. His welcoming smile never reached his haunted eyes. Though his hand had covertly found hers as they'd made their way to the private car, and he pressed his palm against hers with a meaningful deference. Whether he gave reassurance or sought it, Mena couldn't be certain. Either way, it only served to fuel her dread.

Jani had been there, assuring her the telegram had been delivered to London posthaste.

The news did little to uncurl the fingers of dread threatening to squeeze her heart into stillness, which would be preferable to these constant, breathless palpitations of anxiety.

She'd done what she could to keep her growing panic from the Mackenzies and Jani. Much of the journey was spent indulging the children with descriptions of London.

Barraged with endless questions, Liam did take the time to tell her about their town house off Oxford Street overlooking Hyde Park.

"I want to go to the marina to look at warships." Andrew's blue eyes had gleamed with relish. "And to see the Egyptian exhibit at the British Museum!"

"I want to attend a *real* opera, and a ballet, and a play at Covent Gardens. Oh! And then one at Vauxhall Gardens! And we have to go to a real Russian tearoom; and a Turkish bath, they're all the rage, Father."

"And I am going to try my hand at gambling," Andrew speculated.

"You most certainly will *not*," Mena indignantly chimed in.

"Why not?" Andrew threw his father a plaintive look. " 'Tis a gentlemanly pursuit," he argued as he drew his wiry frame to a more erect posture, trying to take advantage of every inch that he'd sprouted in the past few months.

"Sorry, son," Liam rumbled as he shook his head and hid a smile.

"They willna let a whelp like *ye* in the clubs, ye have to be a man first." Rhianna elbowed him in the ribs. "Like Jani."

"I am thinking that even I am too young to attend," Jani had said, more solemn and serious today than his usual jolly self.

Andrew huffed indignantly. "I'll likely be an *old* man the next time we get to visit London . . . if we keep up this rate." He eyed his father accusingly, but the point was lost by the well-timed crack in his pubescent voice.

"We'll have to supplement your wardrobes if you have such lofty goals for the city." Mena'd considered, momentarily forgetting herself.

"Och." Liam grimaced. "And how much is that going to cost me?"

"A small fortune, if I have anything to say about it." She cast a wry glance at the marquess, and blanched as his dark eyes glimmered with hot reminders of their previous night.

As soon as the children had settled, Mena escaped them, finally struck with the idea to beg a need for fresh air, announcing that the rocking of the train caused her to feel unwell.

However, her only malady remained her ever-growing panic. Another lie, however inert, had fallen from her lips.

She despised them, loathed herself for telling them, and detested the need for her dishonesty.

Cursing her fear-driven weakness, Mena remained with her forehead pressed to the cool window and watched the fields of the Scottish Lowlands give way to Northern England.

Mena's thoughts flew faster, trying to keep ahead of the train. If she could ferret out every possible contingency, and formulate a plan to avoid discovery, she might make it to Paris with her guise intact.

God, how she wanted to tell him. Most especially after last night. His secret had been revealed to her and she'd not only understood it, but she accepted his intentions as noble, if his actions had not been.

Hamish had been right about one thing, sometimes great men did evil things.

Even in the name of good.

She'd come close to confiding her own secret so many times the night before, but had decided to leave it to the light of day. The right moment had never truly presented itself. And she hadn't the opportunity this morning.

But what could she do? There was a chance Liam would forgive her if she confessed, but to do so now would be out of the question.

What if his famous temper got the better of him? What if he cast her out, or worse, handed her over to the authorities?

She simply couldn't risk it.

The tiny striations of her veil felt gritty against her forehead, but it did let the coolness of the glass temper the flush of panic heating her face. With Farah's and Millie's help, she just might avoid detection altogether.

Her husband, Gordon, and his parents ran in completely different circles than the Marquess Ravencroft and his former mother-in-law. *Lower* circles, to be sure. Even as a

viscountess, Mena never had the opportunity to meet Lady
Eloise Gleason.

As a high-ranking military officer, a national hero, and
the carrier of a very ancient title, no one would dare to
close a door to Ravencroft. In fact, when word reached
London that he'd arrived, invitations would inundate his
household with startling alacrity.

But Liam Mackenzie attended the parlors of such lofty
people as His Grace, Collin Talmage, the Duke of Trenwyth, and even His Grace, Lord Grosvenor, the Duke of
Westminster upon occasion.

This time of year, the St. Vincents would undoubtedly
have retired to their home in Hampshire for a country
Christmas like a great deal of the *ton* was wont to do.
They'd filter back to the capital for the New Year and the
season, but it didn't seem like the Mackenzie family
planned to linger in London for that long before moving
on to the Continent.

As a lowly governess, she would not be included at any
social event the marquess attended, as Rhianna was not out
in society until she was presented to the queen next year.
Excluding a few shopping and sightseeing outings, there
was really no call for her to leave the house.

She could wear very unremarkable clothing and perhaps hide the color of her hair under a few bonnets, and if
heaven was on her side, she'd avoid recognition.

If it wasn't . . . well, it didn't bear thinking about.

"I know what ye're afraid of." Liam's dark voice echoed
off the wood of the tiny compartment.

Mena jumped from her seat and whirled around, wondering just how a man so large could sneak up on her like
that.

Today he looked every inch the English marquess.
Polished black knee boots complemented his dark gray
wool breeches and waistcoat, making the stark white of his
shirt all the more dramatic. A silver-gray cravat tied loosely

at his chin belied his inherent distaste for English clothing. His hair was bound in an ebony queue gleaming against the white of his shirt and caused his rawboned features to stand out in stark contrast to the implied gentility of his attire.

No one wore their hair long these days, and Mena imagined no one would dare mention that to the marquess.

His uncultured appeal stole her breath, even now, and she found her gloved hand clutching at her own lace cravat as she struggled to reply.

"What—what makes you think I'm afraid?"

One dubious brow lifted, but he said nothing as he stepped forward and slid the silent door to the passenger compartment closed and locked them inside, pulling the blinds down over the window to the cramped hall.

Mena found herself drawn into the circle of his arms, sheltered by his massive shoulders, and she couldn't help but wonder how he could fit through the cramped walkways of the train. His heart thumped a strong rhythm against her ear and his arms settled around her shoulders, cocooning her in his masculine warmth and unfathomable strength.

She leaned on him heavily, breathing in the scent of starch from his laundered clothing, the cedar soap he used, and something earthier. Sharper, like iron and stone. Like he'd been underground.

"How did it go with your brother this morning?" she asked, partly trying to divert the conversation, and mostly because she worried about the shadows she'd earlier seen in his eyes.

"Ye're afraid that whatever ye're running from will find ye in London," he surmised correctly, not allowing himself to be misdirected. "And, though I doona ken what it is, who it is, I want ye to know that I willna let harm come to ye." His words sounded exaggerated in the ear she had pressed against his chest. The resonance of the sound calmed her a little, though she reluctantly pulled back, stepping out of the circle of his arms.

"Why?" she asked, searching his face. "Why would you promise me such things when you don't know anything about it? What if . . . what if I've done something unforgivable?"

Liam stared down into Mena's angelic face, pinched with worry, and couldn't imagine her ever committing an unforgivable sin. She was gentle to the point of demure. Dangerous as a wounded bird and as ladylike as he'd ever seen, even in bed. Though he planned to thoroughly debauch her just as soon as she'd allow. Hell, she'd only ever cursed the once.

She'd make a rather splendid marchioness.

Filled with a foreign tenderness, he traced the brackets of anxiety next to her lips. He wished she'd confide in him, but maybe it was for the best that she left her secrets where they were for now. He had his brother to deal with, and this relationship was all rather new. He was, after all, still her employer.

Trust came neither easily nor quickly to either of them, and the thread they'd woven thus far felt young and tenuous and exceedingly fine. He didn't want to pull the string before it became a cord, lest it snap. Yet, he wanted her to feel safe, to know that if she must fight any sort of battle, the Demon Highlander was on her side. He was her champion, and would ever be.

"Have ye committed murder?" he asked, wondering if they had more in common than he initially thought. "Is Scotland Yard searching the streets of London for ye?" Had she been eager to forgive his own sin on that account because she'd committed one of her own?

"I've never taken a life." He saw truth in her answer, though caution lurked in her eyes.

"Have ye done anything to personally anger the monarchy or any particular member of the royal family?" he queried, feeling his lips curl in an unfamiliar direction.

"No," she denied again, her pale gaze latching onto his mouth as she gave a few distracted blinks.

"Have ye done aught to incur the wrath of Her Majesty's Royal Navy or any branch of the esteemed military?"

"I have not." Her own lips quirked in a reluctant feminine smirk.

"Then, lass, I am confident in my ability to protect ye, and we can save revelations for another time, when all of this is over."

As he pulled her close, she tilted her head back, her careful gaze searching his features for God only knew what. "Truly?" she whispered.

"Aye. Truly," he assured her. "And I give ye my vow as Laird of the Mackenzie clan that if I happen to encounter the man who hurt ye, I'll put my dagger through his eye." He'd done his best to keep his voice light, but he meant every word.

She stepped back into his embrace with an ironic noise. "And they say Highlanders aren't romantic."

"Who needs poetry or diamonds and gems?" He flashed his teeth in a fierce smile. "I find the most precious stones a man can offer are the ones cut from yer enemy while he's on his knees screaming for death."

She groaned, burying her wry laugh in the groove between his pectorals as she furrowed her face against his chest. "What a ferocious barbarian I've fallen for."

They both froze at her flippant admission and her hands tightened in his shirt.

Liam's heart stilled with reverence as he reached in between them and cupped her jaw in his gentle hand, holding it like he would a delicate bauble as he lifted her face to look at him.

She hadn't said *love*. She hadn't needed to.

Unable to speak around a strange tightness in his throat, he bent to run his lips against her forehead, her fluttering eyelids, her velvet cheek.

She was precious to him.

How fiercely he loved her. How afraid he was that she'd be yet another casualty of his accursed blood. And yet, selfish bastard that he was, he couldn't consider letting her go.

"We should get back to the children," she whispered, gently disentangling herself from his grasp. "They'll wonder where we've gone."

"After," he said.

"After what?"

He kissed her swiftly, making his answer abundantly clear. He pressed his hard mouth against the softness of hers again and again, coaxing, enticing, until her moan of response drove him wild with need.

Their tongues tangled, and he tasted desperation on her as she gripped at the solid muscles of his back with a fervency he'd not felt from her even last night.

Her need heightened his, and a rush of desire directed every last drop of blood into his cock. He pressed her against him tightly, rolling his hips to show her what her beauty did to him.

He captured one of her wrists and brought her fingers to his mouth. Gently gripping the tip of her soft satin gloves with his teeth, he pulled each sheath from her fingers until it slid from her hand completely.

With his other hand, he undid his trousers as he distracted her by sliding two of her fingers in his mouth. Her lips parted, glimmering with the leavings of his kiss. Her eyes became stormy and hooded and he watched her relish the memories of how his tongue had slid through the folds of her sex the very same way it now slid in between her fingers.

Leaving her fingers good and wet, he drew them from his mouth. "Touch me, lass," he murmured, lowering both of their hands to where he'd freed himself from his trousers.

He wanted her to know him, to feel what she did to him. To consider his manhood not as a weapon he could use against her, but as an extension of his desire. She could hold him, wield him, drive their pleasure, and use his body to sate her own needs.

They both gasped when her hand closed around him, though his was the sharper inhale. Her lithe fingers encircled his turgid shaft, testing the girth. Her eyes flicked up to his in surprise, but quickly darted away as she used her moist fingers to explore the hot skin.

Liam shuddered as she slid her fingers to the round tip, treading the ridge before sliding all the way to the root. He groaned and shook, lowering his head to her throat, wishing her damned gown weren't high-necked. That they were naked and alone.

But their only bare skin was his cock and her hand, her soft, curious, magical hand that not only held his sex in her delicate grip, but his heart, his black soul.

His salvation.

Lifting up on her toes, she pressed a soft kiss to his panting lips, and when he would have captured her mouth, she pulled away and shocked him by dropping to her knees.

Mena's hand remained gently locked around his cock as her skirts flared around her, creating a puddle of dark silk and muslin. She wanted this. Wanted to give him the pleasure that he'd so lovingly shown her. Wanted to use her mouth to convey the things she could not yet bring herself to say.

She needed to reclaim this act as one between lovers, not as a memory of domination and humiliation.

"Please," she whispered, arching her neck to look up at him. "Don't pull my hair."

"Mena," he groaned, his massive chest sawing beneath his gray vest with wolfish panting breaths. "Ye doona have to—och, Christ," he bit out as she closed her lips over his thick shaft.

Every muscle in his body shuddered and locked in a splendid, animalistic movement. He tossed his head back, baring his thick neck and blindly reached down for her.

Stopping himself just in time, he groped behind him, gripping the molding on the train wall, his fingers turning white with strain.

A victorious thrill shocked Mena as she drew him deeper into the warm cavern of her mouth. Even through the haze of his passion, he'd heeded her request, and she'd reward him for it.

She kept her hand around the base of him, gripping what her mouth could not fit. Slowly, she ran her tongue around the engorged ridge of the blunt head, reveling in the coarse sound he made. He fascinated and tantalized her, such unyielding hardness covered in pure silk.

The rhythm of his furiously pumping heart beat rampantly in the flesh contained by her mouth. She felt giddy, powerful, and astounded by her own body's wet and throbbing response to her bold action.

He tasted sumptuous and salty and completely masculine. Her mouth watered and she used the rampant moisture to ease his cock as deep as she could take him before drawing him out again.

The responding catches and clenches in his abdomen were visible even beneath his shirt and waistcoat.

Her tongue made an expedition of him, finding the curious veins beneath his thin, smooth skin. Stroking him rhythmically with her hand, she allowed her mouth more leeway, pressing kisses to the weeping tip and teasing him with little licks and nibbles using only her lips.

He growled down at her, baring his teeth in wordless demand. Some of the molding gave way beneath his hands, splintering beneath the pressure of his grip.

Foreign guttural words escaped him, though whether blessings or curses, she couldn't begin to speculate.

With a mischievous smile, she pulled away just a little, enjoying the mindless thrust of his hips as he followed. The pleading tilt of his brow. The unbidden sound of protest.

She gave him what he wanted, taking him so deep her jaw ached with the effort of it. Covering her teeth with her lips, she used her hand and mouth to simulate what their bodies had done. Her tongue glided on the underside of his shaft, finding the large, tender vein there and exerting extra pressure.

Now she knew his words to be ferocious blasphemies, as he growled them harshly to the ceiling. When her hand dipped into his trousers, discovering the nest of dark hair and palming the pendulous weight of his potency, his language dissolved into little more than grunts and her name on helpless catches of breath.

Though she knew he fought it, his hips bucked forward, driving himself farther into her mouth. She opened her throat to accept him, held her breath when he reached too deep. He ravished her mouth with desperate thrusts, pulsing, throbbing, growing larger until her fingers could no longer contain him.

Mena prepared to receive his release, to let his seed slide down her throat in glorious pulses and lap like a kitten at what she could not initially take. But she suddenly found herself seized by the arms and hauled to her feet.

His mouth crushed hers in a predatory kiss filled with a paradoxical, worshipful sentiment. He gathered her skirts in desperate, bunching handfuls and she found herself falling, though he caught her before she landed and gently pressed her into the edge of the seat.

Features taut and eyes burning with abysmal flames, he swept her undergarments down and roughly pushed her knees upward and apart, exposing her utterly.

He filled the space between her legs with his wide, hard body, and before she could catch her breath there was a blunt, heavy pressure against the wet cove of her secret flesh. He slid inside her with a long, lithe thrust and, though Mena felt a twinge of soreness from their night of passion, she accepted the massive intrusion with a purr of welcome.

Her flesh felt swollen and soft around his hardness. Eyes glazed with dark need, he withdrew, repositioned, and took her again, this time penetrating so deep that she felt a strange and heady sensation thrill against her spine.

Lids shuttered low with passion, he pleasured her in grinding, circular motions rather than long thrusts. It was as though he couldn't bear to withdraw, to leave her warmth for even a moment.

Feeling just as needy, just as desperate for closeness, Mena reached for his hard shoulders, wanting to pull him against her. But he resisted, pressing a gentle palm to her chest until she relaxed against the cushion of the bench.

Mena might have been wounded had he not instantly brought his thumb to her mouth and dipped it inside with a wicked sound. Drawing it against her tongue, he gathered some of the moisture there and then left her to apply it to the bud nestled in the auburn curls between her split legs.

Mena jerked as he slid the rough skin turned slick against the aching cluster of sensation. She bit down hard on her lip to keep from screaming as he circled it in time to the strong and sinuous movements of his hips.

She was stretched as wide as her legs allowed, helplessly pinned beneath his big, undulating body. She could not press back against him, or meet his rhythm. Her only option was to receive him and submit to his hedonistic onslaught.

He drove her pleasure with his teasing, torturing thumb

as he surged inside of her, watching her with alert and restless eyes. He learned what pleased her and lingered there,
until she clamped her own hand over her mouth and her
thighs began to clench around him as the whispers of pul-
sating release began to threaten to overwhelm her.

His fingers left her sex, digging into the flesh of her
thighs and pressing them wider as he angled deep, deeper,
until a flood of bliss clenched her feminine muscles around
him. Her climax found her in great, cresting waves, each
one more powerful than the last until she writhed and
squirmed to try to escape their unexpected intensity.

His dark sound of triumph was lost in the rush of
sound through her ears, as though the universe had finally
opened to her, and she could hear whatever curious song
the cosmos sang as the earth hurled its way through the
darkness.

The spasms of her body pulled the release Liam had
been trying to hold back. He caught a raw sound in his
throat, and buried his face in the front of her dress, bearing down on the fabric with his teeth. He sank into her with
a few final and powerful thrusts, his large body racked
with great, violent shudders.

They didn't move for a few countless moments after,
neither of them certain their body truly still belonged to
them.

With an incredible sigh, Liam dropped his forehead on
her shoulder and allowed himself to go lax, though he
propped most of his weight with his elbows on either side
of her.

Mena stroked the stubble of his two-day beard and cradled him with her body, wrapping her legs around his
waist as though she could hold him inside forever. He
didn't seem to mind in the least, nuzzling her breast with
his jaw through her layers of clothing. A sheen of mist
blurred her vision as she realized that this was the kind
of closeness she'd craved her entire life. True intimacy.

Mutual regard. Give and take, instead of her merely giving until she was utterly empty. A shell of a woman.

"After this is over, I'm going to marry ye," he announced softly, pressing a kiss to her jaw.

Mena said nothing as she pressed his head tenderly to her, resting her cheek against his forehead as a tear ran into her hair.

CHAPTER TWENTY-ONE

The Euston Rail Station in Camden was considered the gateway rail line from London to the north of the empire. The grand structure consisted of four platforms, a stately great hall, and a Doric propylaeum built after the style of the Acropolis at the entrance complete with resplendent statuary. The borough of Camden perched very close to Regent's Park, almost equidistant to the Strand in the southeast, and Mayfair to the southwest.

Stiff from a horrible night's sleep on the train, Mena stepped down onto the arrival platform and was instantly jostled by a press of humanity in the form of late-afternoon London travelers. A burst of loud steam engulfed her, startling her so much that she hopped backward, her heel stomping down on the foot of whoever was unfortunate enough to have disembarked behind her.

"Oh, Jani," she exclaimed, turning to help him limp to a less crowded spot on the platform. "Forgive me. Are you very badly hurt?"

"No, no, Miss Mena," he kindly assured her through clenched teeth and eyes pinched with pain. "I am only sorry to have been in your path."

"Dear Jani, don't you even think of apologizing, it is *entirely* my fault." She patted the soft violet silk of his shoulder as he tested his weight on the offended foot. Mena was sorry for anyone in her path, nay, her vicinity. She was a bundle of emotion and fear and elation all at once. Her mind could barely process the filigree signs pointing toward the portico, let alone navigate the crowded station.

"I will be fine, Miss Mena," he soothed, straightening. "I feel that I am not myself today."

"Does London make you nervous?" Mena asked.

"Not as nervous as it seems to make you," Jani observed.

Mena would have denied it, but a hand violently seized her arm and she whirled around with a startled gasp.

"Look at all the shops out on the portico!" Rhianna squealed, nearly shaking Mena in her exuberance. "And can ye believe how grand those hotels are? How close are we to Hyde Park? Should we find a paperboy so that we can see what events are happening and decide what we want to do before we get to Grandmama's? I've heard they sell papers on every corner here. Why does it smell like food in the middle of the station, do they have vendors?"

Coming up behind her, Liam playfully clamped his gloved hand over his daughter's mouth. "Breathe, *nighean*," he commanded gently, his dark eyes gleaming with mischief. "We'll have time to see what there is to see."

"Can I take yer carpetbag, Miss Lockhart?" Andrew asked, nudging his sister who still vibrated with excitement, taking in the grandeur of the station as if frustrated that she couldn't look everywhere at once.

"Yes, you *may*." Mena gently hinted a correction of his grammar, handing it to him. "What a lovely offer."

"I think Miss Lockhart is in danger of turning ye into a gentleman, my son." Liam offered Andrew a proud smile, one that the youth returned.

"One of us has to be," Andrew ribbed back.

Liam's warm sound of amusement could almost be called a laugh, and drew the admiring gazes of the few women who weren't already staring up at him with frank appreciation.

"You're our only hope for a gentleman in the Mackenzie family, Andrew, dear." Mena relaxed into the jovial moment, thoroughly enjoying the familial teasing. She appreciated it almost as much as she did the tranquil, heavy-lidded expression Ravencroft wore, and the secret pleasure it brought her to know that she was the one responsible for it.

"Aye, lad," Liam concurred. "Miss Lockhart called me a ferocious barbarian." His eyebrows lifted in ridiculous mockery of an innocent expression, something his sinister features could never hope to attain. "Can ye imagine?"

A blush crept above the high collar of her gown as she recalled the conversation they'd had before their frenzied interlude in the rail car. He not only reminded her of the uncontrolled passion they shared, but also of her admission.

She'd fallen for him. Fallen in *love* with him.

What does he feel for me? she wondered. Desire, of course, and perhaps a bit of protective tenderness. But could his emotions possibly resemble the depth of her own?

"Aye," Andrew chuffed. "Only Miss Lockhart can speak to ye like that." His eyes, a shade paler than his father's, glimmered with mischievous meaning, and Mena knew her color only intensified.

"Well," she said with an overabundance of cheer. "Let's do go see what the footmen are doing about our luggage." Threading her arm through Rhianna's, she bustled toward the growing pile of baggage on the platform, purposely not making eye contact with the wicked marquess. Every time she looked at him, her belly quivered. She knew how tender that hard mouth could feel on almost every inch of her body now. How one would assume his large hands to be brutish and unwieldy, but they could coax such unimaginable pleasure with their surprisingly deft touch.

She'd tasted the barbarian beneath the fine suit, and that knowledge caused her most secret muscles to clench with delight. Though she'd learned to live a lie, she'd never quite mastered the art of deception, and the children were obviously picking up on the thread of heat between her and their father.

They'd have to be more careful until the future could be discussed.

"Where's Uncle Thorne and Russell?" Andrew queried, trailing behind them.

"They had some . . . family business to attend." Mena noted the slight change of Liam's tone as it lost its cheer. "In fact, I must join them once ye're on yer way to yer grandmother's."

"Are ye coming with us, Jani, or are ye going with Father?" Rhianna asked as they threaded their way through the dispersing crowd. Theirs was the last train from Scotland to arrive, and this close to supper, Mena couldn't imagine many other departures.

"There is business I must attend with the marquess after I see to your things," Jani said, a dark shadow of sadness settled over his dusky skin.

Mena reached for him covertly, and gave his arm a reassuring squeeze.

"They *do* have vendors," Andrew exclaimed, pointing toward a steaming cart of what appeared to be candied nuts and caramel-dipped autumn fruits.

"Oh, Papa, please say we can have some!" Rhianna begged.

Fishing coins from his jacket, Liam motioned to a footman. "All right," he said indulgently. "Ross will take ye to the vendor and conduct ye to Lady Eloise whilst I see to a few things. I'll be joining ye shortly."

The press of bodies gave them an excellent excuse to stand close to each other, and Mena enjoyed Liam's proximity while they watched after his children as they bounded through the crowd like frolicking deer.

"Do you remember being so young?" she asked, feeling a little wistful. "When the world held such excitement and curiosity, when everything seemed so possible and wondrous and the days were endlessly carefree."

Liam's hand covertly caressed the small of her back, and though he stood behind her, Mena didn't have to see his face to understand the meaning in his touch. "I never experienced such things as a youth, didna understand what those words meant; though . . . I'm beginning to now." His words brought tears to her eyes that had nothing to do with steam or coal smoke. There was such yearning in his touch, so much gentle reverence in his voice that her heart crested with hope. She wanted to be the reason the second half of his life was carefree. She wanted to give him the peace and comfort he so ardently deserved.

She wanted a future that was patently impossible.

The baggage car sat between the locomotive and the passenger cars. Rail workers unloaded trunks, bags, crates, and boxes of various sizes while passengers handed tickets to the baggage employees to retrieve their things. Jani had taken their tickets and the other accompanying footman to the baggage line.

Even though the crowd of people had begun to disperse, Mena found the bustle a bit oppressive. It surprised her how accustomed she'd become to the remote and bucolic paradise that was Wester Ross. Certainly it lacked the convenience and diversions of the city, but it also lacked the dangers, the cloying smells, the ceaseless noises, and the endless stretches of stone and steam and winter pall of coal smoke.

Mena loved some things about London, but all she could think of now was how unhappy her life had been here. She'd grown up in the country with wood fires instead of coal, with open spaces and sweet-smelling grasses, emerald fields, and stone fences. She felt at home amongst those things.

Here she was a visitor, and it had ever been thus.

"They're waiting to offload Hamish until the authorities arrive." Liam sighed as Mena turned toward him and caught the baleful look he cast toward the train. "I have to remain to see him off and may be yet a while. Go to the portico and take the carriage that awaits Rhianna and Andrew."

Suddenly struck by uneasy anxiety, Mena also regarded the train with distaste. "I hate to leave you to deal with this all on your own," she fretted. "What if something . . . goes amiss?"

Liam leaned down until his warm breath caressed her ear, and sent shivers of awareness skittering along her skin, heedless of anyone who might see his actions as untoward or inappropriate. "Ye are eternally sweet, Mena mine," he murmured tenderly. "But between Russell, Gavin, and me, not to mention the officers they're sending to retrieve him, Hamish willna have an opportunity to cause trouble. Besides, if something dangerous were to happen, I'd not like ye or my children anywhere near."

Mena turned her head slightly toward him, pressing her cheek against his before pulling away. "Very well." She smiled up into the features that had become more precious than any she'd known. It amazed her how much trust and tenderness she could feel for such a big and brutish Highlander. Millicent LeCour's words filtered back to her from the last morning she'd spent in London.

Sometimes . . . the safest place to be is at the side of a violent man.

She hadn't truly understood the actress at the time. In fact, she'd wondered if the woman had fooled herself into believing that, because her own fiancé was the very cold, very lethal Christopher Argent. The man who'd snapped Mr. Burns's neck right in front of her as though he'd done so a million times.

Mena understood now. It didn't get more violent than the Demon Highlander, and she'd never felt more secure in her life than when she was by his side. The power and prowess that used to frighten her had, indeed, become her sanctuary.

"Promise me you'll be careful," she admonished, putting a staying hand on his arm before she could stop herself. "I have this terrible feeling. We've only just . . . there's so much to say . . . and I couldn't bear it if anything happened to you."

Liam turned his head and looked away from her, his features tightening, his jaw working and flexing, and the vein at his temple pulsed like it did when he was trying to hide displeasure. When his gaze met hers again, Mena's heart stopped. A suspicious and shocking gloss shimmered in his dark eyes before he blinked it away.

"Are you all right?" she asked alertly.

He didn't speak for a long time, instead staring at the her hand, still clutching his suitcoat. "It is a new experience for me to part with someone knowing that they might . . . wish me to return."

Her own eyes, already misted with emotion now welled with it. "I not only wish for your return, I do not wish us to be parted in the first place."

His smile was uncharacteristically charming, and a new softness found its way into his hard eyes. "I will hurry as fast as I am able." He reached for her hand and kissed it over the glove. "While still taking the utmost care."

"See that you do," she said primly, adopting a very governesslike expression. "I'll not be disobeyed."

Heat simmered away any vestiges of vulnerability and

Mena feared he'd melt her into a puddle of lust right in the middle of the Euston Station platform. "Tonight, lass, I'll be yers to command."

Flustered, she turned from him with a lightness in her step and a glow in her heart she didn't think anything could extinguish. The children were no longer at the vending cart, nor could she see them in the milling crowd, so she headed in the direction of the portico toward the carriages, hoping they hadn't already left for Lady Eloise's. Though, if they had, that might give her time to stop by Farah's home and commiserate with her about—

A hand clamped down on Mena's wrist and nearly jerked her off her feet. Her scream was lost in the tinny whistle of a locomotive.

CHAPTER TWENTY-TWO

"I've got 'er!" a wiry, unfamiliar man crowed from beneath a grimy hat. His clawlike fingers bit into Mena's arm as she struggled to free herself. "I've got the viscountess!"

A cold fear Mena had never before experienced speared her chest as five men detached from where they stood posted next to every exit to the platform, and began to hurry in their direction. They were dressed to blend with the crowd in plain clothing, but each of them had the demeanor of hired muscle. Two of them brandished clubs and one swung irons much like the ones she'd been subjected to in Belle Glen.

Somehow, they'd found her. They'd *known* that Philomena St. Vincent, Viscountess Benchley, was going to arrive on a train at Euston Station today.

How?

This couldn't be happening.

"Let me go!" she cried, twisting in the thin man's surprisingly strong grip.

By the time Mena processed that the sickening snap she heard before the thin man's scream was his arm breaking, Liam had already planted a knee in her assailant's face with such force, blood exploded onto the white stone floor and sullied Liam's fine gray trousers.

He didn't seem to notice, let alone care. He thrust her behind him, turning to face the others, who sprinted toward them now.

Mena would have thought that the first one to reach them was a big bruiser if he hadn't been advancing on someone the size of Liam Mackenzie. Running at full speed, the man raised his club and prepared a vicious and dangerous swing at Liam's head.

Liam never let him get close enough. He lifted his boot and drove it into the man's chest with such force, the bruiser seemed to collapse around it, folding in on himself. Liam finished him with an uppercut that sent more blood flinging into the air, and somehow he ended up with the man's club.

Chaos erupted after a breathless moment of pure shock. Screaming travelers scattered through the pillars of the portico and spilled onto Drummond Street, or they retreated to the stairs leading to the great hall to avoid the violence.

Mena wanted to lose herself within their ranks. With sickening, detached clarity she knew her ruse was at an end. Even if Liam managed to defeat all these men, there would be questions. Ones she'd have no choice but to answer.

But she couldn't bring herself to run. Didn't take the moment to escape, because the true sight of the Demon Highlander pinned her feet to the ground in pure, unmitigated awe.

Realizing the threat he posed, the three advancing men began to fan out and attempt to flank him, one with a club, one brandishing a pistol, and the other swinging the irons like a mace.

Liam took no time to consider his enemy or formulate a plan. True to his reputation, he lunged forward, an animal of pure aggression and predatory rage. Fearless. Flawless.

And furious.

He didn't seem to hear the screams of the people around him, nor did he note those who may have been in his way. He merely charged forward with all the power of a Spanish bull.

Dropping his shoulder as he reached his first quarry, Liam drove it into the man's chest with enough force to lift him from his feet. Using the momentum, he flung the man up and over his shoulder like a rag doll and dropped him on his back. Turning, Liam stomped the sprawled man very low in the ribs, doubtless breaking a few, before scooping up a second club.

A terrible smile pulled that hard mouth away from his teeth in a wolfish snarl before he turned for the two men only now rounding a small mountain of luggage heaped onto the platform.

Jani and the footman ducked behind the luggage before Liam advanced, striking his two clubs against each other to make ready.

The one with the pistol aimed at Liam's enormous chest and fired. He got two rounds off before Liam reached him and struck him on the face with his club. The pistol clattered to the platform as the man's head jerked to the side with such speed, Mena feared his neck had broken.

After two more swings of Liam's clubs, the irons went flying end over end across the floor right before the man holding them did the same thing in an eerily similar fashion.

The Demon Highlander hadn't a scratch on him. Not one drop of blood was his own. How was that even possible?

It was Mena's scream of pain as a hand wound into her

hair that stopped Liam short. He whirled around, and roared as she was brandished once again as a shield against him.

Mena's captor didn't have to speak for her to recognize him. This grip she knew. This man she feared.

This moment marked the end of all hope.

"How kind you are, Lord Ravencroft, to bring back my missing wife."

She noted the moment the singular word permeated the haze of crimson violence surrounding Liam.

Wife.

Heedless of the blood of his enemies staining his clothes, Liam drew himself up to a regimental stance, long and wide, and undeniably commanding.

"Ye *will* take yer hands off her," he commanded in the voice that sent many a hardened soldier scurrying to do his bidding. "And then ye'll tell me who the fuck ye think ye are."

"I'm well within my rights to subdue my property in any manner I see fit," Gordon St. Vincent, her husband, taunted Ravencroft from behind her, though he released her hair and subdued her wrists, instead. Every movement he made was calculated, and she knew he did this to mitigate any pathos her pain might cause. "Permit me to introduce us both," Gordon said genially. "As I have it on good authority, you've never truly met the fugitive you've been harboring. I am Lord Gordon St. Vincent, the Viscount Benchley, and this"—Gordon gave Mena a firm shake—"is Lady Philomena St. Vincent, my reluctant viscountess and wife of five years."

The marquess stared at her with unblinking dark chasms for eyes. "Ye're . . . *married*?"

Mena strained and twisted against the cruel grip of the man whom she'd vowed to love, honor, and obey in all things. Her master in the eyes of the law. She knew what

Liam saw behind her. An elegant man with impeccable manners and a deceptively mild and trustworthy demeanor.

"Yes." The word ripped from her on a hiss of pain. "You don't understand what I was running from. You can't know what it was like. What he did to me." Even the Demon Highlander couldn't imagine the depths of Gordon's cruelty. Liam was nothing like him, though he was a soldier, a destroyer of life. Gordon had destroyed her *will* to live, and Mena knew that to be the greater sin.

Liam took a step toward them, tightening his grip on the club as if he'd decided to free her.

"What it was like for *you*?" Gordon scoffed, his breath stinking of opium smoke and his father's expensive cigars. "What about me, Philomena? Can you comprehend what it is like to be married to a madwoman? Do you realize how selfish it was to run from the asylum and leave no one with any clue as to your whereabouts? You almost killed poor mother, Philomena. We have been sick with worry."

Liam's step faltered at the word *madwoman*.

"Like hell!" Mena accused, sending a pleading look toward the man she loved as suspicion brewed beneath the tempest in his eyes. "They committed me to the asylum because they'd spent my money and I was no longer useful to them. Because I turned his sister in to the authorities when she had a young actress murdered. I am married to a monster, Liam. And he left me in that place to rot indefinitely. I had no choice but to escape. I am *not* mad. Ask your—ask Dorian Blackwell, he's the one who facilitated my flight."

A dark look crossed Ravencroft's features, one that told her that Liam planned to do just that.

"You witnessed my wounds," she continued, hating how her voice began to climb to a hysterical pitch. "The bruises, the torture. I refuse to go back there. I'll die first!"

"My poor unfortunate wife. She's a delusional woman, Lord Ravencroft, and you're not the first to be taken in by her." Gordon tightened his hold on her and Mena heard the boot falls of someone else bringing chains. "When she escaped Belle Glen Asylum, I hadn't seen her in months. Her wounds were self-inflicted; it was part of why I had to lock her away in the first place."

Twisting and jerking in his hold with all her strength, she watched in horror as suspicion began to drown the anger on Liam's features. The odds were against her. Liam's first wife had been insane, and she could read the doubt that created within him. The reticence to go through something like that again, to put his children through it. Any reasonable man would pause to wonder if he'd been had.

"Your every action has been one of insanity." Mena didn't miss the mocking note beneath Gordon's tone as one iron clamped over her wrist with cold and gritty finality. "A viscountess employed as a governess? Changing your very identity? Seducing a marquess whilst still married? You're seriously ill, my darling, I'm taking you back where they can take care of you."

"This is my secret," she cried to Liam, as desperation cracked in her raw throat. Her shoulders wrenched painfully as she struggled toward him. "This is what I was afraid to reveal. What I was *going* to confess. I'll tell you everything, Liam, just *please* don't let them take me."

Mena never thought she'd see something as human and pedestrian as indecision in Liam's eyes. Mena's desperation became desolation. He didn't trust her, and who could blame him? Guilt and pain crushed any hope she had left. With a cry, she was able to wrench her arm away from Gordon and whirl on him, landing a blow to the aristocratic features she couldn't believe she'd once found handsome.

"Unhand me," she demanded.

Gordon returned her strike with the back of his hand,

and Mena's knees buckled as, for a precious moment, the lights of Euston Station dimmed as shadows danced, threatening her consciousness.

In her periphery, she saw Liam lunge forward, retribution etched onto his features.

Her husband had just signed his own death warrant, and thank God for that. Even if he didn't believe her, Liam's honor wouldn't allow her to be struck.

She turned toward him, anticipating the moment he'd come between her and the man she'd grown to fear and hate.

The unmistakable blast of a pistol shot echoed through the portico with such deafening reverberation, even time seemed to hold its breath.

Mena whirled to see that Gordon was as stunned as she, the two men at his side looking past her in openmouthed astonishment. There was not a pistol among them.

Her heart stalled, then dropped into her stomach as she slowly turned back to see her worst fear confirmed. A pool of red bloomed over the left chest of Liam's gray waistcoat.

Mena cried out and reached for him with her one free hand, burning to go to him, unable to claw herself from her husband's punishing grip.

Liam's expression turned from astonished to enraged in an instant, and he leaped around, his bludgeon lifted to swing at his attacker, heedless of his injury.

Mena saw him hesitate, and she couldn't fathom why. Had they missed one of Gordon's thugs? What did he see that seemed to deflate his lungs and extinguish the inferno of his fury?

The hesitation cost him dearly as a heavy piece of luggage connected with his temple.

Mena screamed and lunged forward as he fell, but someone seized her free wrist and clamped the shackle around it, leaving her to watch in horror as Liam's magnificent body folded to the platform, landing hard enough to shake the ground.

A ragged sound escaped her as it uncovered just *who* held a pistol in one hand, and sharp-edged baggage in the other.

"No," she sobbed, as the resolute anger in Jani's dark eyes was blurred by the storm of her hysterical tears.

CHAPTER TWENTY-THREE

My only means of escape is to be other than I was. You know I have a secret. A terrible secret. You can't imagine the depth of it. The scope of it. You don't know who I am . . . what I've become. To tell you would be the end of me.

Mena's words haunted Liam as he stomped around his private room at St. Margaret's Royal Hospital.

He did things to my body, to my soul. I let him. I had to.

She'd had to let him because she'd been fucking *married* to him.

His head pounded every time he stood upright. His shoulder burned like someone persisted in needling him with a branding iron, even though his left arm had been secured to his chest with a sling. He had enough thread in his hairline and his chest to stitch a quilt.

But none of that mattered. It barely registered. His wounds were more annoyance than pain. They slowed him down when there was so much to be done.

Everything had been ripped open and was falling apart, and he needed to be out there triaging the bleeding damage, not holed up here like a goddamned invalid.

Just when Liam had been certain Jani had become

family rather than foe, the boy had chosen the worst possible moment to exact his revenge. His children were probably worried out of their minds, stuck with a grandmother they'd only visited a handful of times. Had Gavin been able to deliver Hamish to the proper authorities?

And Mena . . .

Mena was in the clutches of that smarmy fuck-wit who'd struck her, shackled her, and dragged her away.

Her. *Husband*.

Christ.

Liam pressed his palm to his throbbing temple with his right hand and kicked the edge of his hospital bed. She'd lied to him in the most fundamental of ways. Not just about whom she was, but *what* she was. A viscountess. A fugitive.

A madwoman? Liam couldn't quite believe it. He'd lived with a madwoman before. Had seen the toll, physically and mentally, that insanity took on a person. Mena had seemed desperate, secretive in the extreme, but never mad.

But did he truly believe that? Or was it his own fervent wish that made it seem thus?

He *had* to know the truth. All of it. Not only to question her, but to see her, and touch her. To know that she was all right. His anger at her, at the whole fucking mess, was knitted tightly with the love that still burned in his heart, and concern, not to mention an intense frustration at his own ignorance. If Lord Benchley had struck her in front of everyone, what had he done to her once they were alone?

His stomach gave a mutinous surge at the thought.

Every moment counted in this situation, and every second apart from her was pure torture. She had much to answer for, but dammit, she'd give him those answers in person.

"Someone bring me a bloody shirt!" he bellowed into the stark and curiously empty hallway. His trousers had been replaced by some flimsy gray cotton pants tied by a string, and his upper half was bared to the chilly hospital air. "*Where* are my goddammed boots?"

The little mouse of a nurse had disappeared when he'd woken violently, and nearly struck her with his flailing limb mere minutes ago. She'd whimpered something about lying still while she fled to find a doctor. Now there was no one to be seen.

Lie still? Didn't they ken who the fuck he was? He hadn't become the Demon Highlander by holding still.

Whirling around, he searched the sparse, clean room for a trace of his belongings and found nothing but a bed, a chair, a table on the far wall with various medical implements on it, and an ugly stand next to the bed upon which a lone glass of water sat.

He reached the table in two long strides and opened its only drawer, finding it empty. Bits of red began to creep into his vision as his heart thudded against his chest, marking the rise of his temper. An image of Mena's pleading, tear-filled eyes swam across his murky vision.

She'd begged him to save her, and he'd let her down.

I'll die first.

Dear Christ, what he if was too late?

His hand connected with the glass, and it went flying across the room, shattering on the far wall.

He wasn't staying here a moment longer, he'd walk the gray autumn streets of London in these flimsy trousers if he had to. He needed to find Mena.

Now.

He turned on his bare heel and had to reach for the bedpost. Not only to counteract the dizziness, but to offset the astonishment of finding his doorway filled by the last person he ever expected to encounter here in London.

Let alone his hospital room.

"You look as though you've been to war, Ravencroft." Dorian Blackwell, the Blackheart of Ben More, stepped into his room with the unconcerned bearing and lithe prowl of a cat, assessing Liam with his one good eye. One that was as obsidian as Liam's own. An eye patch covered the other, hiding an egregious wound. "I've only been shot the once," he continued conversationally. "But I remember that it smarted like the very devil."

"What are ye doing here?" Liam growled by way of greeting.

"I have . . . friends at every train station and on the hospital staff." Dorian shrugged. "They keep me informed of any interesting goings-on in the city, and I'd say the attempted murder of a marquess and the arrest of a fugitive viscountess certainly fit the bill."

"Spies, ye mean?"

With a dismissive gesture, Dorian moved closer. "Technically, I'm your next of kin hereabouts, though very few know it. It'd be ungentlemanly of me not to check on my injured brother."

Christopher Argent's wide shoulders silently filled the door frame Dorian had only just vacated, and the large, pale-eyed assassin stood like a cold sentinel, never making a move to invade Liam's room.

Dorian was *right* to have brought muscle. Liam might only have use of his one arm, but he was still tempted to choke the life from the reigning king of the London Underworld.

"*Ye* sent her to me," Liam snarled, letting go of the bedpost to advance on his criminal half brother. "Ye *knew* who she was, what she'd done, and ye sent her to look after my *children*. Do ye have any idea—" Liam's teeth clenched together with the force of his tumultuous emotion.

Dorian Blackwell had lied to him. But in doing so, he'd sent Mena, the only woman who could have possibly defeated the Demon Highlander. For a man who was used to charging entire battalions, he'd not been prepared for her to come at him sideways. "I'll make ye answer for that," he vowed, stepping up to Dorian.

Though Liam did have a slight height and width advantage, Dorian stood his ground, unperturbed. He was leaner in that feral, hungry way predators were lean, and it lent him a cruel grace.

"I had my reasons, brother, and you'll want to hear them."

Brother.

There was no denying Dorian Blackwell was a Mackenzie. He bore the same broad angles to his forehead and jaw, the same sharp lines etched below his cheekbones. His ebony hair and onyx eyes were an exact replica of Liam's own.

Of their father's.

They'd inherited the same capacity for violence and domination, and it vibrated through the air between them now, underscored by many more painful things.

"Fuck yer reasons," Liam seethed. "Ye only do something if it benefits yer own purposes."

"Not this time," Dorian replied. "Argent and I intervened at the behest of our ladies, and let me assure you that it was more a nuisance than a benefit."

Liam stepped around the Blackheart of Ben More and made for the auburn-haired giant at the door. "I doona have time for yer excuses. I have greater wrath to inflict before I get to any business between us."

"You've arrived at my very reason for being here, Liam," Dorian remarked. "If I've mastered anything in this lifetime, it's the art of settling a score."

There were precious few men tall enough to look Liam in the eye. Christopher Argent was one of them, and they stared each other down with all the menace of two ruling stags about to connect antlers.

"I've defeated entire armies who had a mind to stand between me and where I intended to go," Liam warned from low in his throat. "I suggest ye step aside."

If Liam was fire, Argent was ice, and though his chilly

blue gaze sharpened, he made no move to advance or retreat.

"I owe the vicountess," Argent said in a voice devoid of anger or defense. "She helped to save my fiancée's life, and because of her bravery, she suffered. Terribly."

Liam blinked as that information permeated the anger and the haze of his head wound. "What do ye mean?" he demanded, hating all these secrets and yet dreading any more revelations.

"Lady Philomena spoke out against one of the St. Vincents who'd threatened Millie and her child," Argent said. "And once the debacle had been dealt with, the vicountess had vanished."

Liam was unused to Mena being referred to by a title, but it made such sense. She'd been a ceaselessly gentle lady, so proper and erudite. The perfect tutor to prepare Rhianna to become a noblewoman.

Because she'd been one herself.

Argent's ice-blue eyes narrowed with distaste, though Liam thought it had more to do with a memory than him. "We found her months later half starved and beaten in Belle Glen Asylum. The treatments were equally heinous. We arrived just in time to snap the neck of the orderly who was attempting to rape her."

"His were the bruises she wore when we sent her to you, Liam," Dorian said gently from behind him. "But prior to her incarceration there, we'd witnessed the evidence of her husband's violence."

Liam's stomach knotted and he felt as though he might be sick. His estimation of Argent rose exponentially at the news that he'd killed Mena's attacker, though he wished to bring the bastard back to life so he could kill him again.

Slowly this time.

Liam turned on his brother. "Ye should have told me," he said. "I would have protected her had I known."

"Her family had her declared criminally insane through

the high court," Dorian stated evenly. "You being such an esteemed agent of Her Majesty's, and our father's *legitimate* heir, I couldn't be sure that you wouldn't turn her over to the crown before I could clear her name. Though we are blood, I know nothing other than that, unlike our own father, *you* love your children. If the Demon Highlander would do anything to protect them, then the safest place for her was at their side. Besides, who better to teach my niece to be a lady than a viscountess?"

"I need to see them." Liam lurched for the door again.

"They're safe." Dorian put a hand on his shoulder. "And they know that you are, as well."

But Mena wasn't.

Dorian assessed him with an eerily astute gaze. "I never imagined that you'd even pay her any mind, let alone . . ." He let the insinuation drift unspoken into the air between them.

Let alone fall in love with her.

"How long have I been out?" Liam asked, looking to the window. No light rimmed the drawn heavy drapes, telling him it was night.

"A few hours," Dorian answered. "They kept you sedated while they stitched your wounds. Luckily for you, the bullet passed clean through you, and lodged into a column."

Hours? That gave Lord Benchley all that time to exact his punishment on Mena. The possibilities set his blood on fire with rage.

He brought his face close to Argent's. "Either ye help me, or get the fuck out of my way."

A cruel mask settled over his Viking features as he glared at Liam. "That's why we've come." Argent stepped aside and swept his hand at the hallway. "To settle a debt."

Dorian fell into step with Liam as he surged forward and in the direction of the hospital exit.

"First," the Blackheart of Ben More suggested, "let's

find you a bloody shirt and those goddamned boots you were bellowing for."

The hour approached midnight when Ravencroft, Argent, and Blackwell advanced through the terrace like reapers in search of the damned.

The house still belonged to Gordon St. Vincent's father, some earl or other. The Viscount Benchley resided like a bachelor in a handsome town house in Knightsbridge, though it was set back from Hyde Park in a less fashionable neighborhood. A slight but telling concession to the St. Vincent family's dwindling circumstances.

Blessed little household staff slumbered below stairs where they'd picked the service door lock, lurked through the kitchens, and crept up to the main floor. What was once a handsome and stately home had fallen into shocking disrepair. All was dark but for a faint glow of lantern light creeping from a grand room at the front of the house.

Liam found himself alone in the hall as the once-plush rugs muffled the sound of his heavy footfalls. Soft masculine conversation drifted to him, followed by a feminine reply. It took a moment for Liam to process the false, high pitch of the woman's tone and recognize that it was not Mena's. His shoulder burned like the very devil, and his head still ached, but he'd lived through more dire circumstances than this . . . he'd killed through them, as well.

Lord Benchley's voice was unmistakable, as was the sickeningly sweet aroma of the cloying smoke filtering from the room.

Opium.

Blackwell and Argent advised serpentine stealth to achieve their objective, but try as he might, Liam had never warmed to that particular method. Fingers curling into fists, as though he already held the viscount's neck in his hands, Liam kicked the door to the study open with such force, it shattered.

He'd have thought the sound Gordon made had come from the woman if he hadn't seen evidence to the contrary.

Both occupants of the room were slow and unsteady, even in their panicked state. The effects of the opium exacerbated now, as fear pumped the substance more hastily through their veins. They were locked in a passionate embrace, halfway toward congress on a dingy couch of indeterminate color. On the table in front of them, various mysterious forms of paraphernalia sprawled between half-empty bottles of liquor and uneaten food.

The woman, an exotic beauty, rolled off Gordon St. Vincent's lap and sagged onto the couch, her breasts exposed by her drooping bodice. She was in such a stupor, she didn't even move to cover herself.

"What is the meaning of this, Ravencroft?" Lord Benchley slurred more than demanded. "I saw you shot." He wore the same fine suit he'd sported at the rail station, but now it was disheveled and soiled with God only knew what substances. His hair, fashionably curly with long sideburns, was rumpled in the extreme and slick with some sort of pomade, or maybe with his own oily filth. It was too dark to tell.

That this reprobate, this disgusting, pathetic fuck, had ever put his hands on Mena evaporated the last of Liam's scruples, and left the acid taste of dread and hatred in his mouth.

"Where is she?" Liam snarled, fortifying himself against the stench of opium smoke, unwashed bodies, and sex hanging in a pall over the dim room like a toxic cloud.

"You mean, my *wife*?" the viscount sneered.

"I mean, yer *widow*." Liam stalked toward the shabby couch upon which the two were draped like limp and dirty linens.

The sight of the wan lamplight gleaming golden off the sharp blade seemed to clear some of the murky smoke from their eyes.

Gordon rose unsteadily, and instead of retreating around the sparse furniture, he scrambled over the back of it, placing the couch and the woman between him and the murder etched on Liam's features. He fled toward the door on the far wall and flung it open, uncovering the still, cruel form of Dorian Blackwell.

His cowardice allowed him to recover quickly, and attempt a hasty escape to the French doors that opened onto a veranda. Wrestling them open with fingers made clumsy with drink, vice, and fear, he screamed again as Argent slithered from the darkness beyond and crowded him back inside.

"All *this* over Philomena?" Gordon said as though he couldn't keep his thoughts and his speech separated. "That sallow, barren, miserable bitch?"

"I'll use this blade to dig the answer from your throat before I end your life," Liam threatened darkly. "Where. Is. She?"

A faded dressing robe hung limply from Benchley's shoulders, and his trousers were unbuttoned, but remained aloft around the beginnings of a swollen belly brought on by too much ale and other excess.

"S-she's not here." Gordon stumbled back to the couch and gripped it as though it were the only thing holding him aloft as the three lethal men converged on him and the sloe-eyed, trembling woman. "I had the men Father hired take her back to the asylum."

Liam advanced, ready to strike him dead and race for the asylum when the hooker cried out. Apparently, she'd finally gathered her wits enough to pull her gaping bodice over her breasts. "Don't 'urt me," she begged. "Let me go, and I dinn't see no'fing."

Dorian took a coin from his jacket and pressed it into the hooker's hands. "Fly away, little bird," he commanded gently. "But if I hear of any chirping . . ."

"Everyone knows better than to sing a word about the Black'eart of Ben More." Her fist closed over the coin, and she didn't even pause to collect her shoes as she shuffled away as fast as her muddled limbs would allow, another wraith lost to the night.

Liam seized the sniveling viscount by the lapels of his robe, and hauled him to his feet using only his one good hand. "Why did ye take her only to dump her at an asylum?"

"Because she's mine. She's *my* wife, and as long as I'm alive, she'll belong to me. I must make her pay for what she's done, I'll take it out of her flesh if I have to, but she'll not bring more shame and humiliation on my family."

"Your family doesn't need any help in that regard," Argent remarked wryly.

Liam clenched him harder, unable to fathom the depth of this small man's cruelty. "If ye felt no affection for her, why marry her in the first place?"

Gordon obviously mistook Liam's meaning, as he seemed to find hope in the question. "I liked her well enough, at first," he admitted. "She was from country gentry. Good breeding stock, my father said. Women with hips like that are supposed to be built for birthing sons, but Philomena never even conceived."

An ugly jealousy reared in Liam's chest, and he had to drop the man back to the couch to keep from crushing him with his bare hands. Gordon again misread the action as mercy, and his tongue loosened.

"She was so soft, so unspoiled, so agreeable and malleable, unlike the grasping debutantes in London. Philomena was *good*. Endlessly, eternally, optimistically kind. I found it charming at first, but in the end, I fucking hated her for it."

Every muscle twitched, every drop of blood sang with violence as Liam contemplated breaking every bone in the man's body.

Slowly.

"Steady on," Argent said in a low drone.

Turning away, Liam began to tremble with the force of his emotion.

"You fell in love with her, didn't you, Ravencroft?" Lord Benchley correctly assessed.

Liam remained silent, unable to give voice to the force of his emotion. "The Demon Highlander. She made you want to be a better man, didn't she?" he commiserated with pathetic disgust. "Did she look at you with those bloody big eyes and force you to see your every weakness and every flaw reflected in their depths? I hated *myself* when she looked at me like that, like *I'd* disappointed *her*. Like she still believed I would improve, *hoped* I would be a better man. I began to crush that hope, and revel in doing so."

"But she was never mad," Liam stated, still unable to look at the man without killing him. The void was growing, his humanity was slipping, and he needed to finish this. He knew exactly what the viscount was referring to. He'd seen his own demon reflected in Mena's eyes, and he'd wanted to exorcise it. For her.

She'd made him want to be a better man . . . and he *loved* her for it.

"She was sweet, but she was willful. Her father, the poor sod, educated her for some unfathomable reason, and what she needs is amelioration. It's why I sent her to the asylum. She'd become too erratic to manage, and Lord knows I tried."

"Ye were violent with her." Liam fought to keep the violence from his own voice.

"I only struck her when she needed correction, at first." Gordon leered, as though in a room of like-minded comrades. "Sometimes you have to whip your spaniels to teach them things, a wife is no different. But after this latest stunt, I think a heavier hand is needed. I'm going to teach her a lesson she'll never forget."

Liam had heard *enough* of the truth. Every word was like acid dripping on his heart. The images too terrible to abide, too horrific to ignore.

He had thought he knew what rage was. An inferno of uncontrollable lust for violence and blood. In the past, it had painted the world with a pall of crimson, and flashed fire through his body until his skin burned as though covered in molten steel.

What he felt for Gordon St. Vincent was the antithesis of that. It was a void of ice and darkness. A calculating, glittering shard of dense, hellish hatred lodged in his soul.

A welcome sin.

He snapped, and suddenly he had his knee against the viscount's chest, driving him into the couch as he planted a fist into the man's nose, shattering it beyond repair.

His demon reveled in the feel of the bone and cartilage giving way beneath his fist, and in the choked and pained sounds exuding from the man, as blood exploded down his robe in a great gush.

"She's not at Belle Glen, Liam," Dorian murmured from where he stood behind the couch facing him. "I liberated that hellhole the day I helped her to escape. I worked very hard to have your governess emancipated as a ward of the crown, and she is safely with Farah and Millie at my home."

Liam turned his wrath on his brother. "Why did ye let me believe she was in danger? What sort of bastard are ye?"

"The sort who built his fortune, his entire life, on secrets. The sort who built his name on a lie so *our father* wouldn't try to have me murdered again," Dorian murmured, his good eye burning with its own dark fire. "We may be bound by Mackenzie blood, Liam, but not trust.

Not yet. I needed to be certain you wouldn't take your famous temper out on Mena. She's suffered enough. And *you* needed to hear the truth of your woman's desperate circumstances from the man who caused them. You don't know me well enough to trust my word, and I knew trusting her would be difficult for you."

Liam paused. The veracity of Dorian's reasoning washed over him with chilling precision.

"I knew this was where you'd find the truth." Dorian pointed to Gordon, whose red, bleary eyes blinked up at them from an opium- and terror-induced stupor. "This human heap of rubbish told you everything you needed to know. And now, you can do what needs to be done in order to claim the woman you love."

Liam blinked up at his brother, and found the same demon he saw in the mirror every day staring back at him. Suddenly there were things he wanted to say. Apologies he wanted to make for sins that were not even his own.

But first.

He drew his dagger from his boot.

"D-don't do anything you'll regret," Gordon begged, putting a weak and ineffectual hand out. The man would have been mindless from the pain of his mangled face if not for the heavy amount of narcotics coursing through him.

"I'm a lord of the realm," St. Vincent slurred from behind teeth stained crimson with his own blood. "There will be inquiries. When they find my body, they'll know it was you. There were too many witnesses on the train platform. They saw how you wanted her."

Dorian Blackwell made a dark sound. "What makes you think there will be anything left of you to find?"

"Only the blood you're dripping onto this couch," Argent added blithely.

Liam nodded to them both before pointing the dagger at the viscount's face. "My name is William Grant Ruaridh Mackenzie, I am the Demon Highlander, Laird of the

Mackenzie clan of Wester Ross, and ninth Marquess of Ravencroft. When we meet in hell, ye'll know what to call me. I made a vow to *my* woman that if I ever got my hands on ye, I'd put my dirk through yer eye."

And so he did.

CHAPTER TWENTY-FOUR

"I have to go to him." Anxious agitation drove Mena to her feet and her companions, Millie LeCour and Farah Blackwell, both rose in tandem as she began to pace across the lush cobalt carpets of the Blackwells' Mayfair mansion. "What if he's . . . the poor children . . . I must—"

"Mena, darling." Farah's robin-blue skirts rustled in the heavy, expectant quiet of the house as she put her arm around Mena's shoulders and tried to steer her back to the settee. "Dorian and Christopher left to look after your Lord Ravencroft before Murdoch and I brought your emancipation papers to the authorities. They promised to send a messenger if there was any news to report."

Mena's anguish was a tight fist in her chest, squeezing her heart until every beat seemed as though it might be her last. She hadn't felt this kind of helpless desperation since Belle Glen. For once, her pain had nothing to do with her own hopeless situation.

Even when she'd thought she was going back to the asylum, when she'd assumed Gordon had delivered her to another indefinite hellish incarceration, the only care she had was for Liam. She relived the horror of seeing his blood bloom against the gray of his vest. Of watching such a mountain of a man crumble to the earth.

"It's been *hours*." Mena had never been the hand-wringing sort, but she was certainly doing plenty of that today. "I can't sit here and do *nothing*. I will truly go mad." They'd have to deliver her to the very sort of place she'd been saved from if the man she loved was . . .

God, she couldn't even think it.

What if they hadn't sent word because the news was of the sort that one had to deliver in person.

Tragic news?

The only thing that had kept her away from the hospital this long was an alternate fear. What if Liam refused to see her? Could she face his antipathy? His rejection?

Could she bear the look of betrayal in his eyes?

The answer had been unclear until this moment. And the answer was a resounding *yes*. If he was alive, she could deal with whatever came after. So long as she could see his thick chest expand with breath, and his lithe, muscular body suffused with the almost inhuman strength she attributed to him, alone.

Nothing else mattered. Not until she *knew* he was all right. Until she saw, with her own eyes, that the Demon Highlander stood once again.

Gathering her pelisse, she hurried toward the door.

"Well, if you're going, we're certainly coming with you." Millie LeCour, garbed in violet silk, also retrieved her fur wrapper, her sable eyes snapping. "I know that if Christopher were in a similar situation, the entire Roman Legion couldn't keep me away."

Farah moved to stop them. "I've learned to trust Dorian," she said evenly. "I know what kind of hell you're in, Mena, but if your marquess were in even a hint of danger, my husband would have called you to his side. He asked that we wait here, and I feel there's a reason for that."

Mena paused, seized by indecision, looking to the secure

door beyond Farah's slim shoulders, and then to the gentle gray eyes of the Countess Northwalk.

"Your marquess and my husband are brothers, Mena." Farah's firm tone belied her subtle push back toward the parlor. "Brothers with a long and painful past of their own to sort out. Perhaps they are doing so now, and need the time to clear what is past between them."

She hadn't considered that. Hers was not the only pain Liam had to deal with. There was Jani, their father, Hamish, Dorian, Thorne, and so much more. Mena probably rated rather low on the list of disasters he needed to contain.

Murdoch, the Blackwells' devoted steward, opened the front door, bringing in a blast of chilly November air along with the handsome Gavin St. James, Lord Thorne, looking uncharacteristically somber. Behind his brawny frame, chains rattled as Jani was led into the front entry flanked by two frightening sentinels that looked more criminal than copper.

Blackwell's men, no doubt.

A reckless temper rose within her, and Mena lunged at Jani, slapping him across his dusky cheek.

Hard.

"How could you?" Mena spat.

Jani squeezed his eyes shut, though she didn't know if it was against the pain her slap had caused, or his own guilt. "I did not think you would get hurt, Miss Mena. I did not know that was part of his plan."

"To whose plan are you referring? Explain yourself."

"When Hamish came back from the dead, he found me in the dark halls of the keep, and told me he'd witnessed Ravencroft murder my parents with his own hands. He said it was guilt, not altruism, that prompted the marquess to take me in."

Mena shook her head. *Did the treachery have no end?* Was all this madness because of Hamish's greed?

"Ravencroft loved you like a son. He's known as a demon on the *battlefield*. Not for entering civilian homes. You've spent so many years with him, how could you not know that?"

Jani's chin trembled and dimpled as he valiantly battled boyish tears. "Hamish reported that he threatened to expose Ravencroft, to tell me the truth, to tell everyone what horrors the laird had perpetrated in India. Against my own people. The things Hamish described . . ." Jani looked up, his throat working over a hard swallow as tears enhanced the disgrace in his liquid eyes. "He told me that Ravencroft set off those explosions on the ship on purpose and left him for dead so no one would find out what he'd done."

"Did he offer you any proof of this?" Mena demanded.

Tears ran in fat rivulets down his cheeks. "Hamish described where my house was, where my parents had died and how. I remember . . . I remember their bodies."

Thorne glanced at Mena, regret sitting softly on his hard features. "Once the Duke of Trenwyth got his hands on Hamish, my brother admitted to manipulating the boy. He turned every one of his own war crimes into something Liam had done and filled Jani's head with his poison. After some time alone with Trenwyth, Hamish admitted to killing Jani's parents."

"It is *my* fault, Miss Mena, all of this is my fault. *I* read your telegram," Jani admitted. "I sent word to your husband because Hamish had read your letters to Lady Northwalk and told me to do it. That is why your husband was waiting for you. And that is why I will die here today."

A tear dropped from Jani's chin onto the silk of his kurta, and Mena felt her own eyes well with tears on his behalf.

"How can Rhianna ever forgive what I have done to her father? I will face the marquess and beg for his forgiveness before I am hanged, but I fear I will never see her face again before I am to die."

"Surely you're not going to let him be hanged." Mena turned to Gavin. "Why isn't he with the proper authorities?"

"Because even though this is England, and even though my brother and I have our differences, the first law I recognize is clan law," he said resolutely. "And clan law states that the Mackenzie Laird gets to decide his fate."

"Oh, Jani," Mena whispered. "We've both wounded Ravencroft so terribly."

"Unforgivably." Jani's voice wavered.

She nodded, filled to the brink with a breathless pain. "I would give anything to make things right, but I fear it is too late . . ."

"A kind lass once told me that it is *never* too late to make things right." A familiar voice rumbled from the shadows beyond the still-open door before the Demon Highlander, himself, ducked into the foyer. "I believe, Miss Lockhart, that lass was ye."

Astonished exhilaration at seeing him alive and well made her light-headed with giddy relief. He stood as strong and wide as ever, and though his left arm was tucked into a sling, the rest of him nearly vibrated with strength and vitality.

Apprehension chased the relief away, followed by shame, sadness, and remorse.

Liam looked at her with an intensity she'd never seen before. A dark fire lit behind his eyes, and a grim, resolute set to his already stern features set off alarms of warning in her head.

Mena took a step back, and then another, refusing to believe her own eyes as she backed toward the hall off the foyer and away from those who'd fallen silent as they watched the moment unfold.

Dorian Blackwell stepped behind Liam, followed by the amber shadow of Christopher Argent.

Mena hardly noted any of them. Not Dorian, who went to his wife and reached for her hand, nor Argent, who melted into the shadows as easily as Millie melted into his arms. Not even Thorne, who gaped at Dorian as though looking into a dark-haired mirror, or poor Jani who rattled his chains with the force of his trembling.

Only Liam.

Mena's whole world narrowed to encompass the emotion she couldn't believe shone on his face.

"Doona run from me, lass. There is much to say."

"You called me Miss Lockhart," she realized with a breathless whisper. "Now you *know* I'm not she. That I am Philomena St. Vincent, a viscountess and a . . . married woman."

His obsidian gaze became impossibly darker. "Not anymore."

Her heart stopped. "What do you mean?"

"It is with very little regret that I inform ye that ye're now the widow St. Vincent," he said with not a stitch of remorse.

"Because of you?"

"Don't give him all the credit." Dorian sniffed.

"It was a collaborative effort," Argent said.

Mena wished she could say that she was sorry her husband was dead. The only guilt that seized her was a regret that she didn't feel more distress over the loss of her husband of five years.

But why would she? Gordon had humiliated and shamed her. Terrorized and abused her. Then he'd locked her away and forgotten her.

What he'd done was unforgivable, and she hoped he'd burn in hell for it.

"Laird Mackenzie." Jani dropped to his knees in a clatter of tears and chains. "I must beg of you—"

"Get up, Jani." Ravencroft sounded more irritated than angry as he hauled the young man back to his feet. "It is as Thorne said. Hamish confessed to everything. To what he had ye do, to what he convinced ye of. There are many sins in my past, and I canna say I blame ye for believing yer tragedy is among them. We *will* have words, Jani, count on that. But I ken that ye are more victim than villain."

Jani's eyes widened until they seemed to engulf half of his angular features. "You—you are not going to kill me?"

"Nay." Liam glanced at Mena and their gazes held. "There has been enough of that today."

"You are a more forgiving man than I, brother," Dorian remarked. "Usually if a man shoots me, I shoot him back . . . and then some."

Liam took slow and steady steps toward Mena, whose first impulse was to retreat.

But she was done with that now, Mena decided. Done with being afraid. Of backing away when she should stand her ground. She was no longer helpless, or hopeless.

Or faultless.

The first thing she needed to do was face the consequences of her actions.

"I have recently learned the meaning of such words as *forgiveness* and *redemption*." Liam approached her with narrowed eyes, as though trying to figure a battle strategy.

"Let's retire to the parlor," Farah suggested, shooing her many guests into the azure room they'd only just vacated. "I'm certain we have keys for those chains around here somewhere, and poor Jani looks as though he needs to sit down."

"I could stand here a little longer," Gavin quipped, watching Liam and Mena with sardonic interest.

"Lord Thorne, I presume?" Dorian stepped to Gavin and hesitated before holding out his hand. "I've waited a long time to meet you." The two shook hands, mirror images of each other in all but their coloring.

"Dorian Blackwell." Gavin carefully extracted his hand from Dorian's grip. "Or should I say 'Dougan Mackenzie'?"

"A long and interesting story." Blackwell gestured to the

door opposite the parlor across the grand entry. "Might I invite you to my study for a drink?"

And then Mena and Liam were alone with nothing but the sound of her rapid breath echoing off the grand marble entry.

His stare was relentless but not hard. Aggressive, but not angry. He stood an arm's length from her, towering over her like a monolith of potent masculinity, yet he reached for her with nothing but his gaze. It touched her everywhere, as though she were a specimen he'd never seen before. As if he couldn't make her out, or fathom what—or who—she was.

Mena knew this was her chance, her only chance to apologize for the wrong she'd perpetrated against Liam and his family.

"I cannot excuse what I've done," she began, surprising herself by how her fervency steadied her voice, though the rest of her shook for want of the warmth of his touch. "When I escaped . . . when I accepted the position at Ravencroft as Mena Lockhart, I felt as though this world had truly carved me away from myself. I no longer knew who I was, so becoming someone else seemed permissible. Harmless, even. It was though everyone I ever knew, everyone I should have been able to trust, wanted to tear my very flesh from my bones and feed me to the vultures." Tears she did not feel coming spilled down her cheeks as emotion swept over her, causing her flesh to prickle with it.

"I didn't know," she whispered. "I didn't know there was someone like you in this world of cruel and callous men. I thought . . . I thought my future was a dark and barren corridor with a bolted door at the end of it. And when I ran, my only care was for what I ran from. I didn't stop to think where—or *who*—I ran to. I didn't know it was your arms that would make me feel safe for the first time since I could remember. I didn't know that your face would become so dear. That your children would steal my heart.

That I would learn to trust the very man I so thoroughly deceived."

Mena swiped at her cheeks, despairing at the unchanging expression on Liam's sinister features. She couldn't at all decipher what he was feeling, but he had to know the depth of her regrets, though they did neither of them any good.

"We talked once of forgiveness and redemption, and I want you to know that I neither expect nor deserve that," she continued. "I have wronged you so absolutely, and I wish I could take it all back, but all I can say is that wounding you, Rhianna, and Andrew in any way will forever be my most profound regret and my darkest shame. For I hold no others on this earth so beloved."

Clamping her lips together, she blinked her tears away so she could clearly see what fury was to follow.

"Are ye quite finished?" Liam asked shortly.

Swallowing a fresh wave of hopelessness, Mena nodded mutely, awaiting his wrath like a traitor would the gallows.

He was silent a moment as he studied her with bright eyes, his nostrils flaring with the force of his barely controlled breath. When he finally spoke, it was low and even.

"I am a man who has known little but suspicion and violence. I spent my life too much in the company of competitors or adversaries. I thought I'd been born under a bad star, cursed to live a brutal life. I, too, retreated to Ravencroft Keep, and there I found that I sought solitude, even from those who needed me. I was too much alone . . .

"And then ye came, and ye were in every room. In every corner of my every thought. I could not escape ye, Mena, and then suddenly, I didna want to. I found myself seeking ye out because somehow I knew that I couldna be apart from ye. It was the first happiness I ever knew to look into yer eyes. Ye taught me the meanings to words other than *forgiveness* and *redemption. Desire. Yearning.* And *love.* Ye are my blanket of stars, Mena, my reason to look to the heavens. My map when I am lost and my point of light when all is dark."

Mena released her breath on a sob, and then another as Liam's hard expression melted into the most tender regard she'd ever before seen. Relief didn't seem like a strong enough word for the reaction coursing through her.

Had he said *love*? It was a word that had carefully eluded them until this moment.

Finally, he reached out and hauled her against his body, crushing his lips to hers in a searing, searching kiss. Branding her with his heat before pulling back to gaze down at her.

"I would make ye my wife," he murmured.

The word froze in the air between them and Mena went rigid. She was barely a widow . . . not only that, she was a woman of scandal. All of London knew she'd been institutionalized. That she was barren. To marry her could be his social undoing. She'd been a miserable failure as a viscountess, how in the world could she become a marchioness?

Liam's grip tightened as though he feared her escape. "I know I'm hard man to love, Mena. A difficult man to live with. I'm a flawed brute with a famous temper. But I want ye to know that I'd cut off my own arm before I'd strike ye. That I'd kill myself before I'd ever cause ye harm. Doona fear me, Mena."

Her heart melted into a puddle of warmth in her chest. "Is that why you think I hesitated?"

"I remember how frightened ye were of yer own shadow when ye came to Ravencroft. And now ye said that yer experiences had carved ye away from yourself, but I think ye ken well enough who ye are now. I wouldna be the man who took away yer will, Mena. Still less that husband. I doona mean to ever govern ye. Yer life, yer desires, they would be yer own. I would lay claim to yer heart, lass, and to yer body and soul, as well. But ye see, I canna possess those things without losing myself. Ye own me, Mena. I would never be the master of yer will, but there is no question that ye are the mistress of my heart. And I'd make ye the mistress of the Mackenzie clan as well."

Mena placed trembling fingers over his mouth to stop the flood. She could hear no more or her heart might burst. He was handing her a fantasy tonight, but reality awaited them when the sun rose.

"What about Rhianna and Andrew?" she asked. "What about the fact that I am a barren and disgraced woman? You must think about that before offering me your hand."

He kissed her fingers and offered her a crooked smile that melted years from his savage, weathered features. "Well, everyone would think ye a bit daft to marry the Demon Highlander to begin with."

Despite herself, Mena felt the whisper of a laugh bubble in her throat.

"My children love ye, Mena," he continued. "They are as blessed to have ye in their lives as I am. And even if I had no heir, I'd chose ye to be mine."

"Oh, Liam," Mena breathed, unable to express her joy.

"It's not as though there arena enough Mackenzies under this very roof to take the title if it didna pass to Andrew," he said wryly.

"I love you, Liam," she blurted, unable to keep the words inside. "I thought I'd lost you and I couldn't bear it. It was the one thing I didn't think I'd survive."

"Ye'll never have to," he vowed. "The sun will rise in the west before I stop loving ye, Mena mine." Dipping his head, he captured her lips in a tender kiss.

Mena mine. He'd called her that.

A name she knew she'd always answer to. For now she truly knew who she was, and looked forward to who they would become.

Together.

ΕPILOGUE

Ravencroft Keep, Wester Ross, Scotland,
Late October 1882
Four years later

"Keep your dirty hands off me, William Grant Ruaridh Mackenzie, or we'll never be done with this in time to bathe and meet Andrew at the train," Mena Mackenzie admonished firmly as she slapped her husband's grasping fingers away from where they teased at her waist and were drifting toward her breasts.

"I was under the impression, Lady Ravencroft, that ye like it when I'm dirty." Liam said from behind her where she stood and gathered the orders from the distillery office desk. His lips lowered and danced across her exposed neck, sending familiar shivers across her entire body. "We'll send Jani for the train," he rumbled before nipping at her ear in that way he knew made her instantly wet with desire.

Mena knew what she would find when she turned around. A brawny, soot-streaked Highlander fresh from singing the oak casks over the open fire, muscles thick and bulging from a day's hard work and dark eyes blazing with an even dirtier intent. She'd be lost to his masculine seduction if she gave in to the temptation to turn and admire him, so she did the only thing she could think of to save her dignity. And her time. She called out to the new fore-*woman* of Ravencroft Distillery, whose own office was only across the hall.

"Rhianna!"

Her husband growled and swatted her bottom before he stepped back to a more respectful distance as a great deal of frantic shuffling preceded a bevy of footfalls in the hallway.

"Ye'll pay for that," the laird vowed.

"Promise?" Mena threw a coquettish smile over her shoulder as the office door exploded open and a rather disheveled Rhianna stumbled into the room tucking untidy curls back into place.

"Ye called?" she asked breathlessly, wiping at moist, bee-stung lips and her rumpled blouse. The young lady's lovely eyes widened with panic as she noted the laird lurking behind Mena.

"Father!" she exclaimed rather loudly. "I . . . thought ye were at the kilns burning barrels."

"I was," Liam said slowly, as though trying to piece together whatever information he was missing. "We're finished for the day, and I'm after going to meet Andrew at the train."

"Please inform Jani that we'll need to ready two extra carriages for the ride to Strathcarron Station," Mena told her.

"Jani?" Rhianna squeaked. "I would have to go find him. I havena the slightest idea where he is. I will go and . . . do that right now. Find him. As he is not here."

Mena's eyebrows rose, as she'd seen Jani's tall frame tiptoe past her office door only a quarter hour past and slip into Rhianna's office. A sly smile spread across her lips as she realized just who was responsible for Rhianna's dishabille.

Apparently, Jani had decided to finally throw caution to the wind and claim the woman he loved. After four years, relationships had mended and reparations had been made, and Liam and Jani were close as ever. Jani was once again part of the family, and now Mena wondered if that was going to become more legitimate in short order.

Rhianna, now twenty-one, was a grown woman. A businesswoman. As Andrew had decided that school, industry, and politics interested him more than the family business. Liam had impressed Mena by heartily embracing the idea of his daughter inheriting the distillery rather than his son.

"Yes, do go and find Jani and we'll meet you both at the keep." Rhianna's panicked expression faded as Mena winked at her meaningfully and gestured to Rhianna's office with her eyes.

"Of course," Rhianna said in a breathless huff, backing out of the office. "Thank ye!" Her stepdaughter dashed away, and Mena knew she and Jani would use the side entry as an escape route.

"Why would we need two carriages to pick up my son?" Liam queried, missing the entire subtlety of their interaction.

Mena finally turned to look at him, marveling that even after four years of married life, her husband still took her breath away with his wicked good looks and the demonic glitter of mischief in his eye.

"Because this year for the Samhain celebration, we're having a few extra guests," she said brightly.

Liam's eyes narrowed. "Like who?"

"Oh, just family and close friends. Such as Farah and Dorian, Gavin and his new bride, and then we can't forget His Grace, Lord Trenwyth and his rather scandalous duchess. Argent and Millie can't make it as they're still touring America with the theater company, but they'll meet us at Ben More Castle for Christmas and . . ."

Her grim husband blinked thrice before reaching for her, effectively cutting her off. "Now ye have two things to pay for, and I'll collect my due before I'm inundated with relatives," he said wickedly.

"Very well." Mena pretended to be put out as she bustled to the door to lock it before turning back to her husband with a sensual grin.

"Here in the office?" Liam's dark brows lifted. "That's not very ladylike of ye."

"Well," Mena said as she stepped around the desk and leaned against it invitingly, thoroughly anticipating her husband's raw hands on her soft skin. "We've never been very good at keeping our sport in the bedroom, have we?"

"Nay, Mena mine, no, we have not," he murmured, gathering her skirts in his hands. "And may the gods see that we never improve."